Speak of the Devil

Speak of the Devil

Rose Wilding

BASKERVILLE

An imprint of JOHN MURRAY

First published in Great Britain in 2023 by Baskerville
An imprint of John Murray (Publishers)
An Hachette UK company

1

A CIP catalogue record for this title is available from the British Library

Hardback ISBN 9781399804981
Trade Paperback ISBN 9781399804998
eBook ISBN 9781399805018

Typeset in Perpetua by Hewer Text UK Ltd, Edinburgh
Printed and bound in Great Britain by Clays Ltd, Elcograf S.p.A.

John Murray policy is to use papers that are natural, renewable and recyclable products and made from wood grown in sustainable forests. The logging and manufacturing processes are expected to conform to the environmental regulations of the country of origin.

Baskerville, an imprint of John Murray
Carmelite House
50 Victoria Embankment
London EC4Y 0DZ

www.johnmurraypress.co.uk

For those who made it out alive, for those who didn't,
and for those who are still fighting, with love.

Author's Note

Speak of the Devil is about a group of brilliant women, and all their flaws. It is about the difficulty of finding justice in a society that doesn't often listen when we tell our stories. It is informed by the world around us – by the experiences of women I know, by the news, by my own life – and therefore is very dark in places. I have included a list of resources for anyone affected by the subject matter at the back of the book.

I wrote this novel because I am always, under the skin, under the polite smile, absolutely furious.

1

31st December 1999

Fireworks pop and fizzle in the dark sky above the city, hours before the new millennium, and Maureen watches them for a second before she pushes the window open and closes the curtains. Sarah has already lit the candles, and hands her one as she sits back down.

Eight faces are illuminated, ghastly and sunken-eyed in the flickering light. Seven women sit in a semicircle, their bodies pointing towards a kind of altar in the middle of the room. They all look at him, some of them just glancing now and then, some of them staring, unable to avert their gaze. Only one of them knew he would be here; the others are in varying states of horror at the sight of him. Even the one who brought him is horrified, maybe more so than the rest.

A woman called Ana gets up and kneels in front of him. She hasn't prayed for years, not since she was fresh from Brazil, but the words slip out of her mouth as if they have been waiting for her, the Portuguese fast and slick, almost inaudible over the noise of the party below. Sarah lights a cigarette with the flame of her candle.

'I think it's a bit late for that,' she says to Ana, but does not get a response. Sarah leans back in her chair and crosses her knees, looks around at the other women, but no one pays her any attention.

Kaysha Jackson – the journalist – lurches out of her seat and into the en-suite, where they all hear a retch and a splatter. She comes back a few minutes later, pale, splashes of vomit down her jumper. Sarah takes her hand, and their fingers lace together, brown skin and white almost indistinguishable in the sepia gloom.

Josie, who is the youngest, and is pregnant, is crying. Her pallid face is blotchy and swollen.

'Where's the rest of him?' she asks, her voice cracking.

'We don't know, hin,' Maureen says, reaching across to lay a hand on Josie's arm.

'Someone does,' Sarah says, flicking her finished cigarette onto the floor and grinding it into the carpet with her boot. She looks at him again, meeting his eyes. It's been a long time since she saw him, even longer since they were in this room together. He looks different now, and she feels different now. She loved him then.

His hair is longer than it was, and it's standing on end, as if he's been dragged by it. She supposes that he might have been. His face looks thinner than it did, and his nose looks flat and broken, and dried blood is smeared over the bottom half of his face. She imagines how it must have burst from his mouth, maybe as he tried to say one last clever thing. He was always clean-shaven when she knew him, but he has a short beard now, thick around his mouth and chin, petering out down his throat and stopping abruptly where his neck does.

The rest of him is missing.

The women are in a top-floor suite in a cheap hotel on the outskirts of the city, one of the best rooms once but now just a place to store broken things. Boxes of long-lost property disintegrate under the window and a mattress slumps against a wall.

'Is anyone going to own up?' Sarah asks.

No one speaks.

'We weren't ready,' she continues.

'Ready?' asks Kaysha. 'We hadn't even decided.'

'I never would have agreed to this,' Olive spits. She is a white woman in her fifties. She has grey hair, cut close around her neck, which she smooths and tucks behind her ears every few minutes. She crosses herself with her fingertips and closes her eyes for a second.

'We know, Olive,' Sarah says. Sarah is in her mid-twenties, unusually pale with a mass of unbrushed black hair. She has a rose tattooed on her throat and wears a leather jacket. Her accent is local, but less natural than some of the others, her vowels less flat, as if she is trying to hide where she is from.

'Well, I think we all know who we suspect,' Olive says, her eyes lingering on Sarah.

'You did suggest it,' Maureen says to Sarah, dabbing her watery eyes with a handkerchief.

'I know what I said,' Sarah says. She pulls a hip flask from her boot and takes a mouthful.

Olive nods at Sarah's flask. 'Suppose you did it while you were drunk. You mightn't even remember.'

Sarah opens her mouth to retort.

'Stop it,' Sadia says, cutting Sarah off. 'We don't need a shouting match. We were lucky no one came before.'

When the women had arrived fifteen minutes earlier, the head was covered by a pillowcase. They'd all taken their usual seats, all frowned at the makeshift altar in the centre of the room, all wrinkled their nose at the smell of rot and pennies. There was no small talk, but Josie had asked what was under the pillowcase. When no one answered, Sarah stood and pulled the pillowcase off with a flourish, rolling her eyes, only for them to widen when she revealed what was underneath. Some of the women had screamed.

'It must have been you,' Sadia continues, tipping her head towards Kaysha. Sadia is holding a baby monitor and she drums her fingers on the plastic, letting anger and impatience mask her horror. Sadia has deep brown skin and even features, straight teeth and long eyelashes. In a different life, she'd have been a model or a movie star, not the widow of a dead scientist. 'You arranged all of this. You're the only one who has everyone's phone number.'

'I know how it must look,' Kaysha says. 'But I didn't do it.'

Earlier in the evening, each of the women had received a message from an unknown number: *Meet in the usual place, tonight, 7pm. Emergency.* This followed the usual format of Kaysha's messages, though she'd never called an emergency meeting before.

'How could someone have had all our numbers then? Someone else must know about us,' Maureen says. She is fanning herself with a leaflet from her handbag.

'You said that our information was safe with you,' says Sadia, looking at Kaysha. Kaysha frowns.

'It is, look,' she says, and unzips a pocket on the inside of her jacket, feeling around for the scrap of paper where she jotted down everyone's phone numbers months earlier. The list is no longer there, and she can't hide the confusion on her face. She glances at Sarah, who she lives with. Sarah shrugs.

'You've lost them?' Olive asks.

Ana, still kneeling, crosses herself and stands. She is tall and classically beautiful, with dark hair and golden-brown skin.

'There are ways to find out phone numbers,' she says, sinking into an armchair beside Sadia.

There is silence for a few minutes. The baby monitor crackles.

'I can't believe you brought the bairn,' Sarah says to Sadia, finishing whatever is in the flask and slipping it back into her boot. She lights another cigarette.

'I didn't know what I was walking into.'

'Where is she?'

'Next door. She's been awake since four this morning; she'll be asleep for a while.'

'Some mother.'

'Don't start, Sarah,' Kaysha says. She is in her early thirties but looks younger, and is dressed in a black suit. Her eyes dart around the room, looking for something to focus on other than the head.

'Can we cover him up, please?' Josie asks, looking at the floor. A sequinned dress is stretched across her rounded belly and the glitter on her cheeks sparkles in the candlelight. She was on her way out to celebrate with friends when she got the text.

Sarah picks the pillowcase off the floor and drapes it back over the head. It doesn't cover him completely, but she makes sure she at least blocks him from Josie's view. When Sarah sits back down, an eyeball stares at her through a gap in the fabric.

'Does anyone else think that it's about time we rang the police?' Olive asks, jutting out her chin and glancing around at the others. A silky whisper drifts around the room at the word *police*.

'If you were going to ring the bizzies you'd have done it by now,' Sarah says.

'I think we should ring them too,' Maureen says. A bead of sweat rolls from the hair at her temple down the side of her face and under her soft jawline.

'And get done for conspiracy to murder?' Sarah asks. 'Good plan, aye.'

Kaysha rubs her forehead with her fingertips. 'We can handle this, we just need to be clever about it.'

'What are we going to do then?' asks Sarah.

'Pick those up, for a start,' Ana says, pointing to the cigarette butts by Sarah's feet. 'Evidence.'

'How on earth would they link that to me?'

'We're not in a position to take chances,' says Ana. 'We need some bleach.'

2

Kaysha
31st December 1999

Sarah Smith's house is way out of the city, past the suburbs and the smaller towns and villages, alone in the nowhere land between places. When darkness falls there it falls thick and fast, and it clings like treacle to the grass and the trees to make way for the moon, which is a bright crescent as Kaysha parks by the front door in the last minutes of the old millennium.

They sit in the car for a long time and watch the stars. Sarah traces constellations on the fogged windscreen with her fingertip. Kaysha follows her girlfriend's fingernail, thinking about the blood that is caked underneath it.

'Makes it seem like almost nothing, doesn't it, when you think how big the universe is,' Sarah says.

'No,' Kaysha says.

'Who do you think did it?' Sarah asks. Kaysha gives her a long look, and Sarah cocks her head to one side. 'It wasn't me.'

'I don't know yet.'

'Bet it was the wife. It's always the wife.'

'Maybe,' Kaysha says. Sadia would have had good reason to kill him, but then, they all would.

'If it's her, what'll happen to the bairn?' Sarah asks.

Kaysha says nothing, but reaches out and squeezes Sarah's arm. Sarah turns back to look at the stars.

'I hope it wasn't Sadia,' Sarah says quietly, and then takes off her boots and goes into the house. She comes back out minutes later with a bottle of whisky and a blanket, and they both strip. They pile their clothes onto the grille of a barbecue that has been standing by the front door since their first week together, scorched fat still caked onto the metal. It is beginning to rust. Sarah pours whisky over the bleach-streaked clothes and sets them alight. The women press themselves together under the blanket, skin on skin, passing the whisky back and forth as the flames warm their hands. The cold night numbs them, and they let it.

Fireworks pop against the horizon, and Kaysha's phone rings. Her mother wishes her a happy new year and hears in Kaysha's voice that something is wrong, even though Kaysha is trying to sound cheery. Kaysha tells her that she will explain when she sees her, says goodnight, and they go inside, where Sarah drinks, and Kaysha begins to build a timeline in her head.

3

Nova
3rd January 2000

It's a Monday but the city is quiet as the sun begins to rise. Adults pull heavy blankets tighter around their bodies, enjoying the last long sleep of Christmas break while children finish off tins of Roses for breakfast. Light yawns into a sky the same colour as a peach skin and the river reflects it, yellow-red lapping the muddy banks. The six iconic bridges are lit, one by one, and their shadows sharpen and stretch across the water. The night's frost glitters and begins to melt on the breeze blocks and abandoned cranes of construction sites along the quay, where they are preparing for the arrival of the seventh bridge.

Detective Inspector Nova Stokoe is woken by a phone call about a body and pulls her Escort into a car park near the docks half an hour later. The three floors of mid-sixties brick look odd against the warehouses that have grown around it. Tufts of grass poke through cracks in the tarmac and empty flower baskets hang along the length of the conservatory that fronts the building. A faded sign reads *Towneley Arms Hotel*.

There are two panda cars and a CSI van there already, and Nova glances at herself in the rearview mirror. Ginger curls frame her jaw, messy from the night before, and she spends a few seconds trying to neaten up before abandoning the effort. Her freckles stand out more than usual against her pale skin. She spent the evening in one of the underground pubs off the high street, didn't get home until four, and definitely shouldn't have driven this morning. She swallows two paracetamols to ward off the hangover and gets out of the car.

A man with a serving trolley stacked with boxes clatters across the car park as she approaches the hotel. He grins and a gold tooth gleams in the sunlight.

'Going in here?' she asks, holding the door open for him, and he winks as he passes.

'Morning,' he says to the old man at reception, and then disappears through an archway at the far end of the room without waiting for a response. Nova flashes her badge at the man at reception, and he ignores her for a second while he tops his coffee up with whisky. His hands are shaking.

'Upstairs, hinny,' he says, tipping his head towards a set of stairs to the right. 'Top floor. It's gruesome, mind.'

'Stomach of steel, me, man,' Nova tells him, and goes up. The top floor is cordoned off with police tape and she can smell the corpse from down the hall. She wonders how long it has lain there.

PC Ella McDonald is standing beside an open door with her hat in her hands and a look on her face that Nova knows too well.

'Nice of you to turn up last night,' says Ella quietly, but not quietly enough. Nova looks over Ella's shoulder.

'Have you taken any statements from the staff?'

'Were you with someone else?'

'What about the guests? Any statements from them?'

'Dick!' whispers Ella. She brushes past Nova, who watches her go down the stairs, too tired to feel guilty.

There are baubles scattered across the corridor, and she nudges a couple out of the way with her shoe as she enters the room. Three white bodysuits are moving around, dusting for prints. A floodlight illuminates their workspace. A man's head is on a table. Nova can see no sign of his body. The room is ripe with bleach and decay, and she holds a finger over her nostrils before moving closer.

'Has the body been taken?' she asks one of the CSIs, glancing around for a chalk outline.

'Doesn't look like it was ever here,' he shrugs.

The head is balanced on top of an open book which rests atop a pile of hotel bibles on a bedside table in the middle of the room. Fluids have seeped out of the neck and onto the book so she can only make out a few words around the edges of the page, but by the brown leather cover she can see that it's a bible too.

'When you move it, can you make a note of the page number?'

'Aye, a'll put it in the report,' he says. 'I have had a look though, and I think . . . just based on where the book is opened and the few words I could make out, I think it's the page with Leviticus 2:19 on it.'

Nova lifts her shoulders and the CSI smirks.

'Didn't go to Catholic school, did you?' he says, not really asking, and she shakes her head. 'You'll know the passage. Leviticus 2:19 is *an eye for an eye*. I'll double check it all when they move him, but I'm fairly sure. My dad used to like that one.'

'Revenge,' she says. The page could be random, she supposes, but it seems unlikely. It looks like a revenge killing. She wonders what he did to deserve this.

'I'd imagine so,' the CSI says.

'You're an ugly fucker, aren't you?' she says, turning to the head, leaning close to it. She's seen bodies that were more decomposed, but she hasn't seen one as interesting as this before. His mouth is a little open and maggots slither inside. His eyes and nostrils have started to ooze brown foam, but other than that his skin is grey, as if all the colour has leaked out of him. There's nothing particularly distinctive about him – white man, dirty blond hair, short beard, no tattoos, no scars. Not even a pierced ear. His nose looks broken, but other than that it doesn't seem like he's been beaten up prior to his beheading. She crouches and inspects his neck. Dried-out threads of flesh are twisted and decaying across the book's pages. Certainly not sliced off in one clean sweep. 'How long do you think he's been here?'

The CSI shrugs. 'Hard to tell. The window was open and it's been frosty, so that's probably slowed everything down a bit. Forty-eight hours if I had to guess.'

'Mmm. Don't suppose he had his driving licence?'

The CSI snorts. 'Where would he have kept that, like? Up his nose?'

'Just have to wait for the dentals, I suppose.'

Nova stands back and turns her attention to the wall behind the head. A photographer is taking pictures of a large, round sigil drawn on the wallpaper. Two feet in diameter, it shows the coiled form of a snake surrounded by crude symbols. Nova has been stuck on the cult case for weeks, punishment from the DCI after the business with the women in Gosforth. The sigil has been cropping up all over the region, from city-centre alleyways to the sides of terraced houses in the countryside, accompanied every time by a blood sacrifice. This is usually stolen livestock – a goat or a chicken – but most recently, a snake.

After a tip-off just before Christmas, Nova climbed up to Penshaw Monument – the North-East's answer to the Acropolis – to see the symbol daubed onto the flagstones. It was the same as always – the spent remnants of candles melted around the edge – but the serpent in the centre of the sigil, disturbingly, was real. The carcass of what had turned out to be a Burmese python was curled in on itself, the surrounding runes drawn in the snake's own blood.

Nova moves closer to the sigil. She's studied it extensively during her investigation, and when she sees it on the wall of the Towneley Arms she knows straight away that it's not authentic. A cheap imitation drawn not in blood, but in blue paint. It's well done, good enough to fool the average onlooker, clearly even the police officers who recognised it, but not Nova. The runes are nonsense and the snake is facing the wrong way. This is the work of someone who's seen it in a newspaper or on a street corner and tried to replicate it from memory. An attempt to misdirect the investigation.

Nova wonders who would want to implicate the cult for murder: maybe another occult group, or a local gang. Maybe just a particularly dramatic hired knife. Either way, Nova has no intention of informing anyone that the sigil isn't authentic because this murder is already looking much more interesting than sacrificed livestock; this could be her ticket back into the DCI's good books.

The old man is still sitting behind the front desk when Nova goes back downstairs, sipping coffee and filling in a crossword. He glances up at her over the top of his glasses.

'Areet, hin?' he says, putting his pen behind his ear.

'Has anyone taken a statement from you yet?'

'Aye, er, about five minutes ago. Me wife's just in wi' the lass now.'

'Was it you who found the remains?'

'Nar, not me,' he says with a little chuckle. 'It was Jeffa, the barman. Gary Jeffries. Went up to put the Christmas tree away or summat. Hord the scream from here.'

'Where's Mr Jeffries now?'

'A put him in the kitchen with a bottle of sherry. Easily frightened, wor Gary,' he says, pointing to the archway at the other side of the room. There is a sign above it that reads *Lounge/Diner*. 'Through there, and then through the silver doors, hin.'

'Thanks. Can I have a copy of your guest records for the last two weeks?'

'Aye, nee bother,' he says. 'They're taking statements in the office, like, so A'll have to dee it after.'

'Perfect,' Nova says, and makes her way to the kitchen. A handful of guests are dispersed across the dining room, talking in low voices.

'Excuse me,' says one man as Nova approaches the kitchen. He clicks his fingers at her. 'Do you work here? When's breakfast going to be ready?'

Nova ignores him and goes through the silver doors. She got fired from a local Italian restaurant when she was seventeen for pouring a plate of carbonara over a customer who snapped his fingers at her like she was a dog.

A tall, thin man sits on a bar stool at a steel island that dominates most of the kitchen. The rest of the space is taken up by fridges and racks of shelves stacked with plastic tubs of ingredients. The man glances up as she walks in, his eyes red and his fingers wrapped around a bottle of sherry. He hiccups.

'I don't think breakfast's on this morning, pet,' he says. Nova shows him her badge.

'Mr Jeffries? I'm Detective Inspector Nova Stokoe,' she says. 'How are you feeling?'

'Ahh,' he says, his lips trembling. Tears leak onto his cheeks and he covers his face.

Nova looks around for a kettle. 'Can I make you a cup of tea?'

'I'm okay, thanks, pet,' he says, and tips a tot of sherry into the floral-patterned teacup in front of him. Tears cling to his eyelashes.

'What time did you come across the remains, Mr Jeffries?'

Gary sniffs. 'It was still dark. Too dark to see it, at first. There's no light in there.'

Nova waits for him to carry on.

'But the smell, when I walked in. I'd have walked into it if I hadn't smelled it first. I've never – *never* – smelled anything like it. Awful. I thought a bird must have got in and died. No one ever really goes up there. I didn't want to step in it. The dead bird. So I went back and propped the door open and turned the hall light on,' he says. He breathes out hard before he continues. 'And there he was. I screamed.'

'That's a very normal response,' says Nova. 'Did you go into the room?'

'Did I shite,' he says, with a scoff that turns into a sob. He wipes his eyes. 'I closed the door and came downstairs.'

'Have you noticed anything out of the ordinary in the last few days?'

He shakes his head, turns his mouth down at the corners. 'I don't think so. Nothing strange.'

'No shifty guests?'

'All of the guests are shifty, Detective.'

'Alright, Mr Jeffries. Thank you for your time,' says Nova, standing up and straightening her jacket. She gives him one of her contact cards. 'If you think of anything else, get in touch.'

Just as she reaches the door, he speaks again. 'I did see a woman, she was acting, I dunno, acting strange. Sneaking around.'

'What woman?'

The kitchen doors swing open and the rude man from the dining room bursts in, his face red.

'Where the fuck is breakfast?' he snaps at Nova.

'As I'm sure you're aware, sir, a crime is being investigated. The police are busy questioning the staff and guests, and we'd appreciate your patience and cooperation,' says Nova, her voice calm.

'Well, it takes no effort to put a bit of cereal out, does it?' he says. 'What's your name?'

Nova smiles and gets her badge out of her pocket. 'Detective Inspector Nova Stokoe.'

The man blanches and then tuts, retreating to the dining room. Nova turns back to Gary, who is staring blankly at the doors.

'What woman were you going to tell me about?' she asks him.

He blinks and shakes his head. 'I don't know.'

'You knew a minute ago.'

'It's completely slipped . . . I don't know what I was going to say.'

Nova frowns. 'I'll be back, I'm sure. If you remember anything, write it down.'

The old man behind the desk is now joined by a grey-haired woman who Nova assumes is his wife. Her thin fringe sticks to her forehead with sweat, and a cigarette smoulders between yellow fingertips.

The woman hands Nova a few sheets of photocopied paper. 'The guest records, love.'

'Thanks. Have you got any cameras anywhere?' Nova asks, glancing around the lobby, which is as run-down as the rest of the property.

The woman shakes her head. 'No. We're not that posh. Not much to steal, is there?'

'You might want to consider getting some.'

'Yes, well, I suppose we will now,' she says.

When Nova gets back outside, the sun is properly up. She needs to look around, but she knows the press will likely start turning up soon, so she has to be quick. She walks around the outside of the building, where there is a small overflow car park to the rear, not visible from the road. There are more cars here than there are up front. Nova supposes that the Towneley Arms is the kind of hotel that businessmen take their mistresses to; they don't want their cars to be spotted. She wonders if the old man rents his rooms by the hour for cash. If he does, his books won't have all the names she needs, anyway. She needs CCTV.

There's nothing much more than a fire door and a mossy, padlocked cellar-hatch behind the hotel, and Nova moves on to sweep the surrounding buildings. Opposite the hotel is a used car dealership with plenty of bulky cameras, but all of them point inwards at the building and forecourt. She crosses the road in front of the hotel and inspects the building next to the car dealership. Some sort of warehouse, but no visible cameras. The surrounding buildings are similar, all run down, some empty-looking and some in use, but none with cameras that might capture the hotel's comings and goings.

Just as Nova turns to leave, she spots a man watching her from between the buildings. It's the delivery man from the hotel. He's smoking, but when he sees that she's noticed him he drops his cigarette to the ground and slinks into the building behind him. Nova walks towards the warehouse. It's almost hidden behind the car dealership, but a corner sticks out enough to be visible from the hotel car park. As she nears it, the sun catches a glass disc high up on the corrugated wall, almost hidden in the shadow of a drainpipe. A camera. It points directly at the Towneley Arms in a way that can't be coincidental.

A sign reading *RJ Meats* hangs above the front door, and Nova knocks. Almost immediately the door opens and the delivery man greets her.

'Yep?' he asks.

'Hello,' Nova says, flashing her badge. 'I saw you in the hotel this morning – I wondered if I could speak to you.'

'I don't work there. I just deliver the meat.' He leans against the door frame and lights another cigarette.

'Do you own this . . . factory?'

The man tilts his head to one side. 'I've got shares.'

'I notice you have a camera pointing at the hotel.'

'Mmm.'

‘Why?’

The man shrugs. ‘Security.’

‘They can’t put up their own CCTV?’

‘Better angle from here.’

‘Can I take a look at the footage?’

The man looks her up and down and then stubs his cigarette out on the wall and puts it behind his ear. He backs into the warehouse and jerks his head for Nova to follow.

The inside is lit by dangling overhead lights. Stark beams illuminate certain areas and leave the rest in shadow. Along the far wall, pig carcasses hang by hooks. A handful of people in plastic overalls are working around a conveyor belt, some pushing chunks of meat – bones and all – into a machine’s mouth, others collecting and packaging the ground and reshaped pink that oozes out of the other side. The smell of the place is almost worse than the corpse.

The man leads Nova into a cramped but tidy office. Filing cabinets line the walls and a desk sits below three wall-mounted televisions, each showing the view from a different camera. The one on the right is recording the Towneley Arms’ front door. The camera is clearly zoomed in as far as possible, and though the quality isn’t great, it’s not terrible.

‘There you go,’ he says, gesturing to the screen.

‘I’d like the tapes for the last fortnight.’

The man just looks at her, and it takes Nova a second before she realises that he has his hand outstretched, rubbing his thumb in circles over his first and second fingers. She laughs.

'Alright then,' he says, shrugging and pressing the power button on the TV. 'We don't seem to have those tapes. Must have lost them.'

'You can give me the tapes, and I won't ask any questions about what you're doing filming the hotel in the first place,' she says.

He stares at her blankly.

'I'll also pretend I didn't notice that,' she continues, nodding at a baggy of white powder on the desk.

'Fair enough,' he says, and turns to the shelves of labelled tapes, looking for the right ones.

Nova looks around. Last year's *Page Three* calendar hangs on a wall, turned to June. A topless blonde lies across a garden bench surrounded by flowers and birds. Someone has written NICE TITS in a speech bubble by her mouth.

Nova stretches, and pauses the tape. She's watched footage from the three days leading up to New Year so far and there's been absolutely bollock-all worth writing down. The CCTV shows nothing but staff scurrying in and out for a fag and the occasional pair of afternoon-delighters parking round the back and sneaking in the front. She gets up to get a glass of water and then sits back at her desk, propping her feet up on the corner. There are eight desks crammed into the converted attic above the police station, after a flood three years earlier rendered the second floor unusable. The superintendent always seems to run out of funds before she gets to renovating the offices, so the detectives hunch over desks in the gloom of the rafters, like bats.

‘Coffee?’ Paul Cleary asks her, as he stands. Paul was promoted to DI in September, and Nova has found him insufferable since. They joined the force at the same time, but Nova climbed the ladder faster than he did, and she knew he resented her for it when she beat him to every promotion, solved every case she was given. She’d heard him once whispering to a colleague that she was just being promoted because she was a woman and it looked good on paper, and she’d laughed. She kept getting promoted because she was fucking good at her job, or she had been.

‘Two sugars,’ Nova says, without looking away from her screen. After a few minutes, Paul puts a cup in front of her. She feels him peering over her shoulder.

‘Not doing the crossword today, then?’ he asks, his voice nasal. Nova tenses.

‘My case has taken a turn for the interesting,’ she says.

‘So I hear, so I hear,’ Paul says. He leans closer to her and drops his voice. ‘Between me and you, mate, I’m surprised the DCI hasn’t taken you off it.’

Nova turns and looks at him, bristling. Everyone knows about her last big case. Paul smiles and goes back to his own desk, and Nova resists the urge to tell him to go fuck himself. It’s best that she doesn’t draw too much attention to herself at the moment.

She’s up to three minutes past seven on New Year’s Eve now. People were arriving for the New Year’s Eve party at this point, but no one particularly suspicious, no one with a big enough bag. Nova takes a mouthful of coffee just as a woman hurries across the screen. The woman looks over her shoulder as she goes through the front door of the hotel. She rewinds the tape and the woman walks across the screen again. The tape is too grainy to make out any distinct facial features, but Nova knows the gait of that walk, the shape of her body. Nova puts her face close enough to the screen that the static tickles her nose, trying to make out the woman's features, though she's already sure. She'd recognise Kaysha Jackson anywhere.

4

Kaysha
3rd January 2000

Kaysha sits in an armchair and watches Sarah sleep. When Kaysha came back into the house, minutes before, Sarah was breathing so lightly that Kaysha held a hand in front of her mouth to make sure that she was alive. This is the first time that Sarah has slept properly since New Year's Eve, and Kaysha is not going to wake her, even to tell her that the plan worked – she'd watched from her car as the police and the coroner and the crime scene investigators arrived at the hotel before the sun was up, and then, eventually, there was Nova Stokoe.

It was difficult on New Year's Eve to persuade the group to leave Jamie's head where they'd found it. Most of the others wanted to take it into the middle of nowhere and bury it, burn it, dump it in a lake or hire a boat and drop it into the ocean, clean any evidence from the room and hope that wherever the body was, it wouldn't be found either. They thought that Jamie's disappearance would be in the news for a week or two and then he'd be forgotten, and maybe there'd be a bit of suspicion towards Sadia, because the spouse is always the first suspect, but people would tell the police that they were so happy, deliriously happy, the perfect couple, and she wouldn't go to prison for it, hopefully. Kaysha wondered if Sadia did kill him. It seemed unlikely, because Sadia always seemed so balanced, but if anyone could infuriate someone to the point of murder, it was Jamie Spellman.

Kaysha listened to the women whisper to each other about getting rid of the head, but she couldn't let it happen. It was too risky to leave anything to chance. She had to think fast, join the dots for the others, explain the plan as she was still constructing it.

As a journalist, Kaysha's job is to watch people without them noticing, to piece together little bits of information and weave them into a narrative, and she's good at it. When she's not working, more often than not she is watching people who she shouldn't be watching. She watched Jamie Spellman for as long as she has been watching anyone. She watched each of the women before she approached them. Since they broke up, she has been watching Nova, and because she's been watching her she knows that Nova is currently investigating a spate of animal sacrifices that are popping up around the city, each accompanied by a sigil which features a coiled snake and some runes. Kaysha has been watching this too, and knows that the culprits are a gang of teenage girls. Kaysha would have told Nova this, had they been speaking, but as they aren't, she has been enjoying watching the girls slip out from under Nova's nose again and again.

The women in the hotel room trust Kaysha more than they trust each other, because she was the one who gathered them in the first place. They were the women who Jamie had hurt the most, as far as Kaysha could tell. She'd tried to find the people who would most want to see him locked away. She didn't think it would lead to this, and she realised as she looked at Jamie's severed head that any of these women might have done this. She knew better than anyone that they all had reason to.

She explained her plan to them, leaving out only that she and Nova were lovers, making it seem more like they are just acquaintances who swap unsavoury information. Kaysha told them that if she could make sure that Nova is on the case, they would not be trudging through the dark, they would know how the investigation was going, and Kaysha would be able to feed Nova false leads, draw her away from the women.

Once Kaysha had got a tentative agreement on her plan from the women, she drew the sigil on the wall behind Jamie's head using a can of claggy, blue paint and a stiff paint brush that she found under a pile of dust sheets. The real cult always draws their sigil in red, and she knew this wouldn't be lost on Nova. For good measure, she purposely drew some of the symbols backwards or upside down. She needed Nova to be called to the scene, needed the case to be hers, but she wanted her to know that this was not actually the work of the teenage girls, should she ever catch up with them. She knew that it was a risky move and that she hadn't thought out everything that could happen, but she didn't have time to ponder. She drew the sigil, they cleaned the room, and she would sort out the rest later.

Now that the head has been found, she has two new things to focus on. The first and most important is to seduce Nova again. The second is to figure out which of the women *did* kill Jamie – so Kaysha can help her cover it up.

5

Olive
3rd January 2000

Olive Farrugia was born by accident. Her mother, having had the last of her three children fifteen years before, had been glad when her monthlies stopped. *About time*, she'd thought, and carried on about her life. She pegged her growing belly to the new bakery round the corner and got quite a fright when, one afternoon, after being laid out on the couch all day with what she thought must be a kidney infection, her waters broke. Fifteen minutes later, Edie, who was recently married and pregnant herself, helped her mother deliver a very small child.

The baby grew for the first two months in a glass box in the hospital, and her eldest brother Ted had said she looked like the last little olive at the bottom of the jar that no one wanted enough to bother fishing out. His mother slapped his arm for saying it, but the name stuck.

Olive grew into a skinny and sickly child with mouse-brown plaits dangling down to her waist and a constant cold.

She never really had the patience for friends. Even her niece, Louisa, who had been born only twenty-three days after her, was an irritation. Olive loved her mother, but didn't think too much about it when she plated up Olive's breakfast sporting a black eye or a swollen jaw. Olive's dad was a drunk, and though he was usually kind to Olive when he was sober, Olive knew well enough to stay out of his way when he'd been drinking. Olive never understood why her mother didn't learn the same thing, and thought, in her childish way, that it was her mother's own fault that she ended up on the wrong end of Daddy's fists.

One evening when Olive was eight, her dad came home earlier than usual from the pub. He told Olive to get to bed, and she said she was going, she was just getting a glass of milk first, and opened the fridge. *Get to fucking bed*, he said again, and before Olive had the chance to even close the fridge, he grabbed her by the scruff of the neck and the seat of the pants and threw her bodily up the stairs. The stairway turned at a ninety-degree angle after the first five steps, and her father threw her hard enough that Olive crashed head-first into the wall. Olive rolled back down the five steps and vomited on the kitchen floor, while her mother screamed and her father stormed back out of the house. Olive wasn't allowed to go to sleep that night. Her mother put vinegar on her head and kept her up until morning. Once Olive got past the initial shock of what had happened, she was filled with rage. Over and over again she thought to herself, *I wish he was dead, I wish he was dead*, and a week later, he was.

After Olive's father drank himself to death, her mother grew sick and quickly followed him into the graveyard. Olive stayed with Edie for the first few weeks afterwards, sleeping top to toe in a bed with Louisa, but Edie had recently given birth to twins and didn't have the room or money to care for Olive too, so Olive went to live with her Aunt Sue. Sue was her father's youngest sister and had made her fortune by marrying two very old men, one after the other, and collecting their inheritance when they died. The second one had died two weeks after the wedding, which Olive had been a bridesmaid at, and Aunt Sue called it *a great piece of luck*. She lived in one of the big terraced houses on the seafront at Tynemouth, which was nothing like the cramped cottage that Olive had grown up in. Sue's house had four floors and seven bedrooms, which people often suggested that she filled with lodgers or children of her own, but she always shrugged it off. She liked the space, and so did Olive.

Olive missed her mother, but liked her life with her aunt. Sue was friendly but strict, and attended church on Sunday, which meant that Olive attended church on Sunday too. Before that, Olive had never been, except for weddings, christenings and funerals. She had prayed when she felt helpless to do anything else, though. Olive had prayed for her father to be punished, which he was, and for her mother to get well, which she didn't, and so Olive came to think of God as vengeful. When she joined the church she found that she enjoyed it. She liked the rules of religion, the do's and don'ts, the idea of punishment for those who sinned and then forgiveness for those who repented. For the first time in her life, Olive found that she made friends easily and quickly rose through the ranks of parishioners' children to become their leader, facilitating prayer circles and Bible study groups, her shrill voice cutting through everyone else's until they listened to her. The children knew that they needed to behave in her presence, because she had no qualms about reporting any silliness to one of the adults, or even the vicar. She loved watching people get what they deserved.

Olive loved the church building, too. She loved the way the flock were tinted blue or red when the sun shone through the stained glass during mass and she loved the hand-carved pulpit, which was hundreds of years old. What she liked most about her church were the grey stone arches that kept the building up, like ribs, because they reminded her of the one family holiday she'd taken with her parents. They'd gone to Whitby for the weekend, and wandered along the seafront eating fish and chips as the gulls circled overhead. She'd whined to ride a donkey along the beach and then cried seconds after it set off with her on its back because she didn't like how she wobbled, and her dad had smacked her on the back of the legs for wasting his money.

On the last day they'd climbed the hundred steps up to the abbey and looked out over the town, and a couple were getting married on the clifftop, under the whalebone arch. Olive had been filled with a tingling longing at the sight of the tidy groom and the bride's dress rippling around her in the wind, and hoped that she might one day be married in such a romantic setting. Years later, when she met Alonso and they married under the similarly shaped arches of her church, she remembered the clifftop marriage and knew she was doing the right thing.

Olive sits in the church alone. She is still wearing her wedding ring, though its twin is buried in the churchyard around her husband's long-dead finger. The inside of the church is barely warmer than the street outside. The congregation has been growing smaller for years as the masses turn their back on God, which means the donations have dwindled too. Now they only turn the heating on when there's a service. Olive can see her breath. One of the windows was shattered by a stone a few weeks ago and has yet to be fixed, and snowflakes drift past the gap like ghosts. It was her favourite window too – John the Baptist.

Olive has been in the church for three days, except for the hours when she drags herself home to bed, where she doesn't sleep anyway. She sits where she always does – the front pew, as if being closer to the pulpit is being closer to God. This is where she met Jamie for the first time, and she glances along the row. She can almost see him sitting there like he did all those years ago, in a suit that was too big, early hints of rosacea creeping over his pale cheeks like strawberry juice through fresh cream.

'Still here, Olive?' asks Father Paul, sitting beside her. She didn't even realise he was still here, but she doesn't have enough energy to get a fright. He puts a hand on her shoulder. 'Is there anything you'd like to talk about? I know this is always a difficult time.'

Her face crumples and drops into her waiting palms. He rubs her back. She knows that he thinks she's mourning her family, like she always does at this time of year, but her thoughts are stuck on Jamie. A fresh wave of guilt consumes her with a flash of Kim's accusing stare, the creak of rope from the attic, and with the guilt comes the usual rush of shame.

'Let me take you home,' Father Paul says. His voice is deep and level. It always calms her. She looks up and nods, eyes flickering across his long face for a second. He's been the vicar here for almost twenty years – since before she rejoined the church – and he's become the closest thing she has to a friend through all the loss. He knew Jamie, knew his grandfather – who was also a preacher. Jamie hasn't been part of this congregation for a long time, but she knows that Father Paul will feel his loss too, once the news comes out. She considers confessing as they walk through the empty streets together. She thinks about telling him the truth about Kim. She thinks about telling him about the head, and the women, and the hotel room. She wants to say that she wasn't part of it, not really – she was just spying on them. She is desperate to tell someone. When they get to her house, he gives her one last parting pat on the arm and she closes the door and locks it, her mouth still closed, alone again.

6

Nova
3rd January 2000

The first Christmas after her parents divorced Nova was twenty-two, and she and her brother had been to their mam's new place in the morning. The little flat, though dilapidated and damp, was trimmed throughout with glittering tinsel and garlands of plastic holly, and a tree, sparse but real, stood guard above a pile of brightly wrapped presents in the corner of the living room. The air had been thick with the scent of gingerbread, and though everything was different, it was all familiar. After presents, a mince pie breakfast, and a vaguely sad singalong to a tape of *The Smurfs Christmas Party* – which Nova's brother had given her as a joke – they'd gone to their dad's for Christmas dinner, leaving their mother teary and alone, insisting that she was fine.

Their dad had the money for a better lawyer, so he'd kept the family home, the dishes, the furniture and, in one of the more spectacularly petty settlement arguments, the boxes of Christmas tree baubles and ornaments that his wife had spent her adult life collecting. They weren't worth anything to anyone except Nova's mother; they were her way of documenting where they'd been and what they'd done as a family. It didn't matter whether it was the blistering height of summer in Benidorm or Kos, she'd manage to find a badly painted Santa emblazoned with the resort's name. Sometimes he'd be in his full red garb, sometimes in fur-trimmed swimming trunks, but she always found him. Nova's dad had argued that the ornaments had to stay with the house, so that when that first post-divorce Christmas rolled around, he could put them all up and make the house look like it always did *for the children*, though they were both adults by then. He'd promised Nova that he was going to make lunch, which he insisted was usually his doing anyway, and decorate the house for their arrival at one o'clock sharp, but when they arrived the living room was drab and dark, and the turkey lay uncooked on the kitchen bench with its giblets still in. He'd grumbled something about working all Christmas Eve, he hadn't had time to fuck about with tinsel and turkey. He hadn't bought them presents either, just shoved a crumpled twenty-pound note in a Christmas card for each of them, which was simply signed *love Dad*.

He'd softened since then. Each year he tried a bit harder, cooked the turkey and set the pudding alight, put up the dusty old tree. He'd reluctantly let Nova take the box of baubles to her mother and bought some new ones. He always bought them a gift after that first sad year, though it was usually something cripplingly practical from the central aisle of the budget supermarket he shopped at, often something for her car or some kitchen appliance that she'd use once before it was left to gather dust on top of her kitchen cupboards. This year had been no different; he'd bought Nova a reflective frost cover for her windscreen and a decent bottle of whisky, telling her *it's supposed to be deed frosty owa New Year, young'un*. Nova had rolled her eyes but had gone out to drive home later in the evening to find blooms of ice creeping over her car, and had used it that night.

The windscreen cover worked a treat, but four days after she got it she forgot to tuck the edges into the front seat windows, and in the morning it was gone. She's been using newspaper instead for the last few days, plucking one of the many discarded copies of *The Chronicle* from her back seat and layering sheets across her windscreen when she gets home from work, peeling them off with the frost the next morning.

The day that the head is discovered is the same. She reverses down the tight alley behind her flat and manoeuvres into the space that is hers by the unspoken law of the street, gets out and covers the glass with months-old news, and then goes to bed exhausted. Though the morning was more interesting than usual, the rest of the day has been filled with hours of trawling through missing persons databases, watching the CCTV tape with nothing more interesting cropping up than a glimpse of someone she used to know walking into the hotel. Could be a coincidence, but she doubts it. Kaysha is always the first one to sniff out trouble.

Nova is dog tired, but it takes her hours to fall asleep, and she wakes up forty minutes late the next morning and rushes down the stairs, toothbrush hanging out of her mouth. She slips on the ice but catches herself just in time. It takes until she is in her car and starts the engine to realise that she has forgotten to peel off the sheets of newspaper. She snorts at her own stupidity and glances at the articles through the glass as she opens her door again. A face half hidden behind another sheet catches her eye, an article about some award. It's him.

7

Ana
4th January 2000

Ana, as always, is the first one in the building after the cleaners. The silence is broken only by the clip-clip-clip of her heels on the lino, the wheeze of the boiler as she switches it on, the burr of the kettle in the break room. This is her favourite time of day. She loves the quiet of early morning, so every day she rises before the sun and leaves Tom to deal with the chaos of tipped-over cereal bowls and lost black plimsolls, knowing that the wind-down of bedtime will be hers.

She leans against the bench with her coffee, enjoying the emptiness. It is the day everyone returns from Christmas break and tinsel is still Blu-tacked around the walls, only decorated otherwise with faded health and safety notices, a years-old Slimming World poster and the odd splatter of soup that was never wiped clean. Ana had gone to Slimming World a few times in the year before she got married. She didn't care about losing weight, but she knew that in the churches and community centres where the meetings were held she'd find circles of women who knew how it felt to feel that your body wasn't quite the right fit, and maybe they'd want to be friends. She'd found them welcoming at first, if not a little intense, but when she started turning up having forgotten to fill out a food diary for the week or didn't remember which days were which colour, she was quickly eased out of the clique.

The 'Secret Santa' box is on one of the dozen tables that are dotted around the break room, still holding a few unclaimed presents. Almost two weeks earlier, the Christmas party had been in full swing and gifts were handed out. One by one, the recipients opened them as everyone else watched. People took full advantage of the anonymity that the game provided, and most gifts were entirely inappropriate – but the office Christmas party was the one event when the formality of the workplace was suspended and anything was fair game. When it was Ana's turn, she was handed a three-foot-high gift wrapped in silver paper that was almost entirely covered in tape. It was very light, and she began to unwrap it, smiling as everyone watched. It had taken her an age to get through the wrapping to reveal a male blow-up doll – the kind groups of drunk women drag from bar to bar during hen parties – with a grainy photograph of Ana's face and a cheap black wig taped to its head. Jamie stood across the room, and she caught his eye. He smirked, and Ana forced herself to nod and smile until the next person opened their gift. Ana knew that most people, until recently, hadn't suspected that she was trans. She had never been popular at Parson's, had kept to herself, but lately there had been a definite shift in how her co-workers treated her. She cried in the toilets five minutes later and took Lina from HR to one side before she left the building. Lina had rolled her eyes and told Ana that it was *only a joke. What did she expect?*

Ana hears a door open and close somewhere in the building and Merv the cleaner shuffles into the break room, a newspaper tucked under his arm like always.

'Good morning,' Ana says, tipping the dregs of her coffee into the sink and rinsing her cup. 'Did you have a nice Christmas?'

'Aye, it was alreet. Ha'ya seen this, like, aboot this blowkie without ees heed?'

Ana drops her cup and it smashes on the floor. Merv is holding his newspaper open so she can see the front page, but tuts and thrusts it into her hands. He leaves the room and she hears him clattering around in his cleaning closet down the hall. The front page reads:

BODILESS HEAD HAUNTS LOCAL HOTEL

In the early hours of Monday morning a man's recently decapitated head was discovered by staff in the Towneley Arms Hotel in Newcastle. The body is yet to be found. The man has not yet been identified, but police believe that the killing might coincide with the activities of a cult that has been operating in the area . . .

It is accompanied, thankfully, not by a picture of Jamie, but by a picture of the hotel. She knew the article would be printed any day, she knew what it would say, but she still feels shaken. The announcement of the death to the world in print means that it is real, no longer a secret shared only by the seven women.

Ana puts the paper on the bench and bends down to pick up the biggest pieces of the cup.

'Oot the way, man, A'll dee it,' Merv says, standing behind her with his dustpan. He taps her arm with the handle of his brush to get her to move.

'Thank you. Sorry again,' she says, standing and leaving the room.

Her lab is on the top floor and is smaller than most but looks out over the city, and she spends her lunch breaks watching the ebb and flow of hurrying bodies below, sometimes with Jamie eating a pot noodle beside her. His lab is next door, bigger and filled with new equipment. He recently won a big grant, which has drawn a lot of international attention to the company. The company decked his lab out with brand-new everything as a reward. Everyone is jealous, but no one seethes with envy as much as Ana does. Jamie was supposed to have a meeting with a big German company about an international expansion of his work next week.

Phil, the boss, barges into Ana's office mid-morning, questioning her about Jamie's whereabouts. He glistens with sweat as he stands too close to Ana, growing increasingly purple as the conversation progresses and he doesn't get the answer he's looking for.

‘You must have some idea where he is,’ he says. ‘I’ve got a phone call with the Germans in half an hour, Jamie’s supposed to be here.’

Ana shrugs. ‘Maybe he’s just late? It’s still early, he’s turned up later than this before.’

‘His wife’s just been on the phone asking for him – he’d told her he was working away over New Year, didn’t leave a hotel name or phone number,’ says Phil.

‘I told her, he’s never worked away. Why would he? He works in a lab, what good would he be somewhere else? *You’ve got the wrong Jamie*, she says. *He works away a lot*. Told her there’s only one Jamie, and he’s never once worked away, I see him every day. Must have been pulling the wool over her eyes, poor cow,’ Lina from HR says, standing behind Phil with a smirk on her face. Ana sucks in a breath. She knows how much this will have hurt Sadia. She’s known about his affairs for a while, but Ana doesn’t think she knew the extent of them.

‘You must know where he is, you’re thick as thieves,’ Phil says.

Ana crosses her arms. They haven’t been thick as thieves for a while, but she has no intention of reminding anyone of that. ‘If Sadia doesn’t even know where he is, how should I?’

‘You must,’ he repeats. ‘You must know something. Who’s he shagging this week? Always got a bird on the go, hasn’t he?’

‘No one that I know of. If I hear from him, I’ll let you know.’

Phil huffs out a breath, ruffling his thick moustache, and marches from the room, followed by Lina, a dark patch down the back of his shirt.

There is a door joining Ana's lab directly to Jamie's, which they used to prop open as they worked and turn on their old tape deck, which Ana kept in a cupboard hidden behind her PPE. They'd sing Freddie Mercury lyrics to each other through the gap. Ana leans against the doorway with her arms crossed and looks at his state-of-the-art equipment. It should have all been hers.

8

Sadia
4th January 2000

Shortly after calling Parson's to ask about Jamie's whereabouts, Nova Stokoe knocks on Sadia Spellman's front door and asks her to come and identify a body. Sadia calls Tom, Ana's husband, who picks up Ameera, and then goes with the detective to the morgue.

Sadia turns away after a second and nods. She hears the zip. The sight of her husband's face, slack and discoloured, peering from a flat body bag is worse than it was in the hotel room. The shock had tided her over then. There is no shock this time, just grief. She knows she won't see him again.

Later, the detective questions her. She says that she is sorry, but she has to. The murder, of course, could be ritualistic, but what it really looks like is *passionate*, and who has more passion than a wife? *Yes*, Sadia thinks. *Who has more passion than a wife who has given up everything that ever meant anything to her to be with a man, only to be made a fool of? A wife who trusted that her husband was a good man, and then hears from strangers how he was not. No one.*

Sadia lays out a different version of their relationship for the detective. *Happy marriage for ten years.* Not a lie. *He's – he was – a good dad. Of course, we argued sometimes, who doesn't? He works away a lot. That annoyed me. But I wouldn't have left him over it. I loved him.*

By the time she gets home, and Ana drops Ameera off, it is almost five. Police have searched the house in the hours that Sadia has been out, seemingly haven't found anything to make them think that Jamie was murdered at home, because she was allowed to come back. Ana turns up a couple of hours later, still in her work clothes. She apologises that Ameera's T-shirt is covered in flour – she'd spent the day making biscuits with Ana's husband and children. Ameera presents Sadia with a slightly burned triangle of shortbread wrapped in a paper towel, and Sadia forces a smile, tells her daughter she'll eat it later. Ana brings a lasagne too, and she puts it in the oven while she makes Sadia a cup of tea and puts Ameera to bed. Ana wraps her arms around her friend, keeping all the parts of her together, and then watches as she eats. Before she leaves, Ana runs Sadia a bath.

'I've put lavender in it,' Ana says, then gives her a hug. 'Don't drown yourself.'

Sadia laughs too loud at the joke and then sinks to the floor after Ana leaves. By the time she gets in the bath it's just lukewarm and she lets half of the water drain around her and tops it back up. She lies back and sticks a toe under the tap as it fills, the water so hot that it feels cold until her skin starts to burn. She keeps it there anyway and watches how the water arcs around her foot. She lies there for hours, lets the water cool, drains and fills the tub until there is no more hot water. When the water is as cold as she can bear, she lets it drain around her one last time, feels like some of herself is draining out with it. Lavender sticks to her skin.

Later, Sadia scoops up her sleeping daughter and brings her into the bed she shared with Jamie. Ameera stays asleep, and Sadia curls around her. She can smell Jamie's aftershave on the pillows. He'd spray it on the bed whenever he was working away. So she didn't forget him, he'd say. Clouds shift and the moon shines through the window. Sadia can see Jamie in their daughter now, she doesn't know how she missed it before. She is his in the tilt of her eyebrows and the shape of her jaw, the way she purses her lips when she's angry and the way she tugs her ear when she's sad. Of course she is.

It takes until the following afternoon for Ameera to ask when Jamie is coming home. He has spent a large percentage of her life working away, and she is used to his absence. Sadia gets the axe from the garage and chops some wood, builds a fire in the garden. She waits until the world has grown dark and the sky prickles with stars, then wraps Ameera in a blanket and takes her outside. They cuddle on the bench in front of the fire and rock for a while before Sadia leans back and points upwards.

'See that star?' she says.

'Yep,' Ameera says, and points too. 'That star?'

'Yeah. That's Daddy's star.'

'What's Daddy's star?'

'Daddy's a star now. He lives in heaven.'

'Can we go see him?'

'We can just see him like this.'

Ameera's dark eyes reflect the waxing moon as she gazes upwards. She doesn't speak for a long time.

'Why's Daddy a star?'

'Allah needed him.'

'What for?'

Sadia pauses. A few months ago, she wouldn't have doubted that her husband would go somewhere *good* after death. She didn't know where. She lost that certainty a long time ago. Maybe there is nowhere, but if there is, she'd have been sure that Jamie would go to the good place.

'Because he was so good, Allah picked him for something special.'

'So we can't see him no more?'

'Just like this,' Sadia says, and points up again.

'Just like this,' repeats Ameera, and turns her face into Sadia's shoulder. She is asleep within minutes.

9

Maureen
4th January 2000

Maureen has angled the blinds so that she can see out onto the road from her armchair, but still puts her aida and threads aside every ten minutes to get up and peer out of the window. She occasionally goes upstairs to get a better view of the entire street. Maureen and her husband live in the middle of a long row of terraced houses, built for the miners and passed down through their families. The mines are long closed now, but the century-old houses remain. Maureen has never paid much worry to their position on the street before, but now that she's expecting trouble, she's worried that all the neighbours will see. Even if she manages to get rid of John before they come, she's sure that one of the neighbours will mention it to him. Mrs Lothian over the road always has her nose pressed up against her window. Maureen knows she should just tell him before he finds out, but she can't bring herself to.

'Sit down, for Christ's sake, Maureen,' John snaps eventually. 'What's wrong?'

'Hey!'

'Oh, I know I shouldn't take the name in vain, but you're putting me on edge with your bloody pacing and peering.'

'I'm just restless.'

'What are you looking for?' John asks, craning his neck to see out of the window too.

'Nothing. Look, why don't you just go and play golf if I'm annoying you so much?'

'It's pissing down, freezing, and nearly dark. Why would I go golfing?'

'Oh, then just go to the pub, John. You're getting right on my wick.'

John grumbles and gets out of his chair. 'Fred!' he calls, and a greying Labrador trundles out from the kitchen, stretching in the doorway. 'Howay. We're off to The Prince.'

'I'll have tea ready for half six, hin,' says Maureen, helping John put on his coat and opening the door for him. They wouldn't come after six, surely.

'You're a good'un.'

'I know. Love you.'

'Love you, you loon,' he says. He pushes the dog out before him with the side of his foot, because Fred doesn't like the rain. Maureen leans out of the doorway and watches them down the street, Fred trotting by John's side, John holding his umbrella more over the dog than himself. She smiles, and after glancing around, retreats into the warmth of the sitting room.

As soon as she sits down she stands back up. She wonders if she should just ring the police, put herself out of her misery. She picks up the phone and puts it back down. No, of course not. What would she say? *Hello, I believe what you've found is my nephew's head. How do I know? Well. That's a story and a half.* No. She'll just wait. They'll turn up sooner or later, break the sad news, ask if she knows anything, and she'll act surprised. Upset, but not too upset. She hadn't seen him in years, after all. They were never close. She's worried that they'd recognise her name or her address when they were looking her up and remember that she was married to John Jones – who was ex-police – and just get in touch with him instead – but surely not. It seems unprofessional, especially when it's a death. They wouldn't.

It'll be hours before John is back, but she goes to start the tea just to keep her hands busy. She thought the first couple of days would be the hardest, waiting for someone to find him, but this is worse. Maureen's fingers are awful. She's spent the hours that she'd set aside to sew peeling the skin from around her nails instead. It started with just the dead skin, and once that had gone she moved on to the layers beneath, pulling on the tiniest sore threads, sometimes digging at them with the point of her needle, until each nail was surrounded by a dark pink mess.

A story about Jamie's head is splashed across the front page of today's newspaper, not named, of course. She imagines that when they identify him they'll visit her, she's his only living relative after all, other than his daughter. As far as she knows, they haven't figured out who he is yet, but she still feels on edge, as if the police might turn up at any minute. Maybe they won't come at all.

At least she doesn't have the worry of the candles now. The women had used the same set of candles for every meeting since the first one, when they'd sat in the dark because the light didn't work. Maureen had placed herself in charge of bringing them each week, a small job that made her feel important, like she was contributing something. On the way home on New Year's Eve, she had imagined that each of the women's fingerprints was pressed into the wax, and had visions of the police finding the candles and tracing the fingerprints back to each woman, throwing them into jail one by one. John was already asleep by the time she'd got back from the hotel, snoring after a skinful at The Prince no doubt, and she set the candles out in a row on her hearth and lit them. She watched them burn from her armchair. The last one flickered out as sun filled the sitting room, and she collected the leftover discs and buried them in her kitchen bin under carrot ends and tins of dog food. She'd felt a brief sense of relief that morning when she watched through the kitchen window as the bin men came and tipped the week's refuse into the back of the lorry – but the relief waned as the day went on and by mid-afternoon she was overtaken again by the horrors of the night in the hotel room.

The potatoes are cold in her hands as she peels and slices them. John insists on keeping them in the fridge. One of his little quirks. It took her a long time to get used to living with him after they married. She'd spent so long on her own before that. They've been married for fourteen years now. It was a quiet ceremony; she'd invited a couple of the nurses from the hospital and one of the receptionists. John had been married once before and has a son and a daughter, and they both came. Maureen had worn a smart ivory skirt-suit with a blue handkerchief of Alice's tucked into her pocket. She hadn't invited the farmer or his family because she was worried they'd say something about Jamie, ask where he was maybe; John didn't know about Jamie, and she hadn't ever wanted him to know because she wanted to leave that part of her life behind. Not telling him felt like a stupid decision now it seemed imminent that John would find out, but it was far too late to bring it up; she'd just have to keep lying. She was ashamed of how coldly she had treated her nephew, though most of the time she thought it was justified by his behaviour. Either way, she didn't want John to know that side of her. She was someone different now.

The last time she saw Jamie alive was on his twenty-second birthday, in the only place she ever saw him after he'd left. She'd approached the graveyard that day with a shop-bought bunch of carnations in one hand, and the lead of her poodle in the other. She had taken three buses and walked a mile and a half from the village out to the little chapel in the fields where Alice was buried. She could have paid for a taxi, she had a proper job now, but she liked to take her time with this journey.

She saw Jamie as she rounded the side of the chapel. He was standing in front of Alice's headstone, tall and lithe with his blond hair cropped short and brushed to the side. He was wearing a shirt and suit trousers and looked a damn sight smarter than he had done the previous year, when he'd had a badly cut mullet and looked like he needed a dip in Domestos.

'Good morning,' she said, when she reached the grave. She stood beside him, facing the headstone, and her dog wagged its tail and jumped up to greet Jamie. He bent and extended a hand, but before he could stroke it, Maureen pulled its lead sharply. '*Sit*, Sassy.'

'Aunt Maureen,' he said in acknowledgement, still looking at the dog.

'How long have you been here?'

'Not long. When did you get the dog?'

'I suppose I should wish you a happy birthday.'

'I know that's not what's on your mind today,' he said quietly, meeting her eyes with a look that Maureen thought was almost kind. Almost.

'No.'

'Never was,' he said, his voice harder this time.

'No,' she said, and thought of all his birthdays; no gifts, no cake, just quiet trips to the graveyard. She couldn't bring herself to feel guilty. She imagined how Alice might have celebrated her son's birthday if she'd been alive for any of them – she might have made them special, baked cakes and blown up balloons year after year, made a fuss, let him stay off school and taken him into the city for a new toy that she couldn't afford. Maybe not. Maureen always thought that if Alice had lived she'd have flitted off to live her life while Maureen still raised her son. Maybe she'd have turned up each year on Jamie's birthday, impossibly sparkly and glamorous, each time with a different rich boyfriend, always older with a nice car – swoop into Jamie's life for one day and then be gone by the time he woke the next morning, leaving his world a little more grey without her. Maybe she wouldn't have visited at all, and Maureen would have tried harder with Jamie, been better, because she'd probably have resented Alice then, and not the boy.

Jamie was carrying a small bunch of flowers too, wrapped in brown paper. He laid them on the grave and then lit a cigarette.

'That's a dirty habit. It'll kill you, you know.'

'Would you care?' Jamie smirked.

Maureen smiled. 'She used to smoke. She carried this little silver cigarette case with her initials on it. Some beau or other had given it to her, I imagine. They made her sick when she got pregnant though, so she stopped. Everything made her sick when she got pregnant.'

'Fascinating,' Jamie drawled. They stood in silence for a few minutes, and Jamie dropped the cigarette end to the ground and stamped it out. Maureen huffed, and bent to pick it up.

'Have some respect,' she spat, grabbing his wrist and shoving the butt into his palm. 'Why do you come here, anyway? You didn't even know her. You don't need to come.'

Jamie flicked the cigarette end over the low stone wall of the graveyard into the field beyond and then shrugged. 'Birthday tradition. Wish I had known her. Bet she'd have been a better mother than you.'

'Even if she'd lived, I'd have ended up raising you,' Maureen sneered, looking up at her nephew's face for the first time since she'd arrived. He never did look like Alice. 'She didn't even want you.'

'Would you have hated me less if she'd lived?'

'The only reason she didn't have you ripped out of her womb before you even had fingernails was because I wouldn't let her. Silly me,' Maureen hissed, knowing that she'd gone too far.

Jamie glared into Maureen's eyes for a moment before he spat at her feet and walked away. Maureen waited until he'd gone and lowered herself onto a bench that faced the grave. The dog jumped up and sat beside her, and laid her head on Maureen's leg. Her mouth was wet with puddle water and it made a dark patch on Maureen's skirt. She stroked Sassy's fur as her breathing settled and her heart slowed.

He'd just turned sixteen when he left. She'd woken up at the same time as usual, and crept out of the room to drink her coffee on the doorstep; it was summer, and the sun was already up. She'd only realised when she went back into the house to wake him up for school that he was gone. His clothes had been taken from the wardrobe, and the old suitcase from under the bed was missing too. She remembered with some shame that she was more upset about the absence of the suitcase than she was about the boy – it was the only piece of luggage that she and Alice had had between them when they first arrived at the cottage.

The day before, Maureen had been walking around the perimeter of the farm, which she always did on dry evenings, when she caught Jamie in a shadowy copse with the farmer's granddaughter, Evelyn. Evelyn had just turned twelve, and Jamie loomed over her as she leant against a tree. Neither of them had heard Maureen approach.

'Show me then,' Jamie was saying. 'You said you would.'

Evelyn paused, her mouth open a little, gazing up at Jamie, whom she'd always loved. She moved her hand to the bottom of her skirt.

'Jamie!' Maureen shouted, and they both jumped. Jamie paled. 'Go home, Evelyn.'

Evelyn looked at Jamie and then Maureen, her face screwed up as if she might cry, then bolted out across the field towards the farmhouse.

'What?' Jamie asked. The deepness of his voice still seemed strange, even a couple of years after it had broken. His eyes were wide, as if he didn't know why she was angry. Maureen didn't know what to say, didn't know what to ask or how to broach what she'd seen, or what she hadn't.

'Home,' Maureen said, and pointed towards the tiny cottage they lived in at the edge of the field. Jamie trudged towards it, and she walked two steps behind him all the way, wordless.

'I wasn't doing anything,' Jamie said, when they were inside.

'You were,' Maureen said.

Jamie shrugged in a way that was distinctly teenage and enraged her.

'Whatever you were asking her . . . whatever it was, you are never, ever to do it again.'

Jamie stood in front of Maureen, half a head taller, and gazed at the wall behind her blankly.

'Do you understand?' Maureen asked. She grabbed hold of his jaw and pulled his face close to hers to make him look her in the eye. Before she realised that he had pushed her, she was on the floor. He was looming over her and, for the first time, she was scared of him. She got to her feet and squared up to him despite her fear.

'I pulled you into this world and I'll take you back out, if I have to,' she said, her voice low. For a second, she thought Jamie was going to hit her, but he turned and punched a wall so hard that the bathroom mirror fell off its nail and shattered on the floor. The next morning, he was gone.

The day after he left, she caught the bus into town and bought a new leather suitcase from Fenwick's before returning to the cottage and packing up her belongings. She waited for three days, but the boy did not return, and so, as the sun set over the fields that she'd tended for sixteen years, she moved on.

Maureen puts the panackelty in the oven. John isn't due back for nearly an hour, but it will stay in there just fine until he gets back, the layers of corned beef, onions, peas and potatoes softening one by one until the gravy bubbles through the gaps and the tinfoil lid fills with steam.

A knock on the front door makes her jump. It's a big knock, confident, and Maureen pauses. Dread trickles through her.

She pads into the sitting room, bare feet silent on the carpet, and sees the fluorescent yellow of a police jacket through the frosted glass, someone in black, too. She opens the door to a redhead in a dark trouser-suit and a tall policeman. She doesn't know the police officer, but she knows the redhead. Nova Stokoe. She was at John's retirement party a few years ago, and she's got strands of silver around her temples now, deeper lines joining the corners of her mouth to her nose, but it's her. She doesn't smile.

'Mrs Jones,' Nova says. She shows Maureen her badge. 'Detective Inspector Stokoe. This is Officer Adams. Can we come in?'

'You're a detective inspector now,' Maureen says, standing aside and holding the door open for them. She knows John would be proud of this. He always liked Nova, said she was funny and clever, and Maureen had been briefly jealous until she'd learned that Nova was not interested in men. 'Well done.'

'I didn't know if you'd remember me,' Nova says, as she and the officer step inside and Maureen gestures them towards the sofa, where they both take a seat.

'How could I forget that hair?' Maureen says. She feels faint. 'Are you looking for John?'

Nova presses her lips together and the police officer puts his hat in his lap. 'No. Is he here?'

'No, pet. In the pub.'

'We're actually here to speak to you, Mrs Jones. We have some bad news.'

Maureen hopes that she looks as confused and worried as she's trying to.

'Can I get youse a cup of tea? Coffee?' asks Maureen. She's hovering near her chair, scraping at her fingertips.

'You might want to take a seat,' Nova says.

Maureen nods and sits. She's much more nervous than she thought she'd be.

'It's your nephew, Jamie Spellman. He was found dead yesterday.'

'Dead?' Maureen asks, widening her eyes and hoping she doesn't look too theatrical. Nova is watching her closely, and Maureen thinks she must be looking for traces of guilt on her face. She feels herself flush, and she begins to shake, and she hopes that it looks like grief.

'I'm sorry, I know it must be a shock.'

'How did he die?'

'It was quite . . .' Nova pauses, and Maureen wonders how the detective will describe the state of Jamie's corpse to her. She wonders if telling relatives that their loved one has been decapitated is covered in their training.

Maureen inclines her head, and Nova crosses and uncrosses her legs.

'It was quite gruesome,' Nova continues, glaring at the floor before she meets Maureen's eyes – searching for something, Maureen thinks. 'He was found beheaded, Mrs Jones.'

Just as she says *beheaded*, the front door opens and Fred trots into the house, shaking the rain from his fur, followed by John who is holding a bunch of pink lilies – Maureen's favourite. Maureen goes cold.

'What's going on?' John asks.

10

Kaysha
5th January 2000

A square of sun shines through the skylight onto the woman beside Kaysha in bed. The covers are pushed down around her ankles and every hair across her freckled tummy catches the light, translucent and tiny until the sparse, burnished trail that leads from the well of her belly button to the V of loose-coiled copper below it. The hair thins and lightens across her thighs, grows close again on her calves. She lifts one of her knees so that her foot is flat on the mattress. She has a tattoo of a magpie on her ankle, years old but still bright. Kaysha knows that she has another across her back, the tips of its outstretched wings resting on her shoulder blades. When she moves her arms, the bird takes flight.

She is propped up on cushions reading a book about oranges, which she holds up in front of her face to keep the sun out of her eyes. She is wearing her glasses, only because she thinks that Kaysha is asleep. She's usually too vain, though Kaysha loves the way the round, wire frames rest against her cheekbones. Nova's bottom lip is sucked in below the top one and she frowns slightly as she reads. She makes the same face when she's building up to an orgasm, when she's so close that she goes quiet and wills herself to let go. She finds it hard to relinquish control and give in to her body, but Kaysha always manages to push her over the edge.

Nova's auburn ringlets are clipped away from her face and she winds one around a finger as she reads. Her collarbones are littered with little bites the same colour as dried rose petals, and her nipples are hard in the cool morning air, or maybe it's something in the book.

Kaysha will never admit it, but Nova's cluttered flat is her favourite place in the world to wake up. It's been six months since she was last here, since the argument. They'd always argued and then made up, but the last one was the worst. Kaysha had vowed that last time was really the last time, but needs must.

'I like you in your glasses,' Kaysha says. Nova glances at her and smiles.

'I knew you were watching, you perv.'

'You're nice to watch.'

Nova plucks a hair from her head and uses it to keep her page. She pushes her glasses down to the end of her nose and looks at Kaysha over the top of them.

'Do you know what happens to peeping Toms, Ms Jackson?'

Kaysha laughs but something heavy ripples through her.

She shakes her head and sinks further into the pillows. Nova arches an eyebrow and slips a cold hand under the covers and down Kaysha's abdomen.

'They get punished.'

Kaysha pulls on last night's knickers and looks around the room for the rest of her clothes.

'You can borrow some of mine, if you want, you know,' Nova says as she rifles through her wardrobe. 'Neebody likes a crusty crotch.'

'Nah, Sarah'll notice,' Kaysha says, though she's sure she wouldn't.

'New girlfriend?'

'Yeah.'

'What's she like?' Nova asks, looking genuinely interested.

'She's . . . intense.'

'Do you love her?'

'Some days I think I do. When she's having a good day. Like, I think, I love her, I want to protect her, but I'm not *in* love with her, if that makes sense.'

'Lesbian bed death?'

'Something like that,' Kaysha says, and smirks.

'Maybe you should let her go.'

'She's pretty fragile.'

'Yeah?'

'We moved in too fast and now it's hard to extricate myself.'

'Classic,' Nova says.

'Lesbians, eh?'

'Lesbians.'

'I'll have to find somewhere else to go when we break up,' Kaysha says, surprised at how cold she sounds, but has no deeper feelings about the situation. She needs to keep an eye on Sarah until she's more stable, but she'll leave after that.

Nova looks around the flat pointedly and grins. 'I know somewhere that you could go.'

'Not likely, when you're still with PC Miserybones,' Kaysha says, nodding to a framed picture of Nova and Ella. They're both wearing black-and-white-striped football shirts, and Nova has her arm draped over Ella's shoulders, a pint of beer in her hand. Kaysha suddenly feels sour. The glow of the morning wanes and they're back to where they were six months ago.

Nova's clavicle pinkens and she tips the frame face down. 'She got me that for Christmas. I didn't get her anything.'

'How's she doing?'

'She's fine.'

'How can she be fine?'

'It wasn't cancer after all.'

'Oh, well, that's good.'

'Yeah.'

'But you're still with her.'

'Yeah, I suppose I am.'

Kaysha is furious and sad and disappointed but hasn't got time to be. She wishes Nova wanted her enough to leave Ella. Maybe she got cold feet about moving in with Kaysha, or maybe she just realised that she liked Ella better, or that Kaysha isn't girlfriend material. For one terrible moment, Kaysha wonders if Nova made the entire thing up as an excuse to get rid of her – but no, she knows Nova wouldn't do that. It doesn't matter what happened before, because she can't get sucked back in – she just needs to keep Nova close so that she can keep an eye on her progress with the case.

'Yeah, okay,' Kaysha says, exhaling slowly. 'Let's talk about something else. I didn't come to argue.'

'Thank fuck.'

'What's your day looking like? Anything interesting?'

Nova shrugs. 'Not really. Just trying to get to the bottom of this cult shit.'

'I've seen some of their artistry about. Wrote an article about one of their dead chickens in Whitley Bay a couple of weeks ago. Charming.'

'Mmm. They're slippery. But now . . . well. We need to catch them.'

'What do you mean?'

'I've already said too much,' Nova says. She turns away and grabs her boots.

'Do you think the cult had something to do with the beheaded bloke, then?'

Nova looks up. 'Why would you think that?'

'Little birdie passed me some details about the crime scene.'

'How many little birdies have you got?' Nova asks, putting a foot on the arm of her sofa and lacing up her boot.

Kaysha smiles and ignores the question. 'So you think they're linked?'

'Maybe. Nobody's really that bothered about the goats and that . . . I've just been investigating it because they're spooking all the farmers. We've got to look like we're doing something,' Nova says, squirting hair mousse into her palm. It expands to the size of an apple and she bends over so that her hair dangles in front of her face as she scrunches the foam into it. 'Bigger fish now though.'

'Have you got any idea who he is yet? Is he local?'

Nova shakes her head. 'We're waiting for dental records, but it's slow with the time of year.'

'Yeah, I can imagine,' Kaysha says. She knows that Nova is lying to her, because Sadia has already identified the body.

11

Sarah
5th January 2000

Smoke swirls and gathers against the ceiling as Sarah lights another cigarette from the burning end of the last. She has dragged her favourite armchair across the room, scraping the varnish from the floorboards, so that she can sit in front of the window. The world tumbles away at the end of the lawn, rising again on the other side of the valley, dusted with snow, and she can see the road that slinks between the hills towards the house.

She props her heels on the windowsill. Kaysha said she'd be back in the morning, but the sun rose an hour ago and she's still not here, and Sarah supposes that Kaysha is still curled up in bed with the detective. It's not the fact that her girlfriend has spent the night with another woman that bothers her – it's the lateness. Sarah had been the one to suggest that Kaysha rekindle her affair with Nova, and Kaysha had raised her eyebrows as if she hadn't already considered it. They'd set out guidelines for how it would work, talked about how Kaysha needed to be honest, how she would come home in the morning after a night with Nova and check in before she went to work. Sarah feels a savage pride in herself for the maturity of it, for putting the bigger picture before her own needs. She is letting – *encouraging* – her girlfriend to sleep with another woman, a woman who she's loved before, so that others would be protected. She is being selfless. That's what she keeps telling herself.

It's been a while since she finished the second bottle of the night and the pain of the house starts creeping in again, the dizzying, sprawling emptiness of it, the hatred spread through the walls, darkening the corners like damp. It gets into her lungs. Since she's been back here she can feel it poisoning her, like it poisons everyone. Sometimes she wonders if her parents were the way they were because of the house, if it soured them, or if it was the other way round. Sarah doesn't quite know why she hasn't sold it or burned it down and started again somewhere new, done something with her life instead of rotting there, lurking like some Dickensian ghost. She can't bring herself to commit to the effort. The house weighs her down and her mind weighs her down and she is trapped.

Sarah steps around the shards of a wine glass, the purple stain across the rug, and goes to the cellar to get another. Her dad was a collector and when she first came back there were hundreds of bottles, floor to ceiling against the back wall. She's on to the good stuff now, though she had to break the cabinet with an axe from the shed to get to it. Once when she was thirteen she'd pissed him off and he'd asked her why she couldn't *just be more like David* and she'd said *What, dead?* and then stormed off to her treehouse after a quick trip to the cellar. She remembers her father's face in the hospital as she was lying in bed, hooked up to a drip, and she knew he was more upset about the wine than her. She'd told him she didn't realise it was one of the *very* expensive ones, but she did, and after that he had a cabinet installed and locked them up.

She picks up a bottle at random, blows the dust off it. It's Portuguese, 1964. Her parents had their honeymoon in Portugal in the sixties, and she wonders if it was bought then, saved for a special anniversary or to hand down. She snorts at the thought that they'd be so sentimental about anything and uncorks it.

As the sun climbs and shadows stretch across the hardwood floor, Sarah falls asleep in the armchair. She dreams about Jamie again. Every time the exhaustion overwhelms her she sees him, one way or the other. Sometimes he's like he was in the hotel, grotesque but harmless, silver tongue bloated and still in his mouth. Sometimes he's bodiless but still somehow alive, speaking to them, and they all obey him and only Sarah understands that he's lying. The worst ones are when he's whole, tall and smiling, and everything is happy until it isn't, and he's whispering in her ears and she's turning herself inside out to try and please him, slitting herself in half until there is a tiny cry and he leaves and she is alone again, trying to stitch herself back together, and she startles awake when she realises she's dying.

Sarah hates the entire house, including and especially the bedroom she grew up in. She has started several times, on good days, to paint the walls of the rooms she has to use, but soon the darkness returns and she abandons the effort. She has never been one to finish things, only to start them, and now she lives in a house that is hers in halves; the blue half of the kitchen, the purple half of the living room. The guest room was always plain and unused, so it doesn't feel personal either way.

The night they met, she and Kaysha tumbled out of the pub and down the country lanes together, drunk on each other, temporarily forgetting the dangers of the dark. Sarah had said she lived alone in a haunted old manor, inherited and unwanted, and Kaysha had laughed until she saw it. The ivy-trimmed house stood three floors high, four including the cellar, surrounded by overgrown lawns and backed by a walled garden, and then an evergreen forest. From the top-floor windows you could see for miles across the valley, mainly farmers' fields and livestock, a couple of villages linked by a bridge across the beginnings of the Derwent.

'Thought you were taking the piss,' Kaysha said, eyes wide, as Sarah unlocked the front door. She asked if she could have a tour, and Sarah had obliged, drunk and giddy enough not to be hit by the full force of dread that she usually felt if she thought about going into her parents' or David's rooms. Kaysha had groaned at each new room, cobwebby and untouched since the occupants passed away, and Sarah couldn't tell if she was pleased or horrified, or both. Kaysha said the house felt like a film set, so perfectly preserved that it didn't feel real. Sarah's parents' bed was still unmade, her dad's clothes still around the washing basket rather than in it, a dried-up glass of wine on the vanity desk.

The treehouse was full of spiders and long-rotted men's magazines that she'd stolen from her dad's stash, empty bottles of wine in a corner with a half-finished quart of vodka that she must have forgotten about the last time she climbed up, years earlier. Kaysha kissed Sarah for the first time as they knelt together in the damp, and Sarah felt as dizzy as she had when she was fourteen, sitting in the same spot, a little drunk and thinking about kissing girls. She was allowed to talk about how she'd like to kiss boys anywhere, and she did, but she only allowed herself to think about girls in the same way when she was alone in the treehouse. Sometimes the feeling was sweet and full of potential, and she'd imagine herself in a suit, playing house with a cute wife and a dog. On other days she felt dark and heavy when she thought about it, and on those days she'd drag a pair of scissors across her wrists and then cover the cuts with bracelets.

Two weeks after they met, Kaysha's lease was up and she'd spent so much time with Sarah that she hadn't found anywhere else to live. She'd asked if she could stay for a few days until she found a new place, and then Sarah made sure that Kaysha was too busy to find one. The warmth of someone else in the house with her, someone bright and fizzy, filled the dark corners of the manor so that for the first time since David died, Sarah felt happy there for a while.

When Kaysha comes home, mid-morning, Sarah is waiting by the door. She kisses Kaysha as she walks inside, snow-flakes caught in her hair, and then pushes her up against the front door and kisses her harder, biting her bottom lip and digging her fingernails into Kaysha's shoulders. Kaysha pushes her away.

'What are you doing?'

'I want to fuck you,' Sarah says, tipping her head to kiss Kaysha's neck.

'You're drunk,' Kaysha says, and kicks off her shoes. 'Of course you are.'

'So?'

Kaysha pauses and presses her lips together. 'It's fine.'

'Was she good?'

'What?'

'Better than me?'

'Don't, Sarah.'

'Well, I suppose she has more experience, if she's a full dyke.'

'Stop it.'

'It's alright, you can just say it. You can just say *Sarah, she's better in bed than you*.'

'I'm not having this conversation with you,' Kaysha says, and pushes past Sarah to go upstairs. Sarah winds her fingers into her hair and pulls. She has never learned how to feel pain on the inside without inflicting it on her body too.

12

Nova
5th January 2000

Nova knocks and pushes the door open. The lab is small but bright, and a tall woman in a white coat is sitting on a worktop in front of a window that stretches the length of the wall. She is holding a plastic container full of salad and looks mildly surprised when Nova lets herself in.

'Ana Cortês? Sorry to interrupt your lunch,' Nova says, leaving the door open and walking further into the lab. It's clean and tidy, but everything looks outdated; paint peels from a corner and faults in the lino are patched up with black electrical tape. 'I'm investigating the death of Jamie Spellman. Can I ask you a few questions?'

The woman clips the lid back onto her Tupperware and slides off the bench. She looks Nova in the eye and doesn't smile. She is a couple of inches taller than Nova and seems effortlessly elegant. Her dark hair is swept back in a ponytail with wisps that have fallen free, curling against her long neck. She isn't wearing any make-up save for deep red lipstick, and the top few buttons of her shirt are open. A gold crucifix rests against the tawny brown of her sternum.

'Is everyone being questioned?' she asks.

Nova shrugs. 'Not everyone. They said you two worked together very closely. I thought you might be able to tell me a bit about him.'

Ana nods and leans back against the bench, arms crossed. 'What do you want to know?'

'When was the last time you saw him?' Nova asks, pulling her notepad from her back pocket.

'The twenty-third. We finished work at lunchtime and then the Christmas party happened. I left early, about three. I think he stayed, I don't really know.'

Nova makes a note of the date and time and nods. 'Did you spend a lot of time with him? Here? Outside work?'

'His lab's through there.' Ana nods to a door in the corner of the room. 'So I saw him a lot. We were friends.'

'Was it a strictly professional relationship, Ms Cortês?'

'Mrs,' Ana corrects, tilting her chin up and touching her crucifix with her left hand, and Nova sees her wedding ring. 'We went to university together. He recommended me for the job here. Like I said, we were friends. Nothing more, if that's what you're asking.'

Nova bows her head. 'I'm sorry for your loss.'

'Thank you.'

'Was he particularly close with anyone else here? Romantically or otherwise? Or outside of work?'

Ana hesitates. 'I'm friends with his wife. He had affairs, I think, but I told him I didn't want to know about them.'

Nova nods. 'What about any links to anyone . . . unsavoury? Were you aware of him having links to any underground activities? Organised crime, that sort of thing? Cults, maybe?'

Ana frowns. 'Cults?'

Nova tilts her head. 'It's an unusual murder, so we have to explore unusual routes.'

'He'd have made a good cult leader,' Ana says, and then looks irritated, like she's said something she shouldn't have.

'What do you mean?' Nova asks.

Ana folds her arms and smiles. 'Nothing, really. He was good looking and charming, that's all.'

'Can I have a look around his lab?'

Ana nods, and leads Nova into the other room. It's easily double the size of Ana's lab and filled with a lot more equipment. 'This all looks very complex.'

'It is.'

'I've heard he was doing exciting things,' Nova says, striding around the room and glancing in cupboards and drawers. It was all just books and test tubes, nothing personal. 'I saw that he won a big award a few months ago.'

Ana holds Nova's gaze for a second before she speaks. 'Yes. He was very brilliant. His death is a great loss.'

'What was it he was working on?'

Ana pauses and takes a deep breath. 'He wanted to help with historical rape cases. Finding a way to profile rapists using leftover traces of semen. He made quite a big breakthrough.'

'Impressive,' Nova says. Ana raises her eyebrows and says nothing. 'Worth someone killing him over? A competitor maybe?'

'Maybe.'

'Do you know of any enemies he may have had?'

Ana thumbs her crucifix again. 'He's – he was a complex man. I was his friend, but he didn't have many more. Sometimes he was very friendly, sometimes he was not.'

Nova nods. 'But no particular rivals you can think of?'

Ana shrugs, and Nova wonders how complicated Ana's relationship with Jamie really was.

'Will you take over his projects? You obviously worked very closely.'

'Well, yes – I'd be honoured to, but we'll see how the management feel. I'm not as well respected here as Jamie was. Especially not without his influence.'

'The management treat you badly?' Nova asks, though she knows exactly what Ana means. When she'd turned up an hour earlier, she'd spoken to the general manager of the lab. He'd sweated, tripping over his words as he told her what a devastating loss to the company Jamie was, how they'd lose the funding if they didn't get someone to carry on his project, and – well – they'd already spent most of it. He mumbled about how he could always get *Cortês, knew what she was doing after all, very capable, more so than even Jamie, maybe, but it'd mean countless meetings and interactions with her, and frankly, she gave him the heebs. One of those – you know –* he'd said – *thinks he's a woman . . . we've all got to play along. We all suspected that Jamie was – you know – they were always together. I've already asked but she says she doesn't know how he ended up like he did. Bet she does, though. Can't trust a word they say, those types.* Nova had stiffened and suggested that he have more respect for his staff, and turned to ask the receptionist for directions to Ana's lab as the manager had stood open-mouthed.

'I'm the best scientist here,' Ana says, and then shrugs. 'But you've seen my workspace, compared to this.'

Nova nods. 'It sounds difficult.'

'It's infuriating, but what can I do?'

Nova holds Ana's gaze for a few seconds. She can see the deep, quiet fury in her. It's possible that she could have snapped.

'What do you do outside of work, Mrs Cortês?'

'I care for my children, Detective. I spend time with friends. I read, watch TV. I walk the dog,' she says. 'I grieve for lost friends.'

'Here's my card,' Nova says, and then opens her notebook to a blank page and jots down the address of an LGBT support group that she sometimes attends, where they talk about their experiences. One woman in the group, a blonde femme who was always accompanied by her butch partner, had been a primary school teacher, got fired when she was outed. Of course the school board said it was for something else they'd made up, but everyone knew the real reason. 'Off the record. This is a support group that you might find useful. We mainly just vent to each other but, you know, some of them are lawyers. Just in case.'

Ana takes the scrap of paper and puts it in her pocket, her cheeks colouring. 'I'm fine.'

'I know. You seem very capable,' Nova says, and then lowers her voice to a whisper. 'The manager is a dick.'

Ana doesn't say anything but she smiles and lifts one shoulder.

'I know where to find you if I have anymore questions,' Nova says, and turns to leave. 'Thank you for your help.'

13

Maureen
6th January 2000

The day her nephew ran away from home was the day that Maureen Spellman began her life. When she was young she had often dreamed of how her life would play out. She'd marry at twenty-one – a modestly handsome man, older, but not too much older, who she could dote on, and who wouldn't mind her working after they were married, at least until she had a child. She'd have a son after a year of marriage – she'd call him Jack after her mother's father. Jack would have Maureen's blue eyes and her husband's dark hair. A couple of years later she'd bear a daughter – Susan – who was always clean and obedient, and who people would look at fondly and then say *Aah, Maureen, she'll be a heartbreaker*. Maybe when they were grown she'd go back to nursing. If her husband had money – she didn't mind so much about that – but if he did, they could retire early and go abroad a couple of times a year. She'd always wanted to visit Italy.

When Alice got into her spot of bother, Maureen was already twenty-five and not even courting yet. Time was passing faster than she'd planned, but it was fine – there was a new doctor on her ward whose eyes twinkled when he saw her, or so she imagined. Her eyes certainly twinkled when she saw him. Alice was only just seventeen, and she was nothing like Maureen. She didn't dream of tomorrows, she lived in her today. Maureen knew Alice was much more beautiful than she was – Maureen had big hands and feet, dull coppery hair and eyes that were a bit too small for her round face. Alice was petite and doe-eyed, auburn hair cropped short like that model everyone was obsessed with at the time. A smile like a siren. She was passionate and always ready to argue, but she'd make you a cup of tea straight afterwards to say sorry. Of course she was going to get herself into trouble sooner or later.

Maureen had crouched against a cubicle door in the hospital as she gave Alice the results from her pregnancy test. Alice wept when it said positive, and Maureen had given her a cigarette to calm her down, but it made Alice retch. The cigarette sizzled out in the toilet water when Alice opened her legs and dropped it between them.

'Do you have his telephone number?'

'I don't even have his name.'

'Oh, Alice,' Maureen said, wiping a hand down her face. 'You're going to have to find him.'

'Why?' Alice asked, looking at Maureen as if she were mad.

'You don't want to be sent to the convent.'

'Maur—'

'What do you know about him? Where did you find him?' Maureen asked, possibilities flicking through her head. If Alice didn't know who the father was, she'd just have to trick some poor sap into thinking the baby was his, convince him to marry her. She looked at her sister. Even pale and sickly, she was still beautiful. It would be easy to find someone to marry her.

'I'm not having a baby,' Alice said, taking Maureen's wrist. Her hands were cold, her eyes determined.

'What are you talking about? Of course you are, I just told you.'

'I need you to help me get rid of it.'

Maureen and Alice grew up in a vicarage on the outskirts of the city. Maureen's bedroom overlooked the graveyard, and she often watched from her window as Alice climbed down from her own bedroom onto the kitchen roof, onto the rubber lid of the dustbin and flitted between the headstones, then over the low wall and into the thicket, most often to meet a boy. She'd come to breakfast the next morning with a scarf knotted around her throat to hide the love bites. Maureen disapproved – *No one will marry you if you sleep with anyone you find on a street corner*, she'd tell Alice – but she always covered for her if she needed to.

Their dad was a keen disciplinarian. Maureen had watched him beat their mother since she was small. He'd beat them too, sometimes. Alice more often than her, but sometimes he'd be in such a temper that he'd snap at some little thing Maureen said and slap her and then make her pray for forgiveness. Maureen wasn't always sure what she was praying for, but she'd pray anyway. He wasn't a drinker, he was just angry. Their mother died when Alice was five, and Alice had been Maureen's responsibility after that.

Maureen had seen girls die in the hospital after desperate attempts to induce miscarriages; bleeding out after botched backstreet surgery, or vomiting after swallowing bleach or strange plants. She'd always thought of those girls as silly, reckless. Getting themselves into a mess that could have been avoided if only they'd kept their legs together, a mess so desperate they'd rather risk death than have the child. Not only death, but the wrath of God, because murder is murder is murder. She couldn't bear any of that for her sister, reckless or not, so she convinced Alice to keep the child.

A month later, when Alice's stomach started to bulge, Maureen left their father a note, propped up by the kettle, and they both crept out of Alice's bedroom window at four in the morning with only one suitcase of clothes between them. Maureen had struck a deal with a farmer out in the countryside who had a cottage on his land and would need some help with lambing.

Maureen lived in that cottage for sixteen years. She grew increasingly sour as she pulled each lamb from its mother, feet first, and watched those opening moments of its life. The lambs don't kill their mothers when they come out feet first, but Jamie did. She'd watch the mother lick the baby clean, and then the lamb's first wobbly steps in the hay. A couple of years later she'd help that same lamb birth its own baby, maybe twins, and then eventually trot off to the slaughter. Her own life passed her by, and by the time she left the cottage she was over forty. She didn't meet John until she was forty-five, when he'd come onto her ward with a broken leg and asked her to write her phone number on his cast. That was in 1985, and though she would have loved nothing more than to have a child with John, grow someone inside her that was made of them both, she'd already stopped bleeding.

John has been holed up in the spare bedroom for hours when Maureen brings him another cup of tea. She's been sheepish and overly attentive since Nova visited and Maureen had finally been forced to tell him about Jamie – not the whole truth, of course. Just the necessary bits. John had seemed hurt more than angry. He asked her how she could have kept the truth about her nephew from him. They weren't supposed to have secrets. She'd told him that she'd just wanted to create a life where his name was never uttered, she just wanted to move past it, the memories were too traumatic. They had several long, serious conversations about it, about whether she was hiding anything else from him. She thought of the flickering shadows on the walls of the hotel room, the thickening scent of death in the cold air, the sting of bleach between her fingers, and told him *No, that's all*.

The spare bedroom is a medium-sized room at the back of the house where the sun doesn't often reach, though the long morning rays of midsummer sometimes manage to brush the left-hand wall. It's filled with things that aren't used often – a wooden bunk bed for when the grandkids stay over, a bookshelf filled with coloured plastic boxes of aida and threads, watercolours and half-finished paintings, a few unread celebrity autobiographies, odds and ends that have no other place. Maureen often takes up hobbies and buys all the gear, and then gives up two weeks later, irritated that she isn't good at it yet. In the corner is an L-shaped desk that they'd bought from a car-boot sale. It has KATY carved onto the side of it a few times and the remnants of some peeled-off stickers. It's ratty, but it was the exact right size and was only a fiver. Maureen has been saying she'll sand and paint it for the last year, but she never gets around to it.

Above the desk are wall-mounted shelves, usually filled with dozens of scrapbooks and photo albums and folders, the evidence of John's forty-year career in the police force. He has kept every newspaper article and photograph, photocopies he definitely shouldn't have made of particularly interesting police reports that he filed over the years, the names of the victims and suspects blacked out with a marker, though he can usually remember them anyway. John sits at the desk with his glasses on, the files and folders in piles around him. He's bending over one, trying to read the smudged print of an old article from *The Chronicle*. He flicks onto the next page with a tut just as Maureen picks up his empty mug and replaces it with a fresh one, along with a couple of custard creams.

'Found what you're looking for, hin?' she asks, but John doesn't acknowledge her. 'Let me know if I can help.'

As she walks out of the room John asks, 'Was he a Spellman?'

'Unless he changed his name,' Maureen replies from the doorway. 'Why?'

'What year was he born?'

'Sixty-five.'

John scribbles on a scrap of paper and doesn't say anything else, so Maureen goes back downstairs, teary, to wash the cup and make a start on tea. She should have told him otherwise, told him that Jamie had been called Smith or Black or Davidson, something common, but she can't bear to lie to him more than she has to. Maybe this is her punishment for it all.

An hour later, just as she sits down with her own cuppa to watch *Countdown*, John calls for her from the spare room and she hurries back upstairs. He's been cool with her all day and she's glad that he's willing to speak to her, even if it's about Jamie. He's looking satisfied, legs crossed and mug in hand. He nods her over and points to an article glued into the back cover of a notebook. Maureen picks it up and takes a closer look. It's Jamie alright, but years ago. He looks similar to how he looked the last time she saw him in the graveyard; neat and clean-shaven with a boyish thinness. His face is serious and he has an arm around the shoulders of a slight woman with shoulder-length hair and sharp features. Olive.

The headline reads *LOCAL TEEN LOSES LIFE AT SEASIDE SUICIDE SPOT*. Maureen frowns and takes the book from her husband.

> The lifeless body of a Tynemouth teenager was discovered yesterday at the base of a cliff, in the shadow of the Priory. Kimberley Farrugia (16) was, according to her heartbroken mother, a bright and funny girl who became depressed after her father committed suicide two years ago. Family friend Jamie Spellman and the teen's mother both witnessed the girl fall to her death as they were searching for her after realising she was gone from her bed on Sunday evening.

The rest of the text is illegible. Maureen looks back at the photograph. It's difficult to make much out, but there's something about the way that Jamie has his arm clamped around the woman, something about the way that Olive is leaning on his shoulder that makes her think that they must have been sleeping together. She's wondered before. Olive has never admitted to this during their meetings, saying that they were only ever friends, but she always speaks about him very kindly and insists that she doesn't know why she has been included in the group, though she always turns up.

'Knew I'd heard that name before,' John says triumphantly, jabbing his finger at the photograph. 'I remember this case, did some work on it. Wasn't in my area but someone got fired, or was on holiday, something like that.'

'Did you ever find out what had happened?' Maureen asks. The date on the article tells her that they were together when John was investigating the case, but he always took his job seriously and would never tell her about active investigations, so it doesn't surprise her that he never mentioned it.

John rubs a hand over his chin. 'I had my suspicions.'

'You don't think the girl topped herself?'

'She might have,' John says. He leans back in the chair and puts a hand over his eyes, which Maureen knows means he is trying to remember something. 'I'd heard that she'd been in to the station to complain about him before, *your Jamie*.'

'He's not *my* anything,' she says.

'Well, he was, wasn't he, hen? But that's by the by,' John says, his eyes hard. 'Anywas, apparently the young lassie had been in saying he was following her about, gave her the creeps, but no one ever filed any paperwork. Paul, the officer she'd spoken to, knew the girl's mother and the mother had said to pay the bairn no attention, she was going through a rough time and she'd appreciate it if they didn't make a thing of it. I still thought it was fishy, like, and I had a deeks about in her bedroom, looked for a diary or whatever, but there was nowt.'

'I bet he was up to something,' Maureen says, rage and disgust and shame washing through her.

'Well, you knew him better than anyone, didn't you?'

Maureen flares her nostrils and holds herself back. 'I did when he was a child, and he was awful then. Disturbed. Not normal. Who knows what he grew up to become.'

'Funny. That's the word the girl's mother used to describe her as well. Disturbed. *Kim was disturbed*, she kept saying.'

'Well—'

'Maybe it's something parents say when they haven't done a very good job of raising their kids, and the kid acts like a dick, or when they're just not paying enough attention to realise that the kid is in danger, and they're kidding themselves, and they say *Ah the bairn's just disturbed, nothing to do with my parenting*.'

'You've got no idea what it was like for me.'

'You again. It's always about you, Maur.'

'It's not . . .'

'I did wonder at the time, you know, he was creepy, didn't blink enough, I dunno. I did wonder if he killed her, but when I interviewed them they both swore up and down that the girl fell. Nothing I could do without proof. But if he did . . . what does that make you?'

Maureen's eyes widen. John has never looked at her the way he is now, so cold and accusing. She feels as if something has been lost between them, some understanding of each other.

'If he killed someone . . . if he did, that's nothing to do with me. I hadn't seen him for . . . barely seen him since he was sixteen.'

'Well, that's the question, isn't it? Nature versus nurture.'

'Nature. Always nature.'

'Thought you'd say that,' John says with a small, sad smile. 'I'm going to give Nova Stokoe a bell. I dunno if this Olive will know anything, she mebbes hasn't seen him for years, but she might've.'

A spike of fear shoots through Maureen. They all know that Olive is the one, if any of them, who will get them into trouble. If Nova speaks to her, the entire thing might unravel. They might all end up in prison.

'Oh, I don't think that's necessary,' she says, trying to keep her voice steady. She puts a hand on John's arm. 'Let Nova do her job, hin.'

'A tip isn't going to hurt.'

'It might send her in the wrong direction.'

'What are you hiding?' John says, standing up. He looks down at her, frowning, half a foot taller. She feels tiny beside him, like she has shrunk and he has grown, he fills the room and she is nothing. She feels compelled to just tell him everything. She wonders, if she went to prison, if they all did, if he would respect her again. Maybe it would restore the balance in their relationship.

'Nothing. Nothing else. I just . . . it's just not your job anymore.'

'You must really have hated him,' John says, his lip curling into the closest thing to a sneer she's ever seen on him.

'What do you mean?'

'Well, you'd think you'd actually want your nephew's murder solved, wouldn't you?'

14

Kaysha
6th January 2000

Kaysha arrives at Nova's flat just as the town hall clock chimes nine across the city. Every time they are together it feels like it might be the last time, and they pull at each other's clothes with a desperation that only comes with loss. They only get as far as the fake sheepskin rug in front of the fireplace, where they sweat in the flickering light. They are distracted at a very intimate moment by a repeated vibration from the pocket of Kaysha's denim jacket, which is in a heap by the front door. The phone's movement makes the enamel pins on the jacket rattle against the floor, and Nova pauses.

'Do you want to answer that?'

'No,' Kaysha says, winding her fingers into Nova's hair and pushing her back to what she was doing. The phone eventually goes still, and Kaysha lets her shoulders relax against the rug. Seconds later a tinny ringtone plays from Nova's Nokia, which is on the coffee table.

'Is that the *Inspector Gadget* theme tune?' Kaysha asks, peering over her body at Nova. Nova flushes.

'Shut up,' Nova says. She kisses Kaysha's thigh and pushes herself up.

'Not now,' Kaysha says, grabbing Nova's wrist just as she starts on hands and knees towards her phone. 'I'm so close.'

Nova looks at Kaysha and then at her phone. Kaysha arches her back and tugs at Nova's wrist, and Nova grins and turns back.

Later, when Nova goes to shower, Kaysha adds a few extra logs to the fire and then checks her phone. There is a voicemail from Maureen, who whispers that her husband has found some old article linking Olive to Jamie, and is trying to get in touch with Nova to give her the tip. Maureen doesn't need to explain why this is alarming. If Olive is questioned, the whole messy business will come out. Olive is still in love with Jamie, doesn't believe that he did what he did, and Kaysha knows that she made a mistake when she invited Olive to be part of the group. Kaysha believes that Olive can't let herself accept what Jamie did, because if she does, she'll have to accept that she let the wolf into her house, led him to the feast.

Kaysha deletes the voicemail, and opens Nova's phone to do the same. She is worried that Maureen's husband will try to get in touch again, so she restricts calls from his number and switches off the phone. The sound of the shower stops and she hears Nova step onto her weird, wooden bath mat, which always creaks. Kaysha shoves Nova's phone under the sofa just as the bathroom door opens.

'Shall I order a pizza?' Nova asks, grinning and tying the belt of her dressing gown.

An hour later, they lie across the sofa and watch as Sarah Michelle Gellar and Selma Blair lean in for a kiss. Kaysha picks the pieces of pepperoni off her slice of pizza and eats them first, followed by the cheese, and then, after sucking the tomato sauce from her fingertips, the base. Nova eats her half, veggie, the normal way.

'I saw this five times at the pictures,' Nova says, rewinding the tape and watching the actresses kiss again.

'I knew you would've,' Kaysha says, glancing up at her from her position between Nova's knees. She eats the last of the pizza and wipes her hands on the blanket that she is wrapped in.

'Clampet. Use a tea towel or summat.'

'I can't be bothered to move, so it's this or your dressing gown.'

'Don't even dare, it's silk.'

Kaysha wiggles her fingers near Nova's blue dressing gown and grins. Nova leans over and closes the pizza box.

'That was nice,' Kaysha says.

'Have you ever been to New York?' Nova asks.

'No.'

'I want to go. I want to try the pizza.'

'They call it pie there.'

'I like . . . you know in films when it dangles into their mouths? I always thought it seemed so cool. I just want to try the floppy pizza.'

'So, out of all the galleries, theatres and monuments in New York City, you want to go for flaccid pizza?'

'Yeah.'

Kaysha laughs and Nova wraps her arms around her and kisses the top of her head. They've done this for the last three years, drift together and push apart, over and over. They get a thrill from the illicitness of it, one always looking for information from the other, whispering things they're not supposed to tell at dawn like payment for the night. Kaysha has always been giddy on it, the danger of pointing Nova in the right direction on a case from whispers she's heard in underground bars or drug-front cafes. She is repaid in tip-offs to her next big story, the name of a hotel where a murder has happened. Sometimes she already knows.

Just before Kaysha had found Sarah, she and Nova had decided to have a proper go at their relationship. Nova in particular had grown tired of their clandestine meetings and quick kisses and wanted something real. She'd laid out a life like a map before Kaysha, smoothed the creases and pointed to the places they'd go. They'd move in together, somewhere at the edge of the city where they could rent a house with a garden, or even a top-floor apartment with a roof terrace, they'd have a patio filled with potted plants and their green tendrils would creep up the walls. They'd have a kitchen with an island and it would be such a beautiful room that they'd vow to learn how to bake, though they never really would. They'd stay in bed on Sunday mornings, sometimes hungover, reading the newspaper. They would play Cluedo in the afternoon, and

Kaysha would tip the board over because she doesn't like to lose – but she'd always win at Scrabble. Maybe one day, if it was ever legal, they could get married. Maybe one day, if they wanted to, somehow, they'd have a kid. Maybe two. Kaysha had never really thought about marriage, but the life that Nova proposed seemed so vivid, so cereal-box perfect, that she couldn't help being seduced by the idea.

They both had partners at the time. Kaysha had been with Gillian for four years. She was an old school friend who had turned into a girlfriend, and their relationship had briefly been romantic. For the year before Kaysha broke up with her, they'd slipped back into a sexless friendship and just forgotten to change the label. It had never been a particularly passionate relationship, and the break-up came as no surprise to Gillian. It almost seemed a relief to her. Gillian said she'd met someone else too, which stung Kaysha, though she knew she had no right to be upset. Gillian owned the house that they shared, and Kaysha promised to move out by the end of the month. No doubt Gill's new beau would have the moving van booked by then anyway.

Nova took longer to speak to her girlfriend. She told Kaysha that she kept trying, but Ella would just change the subject. Eventually, two days before Kaysha was supposed to move in, Nova sat Ella down and told her that the relationship was over – so she said, anyway. It didn't stick. Ella told her she had found a lump. She hadn't been to the doctors about it yet, but she was terrified, and Nova didn't feel that it was right to leave her. Kaysha had asked if she couldn't still support her as a friend, or if she thought it was right to stay with someone she didn't love because she might be ill. Nova said that she couldn't break up with someone who might have cancer. Kaysha collected her things and left, heart-broken but determined not to fall back into the same scenario. She promised herself that this was the last time that she'd put herself through this. She needed to move on, throw herself into a project and distract herself. And she had.

Kaysha tracked Sarah down a week later; the first woman on her list of those Jamie had hurt; and they clicked immediately. Sarah had offered her a place to stay – there were plenty of spare rooms in the manor. Sarah was straight-faced and brimming with dark humour, as angry as Kaysha was. She had a bank account full of money she'd only inherited because her parents had no one else to leave it to, but she worked in the pub down the road on the sly for a fiver an hour, *just for the craic*, she said. It hadn't taken Kaysha long to find out how fractured Sarah was on the inside, and how the bottle of wine she cracked open every afternoon both held her together and broke her apart. Kaysha and Sarah had stayed up all night that first night, telling their stories to each other. They both cried, and then they talked more, and they got angry again, started to plan. When dawn came, and they had sex, it was passionate and angry and satisfying. Kaysha found Sarah attractive – she liked a woman who could look after herself – but she knew she couldn't allow herself to get in too deep, not after it had gone so wrong with Nova.

Nova has dozed off. Her head lolls back against the arm of the sofa, and her dressing gown has slipped open enough for

Kaysha to rest her cheek against her freckled chest. She listens to Nova's heart, feels the heat from her skin, inhales her scent. There is something about how their bodies just fit together that stirs something in Kaysha, makes her hope that in some parallel universe where there is no murder investigation and no Sarah and no Ella, they are together without caveats. Nova stirs as if she hears Kaysha's thought and squeezes Kaysha closer to her, and then mumbles something that sounds too much like *I love you* for Kaysha to ignore. She falls asleep wishing she could live in that moment for ever.

15

Sadia
1989

The first time that Sadia felt like she'd lost everything was when she was seventeen, in a musty hospital room that was set aside for difficult conversations. There was a vase of plastic lilies and the windows didn't open, so the room was warm and smelled sweet and chemical, like hospitals always do. The doctor asked Sadia and her mother to wait there for him while he double checked her scan results, and she bit her fingernails until her mother pulled her hand away from her mouth. When the doctor came back and sat down, his face was wan. Sadia wondered how many times he'd given someone a death sentence in this room.

'This is bad news,' he said.

'I'm dying,' Sadia said, and her mother shushed her gently. The doctor smiled.

'Not *that* bad,' he said, and wiped a hand down his face, looking serious again. 'The good news is that you aren't ill.

Everything is . . . working as it should. But the bad news is that not everything is there.'

'What does that mean?' Sadia's mother asked, slipping her fingers between Sadia's and squeezing.

'To put it very simply, you were born without a uterus – which is why your menstrual cycle hasn't started.'

'What does that mean?' Sadia asked, a hand instinctively resting on her abdomen. 'Like . . . what does it . . . what's going to happen?'

'Your uterus is where a foetus would grow,' he said, and pulled a notepad out of his pocket and drew a rough diagram. Sadia had seen diagrams of reproductive systems in Biology classes, but never thought much about them and couldn't remember the labels for the different parts – but he pointed them out one by one, jabbing at them with the end of his pen. She had the two little round ovaries, and they were attached to a mass of useless nothing where her uterus should have been, and the mass carried down to her vagina, which he said was shallow, and would make sex difficult without some manual widening exercises. She blushed at this and her mother hissed *She can worry about that when she's married*, and the doctor carried on as if he hadn't heard. 'The top and bottom of it is that without a uterus, a menstrual cycle is not possible, nor is a pregnancy. I'm sorry, Sadia.'

Sadia's mother's eyes went wide, but Sadia was blank.

'But can't you fix it?' Sadia asked.

The doctor shook his head, rubbed his hand against his rough jaw. 'There's nothing we can do. I'm sorry.'

Sadia asked nothing else, just looked at the tips of her white Nikes peeping from under the hem of her skirt and listened as her mother asked endless questions, none of them with a satisfactory answer, until she was allowed to go home.

Sadia had never particularly thought about having children, other than as an abstract certainty – that her future, far enough forward that she didn't have to worry about it yet, would look something like her own family – she'd go to uni, get married, then have children later. She'd never thought of names, never questioned whether being a mother was her destiny, because it seemed so certain that it was – her adulthood, and motherhood, were gifts that she'd open when the time was right. She'd never particularly longed for it until she was told that it wasn't for her.

She lay in bed for days thinking of names, imagining a son who had her eyes or a daughter whose curly black hair caught the sunlight as she laughed on a playground. Sadia wondered if anyone would even marry her now, knowing that she couldn't provide them with a child, that she'd struggle even to have sex. She saw her new future, barren in every sense, and felt as if what was owed to her had been ripped from her hands before she'd even considered what a gift it was in the first place.

That afternoon was the first time in her life that she ever questioned the will of Allah, or, in fact, His existence. The more she thought about it, this new harsh reality that she found herself in, the more she lost faith. The world threw babies in women's faces, made women who chose not to have children into unfeeling gorgons, told them something was missing from their lives, that they would never know real love, and Sadia had been forced into that sub-womanhood by a God who she'd always felt was with her, who loved her as she loved Him. Whenever she had considered those whose fortunes were less than her own before, she'd just repeated the line she had always heard from others – God works in mysterious ways, trust in Him and help where you can. She was the unfortunate one now, and she didn't trust Him anymore.

Weeks rolled by and she did what she was supposed to; she went to school, she prayed, she cooked and cleaned and cared for her siblings when her parents were at work, but she did all of it without emotion. She felt like the power to feel had somehow seeped out of her. She knew she was trapped now in a life that had been building up to something, some happy ending that wasn't there anymore. She started to drive around the city in her spare moments. Sometimes she'd speed around the ring road, circle Manchester above the speed limit, just to get out of the house. Soon, she started skipping sixth form and driving further out of the city, at first making sure she was home by four as usual, but soon she didn't care anymore. She'd sit through her dad's lectures when she turned up at midnight without caring, take her mother's car if they confiscated the keys for her own. She scoured towns and cities, postcard villages, sped down lanes that dipped and climbed through heather-carpeted valleys, almost crashed a handful of times, looking for the thrill of adrenaline.

One Sunday, she drove for four hours before deciding she wanted to go to a beach, stare out into the vastness of the ocean, and followed signs for a coastal route until she found one. She was outside of Newcastle, and she stood on a cliff edge beside the ruins of some ancient church or castle. The day was clear and people crowded the beach below, ate at cafes tucked into the base of the cliffs. The wind was high, and foam-crested waves crashed onto the boulders gathered below her, and she imagined letting herself fall, the rush of air in her face, the second of absolute freedom before the sharp end. It would be quick. She put her arms out and closed her eyes, let the wind sway her body, and her hair, which she had given up covering weeks earlier, blew wild around her head.

'Careful,' someone said beside her, fingers closing around her wrist. 'You wouldn't be the first to fall from here.'

The man asked her to go for a drink, and she nodded, even though she didn't drink and he was probably too old to be having a drink with a seventeen-year-old. He was taller than her, light hair swept to one side, eyes that sparkled in the sunlight. He seemed confident, nonchalant, as if finding a girl on a cliff and then taking her for a drink were an everyday occurrence for him. She hoped it wasn't.

He took her to a pub further along the cliff, and Sadia sat on a bench outside while the man – who said his name was Jamie – went inside to the bar. He hadn't asked what she wanted, and came back carrying a bottle of white wine and two glasses. It should have felt dangerous, sitting outside a pub in a town she didn't know with a stranger, but something about him put her at ease. She'd felt a swoop of attraction the second she saw him, but by the time they'd finished the bottle of wine, she'd convinced herself that they were meant to be. He'd saved her life. The wind could have swept her off the cliff and she'd have let it, but Jamie saved her life.

They talked all afternoon while the crowds of seaside-goers bustled and then thinned, until the shrieks of children playing in the waves below were long gone and the air grew colder and Jamie offered Sadia his jacket. It smelled good, like expensive aftershave.

'You look good in it,' Jamie told her. She'd sipped her wine after the first glass had made her dizzy, and she felt nice, everything seemed brighter, easier. The world felt more welcoming. 'Do you have a boyfriend?'

Sadia blushed. 'No.'

Jamie's mouth lifted at one side, and he reached a hand across the table. His hands were clean and neat, and she could see the bones and tendons flexing between the skin and he stroked her wrist. 'Good.'

'I've never been in love,' she said, something pushing her to tell the truth, and all of it, more than he needed to know. 'And I never will, because I can't have babies.'

It was the first time she'd told someone who didn't already know, and she expected to feel something when she did, some overarching sadness or feeling of worthlessness, but she didn't, she felt numb. She still didn't quite believe it. Jamie pressed his lips together and nodded.

'How come?' he asked, squeezing her hand.

'Don't have a womb,' she said. 'My mum's going spare, she doesn't think anyone will want to marry me.'

He laughed at that, eyes crinkling at the sides and head tipping back. She saw his pink tongue and imagined it sliding up her neck, grew warm at the thought.

'I think you're so beautiful that you certainly don't need to worry that no one will want you,' he said. 'You'll need to worry about choosing from the line of men that do. There are other ways to have children.'

'That's nice of you to say,' Sadia said.

'I'll tell you a little secret,' Jamie said, leaning towards her over the picnic table. She shifted forward, her face close to his. She could feel his warm breath on her cheek. 'I can't have them either. Maybe we were meant to meet today.'

Their romance progressed quickly, and Sadia only went home the next week to collect her things. Her parents were angry, confused, worried, but she left anyway. Jamie had listened to Sadia talk about her life and her family, her infertility and how she felt like no one around her could understand how it felt, how she felt alienated and suddenly on the outside of a community she had always loved. Jamie had agreed with everything she said, told her she deserved better, that she needed a fresh start in a new place, a new kind of love. They married the day after she turned eighteen, when they had known each other for three months, and Sadia felt whole again, for the first time since she was diagnosed, because Jamie loved her for what she had, and didn't worry about what she didn't.

Their house is a detached three-bedroom tucked into the tapered edge of the woods. It is not visible from the road, though from the bottom of the garden you can hear the cars passing on the country lane beyond. There are no neighbours, no houses at all for a quarter-mile in one direction and only the dense forest on the other. She used to love the solitude of it; she felt cocooned, especially once Ameera was born, and thought of the trees like a womb, providing safety and shelter for her family. Jamie always insisted that she didn't need to work, that he'd provide for her, and she luxuriated in this at first, felt loved and satisfied, especially when Ameera came along. She had no friends, outside of Jamie's friends, and they all worked when he did, so she spent her days alone. Often her only interactions, other than with Ameera, were with the people who worked in the cafes she frequented and the shops she visited. She became invested in their lives, as if she were watching a soap, followed their ups and downs and imagined that they were her own, and she never quite realised how lonely she was, because everyone said that her life was enviable. No work, solitude, a beautiful daughter and a good-looking husband who provided for her.

Sadia is aware now of how desperately alone she is – how there was no one to hear them screaming at each other across the kitchen, the smashing glass of a thrown vase or the thud of a fist against a ribcage. No one to notice a murder.

16

Olive
7th January 2000

The library is always closed between Christmas Eve and January 3rd, but this year, Olive doesn't turn up for her first shifts back on the 5th, or the 6th. When her boss phones her, she says that she is ill, and then pulls the covers back over her head, goes back to not sleeping. On the 7th, the phone rings three times throughout the day, but Olive doesn't pick up. Later, when Julia knocks on her door and calls her name through the letterbox, Olive sinks to the floor and presses herself against the radiator, holds her breath even though the curtains are closed.

Julia knocks for almost twenty minutes, and Olive can hear her muttering to someone between bouts of knocking. She suspects that it is Nancy, Julia's young protégée – a girl whose skin and lank hair are both the colour of watered-down porridge, and whose personality isn't far from porridge either, in Olive's opinion. She hears Julia sigh and announce that she is *going to ring the police, she's worried, this isn't like Olive, something must be wrong.*

'I'm fine!' Olive shouts as soon as she hears this. 'I'm contagious. Go away.'

'Olive?' Julia's fingers appear through the letterbox as she peers inside. Olive has the urge to slam it shut and jam her nosy fingers, watch them turn pink under the pressure until Julia yelps and pulls them back. 'Are you alright? Can you open the door?'

'Go away,' she says again, and forces a cough. 'You'll catch it.'

'Shall we ring a doctor, Olive?'

'It's just the flu.'

'Nance, ring the out of hours surgery, will you?'

'I don't need a doctor!' Olive shouts, her voice growing higher with each word. There is silence for a few seconds and then she hears the two women outside muttering to one another about her.

'We're going. Take a couple of weeks off, Olive. We'll manage. Let me know if you need anything . . . Feel better soon,' Julia says, her voice terse, and Olive hears them retreat. She doesn't move for a few minutes, huddled in her nightgown in the corner beneath the coat rack. It is almost pitch black, only the occasional passing car illuminating the hallway through the window above the door.

Olive can smell herself, can feel her hair stuck to her scalp with days of grease. She usually washes it every morning, but she hasn't been on track for the last few days or nights or the bits in between. It's the silence. She used to love the silence and usually still does. That's why she likes the library, because even when people speak to her, it's hushed, like when she's almost alone in church. People only pray in whispers, pretending to themselves that they are asking for help from God, but Olive knows that, really, they want the help from anyone who is close enough to hear. She's spent her life hearing whispers and pretending that she has not.

Even when Alonso was alive and Kim was small, Olive basked in the quiet hour she'd spend in the morning after Alonso had left for the mines but before Kim was awake, when she'd prepare Kim's lunchbox, cut the crusts off her sandwiches and carefully peel away a strip around the centre of her satsuma, and then tuck it back in, so that Kim's infant fingers could easily open the fruit. She'd do the same to Alonso's lunch too sometimes, without thinking. She'd iron Kim's shirt in front of the television, watching the headlines unfurl without sound, fussing at a grass stain against the white polyester, which was clean and pressed the morning before. If there was muck, Kim was bound to find it. Chaos was drawn to her daughter, who was loud and bright and funny, like her dad. She had his smile, so wide that her big, brown eyes would squeeze shut and almost every tiny tooth in her mouth would be on show. Dimples so big you could fall into them.

The silence is deafening now, and even though the house has been just as quiet for over a decade, she has never felt quite so dreadfully alone in the world. She likes to be alone, but it was nice to know that there was someone, somewhere, who cared about her once. Now, everyone she has ever loved is gone. She presses her fingers against the little gold crucifix that hangs around her neck.

She goes to the kitchen and turns the radio on. The sound of the *Moonlight Sonata* is a shock to her ears at first, but she turns it up as loud as it will go, puts the radio into the sink so it will echo louder. She opens a drawer and pulls out fistfuls of clean, pressed tea towels and throws them into the washing machine, turns it to the longest wash, turns on the empty tumble dryer too. She turns the television on, a game show, turns the volume up as far as it goes and sits on the sofa. Crosses her legs and uncrosses them. Watches as the family of contestants laugh and the host smiles a big, gleaming, bleached-teeth smile. It's so loud in the house. So loud that it's no wonder she can't hear the rhythmic beat of Kim's dance music upstairs as she gets ready for a night out with her friends, in her twenties now, hanging around the beach bars laughing together and with men they might kiss. She doesn't hear Kim clip-clipping round the bathroom in too-high heels looking for her blue eyeshadow, doesn't hear the creak of her sliding down the banister and going to the kitchen for a pre-pub drink, even though she knows Olive disapproves. It's so loud that she can't possibly hear Alonso coming in from the garage, singing the wrong words to a new song, off key, beard more silver now than she ever got to see it. She won't hear the sizzle of oil as he throws a handful of prawns into the skillet, won't hear the chink as he and Kim tap their glasses of wine together before she kisses her father's cheek goodbye and drains her drink. She probably wouldn't even hear the doors slam, caught by the wind, as Kim leaves for the night through the front and Alonso goes out through the back to eat his supper in the garden. She doesn't hear as, in their absence, Jamie sneaks in, young and whole, bible in hand, looking for her, slipping upstairs to meet her in bed. They're still here, she thinks, as she drifts into a light sleep, just creeping through the din, quiet as the grave.

17

Kaysha
7th January 2000

A newsreader's voice on the big telly in the living room is barely audible over the clinking of dishes in the kitchen. The routine is the same in adulthood as it was in childhood. Kaysha, the oldest and most responsible, washes. Deja, eternal bore, dries, and Dev puts away. He dances as he does so, grown now, as they all are. He drops a cup and laughs.

'Dev!' their mum shouts from the living room, because he was always clumsy and she knows it. 'Be careful.'

'It was Deja!' he shouts back, bending to pick up the pieces. 'She did it on purpose.'

They hear a disbelieving *hmm* from their mother and Deja scowls at her twin, rolling her eyes and flicking her hair over her shoulder.

'So childish,' she says, shoving her tea towel into Kaysha's hand and stalking out of the kitchen. Kaysha and Dev fall about laughing and finish putting the dishes away. The two have always been closest, despite the age gap and despite Dev and Deja being twins. They joke that Deja was born without a sense of humour, that Dev stole all the personality genes in the womb and Deja was left with only a fondness for household chores and a penchant for organising things that are already organised.

The twins' twenty-seventh birthday is next week, but Dev will be on a beach in Marbella with friends, so they are celebrating a few days early with a family meal and a supermarket birthday cake. They haven't lit the candles yet, but Dev has already dipped a finger into the icing. Kaysha was invited to bring Sarah, who has only met her family once, but hasn't. Both of the twins are single, because Deja broke up with her boyfriend a few weeks ago, and though Dev goes through girlfriends like they're going out of fashion, each one more beautiful than the last, he is currently single. Kaysha usually likes it best this way, because when it's just the family everyone drifts off to bed sooner or later, and Kaysha and her mother stay up for half the night talking. Kaysha's mother is her favourite person in the world. She thinks of her as a soulmate, they tell each other everything. Almost everything. Kaysha hasn't seen or had a proper conversation with her mother since the brief, loaded New Year phone call, and she isn't looking forward to the conversation that will follow. She knows that she can't lie to her mother, but she doesn't want to implicate her either. Kaysha can see in Roxy's face that she is anxious to talk. She knows something is wrong.

They light the candles on the cake after the dishes are put away, and the twins lean in to blow them out. Deja lights them again because she insists that Dev blew them out before she had a chance, so they all have to sing 'Happy Birthday' again, just to Deja. They play Monopoly, and Dev wins after Kaysha sells Park Lane to him for £1, and then he puts a hotel on it, which Deja lands on, and loses spectacularly, so she goes to bed. At nine, Dev goes outside to answer a call and then leaves a few minutes later, a twinkle in his eye that they all know. Romesh, who is the twins' father, but not Kaysha's, is asleep in his armchair, and then there is just Kaysha and her mother left, and Kaysha feels nervous in a way that she rarely ever has around Roxy.

Roxy pulls Kaysha towards her, and Kaysha rests her head in the space where Roxy's neck and shoulder meet. The television volume is low, but neither of them are really watching anyway.

'What's wrong then, chicken?' Roxy asks, her voice gentle.

'I can't tell you,' Kaysha says, knowing that Roxy will respect this answer, but will worry about it all the more.

'Alright,' Roxy says, stroking Kaysha's hair. 'Is it something to do with work, and it's confidential?'

Kaysha shakes her head, knowing that if she'd said yes, Roxy would have dropped it. She can't lie to her mother, though, never could. Kaysha's stomach churns. She hates keeping things from Roxy, even when it's the right thing to do.

Roxy is quiet for a while, and then asks how Sarah is. Kaysha shrugs. She doesn't want to talk about Sarah. She doesn't like herself very much when she thinks about how she is treating Sarah.

'Not great.'

'On the drink again?' Roxy asks.

'Yep,' Kaysha says. For a month before Christmas, Sarah had drastically cut down how much she was drinking. She was talking about selling up and going travelling, finding somewhere new to start again. Kaysha almost believed it. Since New Year's Eve, she's been drinking more than ever.

'You don't have to stay, you know. You're always welcome here.'

'I know,' Kaysha says, but though she loves her family more than anything, she doesn't want to live with them again.

'She's not yours to take care of.'

'She's just caught up in something at the moment.'

They turn back to the TV, where a suited detective runs across the screen, pursuing a man with a gun.

Roxy says, 'You're seeing the police officer again.'

Kaysha glances at her. 'How could you tell?'

'I always know,' Roxy says. 'I thought you were done with her.'

Kaysha sits upright, turning to lean against the opposite arm of the sofa, and tucks her toes under her mother's thigh.

'You don't have to worry about Nova.'

'I didn't say a word,' Roxy says, but crosses her arms. She closes her eyes and says nothing, and Kaysha knows that she is focusing on her breathing to clear her anger, or worry, or whatever she feels when she thinks of her daughter sleeping with a police officer. Roxy had learned the technique from a Hindu man who lived next door to her growing up. Roxy said the man and his wife were always kind to her, and taught her how to control her rage after her dad left. He'd once sent Roxy and her siblings a Christmas card with a fiver between the five of them in it, but they'd never seen him again.

Roxy's dad was white and her mother was Black. Roxy had the palest skin of her siblings or in her church, and her white friends would tell her that they envied how 'tanned' she was, put their arms against hers in the summer to see if their sun-darkened skin matched hers yet, and tell her that *they thought of her as white*, as if it were a compliment, and Roxy had thought of it as a compliment until she was old enough to understand that what they were really saying was *we think of you as a person*, and knew that if she'd been dark-skinned like her mother they might not have seen beauty in her.

'Think of what they do to us,' Roxy says eventually.

Kaysha groans and puts a hand over her eyes. They've had this conversation dozens of times before. 'I know, Mum. But they're not all . . . you know. She's not like that.'

'Course she's not,' Roxy says, and pushes herself off the sofa. 'Cuppa?'

'Yeah,' Kaysha says, and listens to her mother's hard breaths in the kitchen, then the burr of the kettle and the clink of cups. Kaysha lived in Brixton until she was thirteen, and she knows as well as anyone how Black people are treated by the police.

'Does she know how they treated you when you were raped?' her mother asks. Kaysha flinches, but her mother has never been scared to vocalise what happened. *Not saying the word won't erase what happened*, she'd say. Kaysha agrees with the sentiment and does her best never to mince her words, but when referring to her own trauma, it feels different. She has never told Nova about the rape, telling herself that it is private, that she doesn't want Nova to think differently about her or think of her as a victim.

When Kaysha doesn't answer, Roxy flares her nostrils. 'You haven't told her because you're scared that she'll treat you the same as they did. You know she's the same, deep down.'

'We just don't have that type of relationship, Mum. It's just sex.'

Roxy chokes on her mouthful of tea, and Romesh stirs, then begins to snore again.

'Bollocks. I saw the state of you after she dumped you the last time. That's not just sex,' Roxy says. 'If you don't trust her—'

'I do trust her.'

'If you say so.'

'Well, I can't tell her now, can I?' Kaysha says, and nods to the television. The ten o'clock news is on and Jamie's face flashes up on the screen. He's been all over the newspapers too. It's the kind of story that Kaysha would usually have done anything to cover, but she let one of her colleagues take it. She didn't want to have to write anything kind about him, because you have to when people are dead, even the bastards.

'Police are investigating the death of a local man who was found brutally murdered in a hotel in Byker,' the newsreader begins. Roxy leans forward in her chair, her mouth open. She glances back at Kaysha.

'That's him,' Roxy says, eyes wide. Kaysha nods.

'It's been all over the news for a couple of days,' Kaysha says.

'I heard about it, but I didn't realise it was him.'

'Yep.'

'This is what you've been upset about all week.'

Kaysha doesn't say anything and looks at the carpet.

'Kay.'

'I didn't kill him.'

'Okay.'

'I didn't, I need you to know that. I didn't do it.'

'But you know who did?'

Kaysha rubs the back of her neck. 'I'm trying to find out.'

'Was it Sarah?'

Kaysha feels a brief flare of anger at her mother for even suggesting it, but it subsides when she thinks about how many times she's wondered if it was Sarah too. 'No, I was with her almost all the time over New Year's. She was only alone for an hour or so.'

'You can kill someone in an hour.'

'She's all mouth,' Kaysha says. 'She wouldn't actually go through with it.'

'But she has a motive?'

'There are lots of people who have a motive.'

18

Kaysha
May 1985

The pain arrived in Kaysha's chest, radiating to her shoulders, her clavicle, her neck, the back of her head as it bounced against a hard surface. Her nose ring was pushed into her septum and someone blew into her mouth and she felt like she'd been underwater and the breath inside her had been there for too long, and she had the vague feeling that she must be dying, and she felt calm. The punching stopped, and there were footsteps, and she coughed a small cough, and then she felt someone beside her, and she heard her name, relief in the voice.

She came to again sometime later, fingers pushed into the side of her neck, then into her wrist, and her name again, a low voice. She had more control this time, a little bit more, and she opened one eye, and couldn't see much other than the darkness of a person and the light behind them and she wondered if it was some kind of halo, and then her eyes closed and she slipped away again.

The third time, the light pushed against her eyelids and she could open both eyes and she was in a room that she did not recognise, and panic fluttered deep inside her, somewhere almost inaccessible, and it occurred to her that something bad must have happened, but it was a long time before she began to feel the danger response rise in her body, the desire to run, and even when she did feel it, she could barely move.

Eventually, a person came into the room, the same person as before. He smiled at her, had a cup of water in his hands, and helped her to sit up and take a drink. He was shaking. She coughed because her throat was so dry and so tight, and she wondered if she'd had an allergic reaction to something, and then wondered if she was in a hospital, and then realised that she was not.

The room smelled of sweat and cheap cologne, the sweet rot of damp. As soon as she swallowed the water, she vomited, and the man tipped her forward and hit her between the shoulders. She was sick onto her bare knees and onto the floor, and kept choking on it, because she wasn't bent over enough. When she was finished being sick, she very briefly felt brighter and she looked around and she realised that she knew the man who was caring for her. Jamie. She didn't know his last name. He was a friend of a friend, he went to her uni, she came to his flat for a party once in September before a night out. She couldn't imagine what she was doing there again. She didn't think she had intended to come.

Jamie helped her up, and she retched again as he held her, but there was only bile left. He took her out of the room and across a dark hall, into a bathroom, and he said that she should have a shower, and he turned the shower on, which was above a bath, and it was only when she was sitting in the bath that she realised she was already naked. Jamie lifted the showerhead down and handed it to her and told her to rinse herself off, and then he didn't leave, he just sat on the toilet seat, eyes turned to the floor. He was breathing in through his nose and out through his mouth with purpose, as if he were trying to calm himself down.

'Thank you,' she said to him, and her voice burned her throat as she did. He looked at her, and she pulled her knees up against her chest, hiding herself though he'd already seen her.

'Are you okay?' he asked, his voice quiet and gentle. He wiped his forehead.

'Did I die?' Kaysha asked, directing the lukewarm water over her knees to wash away the vomit. The smell rose and she gagged, and Jamie put a finger in front of his nostrils.

'No,' he said.

'You were giving me CPR,' Kaysha said.

'Yeah,' Jamie said, and glanced at her. He was pale and kept putting a hand on his chest, as if to check that his heart was still beating. 'I thought you were worse than you were. You're alright.'

'What happened?' she asked, and moved the showerhead so that water ran down her chest, which felt bruised. The bathroom was only lit by a streetlight shining through the frosted glass, but she could see darker areas on her breasts, blooming bruises, or bites. 'I'm so sore.'

Jamie made a noise in his throat.

'Yeah, I was really – I couldn't feel your heart.'

'Thank you,' she whispered again. Her teeth were clattering together. She picked up a bar of soap and started to rub herself with it. It slipped out of her fingers and she fished it out of the inch of water that had gathered in the bottom of the tub. As she rubbed her thighs with the soap she realised that they were tender too. She touched her vulva and sucked air through her teeth. The pain took her by surprise, stole the air from her lungs, and she couldn't breathe for a second. Jamie glanced at her.

'You okay?' he asked, and she nodded.

'Can you give me some privacy?' she asked.

'I'm scared to leave you in case you pass out again,' he said, but shifted his body so that his back was towards her and he was facing a wall. She was uncomfortable, but still confused and tired and grateful that he was looking after her. She took a deep breath and raised one heel onto the side of the bath, probed herself, bit down on her lip to stop herself from gasping. The pain was both knife-sharp and a deep ache, and when she pulled her fingers away they were slick.

'Can you turn the light on?' she asked, and Jamie leant over and pulled a string, and the light burned Kaysha's eyes and she squinted until she could see. Her head ached in the brightness but she looked at her fingers. There was blood, bright and fresh, not her period. There was something else, something milky, and she tried to scrape more of it out of herself, just to make sure. Her heart was beating faster than it should, and she rubbed it between her fingers and she knew what it was.

When she glanced up, she saw that Jamie was still facing away, but he was watching her through the mirror, his eyes wide and unblinking. A sob burst out of her. Jamie didn't move.

'What happened?' she asked again, rubbing at herself with soap, despite the pain. She wanted to push it inside herself, wanted to scrape any trace of him out.

'What do you mean?' he asked, crossing his legs. She noticed for the first time that he was wearing a dressing gown, his skinny white legs poking out from under the fabric like the roots of a plant. The water was running cold, and Kaysha shivered.

'Why am I here?' She began to roll her wrists and ankles, bend her knees and elbows, to test how much control she had. Her body was so heavy, each limb felt disconnected and tired.

'You're okay now,' he said, looking away from the mirror and facing the wall again. He wrung his hands. 'Don't worry.'

She wanted to tell him that she wasn't okay, that she could barely lift her arms, didn't think she'd be able to walk, definitely wouldn't be able to run, she didn't know why she was here or what had happened. She didn't say anything.

'Do you want me to help you out?' he asked.

'Can I have a towel?'

There was a heap of towels on the floor and Jamie glanced at it.

'I think I've got a cleaner one in my room,' he said, and left the bathroom, leaving the door open a crack. He was back a few seconds later. 'It's not proper clean, but it's better than those.'

He bent over Kaysha and wrapped an arm around her, helped her to stand. He smelled like old sweat and she gagged but nothing came out. As she climbed out of the bath she slipped a little and grabbed Jamie's shoulder, and as she did his dressing gown was pulled open. Before he pulled it shut Kaysha caught a glimpse of his chest. It was criss-crossed with deep pink lines, some of them deep enough to glisten red, and it took her a few seconds to realise that they were scratches.

Kaysha sat on the edge of Jamie's bed, the air so cold against her damp skin that she shivered, but she felt hot. Jamie picked up a pile of clothes by the end of the bed and put them next to her. They were hers, and she pulled them on, and he looked away while she did. She was missing a sock, and he noticed and looked under the bed for it, and then handed her one from his own sock drawer when he couldn't find it. He was still wearing his dressing gown and sat on his desk chair, his head tipped back against the wall, his bare toes pressed against the floor. After a while he stood and started to put his own clothes on, and as he pulled a black shirt over his head, she remembered him the night before, just a glimpse, in a bar that smelled of vodka, handing her a glass of something pink.

Kaysha wanted to ask what was in the drink. She wanted to ask him what she was doing in his bedroom, dazed, almost dead, covered in bruises and semen. She wanted to tell him she knew she never would have slept with him, not if she'd been normal, not ever. She wanted to tell him that she knew that he wasn't shaky because he'd been worried about her, not because of shame, but because he'd almost killed her. She wanted to tell him that she knew what he'd done, but she didn't, and when he asked her if she wanted a lift home, she smiled and nodded and said *yes, please*.

As soon as Jamie's car had disappeared, Kaysha booked a taxi to the police station. It was just after five and the sun was already climbing. She didn't change her clothes, she just left the house as she was, and the taxi driver said *Couldn't face the walk of shame, pet, eh?* and she didn't answer and he said *No shame in it, done it plenty times mesel'*.

The entire police station was steeped in the scent of disinfectant, so strong that it made the back of Kaysha's nose feel raw and tender, as if she had the flu. She breathed through her mouth to avoid it so that she didn't heave. She'd first noticed it in the reception area while she waited for an officer to acknowledge her after she'd walked in. It had been diluted there with the fresh air wafting between opening and closing doors from the street outside, but in the unlocked cell she had been taken to, which the officer had referred to as the *waiting room*, the air was thick with it.

The room was windowless and the light fixture above was without a bulb. A floor lamp stood next to the toilet, casting amber light across the cell. A pile of tatty magazines were stacked in a corner of the floor and a poster was taped to one of the walls. It read BOBBIES ON THE BEAT BEAT CRIME and featured a cartoon of a grinning police officer, truncheon in hand, standing next to a police box. Someone had blacked out a couple of his teeth.

Kaysha closed her eyes. The echoes of voices and hard boots in the corridors seemed amplified. Even the rasp of her own lungs was impossibly loud. Her body felt heavy. She tried to focus on the headache and on the bruises on her hips, the dull throb of her abdomen, letting the pain expand and fill up every inch of her.

A white-haired officer came into the room after a long time and leant on the door frame, arms crossed. He was tall and broad, with glasses that made his eyes look bigger than they were.

'Ms Jackson?' he asked, looking her up and down. Kaysha nodded, and he jerked his head, beckoning her. They went down the hall to a room with two chairs and a desk. The room was too bright and too hot, and one of the walls was black glass. Kaysha knew that it was a two-way mirror and she wondered if anyone was watching her from the other side. The officer sat down and gestured for Kaysha to sit on the other side of the desk, then pulled some papers and a chewed biro from a drawer. He tapped the papers on the desk to straighten them, lit a cigarette, and then looked Kaysha in the eyes.

'So,' he said, blowing smoke up towards the ceiling. 'Why are you here?'

Kaysha took a deep breath. 'I've been raped.'

'By whom?' he asked, looking at her over his glasses.

'Someone called Jamie.'

'Someone called Jamie,' he repeated, and made a note on his paper. 'And where did this happen? When?'

'Just now . . . hours ago. I was at his house, I think.'

'You think?'

'I can't remember much.'

'What were you doing at his house?'

'I don't know. I just woke up there,' Kaysha said.

'Where did your night begin, if not in his house?'

Kaysha began to recount what she could remember in a flat voice, concentrating on the facts, trying not to let her emotions interfere. She told him about how she was supposed to be meeting a friend in the city for some drinks to celebrate having taken their final exam of the year.

'What are you studying?' the officer asked, his pen hovering above the paper.

'English,' she said.

He raised an eyebrow. 'So you're good at making up stories, then?'

'What do you mean?'

The officer smirked and shook his head, flicked his finished cigarette into an empty bin by his feet. 'Carry on.'

Kaysha continued. She'd arrived at the pub at around seven, and Denise wasn't there yet. The pub was busier than she'd expected because there was a quiz that night, and she'd had to sit at the bar because she wasn't participating. She'd noticed a couple breaking up at a nearby table. The man had cried after the woman left, and Kaysha had felt like an intruder on the intimacy of the moment. The man had sniffed and went to play on the slot machine, pushing the buttons with an unnecessary amount of force, and then eventually, when he must have run out of change, punched the machine and stormed out of the pub. That was when Jamie slid onto the seat next to her, tipped his head towards the slot machine. *Bit of a prick*, he'd said, not even a hello. It had taken her a few seconds to realise that she knew him, vaguely, and he wasn't just some random creep.

They'd talked for a while, and she asked him about his degree, his friends, whether or not he had a job, and he didn't ask her anything other than who she was waiting for and how long they would be. He said he was doing Science, his exams had been really difficult. She told the officer that she kept looking around for Denise, who never turned up in the end, or not that she could remember. Kaysha said at some point Jamie had told her that she was beautiful, like an Amazon, and she'd rolled her eyes and gone to the toilet. When she got back to her seat, Jamie had bought them both a new drink. A paper umbrella and a glacé cherry lolled against the rim of her glass. She had never had that kind of cocktail before and she'd thought it tasted strange but she didn't know what it was supposed to taste like in the first place. That was the last thing she remembered in any detail until she'd woken up.

'What were you drinking?' the officer asked, a fresh cigarette lodged in the corner of his mouth.

'I only had two drinks,' she said.

'What were your *two* drinks of then?'

'The first was a vodka tonic, and the one he bought me was a cocktail, something fruity.'

The officer nodded and scribbled something down. 'And did you leave your drink unattended at any point?'

'No, he just got me the new one when I was in the toilet.'

The officer rolled his eyes and leant back in his chair, folding his arms. 'Miss Jackson, didn't your mother ever teach you never to leave your drink unattended?'

'Nah. She was too busy teaching my brother not to put drugs in girls' drinks,' Kaysha said, the words rolling out of her mouth before she could stop them. The officer scoffed.

'I'm not convinced that you were drugged.'

'I wasn't drunk.'

'Don't students always have drinks before they go out?'

'Sometimes, but—'

'You were probably just drunk,' he said.

'But I wasn't.'

'Do you have any recollection of the alleged incident?'

'No.'

'Do you have any recollection of dissenting to sexual activity?'

'No, but—'

'Then how do you know the sexual encounter was non-consensual? Letting a man buy you drinks sends a certain signal. But I'm sure you know that.'

Kaysha said nothing and looked at her hands, her eyes welling up. She'd come to report it because that's what she always told other girls to do. She was part of a group of women at uni, mostly white, who advocated for better treatment of sexual assault victims, and their main message was to go to the police as soon as possible after an assault, because the more people who reported, the more they'd be forced to listen, to do something about it. The group had held marches around campus and had staged protests at Grey's Monument, where they'd be heckled by passers-by – usually middle-aged white men shouting that they were sluts. Once a man had pushed one of Kaysha's friends to the ground and told her she deserved to be raped. The police didn't help then, either.

'Women like you are dangerous.'

'I'm just trying to report an assault.'

'How do you know it was assault?'

'I woke up on his floor and I was naked and he was trying to revive me.'

'Revive you?' the officer repeated, leaning forward across the desk.

Kaysha nodded, and closed her eyes. 'He was doing CPR on me.'

'So he was trying to save your life?' the officer asked, ruffling his hair and then brushing it back into place. 'This man saved your life and now you're reporting him for rape?'

'He still raped me.'

'Right.'

'Do you not believe me?'

The officer shifted in his seat, rubbing a palm against his grey stubble. 'I don't know what you expected to happen, Miss Jackson. You let a man buy you drinks, you left your drink unattended, and by the sound of it, you went home with him willingly. I can't arrest a man for rape if he thought you wanted it, can I?'

Kaysha dug the heels of her hands into her eye sockets and held her breath for a few seconds. 'So that's it?'

'Look, I want you to really consider this allegation, Miss Jackson. A rape charge could ruin this young man's life. Think about the repercussions that your actions are going to have if you push this.'

Kaysha slumped in her chair, letting the pain of her headache wash over her.

'Would you like someone to give you a lift home?' the officer asked. Kaysha opened her eyes. He was folding his notes in half and tucking his pen into his breast pocket.

'Aren't you going to do the test?' she said, eyes widening in disbelief. 'The swab?'

'Are you referring to a rape kit?'

'Yeah,' Kaysha said.

'We only use those in cases of rape, Miss Jackson, not of sexual misunderstanding,' he said, and chivvied her out of the door. She turned back to look at him just in time to see him dropping the notes he'd made into the bin.

Kaysha leant against the outside wall of the police station trying to get her bearings. She didn't know this part of the city. There were only office buildings and warehouses, a closed-down restaurant that she'd never visited – no shop fronts or women with babies. When she was little her mum had always told her that if she got lost she had to ask a lady with a baby for help. They were the safest. The street was steep, and at the bottom, between buildings, she could see the rising iron cross-hatch of one of the bridges. She could never remember which was which, other than the Tyne Bridge because it was on bottles of beer, and it wasn't that one. She walked in the opposite direction, away from the river, towards the noise of traffic.

A church bell tolled nine somewhere. Relief at having found her way back to a familiar part of the city was smothered by claustrophobia as Kaysha was buffeted by waves of shoppers through the sloping cobbled streets that were lined with navy-and-white-striped canvas stalls. The crowds bustled around piles of fresh fruit and muddy vegetables, rails of knock-off designer jeans, baskets of batteries and Zippos and fag-papers and curtain rings, piles of fresh-cut meat on refrigerated slabs, still shoals of fish. Pastel-coloured power suits lined shop windows and smoking men in overalls sat in front of the burger van at the bottom of Northumberland Street. An orange and white double-decker trundled down the narrow road between shops and

Kaysha followed a crowd across the road in front of it. It beeped and they walked faster, hopping onto the kerb just in time.

'Rough night, hinny? Fancy a ride yem?' one of the men called as she walked past the burger van. She flicked two fingers up without looking at him, and he shouted *slag* after her as his friends laughed. Kaysha pushed her way through the swarms of people. She'd spent all her money on the taxi to the police station, so she walked the forty minutes home. The streets got gradually emptier as she got further from the city centre and deeper into the residential outskirts. Big-name chain stores and cafes petered out and were replaced by over-filled corner shops, contents spilling out in boxes and baskets onto the pavement, greasy spoons advertising three-quid full-Englishes. Takeaways occupied every other shopfront, and endless rows of Victorian terraced houses snaked from every intersection. She'd felt claustrophobic in the crowds, but felt more uneasy in the quiet streets. She imagined hands dragging her down one of the alleys, clammy fingers closing around her mouth to stifle a scream, no passers-by noticing as she was pulled out of sight and beaten and raped and murdered, her body thrown into the void between a garden shed and a fence and never found. As she got closer to home she sped up until she broke into a run. By the time she got to the street where she lived, she was sprinting and struggling to breathe. She lived in a tall house with five other students, a sign taped to the bay window reading COAL NOT DOLE.

The hallway was dark, and the house was quiet. Kaysha locked the door after herself and kicked her shoes off into the pile by the mat and ran upstairs to the bathroom. She stripped off her dress and bra, throwing them into a bin filled with tampon wrappers and tissues and turned on the shower. Her breathing was still ragged. Her lungs felt like they were constricting and her heart was hammering against her ribs; she could hear the pound of it, feel it in her palms against her fingertips. Her eyes were full of tears and dry sobs filled the little spaces between breaths. The bathroom was small and crowded with towels and shampoos, moisturisers, soaps, sponges and loofahs, body sprays, perfumes, hair oils and conditioners, toothbrushes, toothpaste and mouthwash, slippers and worn underwear, pyjamas and mirrors and the unwashed bath mat. Kaysha felt like it was all on top of her and the darkness and the grime of the room and the house began to enclose her, taking up her space, rushing towards her and boxing her in. Just before the world ended, Kaysha scrambled onto the cistern, shoved the window open and pushed her face into the gap, gulping the outside air as if she'd never breathed before.

19

Ana
July 1997

It was after a conversation about Kaysha Jackson that Ana first had the idea. She was in the pub with Jamie, a long lunch, longer than she'd have dared take on her own, and they were reminiscing about university. The conversation started light, and they talked about the bars they used to frequent, the too-sweet liqueurs they drank, old friends and old lovers. A shadow passed over Jamie's face after a while, and he said *Remember that fucker who said I raped her?* and Ana nodded. She did remember. She remembered the morning it all started. She'd found Jamie sitting in the kitchen when she'd gone down for a glass of water, hungover and satisfied after a night out with her first boyfriend, Chris. Jamie was crying that morning, and she'd never seen him cry before, and she remembered the tenderness of the moment, his tears rolling over his cheeks and into his mouth, and she didn't know whether to fall in love with him or mother him, and she felt that she could do either so easily.

When he noticed her, he tried to speak, but only a sob came out, and she wrapped herself around him, pushing her face into his hair, kissing his head, and he clung to her, his breath wet against her collarbone. His body shook for a long time, and she rubbed his back and made soothing sounds, and she was aware that she probably smelled of sex and sweat and old booze, but he did too, so it was okay. She remembered the pile of pizza boxes beside the back door, and how the sink was full of dishes, and the way that Jamie's fingernails dug into her waist as he cried. She knew he wouldn't have cried in front of anyone else, and she always thought of that moment as the moment that really cemented their friendship, because he knew he could be vulnerable in front of her. He trusted her. Later, they'd think of each other as family.

When he stopped crying, he told Ana in a hoarse voice that he'd made a mistake. He'd taken some drugs with a girl called Kaysha, a friend of a friend who Ana knew only to say hello to. He said they'd slept together, he couldn't really remember much but they'd slept together, he said she'd been quite insistent that he brought her home, even though she wasn't really his type. Ana had nodded as he spoke, still with a hand on his shoulder. Jamie said they both passed out after having sex and when he woke up, he'd realised that Kaysha wasn't breathing. Ana had wondered for a second then, with horror, if there was a body upstairs, but he said he'd given Kaysha CPR, the shock sobering him enough to know what to do. He'd breathed life back into her, and then he'd helped her to have a shower after she was sick everywhere, he'd looked after her, and he said he was worried she'd report him for a rape he'd never committed. Then he cried again, and Ana held him.

Ana's instinct, as a woman, was to always believe women. She'd been assaulted before, most women she knew had, in one way or another. She just always believed them, because there was never any proof. She spent a lot of time gently correcting people who talked about women making up assaults to harm men. *No one does that*, she'd say. *Basically no one. Only nutters.* But she believed Jamie. She knew him. He wouldn't assault anyone. Didn't need to. He was so good looking, found it so easy to find women who wanted to sleep with him, he just wouldn't have raped anyone. He just wouldn't have.

She's not even my type, he'd said again. *I probably wouldn't even have slept with her if we hadn't taken the drugs.* Ana had thought that Kaysha was actually very much Jamie's type, but she didn't say anything, because she didn't want to upset him more. She felt so much rage towards Kaysha because her lie was harmful to Jamie, but also to all the women who tried to report real assaults and were ignored. Kaysha, and women like her, were the problem. If not for women like them, maybe the rest would be believed without question.

Ana suggested that she go to Kaysha's house – someone would know where she lived – and have a chat with her, talk her down from her panic, tell her she was just drunk and ask her to not go around calling Jamie a rapist, maybe stop drinking so much or stop taking drugs with people she clearly didn't know well enough to feel safe around. Jamie pressed his lips together and cupped Ana's cheek at the suggestion, but shook his head. He said it would make him look guilty, desperate, and he didn't want Ana to get wrapped up in it. Ana nodded and told him that she was sure it would all blow over quickly – it was, after all, his word against Kaysha's, and the police most often believed the man – something which Ana usually hated about rape allegations. This time it was useful though, because Jamie was telling the truth.

Ana had worried about it for weeks, prayed for Jamie every night, prayed for Kaysha to do the right thing. When she'd heard the first rumour from her friend Evelyn that Kaysha had been raped, she'd asked, *By who?* Evelyn had shrugged, but looked at her feet in a way that Ana knew meant that Evelyn didn't want to be the one to tell Ana that her best friend was a rapist. *Look*, Ana had said, taking Evelyn by the arm, *you know how vocal I am about believing women, but it just didn't happen. I was in the house. I'd have known. She's making it up.*

After that, Ana found herself telling a lot of her friends that Kaysha was a liar when they brought it up, and after a while Ana found herself bringing it up, whispering it to women she barely knew in club toilets, quietly warning men that she saw standing too close to Kaysha in the student union. It became her only topic of conversation, and she felt herself sucked into the approval it got her from the men she warned.

Jamie went to the bar and got himself another bottle of beer, Ana another glass of wine – her third. The afternoon seemed to stretch and shimmer in front of them, the possibilities endless. The horse brass that dangled from the ceiling beams glittered in the light and made Ana think of a seaside amusement park at twilight. She had the same tremble of excitement, despite the conversation, as if something big were coming.

'I wish there was a way to prove she was lying,' Jamie said, peeling the label from his bottle. Ana twirled a lock of hair around her finger as she thought.

'There must be,' she said. She swept the silky ends of her hair across her lips. The wine was making her think in wider circles than she usually would, and nothing was quite linear. 'What about something like . . . some sort of test.'

'Test?' Jamie said. He rolled the beer label into a tube.

'Yeah,' Ana said. She frowned. 'To match sperm samples to an individual, to prove like . . . whether someone is lying about who they've . . .'

'That wouldn't have helped me, though, would it,' Jamie said. 'It would have matched because we – we fucked. There was just no way to prove it wasn't rape. Especially since we'd taken fucking . . . whatever it was. Some date-rape drug. Rookie mistake on my part.'

'Yeah, it wouldn't work for you,' Ana said, still thinking. 'There's no way we could prove that now, but we could help others. Like . . . historical rape cases, a way to profile the historical sperm samples properly.'

'Is that not already a thing?'

Ana shrugged. 'Not in any particularly reliable way, as far as I know.'

Jamie drained his bottle and shifted in his seat. 'You think you could figure it out?'

'It's definitely in our wheelhouse, isn't it? And if we can stop anyone else from being wrongfully accused, it's worth it.'

'Sounds like a lot of work.'

'We could do it together,' Ana said. She tapped her fingernails against her glass. 'If you asked I'm sure you could get Phil to sign off on it as a special project.'

Jamie reached across and put his hand over Ana's, whether to stop her tapping or as a gesture of affection, she didn't know. 'This feels like yours.'

'You don't want to help?'

'You don't need me to. It's your idea, I know you can do it alone. And when you've done it, and your research wins loads of prizes and changes the world for men like me, you'll finally be appreciated. Like, properly appreciated as a scientist.'

Ana squeezed Jamie's fingers, which had slipped through hers. Her brother, her soulmate. Their eyes met.

'Love you,' she said, as she had a thousand times before.

'Not as much as I love you.'

September 1999

Ana was the last one to arrive at the meeting after a power surge had caused her electricity to trip in the night, which meant that her alarm didn't go off, and she was – for the first time in her career – late for work. By the time she took a seat in the back of the conference room, unshowered and sweating from her hairline, all the croissants were gone and the coffee was cold. Phil made a snide comment as she walked in, as if her lateness were habitual and had been irritating him for years, and she apologised, and sat down. Jamie caught her eye and winked, which made her feel less flustered. This was *his* meeting, after all. He'd told her to make sure she was there – *it was important*, he'd said – he had something to announce. She'd been confused because he usually told her everything that he was up to, even when she didn't want to know. She'd wondered with some jealousy if he was being promoted above her. It wouldn't surprise her, though they both knew that she was better at the job – she fucked up much less than he did, and spent a considerable amount of time quietly correcting Jamie's mistakes. That didn't matter to Phil though – what mattered was that Jamie was charming, likeable, *one of the lads*. Ana was not.

Phil cleared his throat and wiped a hand down his permanently ruddy face, before starting to speak. He did the usual weekly updates on the facts and figures of the company, large projects and a bit about the office Christmas party – it would no longer be held at the Fed Brewery as planned, to save money they were going to hold it in the office break room, and provide wine and snacks.

'I'd request,' he said, with a raised eyebrow and a smirk at Jamie, 'that no one in their drunken wisdom tries to photocopy their arsehole. If you break the printer with your fat backside, it'll come out of your pay packet.'

'What about ladies photocopying their bosoms?' Jamie asked with a straight face. 'Is that permissible?'

'Perfectly acceptable, as long as both you and I are given a copy of the resulting image,' Phil said. He pulled out a handkerchief and blew his nose. 'Now, on to the exciting stuff?'

'More exciting than boobs?' Jamie asked, with raised eyebrows. Phil smiled. Even from across the room, Ana could see that he had smeared snot into his moustache.

'Now, Jamie has some very exciting news – both for himself personally and for Parson's. For a while, he's been working on a little project in his spare time.' Phil paused and looked at Jamie, who nodded at him. He had the look of a child who was about to be presented with a certificate at a school assembly. Ana caught Jamie's eye again and pulled a face that said *What's he on about?* Jamie just pressed his lips together and winked at her, and then looked back at Phil. 'And unbeknownst to us, the sneaky little devil submitted it to the Coel Foundation's Scientific Advancement Prize.'

Ana's skin prickled with something that might have been confusion, or jealousy, or anger. The Coel Prize was the big one. She'd been aiming to submit her own research to the prize this time around, but the write-up hadn't been ready in time. The research was done, and she'd have been able to submit it if she wanted to, probably, but she wanted it to be perfect. In an industry where she was consistently overlooked, despite her talent, she knew that if she was going to win it had to be flawless. She'd rather wait another year to submit than submit something sub-par.

Phil paused dramatically, looking around the room to make sure everyone was looking at him. Jamie grinned, showing all his teeth, and even before Phil said *AND HE ONLY FUCKING WON IT*, Ana knew. She knew by Jamie's face, and her stomach dropped and she felt like she might cry, and though she tried to convince herself that they were tears of joy for Jamie because he had achieved something so great, she knew really that she was jealous. Everyone in the room applauded, and the people closest to Jamie clapped him on the back, reached across the table to shake his hand, and Ana wiped tears from her cheeks. When Jamie looked at her, she gave him the thumbs up and then looked at the carpet, trying to compose herself. She should have been thrilled for him, and she hated herself because she wasn't. She felt blindsided, as if he'd lied to her by not telling her that he was submitting to the Coel, by not even telling her that he had a project. She'd updated him on hers every step of the way, even though he hadn't wanted to be involved. She felt like she'd been slapped, because maybe their friendship wasn't what it seemed. Maybe she didn't know him as well as she thought she did, or maybe he just didn't trust her.

'I want you to read out the abstract,' Phil said, handing Jamie a plastic wallet. 'It's . . . brilliant. Didn't know you were capable of something so eloquent.'

'Charming, as always, Phil,' Jamie said, taking the wallet and pulling out the documents.

'Joking, of course,' Phil said. 'Stand up, then, stand up.'

Jamie got to his feet. He smiled, glancing at Ana, and just for a second, he looked hesitant. There was something in the way he looked at her that made her suck in a breath, and the second expanded in the way that time does when you know that you are about to trip, the second that you hang in the air before you hit the ground. When he began to read, what came out of his mouth was her voice, her work, word for word for word, not even tweaked, and the words just drifted around the room, exactly as she'd written them.

20

Ana
June 1988

Tom's version of how he and Ana met always seemed the more romantic, and when people asked, she told it from her husband's perspective. His mother had taken it upon herself to find him a bride after years of longing for a grandchild, while her only child stayed infuriatingly single. She placed an advert in the lonely-hearts column and received twelve letters in reply. She didn't open them, but instead handed them to her son after Sunday lunch one week when he was thirty-one. Tom had sighed and put them in the bin when he realised what they were, but Doris retrieved them and put them in his car's glovebox while he snoozed on the sofa after tea.

Tom found the letters a few days later when he was looking for his sunglasses. He groaned, but he'd had a shitty day and thought they might give him a laugh if nothing else. The truth was, he'd love to find someone and settle down, but he hated the thought of going to pubs to try and meet anyone.

Eight of the letters included a picture, some of them suggestive and some just a headshot, but he was more interested in what they had to say. Some of the women seemed lonely, some just intrigued by the ad, which described him as three inches taller than he was and made his job – a cleaner in a university – seem much grander than it was in reality. His mother had described him as an *academic refuse removal executive* – which every single one of the replies had asked about.

He read and replied to each one over a bottle of beer. Most were pretty generic – describing their hobbies and jobs and asking questions about his life, did he want children, did he have any, did he mind dating someone who already had children, and so on and so forth.

In the first paragraph of her letter, Ana had written that she was transgender, explained what it meant, and said she liked to put it on the table first in potentially romantic relationships so that it didn't have to be a conversation later. She said that she wasn't interested in being anyone's experiment into their own sexuality or an 'exotic' notch on a bedpost. She was only looking for love if it was genuine. And then she didn't mention it again in that letter or the subsequent ones; she wrote about bands she liked and books she had read and how she was a scientist from Brazil.

They didn't like any of the same music or read the same books, but Tom found over the next few days that he returned to Ana's letter again and again. Something about her honesty hooked him, the earnestness of the writing and the feeling that she was – like he was – looking for something real or nothing at all. After a few days of thinking about how to word his reply, he sent back a letter with his photograph, in which he'd trimmed his beard before getting it taken specially at Boots. He told her that he thought she seemed funny and interesting, that he respected her for telling him that she was transgender, and though he'd never thought about dating a transgender person before, he didn't think that he minded, he just thought she seemed nice. He said he'd like to hear more from her.

She sent a letter back the next week, and they corresponded for three months, only by post, until they eventually decided to meet. Tom had wanted to meet her from the first letter, but had enjoyed how deliciously slow and romantic the exchanging of letters was. He wondered if every woman he saw in the supermarket or the library was her, whether serendipity would lead them to meet before they'd planned to.

They decided to go for a drink on a Saturday afternoon in town, somewhere busy enough that Ana felt safe, but not so busy that they couldn't talk. Ana suggested a restaurant on the quayside, which wasn't usually as busy as the city centre but was just as beautiful.

Tom turned up with a bouquet of lilies, ten minutes late, as he always somehow did no matter how early he left the house. He realised that he recognised Ana, though she had never sent a photograph. He'd seen her before at work, though not for a few years. He'd always noticed her in the hallways as he passed, her arms usually full of books. She was often accompanied by a tall white man, who he didn't think was her boyfriend, but they seemed close. He had always thought, offhand, that she was pretty, but hadn't dwelled on it – he wasn't the type to chat up students. She looked different now – beautiful rather than pretty – like she had grown into herself.

The day was unexpectedly sunny and she was sitting at a table for two on the pavement outside the restaurant, a glass of red wine in her hand, looking out over the river, where someone was cleaving the water with a jet ski. She was wearing a sundress and a straw hat, and her black hair was loose over her shoulders, her skin golden in the sunlight. She looked like she should be on television.

'Tom?' she asked when she noticed him. She stood and extended a hand for him to shake and then kissed his cheeks, twice each. 'I'm Ana.'

'These are for you,' Tom said, and felt shy, like he'd somehow got the wrong Ana. She was way out of his league and he knew it. She accepted the flowers with a grin, smelled them, and then asked a passing waiter for some water to stand them in.

'I know you,' she said, looking at him over the top of her sunglasses. He nodded.

'From the university,' he said, sitting down, a bit breathless.

'Yes,' she said. 'I didn't expect to recognise you.'

Tom shrugs. 'People don't usually notice the cleaners.'

'I must have noticed you,' she said.

'I noticed you too,' he said.

Ana smiled, her eyes crinkling together. 'It must be hard work, cleaning up after students.'

'Yeah, it is. Harder than I expected. It's not my speciality. Not that it wouldn't be okay if it was,' he said, aware that he was rambling, and unable to stop himself. 'My degree is in Computer Science and I really wanted to teach, but there was nothing in the department when I graduated, so I just took the first job in the uni that came up so they wouldn't forget about me when they were hiring. I've been doing it for years now, still no IT job.'

'Something will come up.'

'Hopefully,' Tom said, grinning at her. She sipped her wine. 'And you're a chemist?'

'I am.'

'That's cool. Are there many women working in your . . . office?'

'Lab,' she corrected. 'There are some, but they're mainly admin and not scientists. It's quite male-dominated. You don't really see Science Barbie, do you?'

'Yeah, no. Maybe we should write to the Barbie people. Tell them to make one.'

'Let's,' Ana said. Her glass was empty and she asked the waiter to bring the bottle when he passed, and another glass for Tom. 'How's Izzy?'

Izzy was Tom's cat. He had sent Ana three pictures of her with his letters, because Ana said she loved cats. Izzy was sixteen and slowing down, always at the vet's for some ailment or another.

'Still indestructible,' Tom said.

Ana laughed. 'I'd like to meet her.'

'I think she'd like to meet you too,' he said.

'I can't wait.'

'God. Your accent is—'

'Annoying, I know, my friends always tell me. So nasal.'

'I was going to say it was lovely. You speak such perfect English.'

'Well, yeah, I've been speaking it my whole life,' she said, raising an eyebrow. Tom got the feeling he'd said the wrong thing, but she smiled. 'Do you speak any other languages?'

'No . . . well, I did French at school and I was awful at it. Got a D. But I've started, well, I started to learn Portuguese a couple of weeks ago.'

'Portuguese?'

'Yeah, well, you know. I got a book from the library that comes with a tape. There's an evening course starting at the college in September that I was going to take, maybe.'

'Portuguese Portuguese or Brazilian Portuguese?'

'They're different?'

'Brazilian is nicer,' Ana said, and then placed a hand on her chest. 'In my opinion.'

'I'm not sure which I've been learning.'

'Why are you so interested in learning Portuguese, anyway?' she asked, grinning over her wine and leaning back in her chair.

'Well, you know. It's just the way the English – we always expect everyone to just speak our – to speak English. And we never bother to learn any other languages. And you know . . .' he said, blushing and taking a gulp of his own wine. 'I don't want you to think that I expect you to always speak my language.'

Ana smiled, and raised her glass towards Tom, who chinked his own against it, and they both drank.

'Don't take that course,' Ana said. 'I'll teach you.'

September 1999

Most of the community lived in century-old mining cottages, purpose-built in neat rows, spread from the road like a pair of lungs. Those houses had no gardens, just unkempt, concrete yards with washing lines stretched across them like webs, each with a stone shed that was once an outhouse. There was a small cluster of shops and a couple of pubs like an island in the middle of the streets, and a boarded-up church tucked into the mouth of the woods. The valley beyond tumbled down in clusters of fields and copses of trees until the slim river at the bottom split it in two. In the winter, when snow settled across the fields and the rooftops and iced the sheep and the branches of the conifers, it looked like a Christmas card.

Ana and Tom lived on a street that was set slightly higher up the valley than the rest of the houses, next to a golf course and a field of Highland cattle. The house was cheap because the village was known as *rough*, which really just meant that the people were poor, and the drugs of choice there were heroin and resin, rather than the cocaine of the city.

Smoke rose from chimneys into the golden September evening, and a red Mini Cooper streaked over the crest of the hill and pulled up outside Tom and Ana's house as it often did on a Friday night.

'You've got to be fucking kidding,' Tom said, tipping his head to one side to look out of the kitchen window at the car. Ana lifted her head from her hands, where it had been resting for some time. Tom squared his shoulders. 'I'm going to go and tell him to—'

'Don't,' Ana said, laying a hand on her husband's forearm. She sniffed and wiped her face, ran her fingers through her hair. She looked around. The kitchen was still a mess from breakfast. 'Can you load the dishwasher?'

'You're not going to defend him this time?' Tom asked, pulling his arm away. He glanced out of the window again.

'No, but—'

'What a brazen prick,' Tom said. 'As if he thinks he's just going to swan in as usual.'

'Tom,' Ana said, her voice firm. Jamie was leaning against the car as Sadia got Ameera out from the back seat. He had a bottle of champagne in his hand.

'He's not coming in.'

'I'll deal with it,' Ana said. She ducked to look at her reflection in the oven door and scrubbed at the mascara that was smeared under her eyes. 'I'm not sure what he'll do if we cause a scene.'

'What do you mean, you don't know what he'll do?'

'It's fine – just please load the dishwasher,' Ana said, rolling her shoulders back and pulling her hair into a ponytail.

'What's he said to you?'

'Nothing. I just . . . I don't know what he's capable of anymore.'

'You know him better than anyone. What's he got on you?'

'Just let me deal with him,' Ana said. Tom followed her to the front door, and she sighed as she reached for the handle. 'Please don't start.'

'I'll follow your lead,' he said, but he had a look in his eyes that she didn't trust.

As soon as Ana opened the door, Ameera ran to her. Ana picked the child up and dropped little kisses all over her face, pecking at her like a bird. Ameera wrapped her arms around Ana's neck. She smelled of plasticine and bergamot, and Ana blew a raspberry on the child's cheek to make her laugh.

Sadia came through the open door next, looking – as ever – like she belonged on television. Sadia's hair fell in loose curls around her face, shiny and sleek, and her big, brown eyes – so like Ameera's, even though they couldn't be – squeezed almost shut as she greeted Ana with a smile.

'Hiya,' she said, leaning in for a hug. Sadia's gaze rested on Ana's puffy eyes and red nose as she pulled away. 'You alright, lovely?'

'Yeah,' Ana said. She pointed to a bunch of lilies that were in a vase by the door. 'Yeah, I'm fine. Tom got me some flowers, but I'm allergic to them.'

'Goon,' Sadia said, turning to Tom and shaking her head. 'What did you do?'

'What do you mean?' Tom asked.

Sadia laughed. 'What did you do that meant you had to buy her flowers?'

Tom looked at Ana and then at Jamie, who was standing in the doorway, and then back to Sadia. 'Not every man who buys his wife flowers has been up to something, hin.'

Sadia laughed again, and put her hands on her hips. 'You could stand to take a leaf out of Tom's book, Mr Spellman.'

'Oh, I'm sure I could,' Jamie said, looking bored.

Sadia put her hands out to take Ameera, who was sitting on Ana's hip.

'No,' Ameera said, and clung tighter to Ana's side.

'Have you missed Aunty Ana?' Sadia asked, reaching out to stroke her daughter's hair. Ameera nodded and lay her head on Ana's shoulder. Ana squeezed the toddler closer to her and kissed her head. Sadia took off her shoes and went into the kitchen.

Jamie leant against the door frame, ankles crossed. He held out the bottle of Moët and let his head drop to one side, smiled at Ana, his eyes soft – something he'd always done when she was mad at him. Ana used to think he was cute when he did it, like a naughty child who knew he was in trouble, and she'd soften and forgive him. It didn't work on her this time, but she took the champagne and he smiled and leant close to her. He kissed her cheek, and she stiffened under his touch. A gesture they'd performed countless times before, but this time she didn't soften into him, didn't wrap an arm around him, didn't kiss his cheek back. She felt the scrape of his stubbly chin across her cheek, worried, just for a second, that he'd bite her throat like an animal.

Ameera was wrapping the chain of Ana's crucifix around her index finger, and Jamie extended his hand towards Tom, who didn't shake it. He slid an arm around Ana's waist and stared Jamie down.

'No bother,' Jamie said, and followed Sadia into the kitchen. When he was out of sight, Ana shot a hard look at Tom.

'Please, Tom,' Ana whispered, following Jamie into the kitchen.

The twins, who were nearly ten, had heard the Spellmans arriving and had barrelled down the stairs to greet them.

'What are you doing here?' Eloise asked Jamie suspiciously. 'Daddy said you weren't coming over tonight.'

Jamie grinned. 'But we always come over on a Friday night, darling.'

'Yes, I know, but Daddy said you weren't this time,' Eloise said, putting her hands on her hips in the same way that Tom did when he was irritated. Sadia's brow creased and she looked at Ana, who shrugged.

'Well, Daddy was wrong, wasn't he?' Jamie said, and leant down to tickle Eloise. Within seconds he was dangling the child by her ankles, and she was screeching in delight, stretching her fingertips towards the floor and not quite reaching. This was a regular occurrence – Eloise loved Jamie, and he gave her a lot of attention. Ana had always loved to watch them playing, but it occurred to her for the first time as she watched him dangle her daughter above the floor that he might drop her. He could hurt her if he wanted to. She tried to brush the thought aside because she knew that he'd never hurt Eloise, but then, Ana didn't think he'd ever hurt her either. She felt Tom stiffen beside her and knew that he was thinking the same thing.

Alexander was sitting on the kitchen table telling Sadia about some biscuits that he and Tom had made for a charity bake sale during the week, but when he saw Ameera he scrambled off the table and held his hands up to take the toddler from Ana. Ameera squealed and wriggled out of Ana's grip to get to Alex. Alex especially loved to play with her, and often picked her up and carried her around, despite her being half his size and clearly too heavy for him. It made Ana broody – more so than usual. She wanted another child. At least one more. She loved the thought of having a big family, her house bursting at the seams with children and grandchildren, never being far from the gurgling of babies' laughter or sticky fingerprints on her windows. She and Tom had planned to apply to adopt again when Ana was finished with the project, and if she won, they'd use the money to help buy a bigger house. She wasn't sure any of it would happen now – not just the house, but she didn't know if they could risk adoption. Jamie knew too much. She felt it as a loss – the loss of children she didn't know yet but might have done. It was Tom's loss too, which made her feel worse.

'Have you not cooked, like?' Jamie asked, lowering Eloise to the ground and taking the bottle of Moët back from Ana. He put it into the fridge and then took a bottle of beer from one of the shelves.

'We can just get a takeaway,' Sadia said before Ana could answer, and then looked at Ana. 'Or we can go if it's a bad time?'

'No, don't go!' Alex said. He was on all fours with Ameera on his back, playing horses. 'It's not a bad time.'

'Don't be silly,' Ana said, opening a cupboard and taking out a bottle of red wine and two glasses. She passed one to Sadia and then dug around in a drawer for the corkscrew. 'I just fancied Chinese. Is that alright?'

'Wicked,' breathed Eloise, who was sitting at Jamie's feet tying his shoelaces together. Jamie hadn't noticed her and Ana didn't say anything.

'Yeah, that sounds amazing,' Sadia said, holding her glass out for Ana to fill. Ana saw Sadia watching Eloise too. She didn't warn Jamie either. 'I haven't had Chinese food for ages. Jamie always wants to get a kebab.'

A shadow passed over Jamie's face, and Ana wondered if Sadia had found out about the teenager. Ana had seen Jamie seduce the girl in a pub, said he knew her because she worked in the kebab shop he frequented. She was far too young, and Ana had told Jamie that, but when he laughed and told her not to worry about it, she hadn't brought it up again. It was easier not to. Jamie hadn't mentioned her again until a few weeks earlier, when he said that the girl had fallen pregnant. Ana had pretended not to hear, because she wished she hadn't. Ana imagined that when the girl gave birth, the same thing would happen as when Ameera was born – Jamie would bring the baby home to Sadia, and Sadia would be thrilled, and maybe she'd be so happy that she'd never question why Jamie knew so many young women willing to give their babies to him. Ana had tried not to think about what Jamie must have said to Ameera's biological mother to make her give up the baby.

Ana knew that she was selfish. She was furious about the Coel Prize, and she knew that it was the end of her friendship with Jamie, even if he thought he could win her over as usual – even if she had to pretend that she'd forgiven him. She'd doggedly overlooked lots of things about Jamie for the fifteen years she'd been friends with him, taken his side even when she wasn't sure she should, let him get away with things she should have confronted him about, and she realised then that it was easy to forgive him for harming other people because she loved him more than them. He had been, for a very long time, the most important person in her life, until the kids came along. She even put Jamie above Tom, sometimes. More often than she should have.

When the food was delivered, Ana set the foil containers across the table with a pile of cutlery and plates, and they all sat down, as they did most Friday nights, either here or at the Spellmans' cottage. Sadia was making Ameera a bowl of rice and cut up bits of chicken as everyone else started to fill their plates. Tom was sitting as far away from Jamie as he could get.

'So,' Sadia said when they had all started eating. She smiled. 'Jamie has a bit of an announcement.'

'Not another one, surely?' Tom said, not looking up from his satay.

'Oh, you already know?' Sadia asked.

Ana kept her eyes on her food, took a deep breath and held it until she counted to five.

'I told you,' Jamie said, tipping some rice onto his plate and spreading it around with his fork. 'They talked about it at work.'

'Oh, I thought you said . . .' Sadia said, looking momentarily confused. Her face brightened again and she stood up. 'Shall we make a toast then?'

Tom glanced along the table at Ana. He tilted his head, his nostrils flared. She reached over and touched his hand, and then got to her feet too. Sadia got the bottle of champagne from the fridge and brought it back to the table, and Ana retrieved some champagne flutes from the back of a shelf, a wedding gift from Tom's mother. She rinsed the dust off them as Sadia popped the cork from the bottle.

'Can we have some, Mam?' Eloise asked, leaning over one of the glasses to inspect the golden fizz. Jamie laughed.

'Absolutely not, adults only,' Jamie said, ruffling Eloise's hair. Tom opened his mouth to speak, but Ana got there first.

'You can have a *tiny* bit in some lemonade,' Ana said, pouring half an inch into the bottom of two of the glasses. Eloise pumped her fist and then stuck her tongue out at Jamie, who lifted his chin but didn't say anything.

'You're the best, you, Mam,' Eloise said.

'Remember that next time I tell you to tidy your room,' Ana said, topping the glasses up with lemonade and passing them to the twins. When everyone had a glass in hand, Sadia stood again. She raised her glass.

'To my brilliant husband,' she said. 'A major, prize-winning scientist. I'm so proud of you, you've worked so hard for this.'

Jamie grinned, and clinked his glass with Sadia's, and then reached over to do the same with Ana, and then Eloise, Alexander, and eventually Tom. Tom pulled his glass away as civica

Issued

Branch: South Dublin Lucan
Date: 21/02/2024 Time: 6:13 PM
Name: Correos, Babie
ID: D4000000354161

ITEM(S)	DUE DATE
Speak of the devil	02 Mar 2024
SD200000047434	
Item Value: €16.98	
Second act	02 Mar 2024
SD200000056740	
Item Value: €17.21	

Total value of item(s): €34.19
Your current loan(s): 3
Your current reservation(s): 0
Your current active request(s): 0

To renew your items please log onto My Account on the OPAC at https://southdublin.spydus.ie

Thank you for using your local library

Jamie reached over to him, and drank. Ana put a hand on Tom's thigh. A crease appeared briefly between Sadia's eyebrows, but she didn't say anything, and they all drank and refilled the glasses until the bottle was empty.

'How long have you been working on this research, then, Jamie?' Tom asked after a few minutes. Eloise was picking all the peas out of her curry and making a little smiley face with them on the edge of her plate. 'How many hours would you say you've put into the thing?'

Jamie opened his mouth to speak, but Sadia got there first.

'It's taken so bloody long, Tom,' she said. 'Honestly, he's been working on it for years, all hush-hush. He's hardly been at home.'

'Well—' Jamie tried to interject, but Sadia carried on.

'But it'll be worth it when that prize fund comes through,' she said. 'I'm dying to remodel the kitchen.'

'If Ana had been out of the house that much I'd probably think she was up to something . . . extra-curricular,' Tom said, winking at Jamie.

Jamie glared at Tom, and Sadia laughed a little too loud. She turned to her husband, mock anger on her face and gasped.

'Is that what you've been doing?'

Jamie rolled his eyes. 'Obviously.'

'Maybe worth keeping an eye on, Sads,' Tom said.

'Tom,' Ana said, getting to her feet and taking Tom's elbow. 'I've got a box of chocolates upstairs for dessert. Come help me find them.'

'I'll help, Mam,' said Alex.

'No, you stay there. Finish your tea. Daddy's going to help,' Ana said, and went upstairs, Tom following her.

'What?' Tom asked as soon as she'd closed their bedroom door behind them.

'Fucking stop it,' Ana hissed. 'I told you not to stir things up.'

'Why is he here, Ana? How the fuck can you let him take the credit for something you've been working on for the better part of three years, something that you've sort of abandoned me and the kids for, and we haven't complained, not once, and you're just going to let him come back in? And I'm just supposed to sit around and be fucking nice to him?'

'Look—'

'Are you in love with him? I never thought so but . . . I dunno. Is that what it is?'

'You're being a dick,' Ana said.

'Well, what else am I supposed to think? What's he blackmailing you with?'

'He's not.'

'But he could?'

'Of course he fucking could, Tom. He could out me.'

'That's not all though, is it?'

Ana looked at her husband and knew there was no point in lying to him. He knew there was something she wasn't telling him. 'No.'

Tom sat on the edge of their bed and crossed his knees. 'Come on then.'

'He knows about the adoption,' Ana said, and Tom looked at her for a few seconds until he realised what she was saying, and then his eyes widened.

'Not even my mother knows about that,' Tom said.

'I know.'

Tom covered the bottom half of his face with a hand as if to stop himself saying something he'd regret. Ana sat beside him on the bed. When she was eighteen and she decided to leave Brazil, her mother had sold her wedding ring, an heirloom from Ana's father's grandmother – who'd been rich – to get the money to buy Ana a new passport. A fake passport, which listed her as *Ana Maria Cortês*, and had a little *f* under the *sexo/sex* heading, which had filled her with such euphoria that she had burst into tears. She had been back to Brazil only once since then, meeting her parents in Rio for a week with Tom, six months before they adopted the twins. She felt both enveloped in a culture she loved and estranged from it after so long. Her parents had visited twice, the first time a year after she moved to England and again in 1998. When they visited, she was conscious of their foreignness.

She hadn't left the country at all since her visit to Brazil, because using the passport was too risky, filled her with such a sense of dread that she'd be caught and arrested, that it was easier not to, though she'd had to use it when they adopted the twins. If she'd told the truth about herself they wouldn't have been able to adopt children at all. If anyone found out that she'd adopted children using a fake passport, the children would be taken away and she, and probably Tom, would end up in jail. And she had told Jamie about the entire thing, years ago, because she told him everything, though she'd promised Tom that she would never tell anyone.

'I can't believe you,' Tom said. He was crying. Ana put a hand on his knee and he flinched away. There was a knock on the door.

'Mam?' Alexander said from the other side of the wood. 'Eloise has been sick everywhere.'

'I'll be down in a second, baby,' Ana said. 'Two minutes.'

'He'll have been dangling her upside down again,' Tom said.

'I know.'

'I can't fucking believe you.'

'I know.'

'I've never – I've never been so fucking mad . . .'

'I know. I know,' Ana said, covering her eyes with a hand. 'But this isn't the time. We have to just keep him steady until I figure out what to do.'

'Looks like it, doesn't it?'

'We'll talk about it later,' Ana said.

'You're fucking right we will.'

Tom had been right – Jamie had gone back to wrestling with Eloise after she'd eaten and she'd thrown up across the lino. When Ana got downstairs, Sadia was in the middle of cleaning up the sick, gagging as she went. Eloise was sitting on Jamie's knee, looking sorry for herself, and Alex was watching cartoons with Ameera in the living room.

'I'll do that Sadia, honestly,' Ana said, taking the kitchen roll that Sadia was using and kneeling beside her. 'Ellie, Daddy's running you a bath. Go up and get in it, please.'

'I don't want to go to bed though,' Eloise said. 'Can I come back down after?'

'We'll see,' Ana said, folding a wad of kitchen roll around her hand. Sadia got up and stuck her head out of the open kitchen window.

'Sorry, I'm terrible with sick,' she said, taking deep breaths. 'Even Ameera's.'

'Thanks for trying,' Ana said. 'You didn't have to.'

'Well, it was Jamie's bloody fault she was sick in the first place,' Sadia said, annoyed.

Jamie sniffed. 'Everything always is,' he said.

'Right,' said Sadia, closing the window and pointedly looking anywhere other than the bin that Ana was piling the used kitchen roll into. 'I'll sort the bairn out and we'll head home. You alright to drive, J, or shall I ring for a taxi?'

'I'm fine,' he said. His eyes followed Sadia as she went to the living room and then he turned to Ana. It was the first time they'd been alone since she'd found out about the prize. 'Told Tom to wind his neck in, then?'

'He's just tired,' Ana said. She got to her feet and washed her hands, and when she turned around he'd crossed the room to stand beside her.

'We're okay, aren't we?' he asked, though she knew he wasn't really asking.

'Course we are,' she said. Jamie tipped his head back and looked at her, and she looked back. She saw him for the first time then as other people must have sometimes seen him – there was a look in his eyes that she'd somehow missed before, but that she caught then. If she'd seen it earlier, she would have known that he wasn't her friend, had never been. These were the eyes – it occurred to her out of nowhere – that Kaysha Jackson had looked into as he raped her, and for the first time Ana realised that Kaysha had been telling the truth.

The following Monday, Ana and Tom both took the morning off work to attend a school assembly that the twins were performing in. The performance was an amalgam of the class's thoughts on what might happen in the new millennium. Some kids presented drawings of flying cars and teleportation machines, one kid recited a poem she'd written about how the Millennium Bug might make all technology cease to exist, throwing everyone back into the Dark Ages, and another child just stood on the stage and declared that everything would be the same – which Ana was slightly disappointed by, even though she agreed. Eloise had wrapped herself in tinfoil and walked around the stage holding a dustpan and brush, limbs stiff, pretending to be a 'house-cleaning robot'. Alex was narrating the assembly rather than presenting, and stood to the side of the stage introducing each student in his best game-show-host voice, his lines written on some colourful flashcards that he and Tom had made together the night before. Tom leant out into the aisle the entire time, filming on his camcorder.

As Ana watched, it occurred to her that these were the moments that made life good, the little bits between the big events, and she wished that she could draw the moment out a little longer, her kids brightened by the stage-lights, the warmth of her husband beside her. She was just a person in a crowd, living her life the way she'd always dreamed that she would. It seemed too good to be true.

When she went to work in the afternoon, happy despite everything, she found that someone had changed the name on her door plaque to *Man Cortês* with a marker. She slid it from its holder and threw it into the bin with such force that the bin toppled over and an apple core rolled across the lino. When she turned around, Jamie was leaning against the door frame, his arms crossed. He smiled.

'Cat's out of the bag,' he said.

21

Josie
8th January 2000

Buses into the city pass Josie Kitchen's house every ten minutes, but she lets them drive by as she walks. She doesn't bother to step around the puddles, and her Air Maxes are already wet. She lets her hood slip backwards as the snow intensifies, and she imagines that by the time she gets to the police station her hair will hang in dripping strands, framing her face the way it does to women in films when they turn up at someone's door, ready to proclaim their love or their regret. She remembers learning about pathetic fallacy in English and imagines that if she *was* in a film, it would be raining instead of snowing. Pouring down. Josie rubs her eyes, knowing that her mascara will smear and drip down her face. She wonders if she looks like the self-portrait she did for art once, in which she painted herself crying, messy, helpless, but in a pretty way. She'd called the piece '*unrequited*', and it was designed to capture the exquisite torture, the sad beauty of loving Jamie when he didn't even know her name. At the time, she couldn't imagine that any feeling in her life would fill her up the way her longing for Jamie would. She couldn't fathom that anything could be more torturous.

The foam earpads on her headphones are wet, and she imagines melted snowflakes getting into the plastic bit underneath, or dripping down the wire and into the cassette deck in her pocket, frazzling it. It wouldn't matter anyway, because they'll confiscate it once they lock her up. She should have left it at home for her little brother Tony, at least he'd have got some use out of it rather than it being locked up with her damp clothes in some police locker. She imagines Tony lying in her bed, loading and listening to each of her tapes because they remind him of her. She worries about the impact it'll have on him when she is in jail. At least he'll finally have his own room.

She's listening to a tape that she made around the same time as she painted '*unrequited*', songs carefully recorded on a Sunday night from the *Top 40* – only the sad ones that exacerbated her mood rather than cheered her up, and as she walks, she lets the nostalgia wash over her. She lets herself be sucked back into her younger psyche, the emotions simpler and easier to manage. She tries to remember Jamie as she thought of him then – before she knew him properly. She's listened to this tape so many times that she knows the order of songs by heart, knows there'll be a second or two of the DJ's voice between 'Something About the Way You Look Tonight' and 'Torn', because she hadn't pressed STOP RECORD in time. She remembers how she'd purposely recorded them in an order that crescendoed, and that when she'd listened to the tape in bed every night, by the time it finished she'd be so bursting with emotion that she wouldn't be able to sleep, and sometimes she'd drag her fingernails up and down her thighs until they bled, just to release some of the feelings she'd built up.

She thinks she'll probably get to the last song, 'Time To Say Goodbye' by Andrea Bocelli and Sarah Brightman, as she approaches the police station. The song isn't what she usually listens to, but it had been popular when she made the tape, and she likes the noise of it, likes that it is so big that it expands into the space around her and within her, and it makes her feel like there is something bigger than just her. She's going to the police station for something bigger than just her. She's going because it's the right thing to do, she's going to save the other women, she's going to save her baby from herself. Who knows what she'll do if she's left alone with it.

She doesn't cry until 'Un-Break My Heart' starts to play, and when she starts she finds that she can't stop. She slips into the mouth of an alleyway and leans against the wall. Above her, steam from someone's shower or washing-up billows from a pipe into the January night, stark against the dark sky. Another bus passes by, almost empty, condensed windows illuminated by the orangey lights inside. Briefly, just for a second, less than a second, she imagines herself stepping into its path. She imagines darkness, a vast, empty forever that is free from Jamie Spellman and from herself, from what she's done. She doesn't believe in God anymore, despite all the years of Catholic school. God wouldn't have let this happen to her baby.

She feels the twist of the baby moving inside her and she doesn't step in front of the bus. She thinks about walking back through the slushy streets to the flat above her dad's kebab shop. She wishes she could, but she can't be trusted to be around other people. She can't risk it. She needs to be locked up for the safety of everyone around her. Especially, she thinks, touching her belly, the baby.

The cold and damp seep through the fabric of her coat – a hand-me-down from her cousin Jenn, who is a year younger than her but half a foot taller – and she shivers, lets her teeth clatter together as she tries to gather her resolve. 'It's All Coming Back to Me Now' – the first few bars of the song missing because she hadn't pressed RECORD in time – comes on, and she sniffs and wipes her face, and braces herself against the cold. It's the right thing to do. She has to hand herself in. She didn't tell anyone where she was going, because she knew someone would try and stop her. She thinks that she'll ring her dad when she gets her one phone call and explain that she won't be home for dinner, and that he'll have to find someone to work Saturday nights for him.

She realises as she thinks it that she won't be back at the cafe, either. She imagines what will happen when she doesn't turn up for her next shift, how they'll find out what she did. They'll tell the customers, and the nice ones, the ones who gave her a tip at Christmas and who had knitted tiny cardigans for her baby, will be disgusted by her. She imagines

Sadia going to the cafe with her daughter and the baristas whispering in the kitchen after she leaves. *That's her, that's the woman whose husband Josie murdered*.

Josie was fourteen when she first met Jamie, and she remembers the moment with a clarity that is particular to the throes of teenage obsession. It was the first Saturday before the start of spring term at school, early evening in her dad's shop, her legs were cold because she was wearing a miniskirt and knee-high socks, and she was arguing with her dad about the length of her skirt, which she had rolled up as high as she dared. She flashed her palm at him, which she knew pissed him off, and turned the volume of the radio up as high as it went. 'Rotterdam' was playing, and Josie leant against the counter. There had been no customers for the last twenty minutes, and she was furious that she was forced to stand there every Saturday night while her friends all got pissed in Leazes Park.

The song changed to 'Children', her favourite song ever, which awoke something in her every time she heard it, made her want to dance, want to speed down a wide American highway in a convertible full of her friends. She never felt more alive than she did when she listened to it, and Jamie walked into her life as the first few seconds of echoing piano rang through the shop. Their eyes met, and Josie's heart sped up and she forgot to breathe, and it felt like the most perfect moment of serendipity. Her dad leapt across the shop to turn the radio down, and shot an apologetic look at Jamie. *Fuckin' pack it in, man*, her dad hissed, but Josie paid no attention. The man was probably the most beautiful human she had ever seen in real life. He was wearing a leather bomber jacket and sunglasses and she thought he looked like Newcastle's answer to Brad Pitt, or a member of a boyband or something. Later, she always told him that it was love at first sight.

Her dad asked Jamie what he wanted and Josie was relieved that he did, because she didn't think she'd have been able to articulate something so banal as *what can I get you?* to *this* man. Her dad shuffled back to the grills to make the food, and the man dropped a few pound coins into Josie's open palm. She could smell his aftershave across the counter and it smelled expensive, not like the knock-off body spray her dad wore, if he wore any at all. She was self-conscious about her outfit suddenly, wished she was wearing something better, more grown up. She considered just sinking below the counter, or out of the back door into the alley until he'd gone, because she couldn't bear the thought of him looking at her when she was so average.

He leant against the wall while he waited for his order, two chicken kebabs with extra garlic sauce. He had a thumb tucked into his jacket pocket and tapped the rhythm of the song against the leather with his palm, and Josie thought it was the single coolest thing she'd ever seen. For months afterwards she'd mimic him when she was trying to look nonchalant, tucking her thumbs into her waistband and tapping.

When he left, she ran upstairs to her room, drunk on her attraction. She'd never felt so immediately into someone before, and she couldn't help but think *this is it, this is the thing all the songs and films and poems are about*. She laughed at herself, feeling like she'd been hit by a train, and spent the rest of the night on her bed, not even doing anything, just listening to music and staring at the slats of the bunk above, imagining a life with the chicken kebab man, even though she knew that was crazy. She imagined marrying him, having his children, climbing into bed with him every night for the rest of her life.

She kept him to herself like a secret, as if something other than an electric shock as their fingers touched when she passed him his change had happened. The feeling was too much and not enough, and suddenly the boys at school seemed immature and beneath her attention. She was supposed to be meeting Michael Phillips at the cinema on Tuesday but she rang him and told him she'd changed her mind. She didn't have the time anymore – she needed an older man.

To Josie's delight, the man came in again at the same time the following week. She'd pre-empted his arrival and worn some Miss Sixty flares she'd borrowed from her best friend and a T-shirt that she knew was a bit too small for her, so it rode up and showed a couple of inches of her belly. Plus it was tight across her boobs. She smeared creamy eyeshadow across her lids, plucked her eyebrows until they were basically non-existent and doused herself in Body Shop perfume. By the time she went downstairs to man the counter, she felt like Britney Spears.

'A don't care how much you dress up, you're still not going drinking,' her dad said as she appeared at the bottom of the stairs, glancing at her and then turning back to the onions he was chopping. Herman, who worked on the grills, smirked.

'God, Dad, A'm just making an effort for your stupid shop, man,' Josie bit back, and stalked across to the counter, where she rested her head on her palm and tried to look artfully bored. When Jamie came in, though of course she didn't know his name yet, she had to keep herself from beaming at him. It was much better to stay cool than act too interested, as she'd read in a magazine that morning.

'What can I get you?' she asked in what she hoped was a sultry voice. She'd been practising.

'Going somewhere nice, hin?' he asked, pushing his sunglasses up onto his head. His eyes were grey-blue and he smiled at her. His teeth weren't the straightest she'd ever seen, but his incisors were really pointy, and reminded her again of Brad Pitt, but in *Interview with the Vampire*. She decided she was just going to call him Brad in her head until she found out his real name.

He came in every weekend after that, and Josie would sometimes spend a few minutes talking to him about a film that had just come out, or music, and then when he left she'd sulk for the rest of the night. She thought about him all the time, felt breathless and overstimulated when she saw him, moody the rest of the time, and she knew that she was in love. One Sunday she was in town with Lou, her best mate, who was very good at getting a five-finger discount whenever she wanted something she couldn't afford – and she couldn't afford anything. Josie got Lou to steal her a bottle of the aftershave that Jamie wore, once she'd sniffed them all and figured out which it was. She squirted it on her pillow every night and imagined that she was falling asleep next to him.

On Sunday nights Josie would sit in her bedroom with her diary and listen to the *Top 40* on Radio One, writing pages and pages of lyrics that she thought described how she felt, and then she fantasised about Jamie one day finding her old diary, in ten years, and how he'd be touched that she used to sit and obsess over him, and he'd say he did the same thing, sang songs in the car on the way to work and thought of her until they got together.

She thought he was perfect. She liked how he'd run his fingers through his hair and sometimes a few strands would fall back into his eyes. She liked that he asked how her day was, how he'd lean against the bar and show her his mobile phone, which was always the best one out. Her dad and Herman would piss themselves laughing at her whenever she tried to casually bring him up in conversation, just for the thrill of talking about him. They'd tease her for having a crush on him, and after a while they started referring to him as her boyfriend, which made Josie squirm with embarrassment, especially when they said it in front of him. She'd tell them not to be so gross, of course she didn't fancy him, he was ancient, *bleurgh*, and they'd howl.

In her bedroom, when Tony was asleep, she'd write about Jamie in her diary. She'd write quick, sloppy paragraphs about how she knew that he was flirting with her, that the way his fingers touched her palm for a second too long when he paid for his food wasn't accidental at all. The way he smiled at her and looked right into her eyes felt like he was looking right into her soul. She'd lie with the lights off afterwards, under the covers with a hand in her pyjama bottoms, inventing scenarios where he'd come back after they closed, and she'd be round the back having a sneaky tab after her parents were asleep, and she'd get in his car and they'd fuck. She didn't write that in her diary. She invented a code for it, in case anyone read it – which was always likely. Fucking was chips. She'd write, *God I wish me and Brad could go out and eat chips. Loads and loads of chips.*

Two years went by, but Josie didn't lose interest. She occasionally went out with boys from school, usually from the year above and once the year above that, but when she was with them she thought about Jamie. She found out scraps about his life week by week and wove them together until eventually she felt like she knew him. He had a wife whom he didn't like, and a little girl. He was a scientist, he had a nice car, his favourite beer was Budweiser. His favourite film was *A Clockwork Orange*, which Josie hadn't watched, but pretended she had. Once, she saw him pause outside the shop to talk to one of the delivery drivers who was hanging around waiting for his next order. She wanted an excuse to talk to Jamie again, so she took a couple of pound coins out of the till so that she could pretend she'd forgotten to give him his change, though she hadn't. She slipped out from behind the counter, but before she got out of the shop she heard her name and paused, blocked from view by the door.

'Aye, she's got a bit of a thing for you like, the bairn,' the delivery man was saying, and Jamie laughed.

'Course she does, A'm lush, me.'

'She's a bit young, like.'

'Wey, you know what they say,' Jamie said, laughing again. 'If it bleeds, it breeds. See you, mate.'

The delivery driver coughed and spat. Josie knew deep down that what Jamie had said was creepy, that he shouldn't be referring to her as *it*, but she decided that it was funny instead. He was just being funny. He didn't mean it. What he did mean, really, was that he didn't think she was too young. She had hoped for the last couple of years that he would wait until she was sixteen, until she was legal, and whisk her away. Confess his feelings, gush that he'd loved her since the first day he'd met her but he couldn't do anything about it. He didn't. She made a point of announcing that she'd soon be sixteen a few weeks before her birthday, but when the day came and went he acted as he always did.

One Sunday afternoon Josie and Lou were lying on Lou's bed. They had been best friends since they were five, though no one would ever put them together. Josie was a charva, complete with peroxide blonde hair and a pair of Rockports that her dad had got her off the back of a wagon. Lou was a goth. She wore black from head to toe and thought about death a lot. They were supposed to be sworn enemies, really, by the unwritten rules of school, but they'd always been inseparable. Lou was into Smashing Pumpkins and she told everyone she was a Wiccan because she had a black cat, but mainly she was just interested in shagging, like everyone else.

When Josie told her about how Jamie still hadn't made a move, Lou laughed.

'Course he hasn't, man, not with your da hanging around.'

'Nah, sometimes I catch him outside when A'm having a tab,' Josie said, twirling a strand of hair around her finger.

'Fucking men, eh,' Lou said, imitating her mam, who was always going out with someone who later turned out to be a dickhead. Lou pulled some books from a pile under her bed.

'I'm not doing a spell, man,' Josie said, rolling her eyes but picking up one of the books anyway. It had a black velvet cover and even if magic was all a heap of shite, which Josie suspected it was, at least the book was nice to look at. The spells inside were printed in an old-fashioned font and there were illustrations of pentagons and herbs and crystals. There were recipes for revenge spells, potions to make you sleep better, to invite good luck, to invite love. Josie paused on a page with a love potion on it, and Lou made a sound of approval.

'Let's do it,' she said, and ran her finger down the list of ingredients at the top of the page.

Exactly three weeks later, just as Josie was losing the last inkling of disbelieving hope that the love spell had filled her with, it happened. She had snuck into a pub with Lou, both using their cleavage in lieu of ID, when Josie spotted Jamie standing at the bar. The hairs on the back of her neck stood up, and she was going to go and speak to him until she noticed the tall, dark-haired woman that he was standing next to. He said something and the woman laughed, shook her head. Josie supposed that the woman was his wife, and felt sour because it didn't look like they were about to get a divorce like he always said. Maybe it wasn't his wife, maybe he had a new girlfriend, and this was her, someone his own age, with a job and a house of her own, and not some spotty teenager who still shared a bedroom with her little brother. She felt stupid, ridiculous for ever thinking that something could happen between them, she was just a kid to him. Of course he'd never want her.

Josie wanted to leave but Lou ordered them both a cider and black before she could say anything. They sat in a corner hoping that the landlady – who was notoriously good at spotting underage drinkers – didn't notice them, and Josie stared at the back of Jamie's head, willing him to turn around and see her.

'Well, you're full of craic today, aren't you?' Lou said eventually, crossing her knees. She wiped the condensation from her pint.

'That's him,' Josie said.

'Who?'

'*Him*,' Josie said, and nodded towards the bar. 'Light hair, leather jacket.'

'Beside the woman in the white dress?'

'Yeah.'

Jamie turned his head to look at the woman and for a second Josie and Lou could see his profile. His eyelashes looked impossibly long from that angle, and Josie watched the way his cheeks wrinkled as he laughed.

'He's alright,' Lou said, shrugging. 'Bit old, like.'

'I love older men,' Josie said, resting her chin on her fist. 'It's because I'm mature for my age.'

'You think you're Cher Horowitz, you,' Lou said.

'I wish.'

'What's his name?'

'Dunno,' Josie said, blushing. 'I just call him Brad.'

'Brad?' Lou repeated, amused. 'Who round here's called Brad, man?'

'Well, because he looks a bit like Brad Pitt.'

Lou spits the last mouthful of cider across the table and then coughs. 'Shut up, man.'

'He does *a bit*.'

'You need geps, you,' Lou said, and watched the landlady sling her handbag over her shoulder and leave the pub. 'I'm going to get us another pint while she's away.'

Josie still had half of her pint and drank it quickly while Lou was at the bar. She was standing next to Jamie, and Josie was envious of Lou's proximity to him. As Josie watched, Lou tapped him on the shoulder and started speaking to him. Lou pointed to Josie and Jamie looked over his shoulder, glancing around. His eyes stopped when he saw Josie and he smiled, winked at her. The dark-haired woman looked too, then quickly looked away. Lou picked up the fresh pints the barman had placed in front of her and came back to the table.

'What did you say?' Josie hissed, pulling a cigarette from Lou's pack and lighting it with shaking fingers.

'Told him you think he looks like Brad Pitt.'

'You didn't.'

'I did. Sometimes you need to give the magic a little push, but it always works,' she said. She gulped her pint and then took a deep breath and got up.

'Where you going?' Josie asked. Lou pulled two cigarettes out of her packet and put them in front of Josie.

'Well, I'm not being a third wheel,' she said. 'Ring me later and let me know what happens.'

Lou was gone before Josie had a chance to say anything else, and the man slipped into the chair that Lou had just vacated.

'Areet?' he said, putting two brown bottles of beer on the table. He pushed one towards her. Josie blinked, felt like she'd been tripped up.

'Was that your wife?' she asked. He laughed.

'Just a friend,' he said. 'No need to get jealous.'

Josie felt choked up, hot with embarrassment and more excited than she'd ever been.

'Why would I be jealous?' she said, her voice breathy and higher than usual.

He just smiled and took a drink from his bottle.

'So you think I look like Brad Pitt?' he asked. Josie knew that she was blushing and hoped that the pub was dingy enough that he wouldn't notice. 'Better looking, though.'

'I didn't actually say that.'

'Your mate said you fancy me.'

'I don't,' Josie said, mortified. 'I actually have a boyfriend.'

'Do you,' he said, moving close to her. He put his hand on her thigh, squeezed a little, and then leant in to kiss her. Josie felt dizzy. The kiss only lasted for a second, but she felt like it was forever, the defining moment in her life so far. She felt as adult as she'd ever been, desire flushing through her in tingling waves, but she also felt so young, tiny beneath his adult hands.

He pulled back and took a drink, looked her in the eyes with such intensity that she had to look away.

'You're going to get me into trouble,' he said, leaning close to her and pushing a strand of hair behind her ear. She shivered as his nose brushed across her neck.

'I won't,' she said. 'I promise.'

'Let's go somewhere,' he said, his voice low. His breath tickled her ear and he squeezed her thigh again. Josie nodded, breathless, out of her depth but too far in to turn back now.

It was only afterwards, in a damp hotel room, feeling bruised and overwhelmed, but fundamentally unchanged, that she learned his name.

22

Nova
8th January 2000

There is a small courtyard round the back of the police station where they keep their bins, as well as a half-rotten picnic table that they eat their lunches on when it's warm – though it rarely is. Nova flicks her cigarette butt into a plastic bucket filled with slushy rain water and it fizzes out. It's snowing but she never bothers to bring her big coat, so she takes another minute to steady herself and then goes back into the interview room.

The kid is pale and still spotty round her chin like a schoolgirl, pretty even though she's been crying. Her hair is bleached but you can see the mousy brown coming back in at the roots, and her nails are long. She scrapes out the dirt from underneath them while Nova sits back down and pulls her notes out of the drawer.

'Thanks for waiting,' Nova says, and the girl shrugs and glances at the two-way mirror. Nova knows that the DCI is standing behind it, watching them. Josie had declined the offer of a lawyer, and Nova didn't want to make her feel outnumbered by having anyone else in the room. The DCI wanted to sit in but Nova convinced her it would spook Josie – Nova knows that she is desperate to take over the investigation, because she thinks that Nova isn't getting answers quickly enough. Really, Nova just hasn't been filing her paperwork. Something about the conversations she's had with the women seems too personal to report, though she knows she's risking her job. 'Do you need anything? More water?'

Josie shakes her head. 'I'm okay, thanks.'

'Okay, let me know if you do,' Nova says, and leans back in her chair. The girl nods and Nova continues. 'So. Where were we?'

'The solstice.'

'Yeah, okay, so . . . so you took part in the ritual at Penshaw with the snake. I know all about that one.'

'Do you?'

'Oh yes,' Nova says. 'So then what? Because he didn't die that night, did he?'

'And then, I just saw him once more. On Boxing Day.'

'What happened on Boxing Day?' The best guess is that Jamie Spellman died on New Year's Day, maybe New Year's Eve. His wife said she had last seen him on the afternoon of the 31st, so any time before that was out. Unless Sadia was lying, of course.

'He brought some clothes and things to my house,' she says, tearing up again. Nova offers Josie a box of tissues and she takes one. 'For the baby.'

'Right, right, and you had a conversation?'

'Well, I sent him packing,' she says, lifting her chin. 'I don't need anything from him. He wanted to take the baby away. He kept saying he was going to take the baby away, and then he turned up with this box of second-hand baby clothes from his daughter trying to be nice, and I told him to f— I told him to go away.'

'I can't imagine he took that well?'

'No,' she says. 'He got nasty again. He said what he always says, what he was saying before that. He said he'd sue me for custody because who would trust a stupid teenager with a bairn over a grown man with a wife and a house.'

Nova raises an eyebrow. 'Depends on the man, doesn't it?'

'I really thought – I was so scared he'd take the baby.'

'And that's why you killed him?'

Josie nods.

'Josie . . . at least if he'd taken you to court, you know, you'd have had a good chance. You might have got a council flat and even if you didn't get custody, you'd have had visitation. What's going to happen now?'

'I know.'

Nova takes a deep breath.

'So, you next saw him on New Year's Eve?'

'No, that was the last time I saw him alive. Boxing Day,' she says, staring at the desk. 'I told him to drop dead. I was so cocky, because I felt, like, powerful. Empowered. After Penshaw.'

'The last time you saw him *alive*?'

Josie flicks her eyes up to Nova's and holds her gaze for a second, as if she is weighing up what to say. 'That was the last time I saw him.'

Nova frowns. 'Except for the day you beheaded him, Josie?'

'I didn't, like . . . I didn't *physically* behead him.'

'You said you murdered him. Did you kill him some other way and someone else took it from there? Did someone offer to dispose of the body for you?' Nova asks, feeling the DCI's gaze on her through the glass.

'No, well. I don't know what happened to his body. We killed him – I killed him with the ritual. It's really powerful. I didn't believe it either, and it was just to – to get rid of my anger and frustration, and we sacrificed the snake, and obviously I didn't think it was going to work, not really. I didn't believe in it, really, at all, but then he was dead, because I wanted it so much . . .'

'Josie . . . you didn't kill him,' Nova says, trying to sound firm though she feels faint with relief.

'I did,' she says, leaning forward, her eyes wide. 'You need to lock me up. I killed Jamie and I'm scared I'll kill someone else as well, just – I don't know – just by wanting it so much.'

'Josie . . .'

'What if I hurt the baby?' Josie says, and tears spill down her face. 'What if it cries all the time and I can't sleep and I wish her dead, and she dies? You need to take her away from me . . . please.'

'Alright. Let's just take a second and calm down,' Nova says, sitting upright and reaching across the desk to take

Josie's hands in her own. She squeezes the teenager's fingers and Josie squeezes back as she cries. Nova glances at the mirror, aware that she'll be bollocked later, but she can't just let a pregnant teenager have a panic attack in her care. She didn't kill him. 'Just breathe, Josie.'

Nova takes deep breaths with Josie for a few minutes, until the teenager stops crying. She is still shaking, but she wipes her eyes with her sleeve and looks back at Nova.

'Thank you,' she says.

'It's okay,' Nova says. 'So, are you saying that you did not physically, with your hands, with a knife, an axe, poison, or anything physical – you didn't physically harm Jamie Spellman?'

'Well, no, but—'

'All you did was cast . . . cast a spell, wish him dead, and he died? And that's what you're taking responsibility for?'

'Yes, but it's more than just a spell—'

'Okay. Stop there. Let's take five,' Nova says, standing up to leave the room again.

23

Kaysha
8th January 2000

Kaysha speaks to each of the women every day, just a brief call or a text to check that they're alright, to check who has spoken to the police or who has heard anything that she might not have, to search for a note of guilt in their voices or to probe for a confession. Kaysha knows that it would be more sensible not to contact any of them, but there are too many moving parts, too many people to trust with such a big secret, too many lives to be ruined. She needs to keep everyone in check.

Olive hasn't answered a text or a phone call for two days when Kaysha goes to see her. Olive is who she is most worried about, because she has never been as invested in the group as the others. It took all of them a little while to trust Kaysha, and each other, but Olive never quite got there. She'd scoff at the other women's stories, imply that they were lying or exaggerating. She wanted to call the police on New Year's Eve, and Kaysha grows more nervous every day that she still will.

Kaysha stands on her doorstep with her hood up and rattles the knocker and letterbox in turn. She has been here before, when she was figuring Olive out, deciding if she should include her in the group, and she is always surprised by the scale of the house. Olive is a librarian and her late husband was a miner, and these houses – towering Victorian terraces that overlook the North Sea and Tynemouth Priory – must be very expensive.

'Olive, open up,' Kaysha hisses through the letterbox, after her knocking goes unanswered. 'I just want to know you're alright.'

After a few seconds Kaysha hears the lock click, and when Olive doesn't open the door to greet her, she takes it as an invitation and lets herself in. The house is dark but Kaysha can hear the murmur of a television through a door to the left. She takes off her shoes and follows the sound through the living room and into the kitchen, where Olive is sitting at a round dining table. The room is tastefully decorated but aged – the tiles are chipped and the wallpaper is stained in places. One of the French doors leading to the garden is cracked and taped over.

'What do you want?' Olive asks when Kaysha walks into the room. Her voice is hoarse, as if she hasn't spoken in days.

'I just came to check you were alright,' Kaysha says, walking towards the table and using the same slow, calm voice she uses when she goes to see her Aunt Zainab, who is senile. 'I haven't heard from you.'

'Why would you?' Olive asks.

'I need you to just let me know that you're alright, until this blows over,' Kaysha says, and puts her hand on the chair opposite Olive. 'May I?'

Olive purses her lips and Kaysha sits down. It's only been a week since Kaysha saw her last but she is thinner. She is wearing a worn pair of Popeye pyjamas which look child-sized, and they hang off her. She looks as delicate as if she were made out of paper.

'What do you want?' Olive asks again, pushing fingers through her greasy hair. Her movements are quick and jumpy, like a sparrow's. 'I haven't said anything to anyone.'

'I just wanted to check you were alright.'

'I'm fine.'

'You don't seem fine,' Kaysha says. 'I thought I heard a TV when I came in . . . Were you talking to someone?'

Olive glances at the chair beside her and then at the ceiling. 'You talk to yourself more as you get older. Often the only sensible conversation of the day.'

'Have you been at work this week?'

'Have you?' Olive asks.

'Not as much as usual, but I've been working,' Kaysha says. She's written a few small pieces for *The Chronicle* to tide her over until she has time to work on something bigger again.

'Of course you have. Of course,' Olive says. She frowns. 'How can you just . . . how can you just carry on as normal, as if a good man isn't dead?'

'He wasn't a good man.'

'You shouldn't speak ill of the dead,' Olive says. A gold crucifix hangs between her collarbones, and she touches it.

'Are you a Catholic?'

'What do you care?'

Kaysha shrugs. 'I care.'

'Protestant,' Olive says.

'Have you been to church recently?'

'I go to church every day,' Olive says. 'Almost every day.'

Kaysha has read that priests aren't allowed to discuss what is divulged in a confession box, but she isn't sure that the rule stretches to murder. She's not sure Protestants even have confession. She wonders if Olive has told. She wants to ask, but doesn't want to put the idea into Olive's head if she hasn't already thought of it.

'Do you need me to get you anything?' Kaysha asks.

'What?'

'I could get you some shopping if you want – milk, bread, cigarettes . . . anything really.'

'I don't smoke.'

'Anything.'

Olive leans across the table, fingernails digging into the wood. 'Have you figured out who did it yet?'

Kaysha keeps her gaze. 'No.'

'I bet it was your girlfriend.'

'It wasn't Sarah,' Kaysha says, her voice firm, though she knows that some of the others suspect Sarah too. She seems the obvious choice – the mouthiest, the one who suggested time and time again with a glint in her eye that they *should just go Michael Myers on the fucker*.

'You're protecting her.'

'Olive, look, we don't know who it was. But it's done now, and all we can do is look out for each other. He harmed us all, and I'm not condoning what happened . . . but . . . it's done.'

'And what if this murderer, whoever she is, but let's call her Sarah,' Olive says. 'What if she does it again? What if she decides to behead the next man who looks at her the wrong way?'

'Jamie isn't dead because he looked at someone the wrong way,' Kaysha spits. 'He's dead because he was an evil prick and it caught up with him.'

'He was good.'

'He was a fucking murderer, Olive,' Kaysha says, taking Olive's wrist.

Olive's eyes widen. 'Get out.'

'He took everything from you. Why are you still protecting him?'

'Just get out of my house,' Olive says, her face flushed with rage.

24

Nova
10th January 2000

Lou Alderman's bedroom is exactly what you'd expect of a teenage occultist, though the rest of the house is not. The house in general is painted in muted peaches and creams, fake bouquets of white roses and sunflowers are tastefully dotted around in nice vases, and the curtains hang just so, as if they've been ironed in perfect pleats. The day outside is grey but the house is bright.

In contrast, Lou's bedroom walls are a shade of purple which is almost black, and the curtains are drawn. Dried bunches of herbs and flowers dangle from the ceiling by strings, and candles clutter various surfaces in a way that makes Nova nervous that the room is going to catch fire. Incense is burning on a shelf and the room is unbearably stuffy and fragrant. A framed drawing of the cult's sigil hangs on the wall above Lou's bed.

'I take it you're not going to deny your involvement, then?' Nova asks, and nods up to the frame. Lou just smiles and clears a tangle of scarves and a black cat from an armchair for Nova, and then sits cross-legged on her bed, the cat settling in the space between her knees. Nova sits on the chair and leans forward. She doesn't know why she was surprised at first that the entire thing was coordinated by a teenage girl – of course it was. They're powerhouses, and always underestimated.

'Look, I'm not here to arrest you,' Nova says, and Lou leans back against the wall.

'Well, I mean, why would you?'

'Theft, for one. Destruction of public property. The list goes on,' Nova says, and Lou tilts her head in acknowledgement. 'But I don't want to arrest you, like I said. I'm willing to let it go – even though it's caused me countless hours of misery.'

'Why?' Lou asks.

'Why am I not going to arrest you?'

'Yeah.'

'Because you've got your whole life ahead of you, and a criminal record isn't going to help you do what you need to do.'

Lou shrugs. 'Everyone round here's got a criminal record. Doesn't matter if I have as well.'

'Yeah, they have, and then they end up stuck here. It's bullshit, because everyone does stupid shit when they're a kid, it shouldn't fuck up the rest of your life, but it does if you haven't got enough money to get rid of your mistakes. You're clever, you can do well if you push yourself.'

'How do you know I'm clever?'

'How many people you got in your gang? Five? Ten? And you're in charge. You convinced all those people that slaughtering a sheep and saying some magic words was going to fix their problems. That's not easy,' Nova says, leaning back in the chair and crossing her legs. 'Imagine if you put those brains to good use. You could be anything.'

'Like what? A police officer? Upholding bullshit laws that fuck over poor people and anyone who isn't white? Nah, mate. Not me,' Lou says, squaring her shoulders. The force of Lou's conviction takes Nova by surprise, but she can't help but agree. Nova can't find the part of herself that believed in the police force anymore, and thinks that if she could go back, with the wisdom she has now, she'd never have joined in the first place.

'I'm not suggesting—'

'I do this because people need help. I love the spells, but we do it to empower people. The law doesn't help us, round here. It helps people in the big houses keep the nice stuff out of our hands.'

'I don't disagree.'

'And to keep women in their place.'

'Yeah, sometimes.'

'My dad raped my mam. And she was brave and she tried to take him to court, but they said there was no case because it isn't rape if they were married. Did you know that? We're still property. I couldn't let Josie become that to this creepy old man she'd been shagging.'

Nova raises her eyebrows. She'd never really thought that the cult had actually killed Jamie Spellman, but maybe she was wrong. Nova leans forward in the chair.

'Did you kill him, Lou?' Nova asks in a low voice, meeting the teenager's eyes. 'To protect Josie?'

Lou laughs. 'A do a ritual and slaughter a few scabby sheep and A'm capable of hacking some gadgie's heed off? Howay, man.'

'What do you mean you couldn't let it happen to Josie, then? If you didn't kill him. Did you ask one of your followers to do it?'

'No. Look, I don't kill people and I don't condone killing people. I just want to empower people. I just like girls to feel powerful. I wanted Jo to know that she could overcome him. With her own, like, energy.'

'You know she thinks that she actually killed him?' Nova says, looking at her hands and then back at Lou. 'She thinks she's a murderer. She begged me to lock her up so she didn't endanger anyone else. She's worried that she'll accidentally kill her baby. You know that, don't you?'

Lou is wide-eyed for a second and then pushes her waist-length hair away from her face. 'I don't – we just did a spell that, like, that powers up rebounding energy, doubles it. His death is on him, not us.'

'What do you mean?'

'It's like, whatever they've put out into the world will come back on them, but harder. Twice as hard. I didn't know he was going to end up dismembered, did I? Wonder what he did to deserve that, must be more than what he did to Josie.'

Nova has always struggled with religion, neither believing nor disbelieving. She wasn't raised in a church, but she respects the power religion has for people, and she finds herself praying at times when she's most desperate, when she doesn't have the power to do anything else. When she thinks about death, she wishes that she believed in something substantial so that it would feel less terrifying. She does believe in karma, though; the idea that every action has a reaction is mechanical enough to make sense to her.

Nova nods. 'What do you think he'd have had to do to deserve his fate, then? If you don't think just manipulating a young woman into having a child for you would do it?'

'I dunno. More than that? Maybe not. I feel like he's done loads of bad things. He's just got that vibe. Just a bad person,' Lou says, and reaches under her pillow. She pulls out a black, velvet bag, embroidered with a sun and some stars. 'Let's see what the tarot says.'

Nova watches as Lou pulls out the deck and shuffles them, larger than playing cards and more interesting; she catches glimpses of faces and buildings as they move through Lou's hands. Lou stops and takes the first three cards from the top of the deck, and lays them out in front of her, face up. She presses her lips together, and Nova is compelled to know what the cards say, even though she doesn't think she believes in them.

'What do they mean?'

'Well,' says Lou, flicking her hair over her shoulder. 'We've got the eight of swords, the Devil, and then the nine of swords. It's like . . . they're saying that he abuses people.

They're about entrapment and false promises, and then just a feeling of hopelessness that surrounds him. I don't think he's the one that feels hopeless, it just follows him around.'

'Okay.'

'It's not the full story, though,' Lou says, and pulls the next card from the deck and lays it on top of the others. The card is upside down, and Nova reads *The Emperor* across the bottom. Lou scoffs. 'No surprise there.'

Nova lifts her shoulders and Lou carries on.

'The Emperor is about authority and control, but in a more . . . more of a fatherly sense than I'd typically think of for Jamie. He's not a bad guy usually. But, reversed,' she says, drawing a circle in the air with her fingertip, 'he becomes a tyrant. He's lost control, and he's angry about it. He'll do anything at all to get it back.'

Nova nods. 'Is that all?'

Lou pulls one more card from the deck and doesn't say anything for a minute. She taps her finger across each of the cards in turn, and then just the first, third, and fifth.

'Eight, nine, and ten of swords,' she says. 'Like a story, but a tragedy. He made everything bad wherever he was, and then, that ending. It's about defeat, and death.'

'His death?'

'Maybe, but I don't think so, because of the other cards. This is something he's done.'

'You think he killed someone?' Nova asks. She wonders if Lou is using the cards as a roundabout way to tell her that she knows something more than she is saying. She wonders if Jamie really did kill someone, and thinks about the Bible passage his head sat on. *An eye for an eye*. Thus far she's thought of it only as an indication that his murder was in revenge for something, but she supposes that the passage points more to a punishment equal to one's crime. An eye for an eye, a murder for a murder. She tries not to get carried away. She knows she's been drawn in by Lou's influence. The teenager really is powerful.

Lou shrugs, and stares at the cards. 'It might be symbolic.'

'What do you think?'

'I don't know. I suppose you'll find out though, won't you? Eventually,' Lou says, and looks at Nova, unsmiling.

Nova feels her phone vibrating in her pocket and takes that as her cue to leave. For a split second she worries that somehow her phone has been on the whole time, connected to someone who would fire her for letting Lou off the hook. She checks the screen, but it's just Jenna from forensics. 'Right, I've got to go, but remember what I said. No more animal sacrifices.'

'I'll be good,' Lou says, gathering the cards and sliding them back into the velvet bag, and when Nova stands and looks down at her, she just sees a little girl trying to make sense of the world.

In the car, Nova's phone rings again and Jenna tells her that they've got Jamie's blood work back, Nova had better come down and have a look. The lab is on an industrial estate in a wealthy suburb of the city, and Nova hates going there because it always smells of chemicals, like a hospital. Jenna greets her at reception with a coffee, and they go to Jenna's office, where she pulls up some reports on her PC. Nova can never make head nor tail of what the charts and abbreviations mean, but nods along as if she does while Jenna explains them, pointing at lines of jargon with a manicured fingernail.

'What it boils down to,' Jenna says after a while, putting her empty cup on the windowsill behind her, 'is that a lot of drugs entered his system very shortly before he was killed.'

'What drug?' Nova asks.

'Lots and lots of diazepam, which is an interesting choice. It's a powerful anti-anxiety drug. Also known as Valium.'

'Probably not planned in advance then?'

'Seems unlikely.'

'Could he have taken them himself? Overdosed?'

Jenna scrunches her nose. 'A suicide attempt? Seems an odd choice of drug for that . . . Depends on his mental state, I suppose. If it was a smaller dose I'd suspect he took them himself, even just as a sleeping aid, something like that . . . but like I said, there was too much for it to have been a casual dose.'

'Fair enough. Did you find anything else?'

'Alcohol level was pretty high. Doesn't react well with diazepam, so I imagine he was out for the count.'

'Ah, we don't think he was, actually,' Nova says. The autopsy technician had spoken to her a couple of days earlier to tell her what little information they could glean without the rest of the corpse. 'The angle of some of the axe strokes – they think it was an axe, something heavy and relatively blunt for a blade – like, not a carving knife – and they think he was standing up when he was first hit. They said the angle was sort of, upwards, like someone had swung sort of forty-five degrees upwards at him. At first, anyway. Obviously, he was on the floor for a lot of it. There were a lot of strokes.'

'Ah, so you think it's a woman? Because she'd be smaller, I mean.'

'Hmm. Some people don't think so. It's quite a grisly crime for a woman, but there's just something about it that seems like . . . I dunno, a woman pushed too far.'

'Well, it's interesting you say that, actually, because diazepam is a prescription drug, not what you'd usually order from your dealer, unless you were already addicted.'

Later, when Nova checks the list of medicines found in the Spellman house when it was searched, she sees that there was nothing at all present that had been prescribed to Jamie, but five or six medicines that were Sadia's, and Diazepam was first on the list.

25

Sadia
11th January 2000

Sadia plans her husband's funeral – or memorial service – as quickly as she would have been expected to if he had died under normal circumstances, in a move which the police will later think of as suspicious, as if she is too eager to lay the idea of him to rest, because she certainly is not laying his body to rest.

There is no coffin. The vicar offered to display an empty coffin at the front of the church, as he'd done for those whose bodies have been scattered by bombs on battlefields, lost at sea, or just lost. Sadia had said no, she thought it would draw attention to the fact that Jamie wasn't whole. She worried that people would think she was burying his head without his body, though she couldn't even bury that. It was still in police custody, in a fridge somewhere, slowly rotting.

The funeral is in the church where Jamie spent two years with his grandfather, formative years he always said. According to Jamie, he grew into a man here, under the stern watch of his mother's father – the only father figure he ever had. The old man was never loving or particularly kind, but at least took him in at fifteen, having never met him before then. He recognised the teen's cold, grey eyes and weak chin as his own, and knew he was Alice's bastard. He made Jamie pray every day for his mother's sins, made him learn the Bible cover to cover. Jamie's years with his grandfather weren't happy, but he always said that he learned more about right and wrong in two years with Joseph Spellman than in sixteen with Aunt Maureen.

Joseph had even agreed to pay for Jamie's degree, though only because Jamie had promised to study Theology and become a clergyman too. Jamie had actually applied for Biochemistry, and was only caught out when his grandfather opened his acceptance letter. When Joseph found out about the deception, he threatened to cancel his payment unless Jamie changed courses. Joseph was found dead by one of his flock the day after Jamie left for university, keeled over the font with his face in the water. He left nothing to his estranged daughter or teenage grandson, and every penny, except what had already been paid for Jamie's degree, went to the church.

26

Maureen
11th January 2000

The others said it would look suspicious if Maureen didn't turn up to the funeral, so she puts on a knee-length, black dress she's had in the back of the wardrobe for ten years, just in case it ever fit again, and a navy hat that she bought for her stepdaughter's wedding last July. They don't match, but she doesn't care. She feels a little stab of satisfaction when John zips up the dress that didn't come past her hips a few weeks ago. Stress always makes her thinner. Finally, a silver lining. The only good thing to come out of the whole thing, bar, of course, Jamie's absence from the world.

The sense of cold glory quickly dissipates as John drives out of the village and around the edge of the city to the church. She hasn't laid eyes on it for thirty-five years, and she'd have lived the rest of her life happily without ever doing so again. It juts against the sky in sharp edges and needling spikes. It was built, her father said once, in the image of the cathedral in Cologne. He liked how severe and gothic it looked. He said it kept away the easily spooked and unholy.

'This it, then?' John asks, as she points him into the car park. 'Gloomy-looking place, innit?'

Maureen nods. She knows that John is uneasy; the new information he has about her life wedges between them, and he feels like he doesn't know her anymore. He said as much yesterday and she is worried that he will leave her. Still, he is here at the funeral with her, and she appreciates it.

The first few pews are full when they go in, save the front bench, which holds only Sadia and her child. Maureen side-steps into the very back row, and John pauses as she does.

'Do you not want to sit at the front? There's plenty of room.'

'Let's just sit here. I don't want to impose,' she whispers, patting the bench beside her.

'But you're family, you should be at the front.'

'We can just sit here,' she says, and beckons him towards her. He raises his eyebrows but sits down. His breath rattles in his chest and she passes him a blue inhaler from her handbag without a word. She tries to settle down. She thought that the church would seem smaller to her, since she was so much younger the last time she was here, but it feels as big as ever. Cavernous. The church she attends now is small and modern, a warm, clean space where the walls are painted magnolia and the services are led by a vicar who laughs often.

Her father has been dead for over fifteen years now, but she can still feel him here. She always thought that if he'd been American, he would have been one of those that you see on television, shouting and thrashing violently as he claimed to heal the sick with divine power lent to him from the Lord. He always said he had a gift for conversion, and it was true that his pews were always full, and whenever someone died or left the area, he'd manage to fill their place quickly with some poor wretch he'd bullied or shamed into joining his church.

Jamie had always yawned his way through the Methodist services they attended in the little chapel where Alice was buried, and though Maureen had scolded him for it, she could hardly blame him. The deacon was a doddering old man with a reedy voice that barely carried past the first two rows of seats, and in the summer, when it was impossible to keep out the heat, Maureen would often find that her nephew had slumped against her arm, fast asleep, and she usually felt close to drifting off herself.

When he left, he found his way here instead. She had no phone in the cottage, but the farmer had received a brief phone call from Jamie a couple of weeks after he left, to say that he was safe with his grandfather, and for Maureen not to bother coming to find him. When the farmer had passed the message on via the address she had left him when she moved out, she had scoffed. She had had no intention of finding him. She was glad he was safe, but the thought of the boy, already knotted with rage on the inside, being moulded by her father made her uneasy. She knew she hadn't been a good parent, but her father was worse than she ever was. No wonder the boy turned out like he did.

Maureen watches the church fill up the way the funerals of young people always do and feels sour that there are more mourners here for him than there were for Alice. Alice deserved them. He doesn't. She realises, as she glances around, that most of the other women are here too, blending into the sea of black, wearing long faces.

Josie, who looks ready to burst, is crying at the end of the third row. She never seems to do anything else but weep. Maureen is surprised to see that Sarah is in the opposite back row, her head tipped back against the wall, neck tattoo on full display. Olive is four rows in front of Maureen, her head jerking around like a hatchling, hungry for something. Just as the vicar, a kind-looking ginger man with glasses and round cheeks who seems as opposite to Maureen's father as possible, clears his throat and glances around, the doors open once more and Ana walks in with a man who Maureen assumes is her husband. He is the same height as her, not as good looking as she is. Maureen wonders if the husband was ever jealous of her friendship with Jamie, whether he thought they were having an affair, whether he trusted his wife. Ana is wearing a black trouser suit that flows with her movements like an expensive gown would. Maureen is struck, not for the first time, by how elegant she is.

27

Ana
11th January 2000

Sadia is in the front row, of course, and she turns to look at Ana and Tom as they walk into the church. She half rises and beckons them towards her, to sit on the otherwise empty front row. Ana kisses her cheek and then takes a seat, whispering a hello to Ameera, who is curled into her mother's side, a plush rabbit dangling from one small fist. She is wearing a dark blue dress, and is quiet, as if she senses the sadness in the room – which is present, but scant. Many people, Ana imagines, are there out of something like obligation, a sense that you must attend the funeral of someone you knew, even if you weren't really friends. Or you were friends, and then you weren't. Ana isn't at the funeral to mourn the Jamie who died, she's there to mourn the Jamie who came before that: the Jamie who let her sleep on his sofa when she had nowhere else to go, the Jamie who sat a few tables away when she went on first dates, just to make sure everything was okay. The

Jamie who got her a job, who never treated her differently or outed her, until he did. She knows that if she examines any of the kindnesses that he extended her, she will probably find an ulterior motive, but she doesn't look for them. Not during his funeral. In the church, she tries to remember the best of him.

There is a brief lull after Ana and Tom sit down and everyone stares at a large, framed photograph of Jamie that is on a table next to the pulpit. It is surrounded by garlands of white flowers, and in it he is laughing and holding a bottle of beer, Ameera on his hip, a year or so old. Ana knows it's just the setting, the expectation of sadness and the poignant but empty words that the vicar has begun to recite, but she feels tears welling in her eyes in spite of herself.

Ana appreciates that she got off relatively unscathed during her friendship with Jamie, compared to the others. She knew him the longest, other than Maureen. Far longer than Sadia. Ana and Jamie met on the first day of university. Ana was brand new to the country, her parents had scraped together every last penny to buy her the fake passport – one that used her chosen name, *Ana Maria Cortês* – and send her halfway across the world to start a new life.

Ana zones out as the vicar speaks, remembering Jamie in her own way. She cannot articulate to any of the other women the things that she will miss about him. She knows that the terrible things that he did outweigh the small kindnesses he showed her, and she accepts that Jamie was a manipulator. Their friendship probably wasn't real to him. She has recently taken a book out from the library about narcissists and recognises Jamie in the dense paragraphs about befriending and seducing the vulnerable and easily manipulated. She was vulnerable when she met him, new to being who she was, and his friendship often meant more to her than her morals. She felt like his acceptance kept her safe.

She decides to grant herself the length of the funeral to bask in the good memories she has of Jamie, before he took her research, before the meetings began and she found out that he had done so much worse to the others. She thought of him at university, countless nights drunk on cheap vodka, when they'd stay out until the sun poked through the cracks between buildings and the food vans swapped burgers for bacon sandwiches. She lets her memory warm her for a second, and then she remembers what else he was doing on those nights out, the ones where he disappeared with a girl, and Ana walked home alone. She had rejected the idea at the time, but all the signs were there. She refused to notice them then, and in all the years since. When Ana thinks about her blunt refusal to believe Kaysha, her selfishness, her utter disbelief that Jamie Spellman could be anyone other than the man she needed him to be, she is more ashamed than she ever has been about anything else in her life. She feels ashamed for even trying to remember the good things about him, as if they aren't cancelled out by the rest. Instead, she thinks about her own actions, prays for forgiveness. She prays that she'll be able to repay Kaysha, somehow. When Kaysha was young and brave and told her university peers that Jamie was a rapist, told them to stay away from him, Ana had made sure that everyone thought that Kaysha was a fantasist. Sometimes, Ana hopes that it is Kaysha who murdered Jamie so that she can help her cover it up.

28

Josie
11th January 2000

Josie comes to the funeral alone, though she has been told not to come at all. Kaysha said that the fewer of them that were there the better, because you could bet the detective would turn up to see who was hanging about. Killers almost always go back to the body, after all, pick the scabs.

She is so overwhelmed. Detective Inspector Stokoe told her that the murder wasn't anything to do with her, that Jamie was decapitated with a physical weapon and not her spell, but she doesn't quite believe it. She doesn't really know what to believe about anything anymore.

Sadia is sitting at the front of the church with her arm around her little girl, and Josie watches as she strokes the child's hair and rubs her back. She's seen them together before at the cafe, and she always thinks that they seem sewn together, like two halves of something. Sadia always seemed to know what to say to make her daughter laugh, or quieten down, or pay attention. They always seemed so at peace in each other's company, and Josie feels envious that she doesn't have that kind of relationship with her mother, who is chaotic and not maternal. Josie's mother isn't awful, she has never abandoned her children or mistreated them, they are fed and housed, but Josie has always felt that there is something missing in their relationship, as if the depth of love that you are supposed to feel from your mother isn't there, and Josie's mother is angry at her children more than she is in love with them.

Josie worries that she will feel the same way towards her child. She worries that because Jamie is the child's father, the child will come out wrong, twisted, like him. She worries that she is not loving enough to pacify the half of the baby that will be Jamie's half, because she hasn't had a good enough example of motherhood to model herself on. She's worried that her half will be twisted and evil too, because she's a murderer, or she might be. Josie is worried that she isn't old enough to know how to raise a child on her own. Even if she gets a council flat for just her and the baby, like Detective Inspector Stokoe suggested, she'll be alone with it. She won't know what to do. This was never the plan. Jamie was supposed to be with her, holding her hand and showing her how to care for the child, how to love it properly, how to mother it like Sadia does.

Everyone assumes that Josie got pregnant by accident, through some carelessness on her part or Jamie's, because no one gets pregnant on purpose at seventeen to a married man. Josie is always confused when she tries to remember why she stopped taking her pill, how Jamie rationalised her having his baby, before he'd even divorced his wife, before Josie had even moved out of her childhood bedroom, but he had. He'd made it seem like the only right idea. Josie would get pregnant, get a house, he'd move in. They'd be together properly, like a family, they wouldn't have to sneak around. If she had his baby, he would know beyond a doubt that she loved him, if she was willing to do that for him. He'd be a great dad. One night in a hotel room, he'd gently prised her pack of pills from her hand just as she was about to take it. He put them in his pocket. *Trust me*, he said, *everything will be perfect*. Afterwards, he made love to her so gently that she believed him.

Months later, when Josie was too pregnant to change her mind, Jamie changed. He started to tell her how childish she was, just the odd comment at first, followed by a hug, a sympathetic stroke of her cheek. Then he'd spit at her that he'd made a mistake, she was too young. He'd thought she was more mature than this. He'd snap at her for anything. When she cried, which was often, Jamie swung between comforting her and hissing insults, and when she tried to explain that it was the hormones, that her body was changing and it was normal for her to be so emotional, he'd just scoff.

Eventually, when she felt so completely addled by her body and Jamie's ever-changing behaviour, he started to tell her that she wasn't fit to be a mother. She felt it the first time like a slap.

'But you made me get pregnant,' she said, sitting on the edge of the bed in the hotel room where they always met. 'It was your idea.'

'What the fuck are you talking about, Josie?' he said, his eyes wide. 'This is a silly little fling, why would I want you to get pregnant?'

'A fling?'

'You can't really think I'd leave my wife and daughter and home and life for *you*?'

'But you're getting a divorce,' Josie said.

Jamie laughed. 'Am I? When have I ever said that?'

'Loads of times,' Josie said, but she faltered, confused. He was so confident. 'You said . . . You know the things you've said. You wanted this baby.'

'Think about it, man, why would I? I'm happily married, I've got a kid already.'

'Well, why would I want to have a baby? I'm seventeen! You're married. You said you wanted this.'

'You're dreaming, you, mind,' he said, baring his teeth. 'You're not fit to raise this kid, you don't live in the real fucking world.'

Josie's breath caught in her throat. 'We'll sort something out . . . You'll help me.'

'What, you think I'm going to sneak off every day to help you look after this kid when you're still a kid yourself? Grow up.'

Josie's heart was racing. She felt hot and on the verge of tears, confused by Jamie's sudden change in attitude, or confused by her own perception. She was sure he'd wanted the baby. He'd taken her pill off her, he'd talked her into it.

'But it was your idea,' she said, sinking into a chair and looking up at him. He glared at her, disgust smeared across his face.

'Fuck off, this was you trying to tie me down. It's not going to work.'

'Well, what am I supposed to do now?' she asked, voice cracking. He squeezed his lips together.

'You'll have to figure something out. Just stay in your bedroom with your brother, I'm sure one more squeezed into that greasy little flat won't make much difference, eh?'

'You've never even been in the flat,' Josie said.

'Do I need to, like? It can't be fucking big, can it? Howay, man,' he said. He sat on the bed and exhaled. 'You've really fucked up.'

Josie bit her lip. She didn't think she had fucked up, she thought she had done exactly what he wanted her to. Maybe she *didn't* know what was real and what wasn't.

'Maybe I can take it,' he said quietly, running fingers through his hair as if he were thinking.

'Take it where?' Josie asked.

'Home,' he said. 'With me.'

'To your house that you live in now . . . with your wife?'

'We could adopt the baby.'

'Adopt it?' Josie asked. 'How can you adopt your own baby?'

'Well, Sadia can't know it's mine, can she?'

'I don't know what you're saying,' Josie said, on the verge of tears. 'It's my baby.'

'I'll have to – I'll say you're just a bairn I met at a kebab shop, managed to get yourself knocked up and can't look after the baby. It's not a lie, really, is it?'

'And what if I tell her it's yours?'

Jamie crouched in front of Josie, and smiled. She felt relieved for a second, waited for him to wrap his arms around her. Instead, he wrapped a hand around her throat, not hard, but firmly enough for her to know that he meant it. He pulled her face close to his.

'You won't.'

After the service, Josie waits outside the church. It's not warm, but the sun is bright in the sky after almost two weeks of snow and freezing, cloudy days. She can see Sadia, shaking hands and kissing the cheeks of mourners as they pass her, Ana by her side, stroking her back, and Ameera leaning against her leg. Sadia rests a palm on her daughter's head, briefly, reassuring her, checking she's still there. Josie thinks, not for the first time, that Sadia seems like she was born for motherhood.

'What are you doing?' someone asks from behind Josie, and she jumps. The detective is leaning against a tombstone with her arms folded across her chest. Josie puts a hand over her heart.

'You scared me,' Josie says, and takes a deep breath.

'Mm. What are you doing?' the detective asks again. 'Here?'

'I'm just . . . mourning. Same as everyone else,' Josie says, looking at her feet. The detective had told her at the end of their interview not to come to the funeral, because it would both look suspicious and be awful for Sadia.

'You said you wouldn't come.'

Josie shrugs. 'I just needed to put it all to rest.'

'Why are you staring at Mrs Spellman?'

'I just wanted to tell her that I'm sorry for her loss.'

'You didn't do that at the door like everyone else?'

'No,' Josie says, and they both stay silent for a minute, both turning their attention to Sadia. 'She's such a good mother, isn't she? This baby was always for her, you know. I realised that a few days ago. That's what he wanted. He was just using me to grow her a baby, like an incubator.'

'What do you mean?'

'She can't have them herself,' Josie says quietly. She feels like she's telling someone else's secret. 'So he wanted to give her my baby.'

'He told you that?'

'No. Well, yes, but he suggested it later, after I'd realised he wasn't going to leave her and I'd be a single mam. He said he and Sadia could raise the baby, because I wasn't fit to. I think he did the whole thing on purpose. This baby was never meant to be mine.'

'Fucking hell,' the detective says quietly. She lights a cigarette. 'So, now what? You're still so convinced that you'll be a terrible mother that you think you need to give Mrs Spellman your child?'

Josie lifts her shoulders and wipes away a tear.

'Look,' the detective says, laying a hand on Josie's shoulder. Josie turns to face her. 'Go home. Have a bath, really think about what you want. No one else gets to decide if motherhood is for you – especially not a man who treated you like *he* did. Lots of people have babies young, and it's hard, especially when you're on your own, but if that's what you want to do, then you'll be okay. You'll manage. There is help out there if you look for it. If you decide that motherhood *isn't* for you, or isn't for you yet, then there's help for that too. Don't rush into a decision and just give your baby away because that's what he wanted you to do. Think it over properly, because whatever you decide, your life is going to be different for ever.'

29

Sarah
11th January 2000

Sarah slips out of the side door and through a gap in the hedge rather than pass Sadia and Ana at the main entrance. She's not supposed to be here, so she had to wait until Kaysha went to work to leave the house. She caught two buses but she was still early, and stashed herself in a gloomy corner in the back row while the pews filled up. She wonders who all the people are. How many people knew Jamie, and of those, how many would mourn his death? Sometimes the shock of a sudden death tricks people into sadness before they have a second to realise that they aren't sad at all. They're glad for one less awful person in the world, or at best, indifferent.

Sarah isn't indifferent. She has been filled with a perverse, furious glee since she saw his head in the hotel room. Sometimes if someone she hated died she might say *Well, you know, sad for their kids, I suppose*, but she doesn't even feel that now. Ameera is better off without him in her life, and all the better that as she grows, she probably won't remember much of him anyway. Sarah is so happy about Jamie's death that she is being eaten alive by it. She knows that if she weren't already rotten on the inside she wouldn't feel so consumed by dark euphoria. She always thought that if he were truly out of her life, if he died or moved far away, she could move on. She thought she'd be happy. Maybe she'd open a bar or go to uni, do art like she wanted to when she was a kid. Maybe, in a different life, she'd be living in California and teaching drawing classes on a beach with a glass of wine and a beautiful wife. She'd be able to just drink the glass without finishing the bottle, and then the next bottle after that. But she hadn't made those decisions, because she was from a family of fuck-ups, destined to be haunted by the past. He'd been out of her life for four years, and she was still stuck on him.

She stops at a corner shop a street behind the church and buys a quart of gin to top up her hip flask, gulps it like it's water, and then goes back in for another. She smokes a cigarette crouched against the wall where a dog is tied to the drainpipe by his lead. The dog barks at passers-by, and Sarah wonders if she should too, just to frighten them. The wake is in a working men's club down the road where Jamie drank when he was sixteen, or so he told Sadia. Sarah had been there a couple of times before and she found her way there easily, tucked her hip flask back into her boot and walked in.

The room is packed, smoky, and Sarah goes to the bar and orders a drink. Sadia is talking to a short man with a balding head, nodding along as he talks at her. She looks trapped, the way women often are in bars with men they are not interested in. You've got to be polite though because you might end up dead. Maybe Jamie should have been more polite.

With Sadia occupied, Sarah scans the room for Ameera and sees her sitting in a booth with Ana and a man that must be Ana's husband. Sarah goes soft at the sight of the little girl, her glossy brown fringe falling into her big eyes as she plays with the straw in her glass of pop. She's beautiful. So, so beautiful, and Sarah wonders how Jamie produced such an angelic looking child, but even his evil didn't show up on the outside. His beauty lured you in, the long eyelashes and the boy-band hair, the easy smile. It wasn't until you saw him in a rage, when it was too late and you were already trapped, that his eyes gave him away. So much anger in one person. So much horror. Sarah always worried that it was genetic, his darkness and hers combined, poisoning the little body. When Sarah gave birth, she hardly looked at the baby, scared she'd love her if she looked for too long. She is looking now though, really looking, for the first time, can't actually look away, and she crosses the room and slides into the booth beside them. Ana gasps, but Sarah just leans across the table towards Ameera and grins. The little girl's dark eyes flick up to meet Sarah's, and in that second Sarah only sees herself, twenty or so years earlier, so much potential, the world at her feet. Beautiful.

'Hello, sunshine,' she whispers. 'I'm your mammy.'

Ana acts as quickly as if Ameera had been her own child, confronted by some mad drunk. She picks Ameera up and passes the child to her husband, who moves over to where

Sadia is standing. Ameera clings to him, but gazes at Sarah over his shoulder. She still has the straw clutched in her little hand.

'What the fuck do you think you're doing?' Ana hisses.

'Fuck me, that was like some SAS operation or something,' Sarah says, laughing and draining her gin and tonic in one. 'Do you often whip children away from their mothers?'

Ana closes her eyes for a second and touches her temples. 'Not today, Sarah.'

Sarah can feel the gin. She's been drinking since she woke up. She's been drinking for the last four years, more and more every day, until it takes her a whole bottle of gin before she even feels tipsy. She doesn't know how much she's gone through today, though. It's a special day, she's allowed to celebrate. Ana's hands are flat on the table, and Sarah puts hers on top, as if they are lovers, looking into each other's eyes on a date.

'Then when?' Sarah asks. 'If not now, when? She's lost her dad, she needs her mother.'

'She does. But that isn't you.'

'I gave birth to her!' Sarah spits. 'I've still got the fucking scars.'

'And then you gave her up, and you haven't bothered to send so much as a fucking Christmas card since, so don't pretend you're suddenly ready to be in her life.'

'Oh fuck off, it's not like you'd understand.'

Ana's eyes go wide and she moves her hands away from Sarah's. When she speaks, her voice is clipped and low. 'Go fuck yourself, Sarah.'

Sarah laughs – not a real laugh, but the kind of laugh that

lets Ana know that she is not sorry for what she said – and stands. When she looks around, she can't see Ameera anywhere. She feels like a claw is gripping her insides, feels prickling behind her nose and goes to the toilets. They are the usual dilapidated type you find in all working men's clubs, a tampon machine that hasn't been restocked for years on the wall and a cracked bar of soap on the sink. There are three stalls, and Sarah chooses the only one with a toilet that has a seat. She pees, and finishes what's left in her hip flask, and then leans against the wall, the plaster cool on her cheek. She almost falls asleep there, drained, but she hears someone walk in and the other two stall doors bang open as if they have been kicked, and then hers flies open, the flimsy lock clattering to the floor.

'What the fuck do you think you're doing?' Sadia asks, face tight with fury.

Sarah shrugs and pulls her jeans up. 'Having a piss. What are you doing?'

'You fucking stay away from my child,' Sadia says, stepping into the cubicle with Sarah and closing the door behind her.

'You look awful,' Sarah says. She knows she's slurring now, and Sadia's face swims in and out of focus.

'How dare you tell her that you're her mother? How fucking dare you?'

Sarah lifts her shoulders and smiles. 'I am, though, aren't I? I pushed her out.'

'Yeah, you did. And that's the last fucking thing you did for her. You haven't changed a nappy, you haven't been there for her when she's been ill, you didn't teach her to speak or walk or write her fucking name. You didn't have to explain to her why Daddy isn't ever coming home again.'

'I didn't even want her, I was – he made me have her,' Sarah spits back, lurching forward against the other woman, and Sadia pushes her back against the wall with a thud. Sarah feels deflated all of a sudden, the anger seeping out of her. 'She's so beautiful.'

'She's amazing,' Sadia says, quietly.

'I could take her back, you know. I could get her back,' Sarah says, and lifts her eyes to meet Sadia's, fights to keep them focused. Sadia takes her hands off Sarah's shoulders and slides into a crouch against the cubicle door.

'You wouldn't,' Sadia says.

'I could.'

'You wouldn't if you loved her.'

'I love her more than you ever could, she's my blood.'

'And you're your mother's blood, and how did that go?' Sadia says.

Sarah raises her eyebrows in surprise, impressed that Sadia remembers the little things that she has said about herself in conversations in their meetings.

'Look,' Sadia says, rubbing her face. 'You can't just storm up to her at her dad's funeral and tell her that you're her mother. She's been through enough. Maybe you can see her sometime though.'

'You can't tell me—'

'Sarah! I'm offering you an olive branch. You can meet her, we'll go to the park or something. You have to be sober, though. You're not going to be around her drunk, you scared her. You're scaring me.'

'I don't know if I can be around her.'

Sadia tips her head back and groans. 'Make your mind up.'

'It's just fucking hard, Sadia. I didn't want to have a baby and I don't want to love her, but I think about her all the time. And then I just drink and drink and drink until I forget and then I wake up anyway and remember. I just wish that I didn't have to wake up anymore,' Sarah says, and then covers her mouth. She hasn't said it out loud before.

'Sarah,' Sadia whispers, and reaches up to touch Sarah's hair, before pulling her into a hug. Sarah's knees hit the lino and she sobs into Sadia's shoulder. She doesn't know how long she kneels there, with Sadia stroking her hair, but she almost falls asleep. Sadia smells of talc and something sweet, like Parma Violets, and for a moment Sarah feels small, tiny, a child being comforted by their mother, and she wants this for Ameera too. Eventually, she pulls away and rubs her face.

'Sorry,' Sarah says.

Sadia pulls a pack of tissues out of her bag and passes one to Sarah, who blows her nose.

'Look, we'll sort something out. Let's talk about it in a couple of days when you're sober. I'm going to ring Kaysha to come pick you up, okay?'

Sarah nods and lets Sadia lead her out of the toilets, past a ginger woman who follows them out of the club and speaks to Sadia quietly out of Sarah's earshot. Sarah slumps onto a bench outside, which is wet but she doesn't care. She rolls a cigarette and tries to light it, but the wind keeps blowing out the flame before she can.

'Here,' the ginger woman says, standing right in front of Sarah, and cups her hands around the end of Sarah's cigarette.

'Thanks,' Sarah murmurs, and then blows out smoke. She offers it to the woman, who sits down beside her and takes it from Sarah's fingers. After a few drags she passes it back to Sarah and coughs.

'Been a while since I've had a rollie,' she says, grinning. When Sarah doesn't reply, she carries on. 'I'm going to sit here with you till your girlfriend comes to pick you up, okay?'

'Sadia tell you to keep an eye on the village drunk, did she?' Sarah asks.

'Something like that,' the woman says, smirking, and holds her fingers out for the cigarette. Sarah passes it over. The woman is pretty, with a strong jaw and a long nose, and freckles that make her look younger than the fine lines around her mouth and eyes would suggest.

'You a dyke?' Sarah asks, narrowing her eyes.

The woman laughs and chokes on the smoke that comes out of her nose. 'How could you tell?'

Sarah smirks. 'I can always tell.'

'Thank God for gaydar, eh?' the woman says. 'Maybe you've seen me around the scene?'

'Nah, I never go to places like that. I was brought up properly,' Sarah says, stretching out the vowels in the last word so that she sounded like her mother. 'Taught to be good and ashamed.'

'Fair enough,' the woman says. 'It's fun, though.'

Sarah lifts her chin, and they share the cigarette until it's finished, and then Sarah rolls another. It starts to rain, and the woman pulls an umbrella from her bag, and they huddle together underneath it.

'I overheard some of your conversation in the toilets,' the woman says, squeezing her lips together. 'I wasn't trying to listen, just proper needed a piss. Wine goes straight through me.'

Sarah nods. 'S'alright. Shouldn't have been shouting, I suppose.'

'Sounds like you and Sadia have a complicated relationship.'

Sarah laughs. 'Yeah, you could say that. It's – yeah – it's complicated.'

The woman stays quiet, waiting for Sarah to carry on, and something about her seems so trustworthy that Sarah can't help but continue.

'Basically,' she says. 'Well, long story short, I had an affair with her husband, got pregnant, and now she's raising the kid.'

The woman turns her head towards Sarah and doesn't speak for a few seconds. Sarah can't read her face.

'Yeah, it's . . .' Sarah continues, folding her arms. She can't find the right words. 'Yeah.'

'That's awful. She doesn't let you have any contact?'

'No. Well. I never wanted any. Not wired up right to be a mother, me. Pissheed,' Sarah says, breathing heavily out of her nose. 'The bairn's best off where she is.'

'Do you think so?' the woman asks.

'I'd just fuck the bairn up. Be teaching her how to uncork wine before she knew how to talk,' Sarah says, not quite smiling. 'Sadia's alright. Better than me.'

The woman squeezes Sarah's shoulder. 'That's really hard. I'm sorry you had to go through that.'

'Yeah,' Sarah says, pulling the hip flask out of her boot and tipping it into her mouth before remembering that it is empty. Kaysha pulls up at the side of the road and beeps, and Sarah stands up.

'Is that your girlfriend?' the ginger woman asks, narrowing her eyes at Kaysha's car.

'Yeah,' Sarah says, patting her pockets to make sure she has her phone, keys and lighter. 'Thanks for sitting with me, mate. See ya.'

'Bye,' the woman says. 'Look after yourself.'

Sarah nods and gets into the car and Kaysha pulls away without saying hello. Sarah can tell that Kaysha is furious, so she doesn't say anything to further antagonise her, just rolls the seat back and puts a hand over her eyes as they speed through the city. Just as Sarah is dropping off to sleep, Kaysha clears her throat.

'You said you weren't going to go.'

Sarah groans and puts her feet up on the dashboard. 'Don't start.'

'Do you know who you were cosying up to on that bench? What were you saying to her?'

'Nothing particularly interesting, she was just some woman.'

'No, Sarah, that's Nova.'

Sarah opens her eyes and looks at Kaysha. 'That's her?'

'Yes.'

'Well, no wonder you wanted to fuck her again,' Sarah says, her voice flat, though she is angry and upset.

'Stop it.'

'I understand now . . . of course you *needed* her to be the one investigating. Very convenient,' Sarah says.

'You know it's just so that I can keep control—'

'Fuck off. You didn't say she looked like that.'

'What does it matter?'

'It doesn't.'

Sarah knows that Kaysha never tells her everything, she's as deep as space. Everything has been shit between them since Jamie's death, and it's such a stark juxtaposition to how it was before. In the weeks leading up to New Year's, the group met regularly, and although not everyone could agree on what the solution to Jamie's behaviour was, it felt like something big was happening. To Sarah, being part of a group of women who had decided to take action against one man, who had in some way harmed them all, felt like *all women* finally taking a stand. It felt like something big was coming, and coupled with the approach of the new millennium, Sarah couldn't help but feel shook up, overwhelmed by anticipation and joy at what she thought was the beginning of a new era for women. Some small act of rebellion that would lead to something bigger – something that mattered.

Kaysha had orchestrated the whole thing. She told Sarah

that she had been following Jamie's life quietly for a long time, keeping an eye on him, punishing herself again and again when she didn't see what he was doing until it was too late, but knowing that there wasn't anything she could do about it, anyway. Checking what he was up to had become almost a hobby to Kaysha, an obsession, because she felt like she was the only person who saw him as he was, and no one else believed her. The police hadn't believed her after Jamie raped her, she knew that they wouldn't believe any of the other women's lone voices either, but if she gathered them all, unified them, then maybe someone would take notice.

The group gathered for the first time in early November, and Kaysha started by telling them her story. One by one, each of the women explained their relationship with Jamie. Some of them, like Olive, had never quite accepted that he'd done anything wrong at all. Some of them told different versions of their stories as the weeks rolled on, gradually revealing the darker and darker scenes of their lives with Jamie until everything seemed laid bare, and they knew it wasn't a fluke, knew it wasn't a one-off that he'd treated them so badly, that something needed to be done.

Sarah had always felt bad for Sadia, though she resented her somewhere in the basest part of herself, where her maternal instincts, lacking as they were, were hidden. Sadia had been lied to by Jamie every day of her marriage and she'd been tricked into thinking that she'd been treated with kindness and respect for all those years, that Jamie loved her. Maybe he did, but not enough. Maybe he did what he did to Sarah and to Josie for Sadia, because he loved her so much, or maybe that's just what he told himself so that he could excuse his need to exert control over everyone else.

30

Nova
11th January 2000

Nova sits on the bench in the rain after Kaysha pulls away, her skin prickling. It takes her brain a while to catch up with her eyes. The drunk woman must have been Sarah – Kaysha's *girlfriend* Sarah. And Sarah had an affair with Jamie Spellman. And Sadia was raising Sarah's child, and Sarah is mad about it, or maybe just sad. And then there's Josie, another one of Jamie's affairs, lined up to be the next Sarah, to give her baby to Sadia. Josie's confusion over what to do with her baby shifts focus. Before, Nova thought Josie was unsure about motherhood because she was young, but now she imagines that Jamie had planned the entire thing – made Josie feel confused and unprepared on purpose. He fucked all of them over except for Kaysha – as far as she knows – but Kaysha is likely involved because she cares about people too much; she always sticks up for the underdog, even when it gets her into trouble. Big trouble, this time. Four women, all of them potentially involved.

Maybe it was just one of them, or maybe it was all of them together; maybe it wasn't any of them at all.

If Nova hadn't recognised Kaysha on the CCTV tape she might have been fooled by her turning up on Nova's doorstep the next night, asking to try again. Neither of them had apologised, they'd just carried on as if the six months before hadn't happened. Nova knows the entire thing is wildly unethical, their relationship always has been, but this time it's worse. Kaysha has always picked little bits of information from between Nova's teeth, just a location or name, a place to start looking for her next story. Nova gets the same from Kaysha, but Kaysha has to be more careful with what she says – Nova can't show up in the right place at the right time too often. Nova could get fired for tipping off a journalist, but Kaysha could get killed for tipping off the police.

Sometimes Nova wishes that she'd met Kaysha under different circumstances, and their relationship could be real. But then she always wonders if it would be so passionate if it wasn't illicit, whether Kaysha would blend into the humdrum rhythm of daily life and they'd both be bored and dissatisfied. Maybe that's why Nova was so easily convinced out of moving in with Kaysha before – she couldn't bear the thought of the passion fizzling out. Eventually, everything becomes normality, and you realise too late that you overlooked the best thing in your life for so many days, but you can't help it. Everything becomes boring after a while. She doesn't want that with Kaysha. She needs to feel like she is doing something risky. When she is with Kaysha, she sometimes feels like James Bond, sleeping with a woman who is affiliated with the enemy, one of them always luring the other in for information. At the same time though, whenever Nova has her arms wrapped around Ella, and everything is quiet and tender, she closes her eyes and imagines that it is Kaysha instead.

Nova knows that this episode of their fling will be the last, because Kaysha has gone too far. Nova can't ignore a murder. She thinks about what she knows and tries to fill in the gaps. They know from Jamie's blood samples that he'd taken Sadia's medication, or had been spiked with it. Maybe then Sarah killed him and Kaysha hid the body. Maybe Josie was there, maybe not. Covering up a murder seems like something Kaysha might be capable of, if she had to be. More so than actually killing someone, anyway. Nova wonders, with a ripple of jealousy, if Kaysha would hide a body for *her*, then she wonders, not for the first time, whether she is in the right job.

Nova watches the mourners filter out from the working men's club until she sees Olive Farrugia leave and walk towards the bus stop on the other side of the road. She has had her eye on Olive all morning, because she was acting strangely – seemingly muttering to herself, glancing around anxiously like she was expecting something to happen. Nova needed to attend the funeral to keep an eye on everyone, mainly Sadia, whose house was being searched while the funeral went ahead. Nova has had a plain-clothes officer parked close to Sadia's house all week, monitoring her comings and goings, making sure she doesn't bolt. Olive is a different kettle of fish. Nova received a tip-off from a retired colleague, John Jones, who remembered Jamie from a past case. Jamie had had some sort of relationship with Olive at the same time that she weathered a family tragedy, and John thought that Olive might know something, an unlikely friend who might be useful. Someone Nova might otherwise have missed. Strange that John was now married to Jamie's aunt. Strange coincidences all around this case, or maybe not a coincidence at all. She was still piecing everything together. Not for the first time in her career, she considered erecting an evidence board, like in American cop dramas, red string connecting pictures of the women Jamie Spellman knew, a big portrait of him in the middle. She just didn't have space in the office.

Nova watches as Olive makes her way across the road. She seems dazed and almost gets hit twice before she reaches the other side, seemingly unaware of the danger she's in. Nova hurries across the road after her, concerned about her making her way home alone, and Olive barely seems to notice that Nova is at her side.

'Mrs Farrugia,' Nova says, touching her shoulder. Olive jumps. 'Can I give you a lift home?'

Olive looks her up and down, eyes lingering on Nova's hair, before she smooths her own with her fingers. She doesn't say anything, but glances along the road, where the bus will appear any moment. Nova gets her badge out of her pocket and shows it to Olive.

'I'm Detective Inspector Nova Stokoe with Northumbria Police, can I give you a lift?'

Olive narrows her eyes at Nova, but nods and follows her down the road, where Nova's Escort is tucked down a side street. They get in, and Nova turns the blowers on and hovers her hands in front of them before she pulls away.

'Cold out there, innit?' she says.

'It's four degrees warmer than it was yesterday, actually,' Olive says. Her voice is quiet and has the type of reedy quality that comes from being silent for long periods of time.

'Well, who knew, eh?' Nova says, and pulls out into the traffic. 'Where am I taking you, hin?'

'Tynemouth,' Olive says.

'I love Tynemouth. My nana used to take me to the market to buy cheap books on Sundays,' Nova says, a rush of warmth spreading through her at the memory of her grandmother.

'Lovely,' Olive says, sounding bored.

'Do you live near the market?'

'Not far,' Olive says. 'On the seafront. The parade.'

'Okay, no bother,' Nova says, glancing across at her passenger. 'It's tragic, isn't it? About Jamie. He was so young.'

Olive shifts in her seat.

'You were friends?' Nova asks.

'Many moons ago. He attended the same church as I did. Sometimes I'd manage to drag Kim too – my daughter.'

‘Kim’s a great name. My first girlfriend was called Kim.’

Olive gives Nova a long look and then smooths her skirt over her thighs. Nova smiles, thinking of her Kim, who she only met once, on a day trip to Whitby with her class when she was eleven. After wandering around the town, they spent a few hours playing on the beach, paddling in the surf. Another school group was there too, and the kids mingled, building sandcastles together and making new friends while the teachers sat in groups, smoking and drinking cans of Coke. Nova had fallen out with her best friend on the coach that morning, so she sat on her own, staring out to sea and trying to look thoughtful and moody, in an attractive kind of way. A girl from the other school sat down beside her and started chatting. She had bright ginger hair too, pretty blue eyes, and when she smiled, something swooped inside of Nova. They made friends fast, and Nova, knowing she’d never see the girl again, decided to tell Kim that she fancied her, which she hadn’t said to another girl before, even though she’d fancied loads of girls. Only girls, really.

‘Are you a lesbian?’ Kim had whispered, and Nova shrugged.

‘Dunno. What’s a lesbian?’

‘A girl who fancies girls instead of boys,’ Kim said, lifting her chin, and smiling.

‘I didn’t know there was a word for it,’ Nova said, excitement rushing through her. There must be others, too, if there was a word for it, she thought.

'Yep. It's lesbian. Our next-door neighbours are lesbians.'

'Cool,' Nova said, and she had the sudden urge to cry. She scrubbed her eyes with her wrists and Kim put a hand on her back.

'It's okay to be a lesbian, *I* think. The ladies next door are dead nice. My mam doesn't think it's okay, though. She hit the roof when I told her I fancied Miss Larkin,' Kim said, nodding to a young teacher a few metres away who was propped up on her elbows, eyes closed and auburn hair blowing in the breeze.

'Are you a lesbian too?' Nova asked, feeling herself flush, and Kim shrugged.

'Dunno,' she said. 'I just know I fancy Miss Larkin. Dunno who I'll fancy next.'

One of Nova's teachers called her class and said it was time to leave, and Nova pulled her jotter and a pencil from her backpack.

'This is so random,' Nova said, breathless, scribbling her phone number on a page and ripping it out. 'But do you want to be my girlfriend?'

Kim laughed, throwing her head back, and Nova noticed the freckles that were scattered across the girl's face and down her throat. 'Yeah, alright, why not?'

'Cool,' Nova said, and shoved the phone number into Kim's hand. 'See you, then.'

'Bye,' Kim said, and Nova waved as she dashed towards Mr Almond, who was blowing his PE whistle. Nova had waited for Kim's phone call for weeks, told herself that she had a girlfriend – which made a ripple of delight flow through her – but it never came, and she never saw Kim again.

'So you were close with Jamie? Was he a friend of your daughter's?' Nova asks after a few minutes of silence, the city flashing past as they drive.

'A friend of *mine*,' Olive says. 'From church, like I said.'

'Had you seen him recently?'

Olive ignores Nova and turns her head away to gaze out of the window. After a few minutes, Nova asks again, her voice slightly louder. Olive tuts.

'How do you know who I am, again?' she snaps.

'You came up in my background search of Mr Spellman,' Nova explains. 'One of my colleagues remembered that you were close with him, years ago.'

'I was, a long time ago.'

'I was sorry to learn about your daughter.'

Olive is silent.

'It sounds like an awful situation,' Nova continues.

'He was devastated when she . . . well,' Olive says, glancing across at Nova. She blows her nose. 'He was there for me.'

'That's good.'

'He was a good man.'

'It's refreshing to hear someone say that.'

'Well, if you ask the wrong women about him, you'll hear some tall tales,' Olive says, straightening her back.

'Do you think he might have had any enemies?'

They stop behind a long line of cars. Nova can see temporary traffic lights ahead. She looks at Olive, who is tapping her lips with her finger and staring straight ahead, eyes unfocused.

'Mrs Farrugia, do you know a woman named Kaysha Jackson?' Nova asks, pulling up the handbrake and turning to look at Olive. She is not sure why she thinks to ask this, has no proof that Kaysha has ever even met this woman, but she asks anyway, just in case. Kaysha is always one step ahead of everyone, including Nova, and if Olive is a piece of the puzzle, she suspects that Kaysha will have figured it out first. Olive presses her lips together and flares her nostrils, and Nova gets the impression that she is weighing up her response. The traffic begins to thin out in front of Nova, but she doesn't pull away, she keeps her eyes on Olive. Her breath catches in her throat with anticipation. Eventually, Olive shakes her head.

'I don't know anyone with that name.'

'Are you sure?' Nova says, her chest tight. Someone beeps behind her and she groans and pulls away.

'Positive.'

After Nova drops Olive off she goes home. She puts the heating on, changes into her pyjamas, and turns off her mobile phone. She is sick of thinking about Jamie Spellman. She finds herself caring less and less about his death as she puts the pieces of his life together and understands what kind of person he was. She knows she should care regardless, that being beheaded is horrific, no matter what you've done. She isn't a fan of capital punishment, but she finds it hard to feel sympathy for him. His is just another death in a city full of people who will each die eventually.

She feels the resentment for Jamie and for her job filling up her entire body. She doesn't care anymore, or she cares too much, but not about the things that she should. She cares about the well-being of the women who Jamie hurt, feels herself being drawn in by them, even though that got her into so much trouble on her last case. A man's body was found, his wife and her female lover were implicated. There was little evidence that there was foul play at all, and none that either of the women were involved, but it became very clear that the DCI and everyone else at the station were suspicious of the women, found their queer relationship salacious, thought that there must be something fishy about them. Nova felt that the women were being implicated based solely on their sexuality, and fought hard against it. She liked them.

Once Nova noticed the institutional bias against people like her, she began to notice it against other marginalised groups as well – she'd always been aware of it, but thought it came second to the work they were doing, didn't notice how much the bigotry of the officers and the institution affected the way they investigated cases. The more she notices, the less she feels tied to her career. The only reason that she is hanging on at all after being punished and ridiculed when one of the women eventually confessed to the murder is because she worked so hard to get to where she is in her career. When she joined, fresh out of university, she'd believed that she was doing the right thing, that she was upholding laws that protected people and promoted a fair and equal society. She's the youngest female detective inspector that her region has ever had, and she was good at her job before, when she cared. She has spent years trying to gently affect change from the inside, but she never sees any. She understands now why the working-class people she speaks to don't trust her, even though she is one of them. They think she is a traitor, and maybe she is. She doesn't know what else she would do if she left though, hates the thought of having to start again in a new career, but doesn't know how much longer she can be part of an institution she no longer believes in.

She tries to switch off. She has a long bath and then orders food from Mr Lau's using the landline, turns the telly on and flicks up and down the five channels until she settles on some hospital drama that she doesn't really want to watch. Instead, she thinks about Kaysha and Sarah, the look on Kaysha's face as she pulled up and realised who Sarah was huddled with against the rain. Nova thinks about them together; Kaysha, always three steps ahead of everyone else, and Sarah, the unravelling alcoholic who is, somehow, still charming. She imagines how they might have met, imagines them in bed together, tumbling around Sarah's house – some crumbling manor, Kaysha has told her. She opens a bottle of wine and lights some candles, tries to focus on the telly, but she can't. She's always jealous of Kaysha's other relationships, though she has no right to be.

On the Newcastle scene, there is a lesbian called Holly, who is obsessed with the East German Stasi. She recreates their tech as a hobby, and sometimes she sells it, too. Holly didn't ask why Nova wanted the microphone, but when Nova slipped her a fifty, she explained how to use it and how to tune into it with a car radio. Nova could have used police equipment, but she'd have had to sign it out, which means paperwork. If she finds out that Kaysha is guilty, she doesn't necessarily want to have to report her findings. It depends on the why.

Nova has had the microphone for a week but hasn't been able to bring herself to use it yet – partly because she knows that Kaysha will hit the roof if she finds out, and partly because she wants to believe that Kaysha being at the hotel on New Year's Eve was a coincidence. Now that Nova knows without a doubt that Kaysha is connected to Jamie Spellman, she can't lose the chance. She picks up her phone to text Kaysha to come over when someone knocks at her door. She digs through her pockets for money as she pulls the door open, thinking someone must have let the delivery man into the building, but it's Kaysha.

'So you met Sarah today, then?' she says, walking in without a smile and dropping onto the sofa. Nova closes the door and sits beside her.

'Yeah,' she says. Kaysha can't know that she's onto her, and she needs to play it cool. 'So it seems.'

'Did you go looking for her on purpose?'

Nova smirks. 'Get over yourself, Jackson. I was working. Ended up looking after her. She caused a bit of a scene at the pub.'

'Of course she did,' Kaysha says. She presses her lips together. 'She needs help with her drinking. She won't see anyone about it.'

'Seems like it, yeah.'

'What were you doing there if you were working?'

'The funeral was the beheaded guy's. I was there to see if any shady characters showed up.'

'And did they?' Kaysha asks, leaning back into the cushions and crossing her legs.

'No one of particular interest,' Nova says. 'Funny that Sarah knew him.'

'Yeah,' Kaysha says. 'I didn't even know until I picked her up. She's deep as the ocean, that one. Never tells anyone anything, really.'

'Why are you with her?' Nova asks, reaching across the sofa to touch Kaysha's hand. Kaysha rubs her face and then shrugs.

'I clearly like to put myself through difficult relationships,' she says, and shifts to lean against Nova, who puts an arm around her.

'Was she okay when she got home?'

'I put her to bed. She'll sleep it off and then start again in the morning.'

'Fucking hell,' Nova whispers, and kisses the top of Kaysha's head, and Kaysha starts to cry, quietly at first, pretty, movie-star tears that cling to her eyelashes, and then deep sobs that shake her whole body. Nova wraps herself around Kaysha. She's never seen her like this before. She's cried when they've argued or watched sad films, but never like this, and Nova doesn't know how to comfort her or whether she even should. Is she really crying because her relationship is difficult, or is she crying because she murdered someone?

The buzzer goes, and a man's voice crackles over the speaker that he has Nova's food. She doesn't move, but Kaysha pulls back and wipes her face, sniffing.

'Go get it, it's fine,' she says. Nova hesitates, but Kaysha smiles. 'Go on. I don't want you to starve. I know you can't cook.'

'Dick,' Nova says, kissing Kaysha's cheek. When she brings back the food, out of breath because she took the stairs, Kaysha has cleaned herself up. Her nose is still pink, and she sniffs occasionally, but otherwise she no longer seems upset. Nova splits her food onto two plates, knowing that Kaysha will eat some, even if she's already eaten. They both grew up poor, aware that if you're offered food, you take it, and even though they each have enough money now, the habit sticks.

They eat and talk about the cult, which Kaysha has been interested in for a while. Nova tells her some of what she has found out about them, that it's a group of angry teenage girls, mad at the ways in which the world takes advantage of them. Kaysha says she might write an article on them, the modern-day witches, scaring the locals into sharpening their pitchforks. She seems impressed by them, says she likes it when girls fight back, it stirs something up in her. Pride. Who cares if they've killed a couple of sheep on the way?

'They could probably do it without killing the sheep, though,' Nova says. Kaysha looks pointedly at the piece of pork on the end of Nova's fork.

'Pot, kettle,' she says, and smiles.

'Well, that's different.'

'How?'

'Well . . .'

Kaysha laughs. 'I'm winding you up, man. I suppose the sheep haven't done anything wrong.'

Later, they have sex, and it's slow and emotional. Kaysha cries afterwards, as she sometimes does, and Nova just holds her. It used to alarm her, as if she'd done something wrong or Kaysha regretted what they'd just done, but Kaysha would just brush it off. *Just old trauma*, she'd say. *Doesn't mean anything*. Nova goes into the bathroom afterwards and cries, and when she goes back to the bedroom, Kaysha is asleep. Nova wants nothing more than to crawl in beside her and press her body up against Kaysha's, sleep tangled together like they have so many times before and wake up together, and know that she'll be there the next day, and the next, and the next.

Instead, she tiptoes to the couch and picks up Kaysha's jacket. It's battered denim, covered in patches and badges, which she's been wearing for as long as Nova has known her. Nova picks the tiny microphone out of her own coat and slips it into one of the breast pockets. They are stiff and hard to unbutton through lack of use, and Nova pins it so that the tiny receiver just barely pokes out of the pocket. She's confident that Kaysha won't notice it. She's had the jacket for so long that she doesn't even see it anymore, it just exists.

•

In the morning, Kaysha leaves, and it takes Nova half an hour to find her phone under the couch. It's been switched off all night. She has six missed calls, so she rings back as she gets ready for work.

'Stokoe?' It's the DCI.

'Yeah,' Nova says, hairpins trapped between her teeth as she attempts to control her curls.

'Where the fuck have you been? I've been trying to get you since last night. We've got her.'

'Got who?'

'The wife. They didn't find much, she'd done a good job of cleaning up. No wonder they missed it the first time. There were blood spatters under the car in the garage, though.'

'Right,' Nova says, mind whirring. She just didn't think it was Sadia. 'Anything else?'

'Glass of whisky, almost empty but what was left was definitely spiked with diazepam. His fingerprints on it, but hers too.'

'Mm. Circumstantial though . . . She could have just washed the dishes and he could have drugged himself . . . I dunno.'

'They found the murder weapon.'

'Oh shit, what was it?'

'Axe, covered in her fingerprints and her fingerprints only.'

'She hadn't cleaned it?'

'She had, but they found traces of his blood on it. Metal's more porous than you'd think.'

‘Okay, I’m going there now,’ Nova says, pulling on her jacket. ‘Sorry again about the phone.’

‘Don’t fuck this up,’ the DCI says, and Nova pauses. She knows that this is her last chance – if she makes a mistake, she’s out. She isn’t sure if she cares.

31

Sadia
12th January 2000

Sadia gets home from the wake in the early evening and goes to bed, stripping down to her underwear and burrowing deep beneath the duvet. Ana and Tom took Ameera home so that Sadia could rest, and she falls into a dreamless sleep and wakes again at midnight. She gets up only to collect a bottle of wine from the kitchen, and then gets back under the covers where she drinks and spends hours watching the home videos that Jamie insisted on making.

She watches them out of order. On the first tape she plays, Ameera is pink-cheeked, bundled up in a snowsuit and toddling around the garden, tumbling over as she tries to touch the snow. Jamie picks her up and hugs her, kisses her tiny forehead. Then she is a newborn fresh out of her first bath, mewling and damp, and Jamie is filming Sadia running a finger around the baby's face, singing under her breath as she puts on a nappy that seems far too big for the tiny child. Next she is crawling, drawing, crying about something, then her first day at nursery, Sadia crying as Ameera waves goodbye at the door, Jamie turning the camera around to film himself rolling his eyes at his wife. It seems like every moment of their life as a family is documented, and Jamie is in every video at some point, having put the camera down to record all three of them or handed it to Sadia. To anyone outside the family watching the videos, it would look like he was always there. Really, he just didn't want anything to be filmed when he wasn't, as if the endless reels of time that Sadia had spent alone with her child weren't worth recording, as if nothing of note ever happened when Jamie wasn't there.

They look so happy, beaming at each other and at Ameera as they swing her around, or play in the woods or sing 'Happy Birthday', and Sadia supposes they were, before she found out about Josie, and then about everything else. She wishes, in weak moments, that she had never discovered his last affair. He would have told her any day now about another newborn that needed her – convinced her that Josie was just another young woman caught off guard by a baby she didn't want and they were helping her by raising it, just like Sarah. She never would have suspected that the child was his own, and they'd have lived the same way, soaked in borrowed joy. But then she remembers Sarah, and the cost of ripping a baby, wanted or not, from its mother's arms, taking it before she has had a chance to decide for herself whether she wants to raise it or not, and she knows that Josie's baby will never and should never have been hers.

Sadia knows that she closed her eyes to all of Jamie's faults for years, let things that should have disgusted her pass without comment, forced herself to believe whatever excuses he made when he didn't come home for three days at a time. She thinks about what he must have said to Sarah to keep her quiet, or what he must have said to convince her to give up her child. She wonders how far along in the process he must have been with Josie, how he must have convinced her into thinking she didn't really want a baby, just a few months after convincing her that she did, and how she was coping with that now, so close to pushing it into the world. Sadia wonders, too, what her part was in the process, whether she was just a silent accomplice, somehow steering Jamie towards his actions in her grief at her own infertility. She wonders if he did it all because he loved her so much, or just to see if he could.

She wakes up again at eight in the morning with a headache, still clutching the empty wine bottle. The television screen is filled with static. She appreciates that she doesn't have a child to care for that morning – she feels like a sense of clarity has washed through her in her sleep, and she knows what she needs to do.

She wraps herself in her dressing gown and goes down to the kitchen, leans against the worktop as the kettle is boiling and thinks about Sarah. She was shocked by the state of her at the funeral. Kaysha has mentioned before that Sarah drinks too much, but Sadia hadn't seen it for herself. At meetings, Sarah was always alert and sarcastic, with the belligerence of a teenager even though she is well into her twenties, and Sadia found it difficult to feel sorry for her.

Even when Sarah told them her story, prompted throughout by Kaysha, Sadia had fought not to roll her eyes, still so much under Jamie's spell that she didn't believe the details, convinced that Sarah was exaggerating what was only the story of someone who got pregnant with a baby they didn't want. Sadia couldn't help feeling absolute fury at the audacity of an accidental pregnancy, something so precious taken so lightly, when she wanted nothing more than a house full of children and had no womb to provide them for herself.

There was no clean-cut way to do the right thing for Sarah, for herself and for Ameera. Sarah has said again and again that she doesn't want to be a mother, never has, never will. Sadia thinks that despite what she said at the wake, Sarah won't want to raise Ameera, certainly not on her own. Or maybe she will, if she cleans herself up; maybe seeing the child has triggered something in her, and she'll want to take Ameera back. Sadia feels faint at the thought of someone taking the child she has loved for four years. She will do anything for Ameera. Blood doesn't mean a thing to Sadia, only love.

Sadia thinks that maybe if she helps Sarah to get sober, get a job, that they could become a sort of family, and Sarah could have a relationship with Ameera. Maybe they could co-parent. The thought terrifies Sadia, because what if blood does matter after all and Ameera naturally gravitates towards her birth mother? What if Sadia's efforts with her amount to nothing, and she runs to Sarah every chance she gets? There would be nothing that Sadia could do to stop it, because if anyone found out that Sarah had given birth to her, Sadia wouldn't have a leg to stand on. Maybe she'd be arrested for kidnapping. Maybe she'd deserve it.

The kettle is boiled and Sadia takes a deep breath, focuses her entire mind on spooning coffee granules into her cup, pouring the water. The week's snow has finally melted and the morning is bright and sunny. It almost looks warm. She slips her feet into Jamie's taking-the-bin-out shoes, which she hasn't thought to move or throw away, and goes out onto the patio. The garden is flooded with light, and compared to the last week, it feels like summer. Sadia sits on one of the garden chairs and drinks her coffee, trying to keep her mind calm and centred on what is around her – the smell of the pine needles, a breeze that rustles through the boughs, the dark of the forest, even on such a bright morning. She takes her feet out of Jamie's shoes and puts them onto the damp grass, grounding herself. Everything will be okay, she thinks.

The dregs of her coffee are cold but she swallows them anyway, and stands to go back inside. A cloud shifts and something glints in the pond at the bottom of the garden where the treeline begins. The koi must have woken up. She always worries that they'll die when the pond freezes over, but they're always there in the spring, bigger than they were when she last saw them. The pond was Jamie's prize project, one of the only things he'd actually got around to finishing in the house. He often started things and didn't finish them, and after a while, Sadia would hire someone to complete whatever the project was instead. In October he'd pulled the entire garden fence down, saying that it was rotten, and he'd make another, but he'd only got as far as digging the holes for the fence posts. The house is alone anyway, tucked into the mouth of the forest, but Sadia feels more exposed without the fence. She knows it's irrational.

She goes over to the pond, and waits to see one of the koi swimming close to the surface. Her favourite is a large, orange one that they call Goldie Hawn. She sees a glint of something metallic again, and smiles, until she realises that the fish isn't moving, and wonders if they haven't survived the snow after all. She crouches, and realises that the shiny thing isn't a fish, it's a silver watch. As she stares, the body seems to materialise out of the murky water, bone white and lying at the bottom. The longer she looks, the clearer it becomes. She can't pull herself away, his body mapping itself out before her, the blue T-shirt and jeans he was wearing on New Year's Eve, his shoes, his neck. The mug falls from her hand and pondwater splashes onto her feet.

She hears the banging on her front door, but she doesn't register it as something she should respond to. She hears the shouting and the footsteps behind her, and still she can't look away. She doesn't look at the people who are around her, doesn't answer when they speak, doesn't start to scream until her hands are cuffed behind her back and they pull her away.

32

Nova
12th January 2000

'I didn't kill him,' Sadia says. 'But I did drug him.'

Nova hasn't asked a single question yet, but Sadia is clearly ready to talk. It's taken her a few hours to calm down after she was arrested. Nova doesn't know what to believe. On one hand, it seems extraordinarily suspicious that they found Sadia standing over her husband's beheaded corpse, hidden in a spot where he more than likely wouldn't have been discovered for quite a while otherwise. On the other, the woman was clearly disturbed, whether by the corpse or the sudden appearance of police in her garden, Nova doesn't know. Either way, she's in custody and they finally have the body to go with the head.

'Why did you drug him?'

'Because he would have killed me otherwise.'

'He said that he'd kill you?'

'Yes,' Sadia says, her body tensing. 'More than once. I

wanted to leave him and take our daughter. He wouldn't let me. I was scared of what he'd do if I tried.'

'Had he threatened you before that?' Nova asks. Her instinct is to reach over the table and touch the woman's hand, but she doesn't.

'We always had a really good relationship, until I found out about Josie.'

'Josie Kitchen?' Nova is briefly surprised that Sadia knows about Josie, but then, these women all seem to know each other.

'Yes.'

'Did you catch them together?'

'No. I wish I had, it would have been simpler. It was like the universe was forcing me to look. I knew Josie already.'

'Oh, that's interesting. So she was a family friend?' Nova makes a note of this, because it doesn't match up to what Josie has told her about meeting Jamie.

'No, just coincidence. I was a regular at the cafe she works in. I went there all the time, lovely little place, flowers on the tables and fresh pastries each morning. I always had a chat with her while she was making my coffee.'

Nova tilted her head. 'Go on.'

'She often complained about her boyfriend, not necessarily to me, but to the other staff, saying he'd stood her up, or that he was still living with his ex even though he promised her they were separated and waiting on divorce papers coming through. Seems funny now, knowing that that's what Jamie was saying to her.'

'You thought your relationship was okay?'

'It was the same as it ever was. I was happy, I had a family, nice house, didn't have to work. What did I have to complain about?'

'Did you suspect he was having an affair?'

Sadia pulls a face. 'No. But looking back, there were a lot of signs that I think I wilfully looked past. Working away so much when he worked in a lab, you'd think he was a travelling salesman, the amount he said he was working away. Of course, he wasn't. He was staying with whoever he was having an affair with at the time.'

'So how did you find out then?'

'Well, like I was saying, I knew Josie. I'd heard all the trials and tribulations of her relationship with this mystery older boyfriend that she'd met in her dad's kebab shop of all places, and then she got pregnant, and I wanted to – it's awful to say, but I wanted to slap her. How silly of her to get pregnant by this awful man she was seeing. And she was so young too. I was jealous,' Sadia says. 'I can't carry children, and I would love nothing more. I would have loved to give birth to my own children. So I was feeling quite sour, and every time after that when she came to work crying, I would think that she was ungrateful. I was so jealous and I took an awful sort of pleasure at her having bad days for a while.

'One day she was really having an awful time – she had to go into the back because she couldn't settle herself down – and the other waitress told me that Josie was upset because her boyfriend had sworn up and down that he'd be at her birthday party that evening, and then he'd cancelled at the last minute. Josie thought he was doing something with his wife instead. And I was feeling quite smug because my husband was taking me out that night for our anniversary.'

'Carry on,' Nova says.

'Well, whenever I'd finished my coffee I would go and put my cup back on the bar, to save their legs, you know? They work hard enough. A delivery man came up to the counter with a bouquet right at the same time as I did, and he said they were for Josie and then left. Josie wasn't there . . . she was still in the back, upset about her boyfriend standing her up. I was admiring the bouquet because it looked exactly like the one that Jamie always got me for birthdays and anniversaries – always the same arrangement, always from the same florist. I always thought it was a really thoughtful touch, like it was my own special bouquet that he'd designed. I picked up the card, not being nosy, really, I was looking to see if it was the same florist. And then I saw the note.' Sadia falls silent for a minute and Nova wonders if she's said this out loud before, or whether it's something she tries not to think about. 'I can see it, still, I can see it in my head. It said: *To Josie, Sorry I couldn't make it, babe. Love you more than all of the atoms, Jamie*.'

Nova pushes a box of tissues across the table and waits for Sadia to calm down before asking her to carry on.

'I knew his writing, obviously, but the thing he wrote . . . *Love you more than all of the atoms* . . . that's what he always said to me. I knew straight away that it wasn't a coincidence. This was from *my* Jamie. At the time it took my brain a second to catch up, because I thought – for a second – I thought they must be for me, somehow, and the name had been mixed up, the universe had got it wrong.'

'I can imagine.'

'I was just standing there, confused, and then Josie came back out, and saw the flowers, read the card, and she beamed. She said he always said that to her, about the atoms, because he was a scientist and he thought it was funny, and she thought it was beautiful. Poetic.

'I just nodded, I couldn't think straight. I wished her a happy birthday and left. All the way home I kept wishing I'd asked what his last name was or what he looked like, and all day I obsessed over it, tried to remember if he'd mentioned a Josie ever, if the times he'd worked away coincided with days that she wasn't crying at work, but you know, I would never remember even if they did. I don't think that it had crossed my mind that her baby was Jamie's at that point – as far as I knew, he was infertile. That's what he told me when we first met, to make me trust him, I suppose, to make it seem like we had something in common.'

'What happened when you got home?' Nova asks.

'I spent the whole day sitting on the sofa, pacing round the rooms. I didn't get anything done, I couldn't focus. I spent hours and hours going over the note in my head, trying to convince myself I'd got it wrong, it couldn't have been his handwriting, or maybe the florist wrote it, and their handwriting was really similar to Jamie's. Maybe the florist had copied Jamie's line about the atoms because Josie's boyfriend wasn't clever enough to think of anything. I thought that maybe even Jamie hadn't thought of the atoms thing, maybe it's from a film or a poem and it was all this huge coincidence that Josie's boyfriend had watched the same film and thought the same line was romantic, and wrote it on a card on a bunch of flowers for his girlfriend.

'By the time I walked to the school to pick my daughter up, I was in a kind of frenzy about it, I couldn't settle down. We walked home the long way that day, through the woods, because being in the woods always calms me down when I'm upset or angry, and Ameera loves it. She always finds a pine cone or a rock to bring home. So we walked home through the woods, and I made her some tea, and then we played for a while. By the time Jamie got home, I'd calmed down.

'He came into the sitting room where we were, all smiles and kisses, like he always was, *how are my best girls*, you know. He pulled this rose from behind his back and gave it to Ameera, and she was delighted with it, and we fussed around putting it in water for her and displaying it on the mantel-piece, and then he came back in with a bouquet for me – the exact same bouquet he always brought me. The same one he sent Josie. And I looked at the note, and it was the same writing, his writing, definitely his, the stupid line about atoms, the same signature.'

Nova blows out a long breath. 'Oh dear.'

'Oh dear,' Sadia repeats. 'I just felt this rage, like it had been building for years in the moments when he didn't answer his phone and didn't come home, working away for half the year, the times I knew he was lying but didn't have the heart to question it. And it was only the topsoil, really. It took me weeks to start realising how deep it all went. How isolated I was from my family, I had no friends, I had no job, no nothing. Everything was in his name. I had nothing of my own.'

'That's terrible,' Nova says, and presses her lips together. Sometimes when women kill their husbands after a long battle with domestic abuse, they get a lighter sentence, but sometimes the jury don't believe they've been abused at all, they think it's just an excuse. She wasn't sure what a jury would make of Jamie Spellman. Maybe he'd charm them, even in death. 'Did he stop you from seeing your family and friends?'

Sadia makes a noise of faint amusement in her throat. 'Not technically. He was too clever for that. He'd never say that I wasn't allowed to go and see my parents or couldn't do *x*, *y* or *z* – but I'd know because he'd be in a foul mood after I had. He wouldn't speak to me for days – even when I was back in time to have his tea on the table when he got in from work, he'd be quiet for sometimes a week afterwards, go to the pub instead of coming home, leave his dinner to go cold on the table and be thrown away the next day. I would go hungry on those nights too, because I knew better than to eat before Jamie came home. Eventually, even the mention of sending a birthday card to my brother or phoning my mum would bring on one of his dark moods, so my contact with them sort of petered out. I haven't spoken to my family for years. They don't even know I have a daughter.'

'I'm sorry you had to live like that,' Nova says, glad that she has never had to live through anything similar. 'What happened next on the day you found out about the affair?'

'I put Ameera to bed. She was complaining because it was much earlier than usual, still light outside, but she fell asleep eventually. When I came back down he was in a mood. He'd get this look on his face sometimes, and I'd dread it because there was no getting him out of it when he was like that, I had to leave him alone and hope for the best. But I couldn't that night,' Sadia says. She takes a deep breath and rubs a hand over her face. 'I put the flowers in the bin, in full view of him. I always think about that. If I hadn't done that one stupid thing, then maybe he'd still be alive, none of this would have happened. Josie would be . . . I don't know.'

'He didn't take kindly to you putting his flowers in the bin, I imagine.'

'No, of course he didn't. He asked what the fuck I was doing, and I asked him if he knew a girl called Josie. He didn't even have the decency to blush. He looked like he was thinking and then shook his head, asked what this *Josie* had to do with his flowers. I told him about the note on the flowers in the cafe, and he laughed. He seemed so calm that I almost believed him when he told me it must have been another Jamie who had similar taste in flowers. He knew better than to knock up a teenager,' Sadia says. She rubs her eyes and then scoffs. 'And there it was.'

'There what was?' Nova asks, feeling like she's missed a step. Sadia smiles and takes a deep breath.

'I hadn't told him she was pregnant.'

'Shit,' Nova whispers, completely drawn in by Sadia's account, all sense of objectivity lost. She believes this bit, at least. He was having an affair and she found out.

'I replay it in my head all day every day. Just this scene, in the kitchen, every movement exaggerated and deliberate, and I try to pinpoint each moment that I could have shut my mouth and stopped everything that happened afterwards. There are so many moments, but I couldn't stop myself. I just kept going. I could have kept my nice life, had another baby, and I didn't, I kept goading him until he snapped.'

'What did he do?'

'I said that I didn't tell him she was pregnant, and he laughed and told me I did, and I knew I hadn't mentioned it. I've never felt rage like I did in that moment, when he was trying to convince me that I didn't know what was real and what wasn't. I picked up a plate and smashed it on the floor, and then another and another. I felt possessed, and he kept laughing, and I told him I was leaving, he could move his little tart in and Ameera and I would be gone by the morning, and then he hit me. He punched me straight in the face, and I went reeling backwards and hit a wall. I was on the floor before I knew what had happened, and he kicked me in the ribs, just once, but hard enough to wind me,' Sadia says. She wipes her wet cheeks and takes a sip of water.

'Take your time, Mrs Spellman,' Nova says, straightening the papers in front of her. 'Do you need a break?'

Sadia shakes her head and sniffs. When she speaks, her voice is thick, as if she has a cold. 'No. No, I'd rather just get it over with, if you don't mind. Unless *you* need a break?'

'I'm fine, thank you,' Nova says. 'Continue whenever you're ready, no rush.'

'I'm ready,' Sadia says, rolling her shoulders and running a hand through her hair.

'So you were arguing, and he hit you. Had he hit you before?'

'No. That was the first time.'

'Okay. And what did he do after that?'

Sadia takes a second to steady her breathing and blows air from between pursed lips. She looks like she might cry again, but she doesn't.

'He said . . . He got down onto the floor beside me and grabbed my hair, and he said if I ever threatened to take his daughter again that he'd kill me.'

'Did you know at that point that—'

'That she was biologically his? No. So I said that . . . I said she was as much mine as she was his, and he laughed, and let me go, and poured a glass of whisky. I sort of pushed myself into a corner and he sat at the kitchen table and then he said . . . he said, *Have you never noticed that she has my mouth?*'

Nova nods and waits for Sadia to continue.

'Then he went out to the garden, and I just sat on the kitchen floor. I think I was . . . I don't know . . . in shock. He'd never really got that angry before, it was like he was all of a sudden a different person. I couldn't comprehend it. We were together for ten years, and I hadn't ever seen him like that.

'We didn't go out that night, obviously, but nobody cancelled the babysitter, and I answered the door before I even thought to tell her we didn't need her, and she must have got such a fright. I didn't know what I looked like until later when I looked in a mirror and my cheek was all bruised and my lip was bloody.'

'Did you need to go to the hospital?'

'No. It was superficial, I was just bruised.'

'You didn't ring the police or anything?' Nova asks, though she knows that she probably didn't because she hasn't come across any paperwork about it.

'I got into bed with Ameera and hugged her. I didn't know what else to do. I was shocked, more than anything else. I couldn't believe the look in his eyes when he'd hit me. That shocked me more than even the punch, I think.'

'Did he apologise?'

'Oh yes, he apologised and apologised the next morning, but when I tried to talk to him about Josie, about what he'd said about Ameera's mouth, he just denied it all again. He told me I was imagining it. And over the next few weeks it became a cycle – we'd argue, he'd hit me, he'd apologise and deny he'd ever cheated on me, never mind fathered a child. Two children. He started to come home earlier than usual, turn up unannounced at lunchtime, phone the house constantly.'

'Worried you were going to leave?'

Sadia nods. 'I couldn't take it. It got hard to trust anything I thought I knew, because he kept telling me things and then denying them, doing things and telling me they were in my head.'

'It's called gaslighting. He was trying to make you question your perception of events so that you had to rely on him for the truth – or his version of it.'

'I didn't know it had a name.'

'It's vile. So that carried on until when?'

'Until New Year's Eve. I couldn't take it anymore. We'd woken Ameera up the night before, arguing, and she must have snuck downstairs. She was standing at the bottom of the stairs and she saw the whole thing. I didn't see her until I was on the floor, and she was just standing there in her pyjamas watching us.'

'God, that's awful.'

'He wouldn't let me put her back to bed afterwards, even though she cried for me, and he told her that I had hit him first, he was just hitting me back. That it was my fault. I listened from the bottom of the stairs. The next morning she was mad at me, and when I asked why she said that I hurt her daddy.

'That was it. I knew we had to get out, and the next day was Friday, New Year's Eve. He was pissing around with my car. He'd taken bits of it apart so I couldn't drive anywhere, and it was up on bricks in the garage. It's still there.'

'Where were you going to go?'

'I don't know. Maybe to my parents' house in Manchester. He doesn't know where they live. He's always made it seem like seeing them is a bad idea, telling me they wouldn't accept him, and that they were abusing me by questioning my choices. It seems obvious now what he was doing, but I was so wrapped up in him then.'

'Have you spoken to them since he died?'

'No, not yet. Maybe I will. It's difficult because it's been so long.'

'I understand. So what happened on New Year's Eve? Walk me through it.'

'He was in the garage, like I said. I'd been taking diazepam for a couple of months, for stress. It makes you drowsy . . . really drowsy, so I crushed some up, I'm not sure how many. I was scared that if I didn't use enough it wouldn't work, that he'd kill me for trying to leave, so I kept crushing up more and more. I stirred it into a glass of whisky he'd told me to bring for him, added a tiny bit of honey to try and disguise the taste. It wouldn't have mattered. He wasn't a sipping type of man, he'd swig it all in one to prove he could.

'I told him that Ameera and I were going for a little walk in the woods, and he made sure I didn't have anything on me that I could get anywhere with.'

'What do you mean? Like what?'

'Money, bank cards. A phone. Even my house keys.'

'I see,' Nova says, scrawling keywords in her notebook. *Diazepam, whisky, kill her if she tried to leave.*

'I'd already arranged for Ana to pick us up, I was going to leave Ameera with her and then go back while he was knocked out, pack us some basics and then she'd drop us back off at the train station.'

'But something went wrong?'

'We went to her house for a cup of tea, and it started to snow, so we had to wait longer than we thought, and by the time the gritters had been out and Ana took us back, Jamie was gone. Nothing looked suspicious, except that he was gone. His wallet, keys and phone were gone, but nothing else. The doors were still unlocked, the radio was still playing in the kitchen. His car hadn't moved.'

'Why didn't you report him missing?'

Sadia wraps her arms around herself, and Nova notes that this is the first time in the interview that Sadia seems to be considering what she is saying. This is where the story is being woven into something not quite true. She makes a note to question Ana Cortês before Sadia has a chance to speak to her, and compare their stories, though they've had plenty of time to straighten it out since New Year's Eve.

'He'd told me earlier that if I ever involved the police, when he hit me, that he'd disappear with Ameera and I'd never see her again. Other times he said he'd kill me if I tried to have him arrested. Even from prison, he'd hire someone. I'd never be safe again. I didn't dare phone the police, I thought he might be watching, somehow.'

'How long were you away from home after drugging your husband?'

'I don't know,' Sadia says, fidgeting with her sleeves. 'A few hours. We probably didn't get home until close to midnight.'

'And you slept in your own home that night?'

'Yes.'

Nova raises an eyebrow. 'And you didn't feel unsafe, knowing that the husband that you had drugged earlier and who had threatened to kill you was possibly hiding somewhere, angry that you'd tricked him?'

'Well . . .'

'Because I don't think I'd have slept there that night.'

33

Maureen
12th January 2000

Maureen sits in the armchair by the bedroom window and watches as John pulls his suitcase down from on top of the wardrobe. It still has the tags from when they went to the Canaries in October, and she remembers the simplicity of the holiday, days wandering around markets of good food and fake designer goods and nights playing cards on their hotel balcony. They went on an excursion where the bus crawled through seas of igneous rock and up to the peak of an active volcano. There was a restaurant there, alone in miles of nothing, and they ate a spatchcock chicken that had been cooked over the heat of the lava beneath. A man had poured water into specially bored holes, and Maureen had screamed as, after a few seconds, the water had spurted back up, boiled by the heat of the earth. John had laughed at her. She hadn't thought that the holiday was particularly special at the time, much preferring the trip to India they had taken for their honeymoon, but now she longs to be back there, drinking sangria by a pebbled beach as the sun set and worrying about nothing more pressing than mosquito bites.

John unzips the case and tosses a couple of Maureen's swimming costumes into the laundry basket. He starts to fill it with shirts and trousers, just stuffing them inside, and Maureen itches to do it for him. She has been folding his clothes for so long that even now, as he is leaving her, she almost stands up to do it properly for him. She doesn't, she sits and watches, still numb that he is giving up on her. She wonders if she will still function without him. When he puts his socks in the suitcase, she feels a stab of something – jealousy or anger or sadness, she isn't sure what.

'No other woman will search through your pile of black socks to make sure that they're paired with the exact right other sock,' she says.

'What?' he asks, confused, a pair dangling from his hand.

'Your socks.'

'What you on about? They're all the same.'

'They're not all the same,' she says, crossing the room and picking up two pairs. 'Look. These ones are different. The fabric's different.'

'Are they?'

'You once said you hated wearing odd socks because they feel different on your feet, so I go through them and find the ones that are exactly the same in a pair,' Maureen says, her voice wobbling. John's mouth hangs open and he half shrugs, perplexed. 'And I'm just worried that no other woman will do that for you.'

'I don't want another woman,' John says, and goes back to throwing things in his suitcase.

'But you don't want me.'

'I just don't know you. Thought I did. Apparently not.'

'You do know me, John. I'm the same as I always was,' Maureen says. She feels herself getting hysterical again, and she knows that John won't speak to her when she's like that. She feels like she's losing control because he won't listen when she tries to tell him why she hid Jamie.

'No, Maureen, I don't. Not at all.'

'Well, what do you want to know?'

'Nothing. You lied to me.'

'I didn't ever lie, I just didn't tell the whole truth.'

John slams the lid of his case down. 'You said – when we first met – you told me this sob story about how you'd always wanted to be a mother, and you'd just never got the chance. And I thought you were lovely, and I thought, well, I can't give her children of her own, but she can be a part of my family. That was a fucking lie.'

'No – he's not – he wasn't my son.'

'But he was. You were his mother, Maureen, you were all he had, and you hated him. You had the chance to be a mother and you threw it away. No wonder he ended up a wrong'un.'

'Your stomach would turn if you knew the things he'd done. He was a monster.'

'And who created him?' John said. Maureen didn't speak again, and John left without even saying goodbye. She heard him whistle for the dog and then slam the door, and then she heard him drive away. She didn't move for a long time, and the room grew dark around her. Alone again. She'd been alone for most of her life, in one way or another, but it had never felt quite this awful before.

Even in death, Jamie ruined everything.

34

Maureen
March 1965

A late clutch of snowflakes fell from the sky, frosting the furrowed earth between the farmhouse and the cottage, shrouding the day's sins. The farmer's wife was plunging a blood-soaked cloth into a bowl of warm water, squeezing blooming poppies from the fabric and then sliding it again across cold skin. The farmer was outside drinking whisky from the bottle in the chill night air with the young doctor who had tried his best. Dark fingerprints clung to the glass. Their breath hung in front of them like a confession. Stars spattered the ink-black sky and the moon was slung low against the horizon. They watched as two figures made their way along the dug-out road, slumped together, until they disappeared through the cottage door.

'You sit here, love,' said the farmer's daughter, steering Maureen into one of the two worn armchairs and bending to light the fire. 'I'll make up some of that formula for him.'

Maureen sat rigid in the chair holding the tiny bundle of cloth to her chest, not looking at the child even as it began to snuffle and cry. All she could think about was her sister's body growing cold on a bed in the farmhouse, the undertaker on his way. The sounds of the teenager moving around in the kitchen were distant noise as Maureen gazed into the climbing tongues of flame, but the eventual whistle of the kettle startled the child and made him scream, dragging her out of her stupor. When the girl had made the milk, Maureen handed her the child so she'd feed him, and went to draw a bath. She peeled off her stained dress and lay in the copper tub until the water had gone cold around her, and when she emerged, hair clinging to her face and feeling no cleaner than she had before, Dana had made the child a makeshift cot from the suitcase that had been stashed under the bed and a couple of woven blankets. He was asleep.

'There's enough powdered formula to last you through the night,' Dana said. 'Lucky we had it, really. We use it for the lambs when their mothers . . . well, anyway, he's a hungry one. My dad will drive to get more in the morning. Will you be alright? Do you want me to stay?'

Maureen shook her head. Dana left, and Maureen climbed into Alice's side of the bed and shivered until her body warmed up the sheets. The child slept in the suitcase on the floor beside her, and she watched as the firelight flicked shadows over his tiny face. It was impossible to see yet if he looked like Alice. Maureen wondered what would happen if she were to zip up the suitcase and throw it into a river, return him to the mother that he'd murdered on the way out. She fell into a clammy, shuddering sleep, broken quickly by a small pair of lungs.

Six years later, Maureen had learned to avoid the floorboard that groaned as she climbed out of bed so that she wouldn't wake the boy. She lived for that hour before dawn when she'd sit on the kitchen doorstep with her coffee and listen as the stillness of the night was broken by the first songs of the wrens.

Every day she collected the bacon rind and scraps of stale bread from their meals in an old biscuit tin by the door, and then in the morning she'd lay them out for the birds and watch as they gathered and ate while the sun rose. Over the years a particularly brazen crow returned often and sometimes sat on the step beside her, and he'd peck at the offerings and let her stroke his feathers. She occasionally found shiny trinkets on the outside kitchen windowsill. She had always assumed they were things that Jamie gathered, until one afternoon she'd seen the crow leaving a shard of broken mirror. She kept the gifts in a pocket inside her old suitcase under the bed, along with other trinkets she'd collected over the years: some pressed flowers, a handkerchief that had once belonged to her grandmother, and Alice's last, half-eaten bar of chocolate, carefully hidden inside a little silver cigarette case with her initials on it. The crow was a secret she kept for herself.

One morning, Maureen was running a finger over the silky dome of the crow's head when she heard the child's voice behind her.

'Can I stroke him?' he asked. Maureen and the crow were both startled, and the crow ruffled his feathers and flew off. Jamie stuck out his lower lip and sat down on the step beside her, his little toes curled against the cold, and his pyjama bottoms two inches too short. He leant against her, yawning and wiping sleep from his eyes.

'Go back to bed now, James,' she said without looking at him. 'It's too early for you to be up.'

'I'm awake now, though,' he said, ducking under her arm so she'd wrap it around him. She rubbed his arm for a second and then stood.

'I'll make you some breakfast then, if you're so awake,' she said, and stepped back into the house, leaving the child alone on the doorstep. When all the birds had flown away he came and sat at the kitchen table as she filled a pan to boil some eggs.

'Is it today?' he asked.

'Yes, it's today,' Maureen said. 'Get dressed, we'll go when we've eaten.'

The chapel was a two-mile walk from the cottage. They followed a narrow path that threaded between the edges of the sheep fields and a silver ribbon stream, which was swollen and fast after the night's rain. They made slow progress because Jamie insisted on stopping to talk to every sheep and horse that was close to the fence. Maureen's head was heavy with the whisky she'd drunk the night before, and she quickly got tired of waiting for Jamie as he got sidetracked every few steps. She grabbed the child's wrist as she passed him and pulled him along beside her, which made him howl.

'You're hurting me,' Jamie shouted, writhing under her grasp until he was free, and then ran a few feet ahead. He made a show of rubbing his arm as he walked and periodically glanced back at Maureen with narrowed eyes until he tripped over a rock and fell forwards into the mud.

'Watch where you're walking,' Maureen said, pulling him back to his feet by the upper arm, barely slowing as she trudged onwards.

The headstone was tucked into a corner at the back of the graveyard. The chapel had a small congregation and barely any money, so the graveyard was usually overgrown. Maureen brought a pair of scissors with her occasionally, to trim the tall grass in front of the headstone, and when she'd snipped away the weeds, she let Jamie place the flowers against it, and they stood in silence for a few minutes. Maureen said a prayer.

'Is there anything you'd like to say, James?' she asked. The child shrugged and twisted his hands.

'Hello, Mam.'

'Is that it?'

'Yep.'

'Go wait over there, then,' Maureen said, and pointed towards a wooden bench a few feet behind her, which faced Alice's grave. Jamie trotted away, and Maureen squatted down, a hand on the headstone for balance. She sniffed, and bit her cheeks to stop herself from crying, and began to cry anyway.

Maureen hunched over the grave for a long time, and only stood up when her calves were so numb that she was about to topple over. She straightened the flowers that Jamie had laid, blew her nose, and sat down beside the child on the bench. He yawned and slumped against Maureen. The morning was unseasonably warm, and the churchyard was empty. A few early insects buzzed around the dandelions, and a herd of Highland cattle were bleating from a couple of fields away. Even the boy was still and quiet for once, though he wasn't asleep, and Maureen basked in the serenity.

The sun was bright against her closed eyelids, and she drifted almost to sleep, lulled by the warm breeze, until Jamie sneezed and wiped his nose on her shoulder. He was twirling a loose string from her cardigan around the crease of his index finger, and picking a scab on his knee with the other hand.

'Stop that,' said Maureen, pulling her cardigan away from him, which only pulled the string tighter around his knuckle.

'Ow!'

'Well, don't be silly, then,' she snapped, untangling him and turning her face away.

'You're nasty,' Jamie said, hopping off the bench and going to sit cross-legged on the grave with his back to Maureen. She could hear him muttering, and it made her uneasy that he was sitting right above Alice's cold bones, but she appreciated that he'd moved away from her. After a few minutes he came and sat beside her again.

'Told on you,' he said, raising his eyebrows and jutting his chin forwards. 'Told on you to my mam.'

'Oh, did you now? What for?'

'Hurting me and being horrible.'

'I see.'

'Mam says you've got to be nice to me or she's gonna haunt you.'

'Haunt me?'

'Yeah. Dana says that when people die, sometimes they make ghosts and haunt people and Mam's going to haunt you if you don't be good.'

'Your mam's not a ghost, she's in heaven.'

'Well, that's not what she said, she said she's a ghost and she'll haunt you.'

'And how would you know what she would say? You never even met her, stupid boy,' snapped Maureen, a hot flush of shame burning her cheeks as soon as she'd finished the last word. Jamie stuck his lip out again. It wasn't often that Maureen felt something like maternal instinct for him, but she leant over and wrapped Jamie in her arms. It was strange, and she felt him stiffen at her touch, and she let go quickly. The child wiped his eyes.

'Well, are you not going to tell me it?'

'Tell you what?'

'Tell me the thing,' Jamie said, crossing his arms.

'I don't know what you mean,' Maureen said, though she did. She could never bring herself to make the day a happy occasion.

'You're supposed to tell me happy birthday.'

•

The next morning when Maureen woke, Jamie was already awake. He was sitting at the kitchen table with a cup of water and a slice of buttered bread. He smiled at her as she made herself a coffee and opened the door to sit on the step to drink it. She took the tin of scraps but found that it was empty. Jamie had fed the birds and they'd been and gone. She looked at him, and he smirked into his water, and she went to sit on the step anyway.

It was a dark, drizzly morning and Maureen kept her feet tucked up under her so that they stayed under the small awning above the door. It took her a few minutes to notice the ruffled black shape at the foot of the steps, lifeless.

35

Nova
12th January 2000

Gary Jeffries is behind the front desk of the Towneley Arms, polishing the varnished top. He smiles when he sees Nova.

'Officer . . . Stephens?' he asks, holding out a hand for her to shake.

'Detective Inspector Stokoe,' she says, shaking his hand. 'How are you feeling after last week?'

'Ah, sorry. Detective. Of course,' Gary says, putting his hands on his hips. 'Much better, thanks. Still having nightmares, but . . . never mind. What can I do for you?'

'I'm looking for the owner. I just have a few more questions to ask.'

'Harry's in the bar,' Gary says, and points to the archway that leads to the dining room. 'Go straight through the door on the other side, past the kitchen.'

'Thanks.'

The room is smoky and there are only two customers, both sitting at the end of the bar playing cards with the proprietor and his wife. The wife notices Nova first, and nudges her husband, who peers over the top of his glasses. He nods at Nova and then plays his hand, which makes the two customers groan and throw down their cards.

'Detective,' Harry says, gesturing for her to come closer with a jerk of his head. His wife lights a cigarette and leans against the back counter.

'Any news?' she asks.

'I've had some fingerprints back from the room,' Nova says, pulling a folded piece of paper out of her pocket. 'There weren't many – looks like whoever left him there cleaned up after themselves, but there were a few here and there. Most of them matched the samples that you and your staff gave us, but we also found someone else's. I just need you to confirm that she doesn't work here, or if you recognise her at all.'

'Gi's a look then, hin,' the man says, leaning forwards. Nova unfolds the paper. A picture of Sarah is printed on it, and the man and his wife glance at each other. They both smirk. One of the customers leans across the bar and looks at the photograph before Nova can pull it away.

'Ahh, that's sexy Sarah, that,' he says, and drains his pint. The landlady starts to pull him another, cigarette hanging out of the corner of her mouth, before he even asks. 'Worst barmaid A've ever met, her. Prettiest, like, but foul attitude. Foul.'

'Sarah worked here?'

'Aye, for a while, a few year ago,' the landlady says.

'Years ago? So there would be no reason for her fingerprints to still be up there, then?'

Harry shrugs. 'We haven't cleaned that room in mebbes a decade, we just use it for storing shite. She spent a lot of time up there when she was here. So I dunno, you tell me.'

'You haven't seen her around lately?'

'Nah, nah. I fired her, hasn't been back since.'

'I see.'

'Aw, aye,' the customer who hasn't spoken yet says, as if he's only just realised who they're talking about. 'It was her that was shagging that gadgie when she was supposed to be working, wasn't it, Harry?'

The landlady's eyes go wide, but the man carries on.

'The one withoot ees heed?'

Nova snaps her head around, but the man just smiles at her, eyes slightly unfocused.

'Aye, in the very room where ya's found him, wasn't it? Sounds like a scorned missus to me, like,' the first customer laughs.

Nova looks at the landlord for confirmation. His face doesn't give away anything.

'Jamie Spellman was a customer?' she asks.

'Aye, well. Aye, he used to come in years agan like, haven't seen him for a lang time. Not since we got rid of Sarah,' the landlord says. He takes his glasses off and rubs his face. 'Not till he torned up again, anywas.'

'And you didn't think to mention that you knew who he was when you found him?'

The landlord gives Nova a long look, which makes clear his attitude on the matter of *grassing* to the police. 'Like A said, it's been a lang time, he was never a proper regular, and to be honest, hin, A didn't look at the heed for lang enough to recognise him.'

'And it didn't cross your mind to get in touch since?'

The man shrugged, and his wife dipped the burning end of her spent cigarette in one of the drip trays so that it hissed out.

'Look, love, it weren't nowt to do with us,' she says in a thick Yorkshire accent. 'We din't know owt were going on up there, could have been anyone. We had a big New Year's Eve party that night. If she did it, nobody saw her. You're best off talking to her, love.'

Nova nods, irritated. 'I'm sure I'll be back.'

She walks out of the bar, raises a hand at Gary on the way past, and gets into her car. The sun has already set, though it's barely five o'clock. It can't be a coincidence that Jamie's head turned up at the site of their affair. It's completely unfeasible to Nova at this point that Sarah isn't somehow involved. She knows that Kaysha is involved, even if she's just protecting Sarah, and she suspects that Sadia has had a hand somehow, too; she just can't figure out how they all fit. She remembers Josie turning up at the station days before, guilty as sin for a murder that Nova was sure she had nothing to do with, but also sure that she knew more than she was saying. They all slot in somewhere, but it's so complicated. She tries to piece all the clues together, but there are so many women and so many moving parts that every time she thinks she's close, something new comes up and throws her off track. She's desperate to figure it out, feels like she's on the edge of a revelation.

Nova makes a phone call and gets Sarah's address, jots it down on the back of a receipt and starts her engine. She knows vaguely where it is, but gets her road atlas out from under the seat just in case.

Sarah lives near to one of the little mining villages in the countryside, usually about half an hour's drive out of the city, but the traffic is manic. The Tyne Bridge is closed off, probably due to an accident, so Nova has to go the long way, and the traffic is dense and slow until she is out of Newcastle. The roads clear as she passes through the suburbs and then out into the green belt, fields stretching away from the road, villages flashing past here and there. She finds herself driving too fast, feeling like she's finally getting somewhere with the case, tension and morbid excitement building within her because she thinks that she might get some answers from Sarah, and find out why these women, all tangled up with the same man and the same child, would turn to murder.

Nova finds the right village. She knows she's looking for an old manor, but she can't see one anywhere. She keeps taking wrong turns and at one point ends up on a farm track, which leads her back to a road she had been on twenty minutes earlier. Eventually she stops and goes into a corner shop for directions to the manor, which she has apparently driven past twice, but it's so covered by ivy that in the dark it's almost impossible to spot against the trees.

The iron gate at the end of the drive is open, and a small gatehouse sits just inside, foliage poking through the long-broken windows. Everything leading up to the house is wildly overgrown, and then Nova sees the house itself up close, looming out of the dark. The front door hangs open, and for a minute Nova wonders if they've got an old address for Sarah, because it certainly doesn't look like anyone lives here.

She knocks at the door several times, but no one answers, so she goes in.

'Sarah?' she calls into the dark. The house seems like an endless tunnel of corridors and rooms that lead to other rooms, and Nova knows that Sarah, or anyone else, could easily hide from her if they wanted to. There are signs in the kitchen that point to someone having been here recently – half a pan of soup on the hob, a loaf of bread that's still soft. The tap drips every few seconds, and the sound echoes through the room. After trying a few doors, Nova finds a room which looks lived in. Empty wine bottles and crisp packets are strewn across the floor. There is an armchair pulled close to a large television, which is on, but muted. Nova looks around the room for any clue as to where Sarah might be, but there is only dust and an overflowing ashtray, nothing particularly catching her eye. She picks up the remote control from the armchair to turn off the TV as she leaves, out of habit, and pauses as she notices what is on the screen. The *Six o'Clock News* shows footage of the Tyne Bridge, which has police cars blocking each end, like it did when Nova passed it an hour earlier. Someone is on the wrong side of the railings, face to the river and wind blowing through long, black hair. There are police officers trying to talk her down, and though the woman's face is pixelated when the camera zooms in on her, Nova recognises the jacket and the throat tattoo.

She runs out of the house and back to her car, digging through the boot for her blue light, and tears out of the estate when she finds it, back through the villages and towns and into the city, lights flashing, her pulse racing. She has to get to Sarah. That's all she knows, she can barely think of anything else, she just knows that she has to get there in time. She thinks that if Sarah did this to Jamie, maybe he deserved it. She's sure there must have been more to their relationship than just an affair, something so scarring that she is losing her battle with the memory of it. Maybe, Nova thinks – and her stomach drops – Sarah found out about her affair with Kaysha. Maybe she's so utterly devastated that the one person in her life whom she could rely on has betrayed her that she wants everything to end.

Nova's tyres screech as she slams her brakes on, jolting herself forward, as close as she can get to the bridge in the car. She gets out and sprints up the road, manoeuvring between panda cars and officers who try to speak to her as she passes. She's out of breath quickly and her limbs ache, but she carries on, darting through the freezing air towards the lit arch of the bridge. She can see Sarah, she can see the white of her hands on the safety railing, her body so small and fragile against the massive iron curve. The river is swollen and turbulent hundreds of feet beneath her, and Nova keeps running.

'Sarah,' she shouts, and she could swear that Sarah turns to look at her, their eyes meeting for just a second before

Sarah throws herself off the ledge. She seems to hang in the air as Nova keeps running towards where she is, where she just was, as if there is still a chance that she can save her. She is gone when Nova gets there, the river swallows her and carries on its way like she was nothing.

36

Sarah
1995

Sarah stepped into the empty car park. A series of commercial buildings spread out in a row before her until they melted into cul-de-sacs of tidy suburban houses at each end of the road. Two young men in white shirts and ankle-length black aprons were clattering chairs and tables onto the patio of the trattoria under Sarah's flat. They shouted and whistled at her as she stalked towards them but stopped when she glanced pointedly up at her kitchen window. It was bright against the evening gloom.

'Areet?' asked one of the boys as she slumped into a chair under the awning, out of sight of the window. They were both in their late teens and had been working with Sarah in the restaurant for a few months. On nights when Jamie wasn't around, they often came up to her flat and drank wine that they'd taken from the restaurant kitchen. They both still lived with their parents, and Sarah's flat was a safe space. She didn't care if they held hands.

'Aye, are you? Can you get me some water?'

'Get yourself some, lazy cow,' Adam said, rolling his eyes. He went into the restaurant and brought her a glass anyway.

'Good job you're not at work the day, Luigi's on the warpath after the palaver with that woman the other neet,' said the other, Stevie, and then nodded up towards Sarah's window. 'Thought you'd got rid of him?'

'So did I,' Sarah said. 'Did that woman complain, like?'

'They usually do when you spill a glass of red wine over them.'

'Silly cow,' Sarah said, crossing her legs. 'She knew it was an accident.'

'Didn't help that you howled about it, though,' Stevie said, laughing.

'It was funny. Have you got my stuff?'

'Are you sure you should be on the baccy, like?' asked Adam, the stockier of the two, putting his hands on his hips and nodding at her swollen belly.

'Er, mind ya beeswax,' said Sarah. 'Herbal, innit. Be fine.'

'S'pose,' Adam shrugged, and after glancing around the empty car park, slipped her a small paper bag from his apron pocket. Sarah looked at it with raised eyebrows.

'What's this, like, a tenpence mix-up?' she asked, opening it to see a tangled green lump the size of a chestnut. She gave it a sniff.

'I've decided to switch to paper. I want to be more sustainable.'

'What the fuck are you on about?'

'We'll all be drowning in plastic bags in twenty years. You'll see,' he said. 'So I nicked those from the corner shop to use instead.'

Sarah laughed and put the paper bag in her back pocket. 'You're a reet hippie, yee, mind.'

Adam winked and carried on laying the tables.

'Are you gonna keep it, then?' asked Stevie, flourishing a white cloth over the nearest table and dumping a handful of cutlery on top. Sarah shrugged.

'Not if A can help it. Wanna adopt a kid? Homemade, fresh out the oven.'

'A'm a bit worried that it's ganna be half-demon with that knacka for a dad,' he said.

'Aye, A kna',' said Sarah. She pulled a battered tin from her inside pocket and opened it on the table.

'Got a filter?' she asked him as she took a pinch of tobacco and pulled it into a stripe across a cigarette paper.

'Does a bear shit in the woods?' he said, handing her one from a pouch in his apron pocket.

'Ta,' Sarah said, putting it in place. She rolled the whole thing into a slim cylinder and licked along the edge of the paper to seal it. Stevie held out a lit Zippo for her and she leant towards him, sucking in the first sour lungful. Stevie sat down beside her and put a hand on her shoulder.

'Are you alright though?' he asked, taking the cigarette from between her fingers and taking a drag, before passing it back. Sarah smirked. 'Is he being a bastard?'

'He's always a bastard.'

'You can do better, you know,' said Adam, sitting down on her other side and resting his chin on his fist.

'Yeah,' she said, clamping her cigarette between her lips and standing up. 'Right, get some work done, you lazy fuckers. A'm away.'

'Lazy? Says bloody you?'

'Aye, says me,' Sarah said, flicking two fingers at them as she turned towards the alley between the restaurant and the pharmacy next door, sticking close to the wall so Jamie wouldn't see her smoking. The door to her flat was surrounded by broken chairs stacked up beside overflowing dustbins. The binmen were on strike again, and the scent of three weeks' worth of rotting pasta made Sarah retch. She spat out a mouthful of bile and flicked her half-smoked cigarette into one of the bins. She pulled a body spray and a packet of Wrigley's out of her bag and sprayed herself until she coughed, and then emptied the remainder of the gum into her mouth. The bare lightbulb dangling in the nook between the door and stairs had popped a while ago and no one had bothered to replace it, so the stairway was completely dark, but Sarah knew her way by touch. She climbed up to her flat and took a deep breath before she pushed the door open.

Jamie was chopping tomatoes with the large kitchen knife that Sarah had stolen from downstairs. Luigi, despite her constant nagging, hadn't bothered to fix the broken lock on the outside door, so she had taken it from his kitchen for protection. Seemed fair. The slimy innards of the tomatoes seeped across the chopping board and dribbled onto the hob, where a pan with too much oil in it was spitting. Jamie didn't look up.

'Hiya,' Sarah said, standing in the doorway. 'I didn't know you were coming over.'

'I told you I was,' he said, sweeping the tomatoes into a pan with the edge of the knife and moving on to slicing some mushrooms. 'Have you forgotten?'

'Must have,' Sarah said. She didn't think that he *had* told her, but it wasn't worth the argument. 'I hate mushrooms.'

Jamie shrugged and dropped a few into the pan. 'I don't.'

'What are you making?'

'You can just pick the mushrooms out.'

'I know, I will, I'm just asking,' she said. She was too tired for this today; she knew this mood. He was ready for an argument and he knew he'd get one if he pushed her. She wanted him to leave her alone and she wanted him to stay. She felt a pull towards him, more like obsession than love, a determination to dig until she found the laughing person she'd fallen in love with in the hotel bar the year before. She could never reach him. She'd see flashes of it sometimes in his smile, or if he was tipsy, before she said the wrong thing and he'd change again, the smile turning into a sneer. Sarah thought about changing her locks every day, but then she thought about a life with him, a proper life, not the strange part-time coexistance they shared in her tiny flat when he'd snuck away from his wife. Sarah always felt a lurch of guilt when she thought about her – Sadia. She sounded alright. Stupid though. Believed anything he fed her, by the sounds of it.

'Do I not get a kiss today, then?' he said, slicing an onion into uneven chunks. Sarah hung her coat up and leant towards him, their lips pressing together for a second before he pulled away. 'I told you to stop smoking.'

'I know,' she said. 'It's hard, though.'

'I know you don't want this kid, but I'd think you'd have enough respect for its life not to try and poison it every five minutes.'

'It's okay, you know. My mam smoked when she was pregnant with me and I was fine. I think it's just all this New Age bullshit.'

'You think you turned out fine?' he asked, scoffing. Sarah took a deep breath and kicked off her boots.

'Can I help you with anything?'

'No.' He took the pan off the heat and put it into the oven, and then dropped onto the sofa. Sarah sat beside him, being careful not to touch him, and rubbed her feet. They were swollen and sore.

'I am sorry, you know,' she said, leaning back. 'This is what I mean, I'd be a shit mother. I'm too selfish.'

'You could be okay if you wanted to be.'

'Yeah, but I just don't. I never wanted a kid.'

'Oh, and don't we know it. Poor little Sarah, got herself up the duff and now doesn't want the kid.'

'Well, I didn't get *myself* up the duff, did I?' she spat back.

He shrugged. 'As the old saying goes, if you don't want a kid, keep your legs closed.'

'You're as much to blame as I am,' she said. 'It was you that refused to wear a rubber and *forgot to pull out*.'

'Well, I thought we wanted a baby together,' he said. 'Silly me.'

'Well yeah, silly fucking you, Jamie. I never, ever told you I wanted a baby. And even if I *did* want one, which I don't, why would *we* have one together? Look around, man. I live in a glorified stockroom above a restaurant and you're fucking married to someone else. We can't raise a bairn like this.'

'Who cares? We love each other, that should be enough.'

'Well, it's not. You can't feed a baby on love.'

Jamie stood up. 'When you're not being a bitch, I actually think you'd be a good mam.'

'And even if I was, even if I wanted it, where would you be? How am I gonna explain to the kid that Daddy's only here when he can get away from his wife? Fuck off, man, Jamie.'

'If you wanted to raise it together, I'd leave her for you,' he said, his voice clipped. Sarah tipped her head back and groaned. She'd heard this a million times before. She used to believe him, but she'd long since realised that he'd never leave his beloved Sadia, kid or not. 'Do you know how lucky you are, Sarah? To have the fucking privilege to have a baby? Do you know how much she wants to have my baby? The amount of nights I've stayed up with her, holding her while she cries because all she wants is a kid, and she hasn't got a fucking womb to carry one? Grow up and be grateful for what you've got, man.'

'I know! I know she does, that's not my fucking fault, Jamie.' Sarah wiped tears from her cheeks. 'She can have it. I'd give her my womb, too, if I could. I wish I could just give it to her.'

Jamie said nothing for a long time, eventually crossing the room to take the food from the oven and spoon it onto a pair of mismatched plates. He took them to the table and then went into the bathroom, slamming the door behind him. Sarah cried into her hands, letting herself sob for a few seconds before she wiped her face and went to get some cutlery from a drawer. She laid it out and straightened the table up, got Jamie a bottle of beer from the fridge and poured herself a glass of water. She wanted a beer, but it wasn't worth the hassle.

A candle shuddered light across the table, and their shadows loomed up opposite walls. Sarah had dragged the table and two chairs up the staircase one by one a few months before, reappropriated from the alley behind the restaurant where the manager dumped broken things. She'd fixed them with superglue, determination, and carefully folded bits of cardboard. She'd taken a wine-stained tablecloth and some bent cutlery to lay it with too. When she'd first moved into the flat, after she was fired from the Towneley Arms and got a job at Luigi's, Jamie had laughed at the way she balanced her plate on her knees every night as she ate, so she'd taken the table, though there was barely any space for it in her one-room flat, and after that they sat there and ate. Their dinners, which were scattered through the week, whenever he could get away, had started off brimming with laughter and fizzy lust.

'Can you pass the salt?' asked Jamie, without looking up from his plate. The table was small and the salt was closer to him than it was to Sarah, but she reached out and pushed it towards him. He didn't use it, and she went back to fishing out all the mushrooms, making a little pile of them on the side of her plate. He took a long drink from his bottle of beer, and sighed, pushing away the full plate of food in front of him. He tipped his head back to stare at the ceiling and folded his arms. Sarah's chest tightened and she let out a slow breath before she spoke.

'What's wrong?' she asked. Jamie shook his head and stood, avoiding Sarah's eyes, and took both of their plates to the bin, tipping the almost untouched food inside. He dropped the plates into the sink and turned the water on, glaring out of the window, down onto the restaurant patio below.

'What a waste, eh?' he said, glancing at her over his shoulder, eyebrows raised and grey eyes wide.

Sarah looked at the carpet, trying not to cry again. It would only be worse if she did.

'Look at them two down there,' he spat, 'fucking mincing about.'

'Don't start.'

'Oh, I forgot, they're your *best friends*,' he said, smirking. 'How dare I?'

'There's just no need to have a go, is there? They've done fuck all to you.'

'Is the kid one of theirs, is it? That why you're so reluctant to mother it? Scared it's gonna be a little mincer as well?' he asked. 'I know you've got a thing for the ginger one.'

'Oh fuck off, man, he's gay! You know he is. The other one is his fucking boyfriend.'

'Well, you still fancy him,' he said.

Sarah laughed, brave and reckless on a wave of anger. 'You're an absolutely ridiculous excuse for a person.'

'*I'm* the ridiculous one?'

'Yeah, you are,' she said. 'Just fuck off, J. I'm not in the mood for your shit tonight.'

'Fine,' he said, pulling his boots on and grabbing his coat. He left, slamming the door behind him. Sarah burst into tears, furious, but already wishing he'd come back. She fought the urge to go after him and rolled a joint instead. She lay on the sofa with it and turned the television on to distract herself. A nature documentarist's voice filled the room. Sarah took deep breaths, trying to remember what her therapist had said when she was a teenager. *Don't let it escalate.* She felt hopeless, trapped, growing a child that she knew she couldn't keep. It moved inside of her and she felt sick.

She'd wanted an abortion. As soon as she'd realised that she was pregnant, her first instinct was that she had to get rid of it. Sarah was a failure, she always had been. She had never managed to do anything right in her life, and her parents had always made sure she knew it. She had never been interested enough in school to pass exams. She'd never stuck a job out for more than a few months. She left every relationship the second it started to get serious, until Jamie. *I love you* had always sent a ripple of disgust through her body, it was so foreign to her, and so, usually, the second she heard it she ran.

Jamie hadn't told Sarah that he loved her for almost six months after they got together, but he made sure she felt it. They met when she worked behind the bar in the Towneley Arms, and within a few weeks Sarah would spend any spare seconds she had on her shifts standing at the end of the bar with Jamie, while he'd make jokes about all the other customers, about the family who ran the hotel, about his wife, about himself, and sometimes about Sarah – though the latter were always followed by a smile and *just kidding*. He'd buy her drinks, more than she should have drunk when she was working, made sure she was always more drunk than he was, and she was happy like that. He'd bring her flowers, and she'd balk, and he'd tell her he found them in a bin on the way in, or that they were in condolence for her being such a miserable fucker, and she'd roll her eyes and put them in water and call him a creep and he'd say yeah, but you love me, and eventually he said it so much that she realised it was true.

Six weeks after they met, Jamie arranged with the manager that Sarah would get her birthday weekend off work without her knowing. He picked her up when she turned up for the Friday night shift and they drove to Scotland, to a cabin with a hot tub and a view across a valley dense with gorse and heather. She was surly at first because she hated surprises and she hated anyone paying attention to her when she hadn't solicited it, and because no one had ever done anything so nice for her before and she didn't know how else to react than with resentment. Jamie had packed the boot with bottles of wine and bags of crisps and he'd kissed Sarah for the first time as she sat in the cabin with tears in her eyes, and the kiss was so gentle that she forgot to be mad.

When Sarah had eventually stopped crying and settled into her sadness, the door opened and Jamie walked back into her flat. He had a couple of plastic carrier bags in one hand and a bunch of flowers in the other. Sarah was angry at the rush of happiness that she felt when she saw him.

'Thought you'd fucked off,' she said, turning back to the television.

'Charming,' he said, closing the door and putting his bags down on the kitchen bench. 'I only went out for milk.'

'What are you on about?'

'I told you, I just went for milk. Got a few more things while I was there.'

'No, you didn't, you went home because I told you to fuck off.'

Jamie sat down on the sofa beside her feet and put a hand on her leg. 'No, Sarah. You're confused. I just went out for milk. I got us some food while I was there, since you refused to eat my cooking.'

Sarah frowned at him. He was rubbing her leg, and he didn't seem angry. But she was sure he had been when he left. 'Are you sure?'

'Yeah, I am. You've just got that – what do you call it? Pregnancy brain, or whatever. You're getting mixed up,' he said, smiling and standing up. 'Look what I brought you anyway.'

'Okay,' Sarah said, pushing herself upright, confused. He didn't seem like he would have been angry enough to storm out an hour before. Maybe she was thinking of another time. She didn't know. He pulled a couple of bottles of beer from the carrier bag. He handed her one and put one in the fridge.

'Alcohol-free,' he said. 'I know you're dying for one.'

'Thanks,' she said, putting it down on the table and glancing around for a bottle opener.

'And I got this, and this, and this,' he said, pulling bread, milk, and juice out of the bag, his voice high and bouncy, being silly to make her laugh. She smiled.

'Thanks.'

'And I got you these,' he said, brandishing the bunch of carnations at her. He pushed them into her face. 'Smell.'

Sarah laughed, pushing them away. 'Yes, lovely. I'll put them in water.'

'No, no, I'm doing it,' he said, filling a pint glass from the bench with water and balancing them in it, still wrapped in cellophane. He opened the other bag, and pulled out a few cardboard containers of Chinese food. 'And I got you this.'

'Oh my God, thank you. I'm so hungry,' she said, pushing herself up.

'No, no, stay where you are,' Jamie said, pushing her hair out of her face and kissing her head. He handed her an open container and a fork, and then sat down with his own. 'Let's just eat here, you don't need to move.'

The container was full of nothing but beansprouts. Sarah had been craving beansprouts her whole pregnancy, something about the crunch, and almost cried at the sight of them. He did love her, really.

'You've appeased it, for now,' she said through a mouthful of food, prodding her belly.

Jamie rolled his eyes. 'Don't call him *it*, man. That's a tiny person in there.'

'Yeah. Sorry.'

'You know, you think that you won't love him now, but wait till he's here. Wait until you see him. Wait until he comes into the world and you see his tiny fingers and toes, till he cries and you know that he needs you. You'll love him when he gets here, I promise.'

'I won't. In four weeks' time he's going to be out of me and I'll have my body back,' she said. 'It's not – *he's* not my baby. He's someone else's. I'm just cooking him.'

'Whose is he then, if not yours?'

'I don't know, I'll find someone who wants a baby but can't have one, I suppose,' she said, and thought about Stevie and Adam.

'What about Sadia?' Jamie asked, stroking his fingers across Sarah's belly.

'What about her?'

'It just seems like the obvious solution,' he said.

'You think she'll want to raise it?' Sarah said too quickly, too eagerly, a wash of relief flooding through her followed by a pang of jealousy. Not for the baby, she thought, but for Jamie.

'Him.'

'Him,' Sarah repeated, putting her hand on top of Jamie's. 'Sorry.'

'I know she will.'

37

Sarah
1996

Sarah was sitting on the restaurant patio with Stevie when her waters burst, two weeks early. Stevie had already drunk three glasses of wine, but he packed Sarah into his battered Fiesta and drove her to the hospital on the other side of the city. When they got there, Sarah used a payphone to ring Jamie at work and tell him that the baby was coming. By the time he arrived, Sarah had already split herself in half and the child was mewling in a cot beside her bed. Tiny and perfect, the nurse had told Sarah, but Sarah couldn't look at her. She'd held her, felt the weight of her against her chest, the pull of her as she latched on to a nipple, but Sarah kept her eyes closed the entire time.

Jamie looked irritated for a second when he walked into the room and saw the baby.

'I missed it,' he said. 'I thought I'd get here in time.'

'Sorry.'

He took a deep breath and then smiled, leaning over Sarah to touch the child's cheek. He kissed Sarah like the first time he'd ever kissed her, like he meant it, and for a second she thought *maybe it could work*. Maybe it would go back to how it was at the beginning. She looked at the baby for the first time, met her dark eyes and felt a rush of something so powerful she felt like she might faint. *Maybe it could work*, she thought again.

'Sadia's on her way,' Jamie said, walking to the other side of the bed and taking the baby from Sarah's arms. 'I've told her that you work in the lab, remember. Just as a cleaner, just so you don't have to sound . . . you know. Clever.'

'You need to support her head,' Sarah said, reaching out and gently adjusting the baby in Jamie's arms. 'The nurse told me.'

'She's a girl?'

'Yeah.'

'I said you didn't know who the dad was.'

Sarah nodded, biting the inside of her cheeks.

Jamie looked at her, the furrows above his eyebrows deepening. 'You're not having second thoughts, are you?'

'No,' Sarah said, sniffing. 'It's just hormones.'

Jamie smiled. 'You'll feel okay about it when you see. Sadia. She's not like us.'

'What do you mean?'

'I mean, she's just . . . good. Really good.'

'If she's that good, why's she with you?'

Jamie glanced away from the baby and frowned. 'Why wouldn't she be?'

There was a tap on the open door. A woman stood in the doorway, a wide smile slung across her pretty face. She wore an ankle-length floral dress and her hair was swept up in a ponytail. She was holding a wicker basket in one hand and a bouquet in the other, and Sarah thought that she looked like she'd just stepped off the front cover of an expensive women's magazine, something middle-class about housekeeping and motherhood. Sarah wondered why Jamie ever wanted to have an affair with *her*, when his wife looked like this. She supposed cheating wasn't anything to do with looks, really. Just power.

'Hello,' Sadia said, her voice soft as she walked into the room.

'Look who I've found,' Jamie said, flashing a smile at his wife and nodding down at the baby.

'Hello,' Sadia said again, laying a hand on Jamie's shoulder and gazing at the baby for a second before she turned to Sarah. She took Sarah's hand and leant over to kiss her cheek. She smelled like clean washing. 'How are you feeling? I'm Sadia. You look really well.'

Sarah smiled, and Sadia carried on before she could answer.

'How was it, did everything go okay? Are you feeling alright? I'm sorry I couldn't be here sooner,' Sadia continued, still grasping Sarah's hand with both of hers. Sarah hated physical contact, especially with strangers, but she was so exhausted and emotional, and this woman so warm, that the touch comforted her.

'Everything was fine, I think,' Sarah said. 'She's a girl. Five pounds three, they said.'

‘A girl!’ Sadia said, giving Sarah’s hand a final squeeze and turning back to the baby. She took her from Jamie’s arms in exactly the way the nurse had shown Sarah, cradling her head. Jamie watched Sadia as she gently rocked the baby, looking at her in a way that he’d never looked at Sarah. Sadia kissed him.

‘We’re a family,’ she whispered, her eyes filling with tears and spilling over. Jamie wrapped his arms around his wife from behind, looking over her shoulder at their baby. He kissed her cheek and Sarah felt like an intruder on the moment.

That night, Jamie left so he could sleep for work the next day, but Sadia insisted on staying with Sarah and the baby. Jamie had given Sarah a warning glance as he left the room, but she knew better than to tell Sadia anything she shouldn’t. She didn’t want to. She knew that Sadia was the right person to raise the child, she didn’t want to alienate her. The flowers and basket she had brought when she arrived were for Sarah. Sadia hadn’t let Sarah open the basket yet, but said it was full of things that she’d read were good for a postpartum body, just some little luxuries, the least she could do.

Sarah drifted off periodically, but whenever she awoke, Sadia was sitting up in the visitor’s chair reading a magazine, or leaning over the crib, watching the baby. When the baby needed to be fed, Sarah asked if Sadia wanted to feed her with a bottle, but Sadia shook her head.

‘If you could feed her, just for tonight – it’s so good for her, you know. I wish I could do it.’ She said it so earnestly that Sarah couldn't refuse. When the sky outside began to brighten at last, Sadia pulled her chair closer to Sarah.

'Sarah,' she whispered, stroking the baby's head. She'd fallen asleep on Sarah's chest. 'Are you sure you want to do this?'

Sarah took a deep breath and felt the weight of the baby on her. She was making little noises that made Sarah's breasts ache.

'I'm not her mother,' Sarah said. 'You are.'

Sadia squeezed Sarah's hand. 'I never thought I'd hear that, you know. Not since I found out that I couldn't have my own. And then when I met Jamie, the day I met him I just knew that he was the one, but he's obviously, you know, he's infertile too, so our options were very limited. But now we have her.'

'He's infertile too?' Sarah repeated, frowning. She was confused for a second, wondered if he'd really believed it, and that's why he'd always insisted that they didn't need to use protection.

'Oh, didn't he ever mention it? I'm sure he won't mind me saying.'

'Are you sure?' Sarah said, before she could stop herself.

'I don't think he'd lie about it,' Sadia said, her eyebrows furrowed. She crossed her arms.

'Sorry, I don't know why I said that,' Sarah said, blushing. 'Hormones. He seems like he really loves you.'

Sadia smiled. 'He does.'

The next day, Jamie came back and Sarah and the baby were discharged from the hospital. Jamie and Sadia took the baby in their car, and Sadia kissed Sarah on the cheek and put her in a taxi with the basket and the flowers. Sarah felt like a part of her body had been removed. When the driver asked where she wanted to go, she didn't tell him to take her to the flat above the restaurant – the address she'd given the hospital for follow-ups and midwife visits she'd never attend – she told him to take her to Heather Hall. He didn't know where it was, and she had to direct him way out of the city. When they pulled up outside he whistled.

She hadn't been there for years, and it was exactly how she remembered it – cold and lifeless. She found the key, still under the clematis, and let herself in. It had been five years since her parents died and no one had broken in. Her dad's watch was on the console by the door, where he always used to forget it, and pairs of shoes with cobwebs stretched between them were still lined neatly along the rack. David's picture was still on the wall where it always was, so that it was the first thing you'd see as you walked into the house. It was in a smaller frame than it had originally been, because in the picture she'd been next to him, and she'd been cut out sometime since she'd run away, and the only part of her left was her hand, fingers laced with her brother's.

Her parents had been rich and cold, disappointed that she wasn't a boy. Sarah had been too, when she was a child. She knew that was where the power in their household lay. Her brother was tall and strong with a tousled mess of golden hair and an easy smile that made everyone else smile too. He did well at school and he played sports, and he was kind to

Sarah, even when their parents weren't, because the only thing that Sarah was good at was getting into trouble.

When David was sixteen, he started to complain that his bones were aching. *Growing pains*, the doctor said. *Sports injuries. Deep tissue bruises*. Eventually, and far too late, they realised it was cancer. He was dead within six weeks of his diagnosis. Sarah had spiralled after that. Her relationship with her parents grew even more distant, and though they never said they'd wished it had been Sarah instead, she knew. She packed a bag and moved out when she was seventeen, and no one came after her. She never saw her parents again.

Three years after she left, her parents both died when her dad crashed the Merc into an oak tree as they were driving home drunk from some benefit. They had, surprisingly, left everything to her – the money, the house, the cars. She hadn't touched any of it, until now, and she wondered why she was eventually drawn back to the place that had made her so miserable when she was already at her lowest ebb, and she thought that maybe she and the house belonged together, both so full of ghosts.

38

Kaysha
12th January 2000

Kaysha drives the road to the coast, as she has done so often recently. She lets herself into Olive's house without knocking and goes to find her in the kitchen, where she always seems to be. Tonight she is leaning over the sink, fingers grasping the windowsill. Her head flicks around to Kaysha for a second and then back to the garden outside.

'What are you looking for?' Kaysha asks. Olive waits for a few moments to answer.

'The birds.'

'They're probably in bed,' Kaysha says, quietly. Olive seems calmer than usual, and Kaysha doesn't want to set her off. She stands beside her and looks out into the garden too. It's small, and surrounded by high walls, covered in moss. It's neatly manicured, and the furniture is covered for the winter. A bird feeder hangs from a tree, and an old bird house is nailed to the trunk. 'I bet this is full of birds in the summer.'

‘They’ll come back, won’t they?’ Olive asks, glancing at Kaysha, and it strikes Kaysha again that she is almost child-sized, shrunken, drowning in her nightdress. She’s dwindling by the day, and Kaysha thinks it likely that one day she’ll just disappear altogether, and only her nightie will be left, draped over the kitchen bench of the quiet, quiet house.

‘I’m sure they will, yeah,’ Kaysha says, resting a hand on Olive’s shoulder. Olive eyes it, but doesn’t shrug her off. ‘What kind of birds are they?’

‘Sparrows. Dozens of them. They all hide in the bushes over there,’ Olive says, pointing to the back corner of the garden. ‘Next door always has cats, always at least three, four cats and once one of them caught one of the birds as I watched, ripped a wing off. I ran out and shouted at it but it was too late, and it took the poor bird over the fence and all that was left was its wing. I buried the wing under the rhododendrons.’

Kaysha is half listening, half watching the news on the TV behind Olive. A helicopter circles the Tyne Bridge, which is blocked off and full of police. There is a close-up of a police boat sailing down the river, a diver suiting up.

‘Are you listening?’ Olive says, waving her hand in front of Kaysha’s face.

‘Yes, Olive. Birds, cats. That’s aw—’

‘I was mad and I told next door that I’d shoot their cat if it came back and they said they’d phone the police if I did. So I bought a water gun instead. A big one, one of those huge ones you have to pump up to get a good shot. And the next time it came in I crept up behind it when it was waiting for the birds again and I shot it with my water gun. Didn't see it again,' Olive says, barely blinking.

Kaysha's phone starts to vibrate in her back pocket. She's hoping it's Nova, who seemed cold that morning, so she steers Olive into a seat and goes into the living room to take the call. When she takes her phone out of her pocket, she sees that it is Nova, and answers it.

'Hey,' she says.

'Kay . . . can I meet you?' Nova says. Her voice sounds odd, and fear floods Kaysha's body. She's found something out. Maybe Sadia has cracked under questioning, maybe they're all going to be arrested.

'What's wrong?'

'I need to see you.'

'I can't,' Kaysha says, looking at Olive, who is peering around the doorway at her. 'What's up?'

'Fuck. I can't . . . I didn't want to tell you over the phone. Are you sitting down?' Nova asks, and Kaysha slumps onto one of the couches behind her.

'I am now, why?'

'It's Sarah,' Nova says, and her voice cracks.

Horror whips through Kaysha, and she wonders if Nova has arrested Sarah, found out something that Kaysha couldn't. Olive sits down right beside Kaysha, far too close. Kaysha covers the mouthpiece with her hand.

'Olive, hold on. I'll just be a minute,' she whispers, and moves to the other couch to resume the call. She tries to sound bold and unworried. 'What about her? You found her drunk somewhere?'

'Are you with someone?'

'No, it's just the TV. What's wrong?'

'Sarah . . . I just watched her . . . she's – Sarah's dead. She jumped – she jumped off the Tyne Bridge.'

Kaysha can't take in what Nova is saying, and Nova keeps asking if she's okay, but Kaysha's hand goes loose and she drops the phone, and as it hits the hardwood floor the back pops off and the battery comes out, and the call goes dead.

When, eventually, Kaysha drops to her knees and puts the phone back together, she doesn't call Nova back. Instead, she sends out a text containing the address, instructions just to come in, not to knock, and to be here as soon as possible, there's an emergency, and then she waits. Olive seems to read the moment, and is almost normal for a while. She tells Kaysha that she knew a girl once who jumped from a ledge and left her alone in the world, and she's never forgiven her for it. Kaysha can't bring herself to say anything, can't bring herself to tell Olive that it isn't the fucking same at all, because Kim didn't jump and Olive knows she didn't. Olive seems to click into mothering mode, and starts to fuss around Kaysha, wiping her face and gently taking off her denim jacket, hanging it up and putting a blanket around her instead. She makes a cup of tea and puts it into Kaysha's hands, and then rubs her back.

Josie is the first to arrive.

'Oh good,' she says, taking off a woolly hat and looking around. 'I was worried there'd be another head.'

'No one followed you here, did they?' Kaysha asks Josie.

Josie shakes her head. 'What's the emergency? Has Sadia told them about us?'

When Sadia had been arrested that morning, she'd been allowed to phone Ana to ask her to keep looking after Ameera while she was in custody, and Ana had informed Kaysha, who had told everyone else. They had all been on edge all day, some of them wondering if Sadia *had* killed him, some of them just worried that she'd implicate the entire cohort.

'No,' Kaysha says, and motions for Josie to sit down, which she does. 'Not that I know of. It's Sarah . . . Sarah's . . .'

'Dead.' Olive finishes the sentence for her, and smiles as if she's just announced something mildly amusing.

Josie looks alarmed at Olive's behaviour, and turns to Kaysha for verification, eyes wide. Kaysha nods, and leans back against the cushions, pinching the bridge of her nose, willing herself not to unravel, not yet. Every time she closes her eyes, she sees Sarah falling through the air.

Ana comes next, and then Maureen an hour after that, and Kaysha lets Josie explain what has happened. Kaysha takes herself into the garden for a few minutes, still with the blanket wrapped around her, just to calm herself down, brace herself for the conversation that will follow. When she walks back inside, everyone looks away, like they'd been talking about her, or like her grief is too much for them to witness. Only Olive keeps looking.

'Do you think she did it, and that's why she . . . because of the guilt?' Ana asks the room in general.

'She didn't,' Kaysha says. 'I'm almost sure. I only left the house to go to my mum's an hour or so before we got the message, I don't think she'd have had time.'

'She wanted to,' Olive spits. 'She kept saying *he deserves to be dead, let's just off him and be done with it, do the world a favour.* She made me sick.'

'Yes, Olive, we all know how much you don't like Sarah, but now isn't the time, is it?' Josie interjects, her directness surprising everyone. Olive purses her lips and doesn't respond. Everyone is quiet for a few minutes. There are only two women missing from their group, but it feels like there are far fewer of them than usual, much less powerful, less purposeful.

'This is my fault,' Kaysha says eventually, folded over herself with her head in her hands. 'If I hadn't been so fucking hellbent on retribution, none of this would have happened.'

'Don't be silly, pet,' Maureen says, though she thinks that maybe Kaysha is right. She gathered them all. She poached them one by one, followed their lives and interjected eventually, choosing six other women who she thought would want to see him punished too, who he'd damaged the most. They'd met four times before New Year's Eve, always in the same hotel room that Sarah had still had a key for, through the back door which was never locked and up a set of stairs that was used for storing rusty mop buckets and brooms. It always took all of Maureen's concentration not to send everything cascading down when she tried to navigate it. They never bumped into a single member of staff, as Sarah had said they wouldn't, because no one used the back staircase or the entire top floor, other than for storage. She said once she'd lived in the room for two months and not a single person had noticed.

'You didn't know that any of this would happen,' Ana says. 'This – all of this – is on Jamie.'

'Is it?' Kaysha asks, glaring at the floor. No one answers.

'What are we going to do about Sadia?' Josie asks, and they all look at her. 'We can't just let her take the blame. Unless she actually did it, I suppose, but even then, we'll have to stand up and tell the courts what a bastard he was. How it's not her fault.'

'She didn't do it,' Ana says, and explains to the rest of the women about the drugging of his drink and how Sadia was planning to leave, how Ana was with Sadia during the time-frame for his murder.

'Could she have done it earlier in the day, and then come to meet you after she'd cleaned up? Just snapped, and killed him?' Josie asks. Even Olive is listening intently now, eyes darting from speaker to speaker, soaking up the information.

'Ameera was with her all day, so no,' Ana says. 'And why would she leave half of him in her own pond and bring the other half to the hotel? It makes no sense.'

'Why would *anyone* do that? I don't understand why whoever did it would have brought his head to the hotel. Why didn't they just bury him in the woods? I think about it every day,' Maureen says. She takes a pack of cigarettes and a lighter out of her bag – an old habit that she's recently taken up again.

'I know why,' Josie says. 'It's like a warning, isn't it? I thought that was really clear.'

'Did *you* . . .?'

'No, of course not,' Josie says. 'I know I'm hormonal, but I don't think I could hack his head off. No, I just mean, like . . . it's like in the olden days, medieval or whatever, when they'd, like, leave the bodies of criminals hanging about in the street or display their heads on spikes. I thought it was like that. That she – whoever did it – was, like, *This is what we do to rapists. Be warned*.'

'That's what we should have written on the wall,' Maureen says, a bit breathless and inspired. '*Rapists, be warned*. Instead of that drawing.'

'The drawing worked, though,' Kaysha says. 'And if we'd called him a rapist someone might have thought – someone might have remembered and pinned it on me.'

'That's what I'd have thought,' Ana says, looking at Kaysha and then bowing her head. Ana's younger self haunts her now, and she hears herself in the dead of night, when there is nothing else to think about, arrogant and convinced that she was right, telling people *it's so sad, so, so sad, that she needs to lie about something like this to get attention. I don't think she's really thought of the consequences. This could ruin Jamie's life. It's just really sad, I feel sorry for her, honestly*.

'Yeah,' Kaysha says, remembering the younger version of Ana too. When she'd gathered the women, she'd found Ana the most difficult to approach. She was still hurt, still so angry that Ana had spent so much energy discrediting her at university. It took Kaysha a long time to reframe Ana in her head as someone older, someone who had changed and grown as she had, someone worth her time, and someone who had been hurt by Jamie too. It was always a risk to include Ana – she had seemed like a much bigger risk than even Olive, at the time – but Kaysha was glad that she had. She doesn't think she'll ever be friends with Ana, but she knows that Ana is trying to be better, and that's good enough.

'So,' Josie says, clearing her throat. 'What *are* we going to do about Sadia?'

Olive grasps her knees. 'We should say that Sarah did it.'

Kaysha glares at her. 'Don't be fucking gross.'

Olive shrugs.

'The air grows thick, and no one speaks for a while.

'It might be the most sensible thing to do,' Maureen says eventually, after a deep breath.

'It's too disrespectful,' Josie says. She wonders if she'd have ended up like Sarah, if Jamie was still alive and he'd taken the baby, and she'd have felt empty and used. She wonders if she will anyway. She wonders if she'll love the baby, or whether she won't be able to because it still feels like it is more Jamie's than hers. She imagines this is exactly how Sarah felt too, and she imagines what Sarah might have been like before everything with Jamie and the baby – imagines her laughing and happy, not so jaded, not so hard – and hopes, even though she tells herself that she doesn't believe in God, that she's like that again now, somewhere.

'Not that I think she did it, necessarily,' Maureen continues, speaking in a quiet, low voice, the way she would speak to a person on the edge of breakdown or death when she was a nurse. 'I just mean – we don't know who *did* do it. And I don't think Sadia deserves to be in prison.'

'Even if she did it?' Kaysha asks.

Maureen shifts in her seat, and thinks about the little girl who looked so solemn at Jamie's funeral. Her father is dead. Her mother is in prison. Now her birth mother is dead too. Maureen is her only living relative, and if Sadia stays in prison, it'll be down to Maureen to take the child in. Of course, she'll do it if she has to – she'd rather look after her than see her go into the care system – but Maureen knows that she shouldn't if she can help it. It's tempting, to take Ameera as a chance at redemption, a way to lure John back home to play happy families – but she knows it's a bad idea. If Ameera turns out like Jamie, Maureen will never know if it's genetics or if it's somehow her fault. With Jamie, she always blamed the boy's father – a faceless man whose name Alice said she didn't know.

Maureen had only considered afterwards, with Jamie in her arms and Alice in the ground, that Alice might have been raped, and if she had, that meant Maureen had made her sister carry a child that was conceived by force. She tried not to think about this, reminded herself that Alice was promiscuous and it was probably her own fault that she'd fallen pregnant. But either way, it was still Maureen's fault that Alice was dead, and it was Maureen's fault that Sarah was dead, and that Kim was dead, and that Kaysha had been raped, and that Josie was in the same position that Alice was all those years ago, and everything else that Jamie had done was her fault too. If she'd let Alice have the abortion, none of this would have happened. The guilt crushed her, when she let herself think about it.

Since Jamie's death she's thought of him more than she has in the last ten years, thought about every facet of his childhood, and she's given in to the idea that maybe she didn't treat him as well as she could have. Maybe he'd have been better with a bit more love. A hug now and then. Maybe he wouldn't, she didn't know, but sometimes in the dark of night she felt the incredible weight of responsibility press her down into the mattress.

'Even if she did it,' Maureen says quietly.

'It feels awful to do that to Sarah,' Josie says. 'But, yeah. Maybe . . . I don't know. I don't think it was Sadia, and I don't know if it was Sarah, but someone has to take the blame. I don't really believe in capital punishment, but I think that whoever . . . I think it was probably more like a reaction to something he did than just, like, a cold-blooded murder.'

'I agree,' Ana says. She feels like someone is standing on her chest, the grief and the desperation of the entire thing settling over her. 'Sadia can't stay where she is. We could type a suicide note, so that the handwriting won't be questioned.'

'This is sick,' Kaysha says. She feels like her whole body is bubbling beneath the surface, as if she might explode, or pass out. 'She's just – two hours ago. She's not even cold.'

'None of us *want* to do this, Kaysha,' Josie says, leaning forward and touching Kaysha's knee. 'It's sick, you're right, it is. Completely . . . just, yeah, sick. I don't know what else we can do, though.'

Maureen thinks that, if she were a braver person, or a better person, she would volunteer to take the blame, as penance, but she's not either of those things and so she stares at the pattern of the carpet until someone else speaks.

'Anyone want to confess?' Kaysha says, looking at them one by one. 'Before we pin it on a woman who was so haunted by what he did to her that she . . .'

Kaysha's voice breaks and they all look away as she gathers herself.

'Look,' Ana says, rubbing her face. 'It wasn't Sadia. It just wasn't. She didn't have time. She didn't want to. Jamie was all she had. I was worried that she'd forgive him, to be honest. If we leave her in there, what's going to happen to Ameera? I'm happy to keep her with me and raise her like she's my own, but she needs her mother. Sarah would have wanted her daughter to be happy and safe with Sadia. Think of it like that. We're not doing it to disrespect Sarah, we're doing it for Ameera.'

'I need a minute,' Kaysha says, and stands up. She goes out into the garden again, pulls the blanket tighter around her shoulders and sits on a bench beneath the kitchen window. It is warmer than it has been for weeks, but Kaysha can still see her breath. She folds her body in on itself and begins to sob. She wants to scream into the night. She can hear the rush of the waves on the beach beyond the street and the cliff, and she imagines wading in, the cold of the ocean washing away the sadness, the water sucking her under, back to Sarah.

Kaysha covers her face with her hands and breathes in the salt of her palms. She can't concentrate, and she has to. She wonders what Sarah was thinking. She wonders what the tipping point was – whether it was the affair with Nova, or the promise Sadia had made her that she'd be able to have a relationship with Ameera if she sobered up and her worry that she couldn't; whether it was the head, whether Sarah actually had killed him and not told Kaysha, just let her clean up the mess. She wonders if it was the drinking, or whether it was all of it, all the broken pieces of her life mixed up in her head while she was living in a house where every memory was sad. Kaysha wonders if she could have saved her, if only she'd paid closer attention, if only she'd loved her properly. She wonders what Sarah would do now, whether she'd want them to let her take the blame, whether she'd want them to keep looking, try and find who it really was. Kaysha doesn't think that Sarah cared who it was, only that she was glad someone had done it. She thinks that Sarah would have come up with Olive's solution too, had it been one of the others who had jumped. She'd have been needlessly brash about it but worried about it quietly later, because she was practical and liked to present herself as someone who knew what to do and wasn't encumbered with needless emotion, but really, underneath, she was kind. Kaysha wonders if Sarah did it on purpose to give them a way out, whether she wanted them to blame the murder on her. Maybe she'd get to the manor and there'd already be a note.

Kaysha should have known that Sarah was on the verge of collapse.

She takes deep, shuddering breaths that cloud the air in front of her. If they blame the murder on Sarah, and she didn't do it, the real murderer is going to walk free. If it's one of them, and she thinks it must be, then it doesn't matter, because it won't happen again. It was a one-off, stirred up by all the old anger and sadness at Jamie, which was Kaysha's fault. She'd wound them up, so determined to punish him, so desperate for someone to listen to them all, finally.

'Fine,' she says, when she goes back inside. 'There's an old typewriter in the house, I think. I'll write something on that and then I'll say I found it. It's all just . . . sick.'

'It is sick,' Josie says, wrapping an arm around Kaysha's shoulders. Her face tightens as the baby kicks. 'But what else can we do?'

The women leave, one by one, until only Kaysha and Olive are left. Olive stays quiet, and Kaysha looks at her, her papery white skin and colourless hair. Olive looks like the life has drained out of her. Whenever she speaks there is a brief burst of colour, but then it dwindles again. Kaysha knows that she should call someone, or stay with her, something, because she's not right.

Kaysha was surprised that Olive had held it together for so long, all the times she'd been knocked over by tragedy. She's surprised now that it's the death of Jamie, a man who was – as far as Kaysha can tell – only very briefly in her life, that has finally brought her down. Kaysha knows she needs to get Olive some help, but she's worried that the whole story will spill out of her.

'I need to nip off, Olive,' Kaysha says, but Olive doesn't seem to hear. 'I'm going to come back in a bit. Do you want to come with me?'

'I don't need looking after,' Olive says, without looking up.

'I know,' Kaysha says. 'Will it be okay if I come and stay here with you for a few days? I don't want to be alone.'

Olive looks at her suspiciously, and then rolls her eyes. 'There are lots of rooms here. Haven't been in some of them for years. You could go up onto the top floor. Don't even know what's up there anymore.'

'Thank you, Olive. I just need to go, but I'll be back, okay?'

Again, Olive doesn't say anything, but Kaysha takes the blanket she's had wrapped around her all night and drapes it over Olive's shoulders instead, and then leaves. When she gets into her car she shivers and realises that she's forgotten her jacket. She turns the heaters all the way up. She'll be back soon anyway.

Olive pulls the blanket tighter around herself. Sometimes she gets a chill even when the heating is on, and she knows that Kim is beside her when that happens. It could be Alonso, but she likes to think that it's Kim. She still hasn't been able to face Alonso, after the romance with Jamie. She feels like she betrayed him, even though he was long dead when Jamie arrived in her life. Too guilty to speak to him, so even if it is Alonso who is sitting beside her on the couch, cold as death, she decides it's Kim instead, because she knows that she did what she could for Kim, especially now.

'They're gone again,' she says to Kim. 'They just wanted him dead. Didn't know him like we knew him. I didn't believe a word of what they said about him. Just like I didn't believe you.'

Olive stretches out an arm to wrap around her daughter, thinks she feels the chill of the ghost against her skin, and pulls the invisible girl to her chest, strokes her invisible hair.

'He was a good man. But you lied about him first, and look where that got you,' Olive says, and then pauses. 'I went to see him, you know, a few days ago. I don't know. A week or two ago. I needed to warn him about them plotting. I found his address, and I had to get the metro and then two buses, it took a long time to get there. I thought about you the whole way.'

39

Olive
20th September 1987

A family of sparrows lived in a clumsy bird box that Kim had made at school a few years earlier. Olive had been dead against putting it up in her nice garden but Alonso had nailed it to the tree anyway. For a year or so it had stayed empty and Olive had made comments about even birds refusing to live somewhere so ugly, and had nagged Alonso to take it down. He never did, and not long after he had passed, the sparrows had moved in, and in those aching moments of early morning silence, when Kim was still asleep and the weight of the grief almost made Olive's knees buckle, she found some stillness in watching the birds. She'd often look for them as she washed the dishes or waited for the kettle to boil, and would find herself still standing there long after she'd forgotten what she had come into the kitchen for. They'd even got a bird table in the winter, and Olive had made balls of fat and seeds from a recipe she'd found in a gardening book. She'd felt a strange swell of pride when there had been some fledglings in the spring, and she'd sat very still with Kim in the garden one morning as they took their first flights. The babies were long gone now, but one of the parents was flitting around under a rose bush. She watched it until it took off and disappeared into the sky. A dark bank of clouds approached from the west, though it had been beautiful all day. Olive had thought that morning, as she walked to church, that it was the last day of real summer heat, the last one before autumn would cast her golden fingers over the leaves and the flowers packed up their blooms for winter.

Jamie broke her reverie, tugging on one of her apron strings.

'You're burning the gravy,' he said, taking her wrist and moving it in circular motions so that the whisk she was holding disturbed the thick, brown liquid. The flame beneath it was low, and the gravy had barely even started to warm. She raised an eyebrow at him and he winked. 'Just keeping you right.'

'I don't know why you insist on making the gravy first anyway,' she said, stirring the pot as he moved back to the chopping board to finish slicing his carrots. 'It's the last thing you're supposed to make, really. With the juices from the joint while the meat's resting and the puddings are rising.'

'I know what I'm doing,' he said.

'Oh, do you really?' she asked, smirking.

'I do.'

'Who taught you to cook?'

'Taught myself,' he shrugged, dropping a fistful of carrots into a pot of boiling water. He hissed as water splashed out and scalded his hand. Olive gasped and pulled him over to the sink and turned the cold tap on.

'Put your hand under there. It'll stop the burning.'

'I'm fine, man,' he said, shaking his hand and turning off the tap.

'No, really, it works,' she said, turning the tap back on and trying to push his hand under it. He turned it back off.

'I said I'm fine,' he said, raising his voice a little. 'Stop trying to be my mam.'

'I'm just trying to help.'

'I'm a grown man, Olive, I don't need you to tell me what to do.'

'Alright,' she said, laying a hand on his forearm. 'I'm sorry, you're right, I just wanted to help.'

Jamie took a deep breath and closed his eyes for a second. 'Sorry.'

'It's okay,' she said, her hand sliding up to rub his shoulder and then cup his cheek. It was smooth; he always shaved on a Sunday. Olive appreciated that he made an effort for church. Every week he strolled into mass wearing his best suit and polished shoes. He was often the first one there, having a chat with Father Paul before the service started, or making sure the pews were tidy before the rest of the congregation arrived. Now he was just in his socks and shirt-sleeves, his tie taken off and the top few buttons of his shirt undone. 'I know you've been stressed.'

'I have.'

'Work?' Olive asked. 'Or Kim?'

'Both,' he said, and bent to slip his arm around Olive's waist. He pulled her close, his face against the place where her neck met her shoulder, rubbing his nose against her and kissing her collarbone. She softened into him. These moments with Jamie warmed her, feeling his body flush against hers, the push of his chest against her as he breathed, the clutch of his fingers on her back or in her hair. She didn't get much other physical contact these days, with Alonso gone and Kim the way she was. This was different though, this thing with Jamie. When she'd first met him, and he told her how he was motherless, she had tried to make herself into a safe harbour for him. She'd long since admitted to herself that she didn't love Jamie like a son. He ran his hands over her backside and she groaned, tilting her chin up towards him. A peal of laughter escaped him and he gave her a light kiss on the lips before slapping her behind and disentangling himself.

'You really are going to burn the gravy now,' he said, opening the freezer and pulling out a bag of peas. Olive brushed her fingers through her hair, trying to regain her composure. Being let go unexpectedly always jarred her in a way that Jamie seemed to find so easy. She supposed it was something to do with youth, the idea of sex being unattached to love or commitment. She went back to stirring the gravy.

Jamie checked his watch and frowned. 'Where's Kim? Didn't she finish work at four?'

Olive looked at the oven clock. Twenty-past four. 'She should be back any minute.'

‘It only takes seven minutes to walk back from the ice cream parlour.’

‘Maybe they were busy and it took longer to clean up,’ Olive said, shrugging. ‘Or she’s seen a friend. She’ll be back soon.’

‘It’s just fucking rude. She knows you’ll have her tea on the table ready for her.’

‘It isn’t ready though,’ Olive said, opening the oven and checking the chicken with a small knife. The juices were still pink. ‘It’s fine, she’ll be back by the time it’s ready.’

‘And the state she’s been in lately, who knows what she’s capable of?’ he said, draining a pan of disintegrating potatoes into the sink and dumping them into a serving dish.

‘She’s been much better for the last few days,’ Olive said, and it was true. Kim had been brighter and more chatty than she had been in months.

‘Because I haven’t been here,’ Jamie said. He scowled and then closed his eyes for a moment, and when he opened them the anger that had gathered in the creases of his face was gone. He pulled Olive into a hug and kissed the top of her head. ‘I don’t mean to keep snapping at you. I’m just worried about the whole thing. I know I’m being grumpy.’

Olive rubbed Jamie’s back. ‘I’m sorry she’s like this. It’s not your fault. I don’t think it’s hers either.’

‘I’m just . . . You know I love her, Olive, like a daughter almost, I want the best for her. It’s just that she’s going to end up getting me put in prison, for fuck’s sake. What if she’s back at the station now?’

'You're not old enough to be her dad,' Olive said, smiling a little sadly. 'I've thought about what you said the other day.'

'And?'

'And if she doesn't settle down, I'll consider it.'

'That's all I'm asking,' he said, squeezing Olive and then holding her at arm's length. 'You know I'd never—'

'I know.'

Olive found some charm in Jamie's stout belief that he knew what he was doing in the kitchen. She left him to finish preparing the food while she busied herself washing the pots and pans that had already been used. She set the dinner table and poured a bottle of wine into a carafe. He cooked everything in the wrong order, and when they dished it all up and laid it out, most of it was already cold. Still, he smiled knowingly as he sat down at the head of the table and began to carve the chicken. Just as the knife sliced through the first ring of flesh, which Olive noted with distaste was still a bit pink in the middle, the front door opened and closed, and Kim's footsteps echoed through the hall. Olive stiffened.

There was a quiet moment when Kim was taking her shoes off and the air around them seemed unbreathable. Olive and Jamie shared a glance. Jamie squared his shoulders and plastered a bright smile across his face. Kim froze in the doorway when she saw him.

'What's he doing here?' she asked, glaring at Olive.

'Don't start, please,' Olive said, tilting her head to one side. 'Jamie's made a lovely Sunday dinner, look.'

'I'm not eating that.'

'Why are you so late? You finished work an hour ago,' Jamie asked. Kim looked at the floor.

'Kim,' Olive said, reproachful.

Kim shrugged. 'I was on the cliffs.'

'We were worried.'

'Yeah, I bet,' Kim said. 'He likes to know where I am, doesn't he?'

'I said don't start. Sit down and get some tea,' said Olive.

Kim shook her head and walked through the kitchen and out into the garden. Olive laid a hand on top of Jamie's. His eyes were fixed on the kitchen door.

'Sorry,' she whispered, getting up. 'I'll go and sort her out. You just eat.'

Olive went into the garden and closed the door after them. Kim sat down on a bench and pulled her knees up to her chest. Olive sat beside her, and they didn't speak for a few minutes. The air had grown cold.

'Why are you doing this, Mam?' Kim asked after a while, her voice strangled.

'We've been over this.'

'You won't listen to me,' Kim said, wringing her hands.

'Darling,' Olive said, taking one of Kim's hands and noticing that her nails were chewed to the quick. 'No one is trying to replace your father.'

'Mam,' Kim groaned, tossing her head back in frustration. 'Why won't you listen? I've told you a million times, it's got nothing to do with Dad.'

'No one ever could replace him, he was a great man,' Olive continued. 'Our family is different now, and Jamie isn't trying to replicate anything.'

'I don't care! I don't care who you shag, Mam. Sleep with every man in the North-East if you want. I do not care. But *he* –' she jabbed her finger back towards the house and dropped her voice to an urgent whisper – '*is a fucking psychopath*.'

'Language,' Olive hissed. Kim's eyes were wide and earnest, and she gripped Olive's upper arm. Olive felt helpless. She knew that her daughter really believed it all – she'd read her diary. Olive knew that it was a terrible breach of trust and it was something that she'd always sworn to herself that she'd never do, but being the parent of a teenager was difficult and terrifying. She was looking for a sign, a confession that Kim was acting up on purpose. She wanted to see in Kim's handwriting something like blind hatred for the new man whom her mother loved, but she didn't find anything like that. She'd found a 'log' of all the times Kim had seen him, the days she'd been convinced he was following her or he'd turned up somewhere unexpected. Olive hadn't told Jamie about the diary because she knew that it would break his heart. He really did love Kim. He was just as concerned about her as Olive was, if not more so. He understood how Kim felt, he said. He'd told Olive about his childhood one night when they were wine-drunk in the garden. He was raised by a cruel aunt. His mother was a teenager who had died in childbirth and no one knew who his father was. He'd left his aunt behind when he was sixteen, ran away to live with the grandfather he'd never met. Olive wished Kim would just talk to him, they had a lot in common. She wished that Kim could see the sparkle in Jamie that she did, the charm that dripped from him almost carelessly.

Kim rested her forehead on her knees. She was thin as a rail, these days. She'd always been a chubby child, and had kept the extra weight well into her teenage years. Alonso's genes, Olive had always thought when she looked at her. Olive had always thought of herself as scrawny, unable to gain weight even when she wanted to. The older she got the more she noticed the bones jutting out from under the skin of her wrists and hips, the shelf of her collarbone and the sharp sweep of her ribs. She felt frail and breakable, more skeleton than woman. She envied her daughter's soft curves and dewy skin, but the weight had dropped off Kim over the last few months. At first everyone had complimented Kim and she had nodded and thanked them in the uncomfortable way that women do when people comment on their weight. The woman who worked in the post office had said that Kim looked like *a glowing picture of health* last week. Olive couldn't disagree more. Everything about her daughter had dulled; she was thin and quiet, jumpy and sensitive. She would burst into tears at the smallest thing. Her body had withered and so had she.

Olive knew that it was all because of Alonso. Kim had been the one who found him swinging from the rafters in the attic one evening in the middle of the miners' strike when everything had seemed so hopeless. She was thirteen at the time. It hadn't seemed to affect her too much at first; she'd been the one to hold everything together. She had arranged the funeral almost single-handedly while Olive fell apart. There hadn't been enough money for a wake, but there wasn't much family to invite to one anyway, and as for friends – Alonso had been crossing the picket line for weeks, so those were thin on the ground too.

Kim had taken the whole thing very well, considering. She had remained calm and balanced after the initial shock. Her schoolwork hadn't slipped and she'd barely seemed to grieve. Olive had worried at the time that she was in denial and when the realisation eventually set in she'd buckle. By the time she'd introduced Kim to Jamie, Olive had stopped waiting for the meltdown. When Kim and Jamie first met, Kim had been fine, even seemed happy for Olive. Her fall into madness had been slow and creeping, difficult to notice at first. At the beginning, she'd just avoid Jamie, stay quiet when he was around, mention that she'd seen him around a lot or complain that he was spending too much time at their house. Over the summer it had grown into full-blown paranoia that Jamie was stalking her, and she and Olive would have regular screaming matches where Kim would repeatedly tell Olive that Jamie was a psychopath, that he was using Olive to get to Kim.

'Kim, look at me,' she said, grasping her daughter's shoulders. 'You need to stop this. Jamie does not have any kind of unhealthy interest in you.'

'He has, Mam,' Kim said, rubbing tears from her eyes and smearing mascara across her face. 'He's everywhere I go.

Everywhere. He's always just hanging around, watching me—'

'Kim—'

'And then you just keep on letting him into our house and you won't listen to me, Mam. The fucking police won't even listen,' she said, tears spilling down her face. There was urgency in her voice and her breathing was becoming erratic.

'Everything okay, girls?' Jamie was standing in the doorway holding two glasses of wine.

'We'll just be a moment,' Olive said.

Jamie stepped out onto the patio and stood beside Olive, placing a hand on her shoulder and passing her one of the glasses.

'Kim,' he said. 'Your mother and I are worried about your welfare.'

Kim picked at a loose thread on her sock and didn't look at him.

'We think you need to get some help,' he continued, taking a sip of the cheap Merlot. 'Proper help. We know that this isn't your fault.'

'No,' she said, her voice quiet. Her gaze flashed up at him for a second, hard and angry. 'It's yours. You've got her wrapped around your little finger, haven't you?'

Jamie smiled and sank into a crouch, putting himself into her line of vision. 'I know you're hurting, Kim, I've been there, believe me. I don't have any parents at all. You have a fantastic mam who'll stop at nothing to make you better. And you have me, Kim. Despite what you think, I'm here for you. We both love you very much.'

Olive squeezed Kim's knee, gazing at Jamie. He was so mature for his age. She admired that he put so much effort into mending his relationship with her daughter, and watching him speak to Kim with so much patience made Olive flush with attraction to him. Kim clenched her jaw, refusing to look at him.

'Which is why we've decided—' Jamie continued, before being cut off by Kim.

'You're only five years older than me.'

'Which is why your mother and I have decided that you need some proper help.'

Olive took a breath so deep that her lungs hurt and held it for a few seconds while she waited for the explosion. She found herself vaguely annoyed that Jamie had taken it upon himself to tell Kim this, but she supposed that he was the one bearing the brunt of Kim's illness. A few weeks earlier Kim had gone to the police station when she was supposed to be at school. She'd told the officer that Jamie was stalking her and that she was scared of what he would do. The police officer, Paul Fletcher, happened to be a member of the church that Jamie and Olive attended. After he had listened to her concerns, he took Kim to the library where Olive worked. Olive had sat Kim down in the office with a cup of tea and explained what was going on to Paul. Paul had nodded sympathetically and said that he thought Kim was probably just making things up to get her mother's new boyfriend into trouble – *Dangerous game*, he'd said, *could ruin his life*. Olive had smiled, and thanked Paul. She knew that Kim wasn't lying, not intentionally. She was hallucinating, she'd fallen into some strange mental state where she didn't know the difference between what was real and what wasn't. It was so out of character for Kim that if it had been anyone but Jamie she was accusing Olive might have believed her. There had been moments when Kim was so sure of herself that Olive almost did believe her – considered just for a second that Jamie might not be who she thought he was, before she shook the feeling off. She knew she couldn't indulge Kim's delusions if she wanted her daughter to be well again.

The clouds shifted across the late afternoon sun and the garden was suddenly chilly. Kim's eyes were fixed on her feet, and she still hadn't said anything.

'These hallucinations, these visions you're having, Kim, darling,' said Olive. 'You know, they're quite dangerous. Jamie could be put in prison if anyone took you seriously. It could ruin his life.'

'You probably won't be there for long, Kimmy, you just need to take a break. Find a way to recognise what's real again,' said Jamie, reaching out and stroking her arm. Kim flinched away.

'What are you talking about?' she asked, frowning at her feet and then turning her gaze to Olive. 'What's he talking about? I'm not going anywhere.'

Olive clasped her hands together. 'We've been thinking that maybe you should go somewhere to recover, Kim. It's nothing to be ashamed of.'

'Recover from what?'

'Your illness, darling. Your paranoia . . . your hallucinations.'

Kim wound her fingers through her tangled hair and pulled, groaning. Jamie took a step back and Olive grabbed Kim's wrists. She looked exhausted, grey half-moons stamped under her eyes.

'You're the one who needs your head looking at, Mam,' she said. 'Believing him over me. What's it going to take for you to realise that I'm not lying?'

Hot tears spilled down Olive's face. 'I know you're not lying, darling. But what you're seeing and feeling, it's just not real. Jamie doesn't follow you anywhere. He doesn't stand in your bedroom at night. He doesn't threaten you. Your brain is just making you believe those things. You can't trust your senses at the minute, Kim.'

Kim's face contorted in sadness and confusion, and she dropped her head to her knees and wept. Jamie slipped back into the house, and Olive enveloped her daughter in her arms. When Kim had settled down, Olive led her upstairs and they climbed into Kim's bed together. Olive stroked Kim's hair until she fell asleep, and then crept out of the room, leaving the door ajar.

Jamie was sitting in an armchair reading the *News of the World*. He'd lit the fire and poured himself another glass of wine. The untouched dinner was still spread across the table, bright piles of vegetables in mismatched dishes and bowls. Olive usually just plated everyone's food up straight from the pans, but Jamie had insisted on doing it the way the

Americans did in films. *More washing up*, she thought, but there was something about it that made her smile, something about him doggedly trying to replicate the image of the nuclear family presented to him on cereal boxes. She'd wait until he left to clean it up.

He didn't look up as she came in, but when she sat on the arm of his chair he put down his paper and pulled her onto his lap. They sat in silence for a while, her head on his shoulder, his arms wrapped around her. Olive was exhausted. Jamie's head was tipped back against the chair and she lost herself in the creases of his eyelids, the silky fuzz on his earlobes. His eyelashes were impossibly long and dark, the kind of eyelashes that people always said were wasted on a man. Olive didn't think they were wasted. The first time they met, Olive had found herself caught in them like an insect in a spider's web, on the end of a gaze so intense that it seemed impossible not to fall in love with him.

She'd first seen him at church. Jamie sat alone and sang quietly, left without a word to anyone but the vicar as soon as the service was over. The congregation was mainly made up of over-sixties and Olive was intrigued by the young man. When she asked the priest who he was, he told her that Jamie was new to the area, moved here for a job. The vicar had known his grandad, who was also a clergyman, but on the other side of the city. *A bit fire and brimstone, his grandad*, he'd said, *but he was alright really. Jamie's a nice kid.*

Jamie turned up for the sermon every week but always

left before Olive had a chance to invite him for a coffee at the church. She had never been the type of woman who befriended the lonely or rooted for the underdog, but something had changed in her since her husband had passed. She hadn't attended church for over twenty years while she was married, because Alonso had been an atheist, and when they married – and they married young – she'd slipped out of her faith. She hadn't missed it particularly; their marriage was full of love and the joy of raising Kim. They had laughed together and wept together for twenty years and there had been nothing missing in her life. When Alonso died, and she was alone again, she rediscovered a space within herself that she'd forgotten, and she returned to God. Olive realised that she'd softened since she was last in the church, and soon found herself drawn to the lonely young man who was always out of her reach.

One Saturday afternoon when Jamie had been attending the church for a few months, Olive and Kim ate at a cafe on the seafront. It was Alonso's birthday, and they both needed to get out of the house and break their usual evening routine of *homework–tea–TV–bath–bed*. They sat at a metal table on the pavement, each with a pile of chips on a crumpled sheet of newspaper, translucent with grease. Olive watched people picnicking in the sunshine atop the cliffs, dog walkers and children far below on the beach, plodging. Kim occasionally flung a chip in the opposite direction to lure away the seagulls. Olive had spotted Jamie through the fingerprint-smeared glass as he stood to leave the table he'd been occupying inside, and when he came out of the cafe Olive had taken the chance to introduce herself and Kim, telling him that she'd seen him in church. He nodded politely and shook both of their hands. He'd even kissed the back of Kim's, and she'd curled her lip and wiped her hand on her jeans the second he turned away. The next Sunday at church he sat beside Olive, and after the service he accepted her invitation to come over for a coffee.

When they got to Olive's house, Jamie had whistled and looked the townhouse up and down as she opened the door. Olive laughed and told him it was inherited and that she could barely afford to heat the place, but she couldn't bear to sell it. Kim had been sprawled upside-down on the sofa watching television when they walked into the house, wearing a leotard with fluorescent yellow leg-warmers and a matching headband. Her ginger ponytail dangled beneath her, brushing the carpet. She had a half-eaten doughnut in one hand and was watching a lithe American woman in an outfit similar to her own leading a group of women in a routine that was mainly gyrating to a light pop beat. She hadn't noticed them come in.

Jamie had said something like *I think you're actually supposed to do it along with her*, and Kim had got such a fright that she'd fallen off the sofa and dropped her doughnut. She blushed and stormed into the kitchen, and Olive and Jamie had laughed. *She'll be a heartbreaker*, Jamie said, and then asked how old she was. *Sweet sixteen*, Olive had told him, *and still not interested in boys*.

•

'Did you ever think of falling in love with Kim rather than me?' Olive asked, head still on his shoulder. She felt the rumble of laughter shake Jamie's chest.

'You know I like older women,' he said. 'Mammy issues and that.'

Olive kissed his cheek, and he turned his head to kiss her on the mouth. He gently bit her bottom lip and the arm that had casually rested around her waist tightened and pulled her towards him. The smell of the wine on his breath mingled with his aftershave, and Olive inhaled it as he unzipped her dress. She felt a tightness in her hips, a need to push herself closer to him. She could feel how hard he was through his trousers. One of his hands slid up her thigh and under her dress, and she moaned and started to unbutton his shirt.

Afterwards, Olive drifted into a light, satisfied sleep, and when she woke the sky outside had grown dark and raindrops tapped on the windows. She felt a jarring sadness when she realised that she was alone. Jamie's clothes and shoes were gone too. It wasn't the first time that he'd left as she slept without saying goodbye. He didn't like to wake her, he said, but it still stung. She'd felt like she was in a film earlier, making love on the rug in front of the fire in her bedroom, but when she woke she felt foolish lying naked on the floor alone, cold in front of the embers.

As she pushed herself upright, she imagined what she must look like to him, her body so much older than his.

Jamie was so young. Too young for her, really, despite what she told herself. He was just a passing indulgence. She wouldn't tie him down, though he soaked her in promises of marriage and eternity whenever she was unsure about their relationship. Her eternity felt so much shorter than his. Twenty years shorter. He deserved more than her, and she would set him free to find it. If Kim found peace from his absence, then that would be good too.

It was after ten and Olive was desperate to climb between her sheets and leave the day behind. The untouched dinner was still spread across the dining table. She thought about the possibilities that the dinner could have brought, the three of them sitting around it and passing a bowl of peas to one another, laughing when Kim dropped the spoon and sprayed them across the tablecloth. Maybe there'd be another child one day; adopted, of course. A boy. Kim would tickle him as they waited for the beef to rest and Olive would tell them to settle down while Jamie laughed. The boy would grow into a teenager, and by that time Kim would bring a boyfriend back for Sunday dinner, a doctor she'd met at university, who would bicker with Jamie about politics over the mashed potatoes. Kim would marry her beau soon enough, a beautiful wedding, and then he'd eat with them every week too. One Sunday she'd announce that she was pregnant and Olive would drop the gravy jug in surprise. Every year the table would grow with another loved one, eventually countless grandchildren and great-grandchildren would fill the room, and Olive would find, as she glanced at her reflection in the kitchen window while she brewed the after-dinner coffee, that, somehow along the way, she'd grown old. She'd bring out the coffee with slices of cake and see Jamie sitting at the head of the table where Alonso once sat, beaming around the room at their overflowing family, still twenty-two. He'd slide his fingers through hers and tell her he loved her. But the food lay uneaten, and Kim was mad, and Olive was going to let Jamie go. The stairs seemed like a mountain that night.

Olive opened her pyjama drawer to see it almost empty; she hadn't done any washing in days. Only a single pair lay squashed against the back of the drawer, almost forgotten. Olive pulled them towards her and smiled. Alonso had bought her these for their anniversary years ago as a joke, but she'd loved them. He'd had to get them from the teenage boys section. They were brushed cotton and printed with illustrations of Popeye and Olive Oyl, surrounded by little anchors. That had been their joke, in the old days. He was Popeye, big and strong, though he'd never been on a boat in his life, and she was his Olive Oyl. She put them on and climbed into bed. It had been good with Alonso, up until the very end. Their love was steady and constant, the kind of love that makes people think that soulmates must exist. Different to how it felt with Jamie – everything was new and exciting, but for every teaspoon of love for him she felt a tablespoon of guilt. Guilt at Alonso's memory. Guilt that she was somehow stealing Jamie's youth, as if she'd tricked him into loving her. Guilt that their relationship seemed to affect Kim so much, and that she still continued to see him.

Just as Olive was drifting off, she realised that she hadn't checked on Kim before she came to bed. It had become a habit recently, since Kim's decline. She slid her feet back out of the warm sheets and padded through the house to Kim's room, tiptoeing around the squeaky floorboards so that she didn't wake her. Her bedroom door was ajar as Olive had left it, and she pushed it just wide enough to slip her head through the gap and look for Kim's bulk beneath her covers. The curtains were drawn and Olive couldn't see her in the gloom, so she crept further into the room, fear spreading from her fingertips up her arms as she got closer to the bed and realised that it was empty. She hadn't heard Kim go to the bathroom but she went to check anyway, and when she wasn't there either Olive checked the spare rooms, and then she checked downstairs and the garden, but Kim wasn't anywhere. Olive noticed that her boots were gone from beside the front door and wrenched it open. The rain had got heavy, and a rumble of thunder rolled through the clouds.

She rang Jamie's house first, but he didn't pick up, so she rang the police station.

'Tynemouth Police Station, Officer Fletcher speaking.'

'Paul, it's Olive,' she said, breathless. 'Kim's missing.'

'Missing?'

'I can't find her. She's not in the house.'

'Well, she's a teenager, Olive, maybe she's snuck out to drink with her friends or—'

'She's not well. You need to help me find her. Please.'

'Have you checked at all her friends' houses? That's most likely where she is, pet.'

'She isn't – she doesn't really have any friends . . .'

'A boyfriend then?'

'Please come out and help me look.'

'Olive, pet, settle down. All teenagers sneak out. Give all her friends a ring and see if they know where she is, and if you still can't find her, give me a ring back.'

Olive slammed the phone down in frustration and went to the front door. She dragged her shoes and raincoat on. The rain came down in sheets and she couldn't see six feet in front of her. She zipped her coat and pulled her hood up but within seconds her pyjamas were soaked through and her feet were sliding around in her pumps.

'Kim?' she shouted into the darkness, making her way out onto the road, squinting around for any shapes moving through the gloom. Jamie must have been asleep, she thought; why else wouldn't he have picked up? A quick wave of jealousy washed through her, despite her worry. Maybe he was with someone else. A denser wave of jealousy. Maybe he was with Kim. Maybe Kim was such a mess because she loved him too. Maybe Kim was making up the stories about him so that Olive would get rid of him, so that she could have him for herself.

'Kim?' she shouted again, peering down an alley at the end of the street. There was something bulky at the end of it; movement, she was sure. Olive started to make her way into the narrow space, her mind casting images of Kim and Jamie gyrating against a wall, slick with rain water, laughing at her.

It was just a couple of dustbins. A cat darted out from behind them as she approached. Olive jumped and clutched her chest. She put her face in her hands. She was being ridiculous. Of course they wouldn't be together. He wouldn't do that to her, and Kim hated Jamie. She squared her shoulders and marched back out of the alley just as the first flash of lightning illuminated the road. There was no one around.

Kim's favourite place was up on the clifftops, where they'd spread Alonso's ashes. He'd always loved it up there. Since Alonso's death, Kim had gone there almost daily to think and watch the sea. Surely she wouldn't be up there now though, in the storm? Olive imagined Kim trapped on the cliff, scared to stand in case she was blown over the edge by the wind. Olive remembered all the times she'd told Kim off for getting too close to the edge when she was a child, but her daughter seemed to have no fear of the sheer drop to the rocky beach below. As soon as the thought was in her head she knew she had to check. Another flash of lightning illuminated the ruins of the priory. She shouted Kim's name again, but the word was whipped from her mouth by the gale and lost. Olive stumbled over the crest of the hill, and a fork of lightning struck the sea, impossibly close, and lit up the clifftop for a second. The scene burnt into her retina like a snapshot. Two figures at the edge of the cliff. A man and a girl. Relief and fear soaked through Olive, and she kicked off her slippery shoes and began to run through the darkness towards them. Lightning. She realised how close they were to the edge. The clifftop was wider than she'd ever realised. She wasn't getting any closer. Lightning, striking the priory this time. The figures had joined, moving, struggling. Passionate. Olive slipped on the grass and landed on her front. Her breath was stuck in her lungs. A scream caught in the wind reached her. Lightning. The girl was gone, and the man stood at the edge of the cliff, arms outstretched. Darkness.

Later, when the police officers left her house and Jamie was still being questioned, Olive rekindled the fire. As the first shafts of grey light cracked between the churning sea and the heavy, starless sky, Olive kissed her daughter's diary and tossed it into the flames.

40

Nova
12th January 2000

Nova rubs her hands together. The car is freezing but she turns the heat off to better hear the conversation that is happening inside Olive's house. She had driven straight there after she'd spoken to Kaysha on the phone, heard her mutter Olive's name and knew that if they were together, something worth hearing was happening. She doesn't remember the drive, but she is outside now. She tunes her car radio to the right frequency and listens.

It is difficult to distinguish the voices at first, but she hears the entire discussion and when they finish talking she watches them slide out of the house, one by one, hoods up, each woman glancing around to make sure no one notices them. Nova sinks low in her seat, hidden by shadows, and none of them see her. Kaysha is the last to leave and even she doesn't spot Nova's car parked opposite the curved terrace. When Kaysha drives away, Nova's whole body goes weak, and she sits and tries to process what she's heard. She doesn't even think to turn the radio off, the quiet static is almost soothing, and she doesn't notice that she didn't hear Kaysha's wet steps to her car, the car engine, her breath. She knows that Kaysha is on her way to write Sarah's suicide note, and Nova hasn't decided whether she is going to stop her yet.

Just as Nova is about to drive away, she hears a voice. It takes her a second to figure out what has happened – she thinks that Kaysha must have driven back towards her or that the radio can pick up the signal over a much larger distance than she thought, but then she realises that Kaysha wasn't wearing her jacket when she left the house. Maybe someone is still in there with Olive, but as she listens, she realises that there is only one voice, one half of a conversation, and she remembers Olive muttering to herself at the funeral. Nova leans closer to the radio and listens to Olive recount what she did on New Year's Eve.

41

Olive
31st December 1999

Olive Farrugia was not the kind of woman who could be easily swept up in conspiracy theories. She didn't believe in alien abductions, she wasn't convinced that the moon landings were a hoax, and she certainly didn't believe that the Queen had ordered anyone to be killed. Olive was the kind of woman who lived her life by things that she could be sure of, things she could trust, and the only person she knew she could trust, other than herself, was God. She was sure that God existed, because she had felt His presence in her life; she'd felt the sting of His punishment when she'd stepped out of line and she had felt the warmth of His grace when she'd submitted. She was sure that, if she was good, she would be reunited with her daughter, and maybe her husband, on the other side. Maybe it would be the other great love of her life she'd be reunited with in paradise, but she knew she'd get there long before he would. She was sure he would be there eventually, though.

She felt a little sick as she sat on the bus. She slid her hand into her handbag and touched the things that she had brought with her. She moved her fingers over her purse, her phone, her house keys, her work keys, a packet of mints, the cold glass of her perfume bottle, and then she unzipped a pocket in the lining of the bag and glanced into it. There was a cardboard envelope which contained a brand-new, pay-as-you-go SIM card that she'd bought from the supermarket a few days earlier, pre-loaded with ten pounds' worth of credit. When she'd said what she had to say to Jamie, she wanted to start afresh and move on. She didn't want anyone from the group to be able to contact her. She'd even considered moving house, even moving city, setting up somewhere new.

As well as the SIM, there were three pieces of paper in the pocket. The first was Jamie's address, which she had found on the North Tyneside Libraries database at work, because his wife was a member of one of their sites. The second was a page cut out of a book of local maps, his house circled in red biro, and the third was a list of telephone numbers, stolen from Kaysha's jacket pocket two weeks earlier, when she and Kaysha had been the first ones to turn up in the hotel room, and Kaysha had gone to the toilet and left her coat on the back of her chair.

He'd been just on the other side of the city all these years, and Olive had never bumped into him. Really, she was glad she hadn't known. She would have been tempted to visit sometimes, she thought, not to let him see her, but just for a glimpse. The memories of him were delicious, but not substantial. Today would be torture, but it would be worth it. She was going to save him. She smiled to herself.

The bus wound through the city, which Olive usually avoided if she could. People said that it was the most beautiful city in the country, something about the architecture, but she didn't care for cities. She found herself unnerved by the crowds and belittled by the towering buildings. Even the town she lived in was sometimes too crowded for her liking, especially in the summer when people swarmed to the usually deserted stretch of beach in front of her house. The screech of children and the inane chatter of bikini-clad women irritated her to the point she'd close her windows and turn the television up, even though the house would grow unbearably stuffy in the August heat. The bus trundled over one of the bridges, and eventually the looming buildings melted away and there were only farmhouses and detached houses, rows of squat miners' cottages separated from one another by wide strips of grass.

'This is you, missus,' the bus driver called as he pulled up to a stop opposite a cul-de-sac. She thanked him as she alighted, and then stood on the kerb as the vehicle pulled away. Behind her was a field of horses and then the beginnings of a forest. She pulled the map from her pocket and opened it. She'd marked the path she needed to take, and began walking along the edge of the road, and then into the woods.

His house was nestled by conifers and quite alone, and Olive stood in a dark clutch of trees, just watching to see who was around. After a while, the garage door edged upwards, and there he was, leaning against a red Mini, propped up on bricks, with his arms crossed. His wife came into the garage after a minute, wearing a coat. Her little girl was on her hip, bundled up for the cold too. She handed Jamie a glass, and he swallowed the drink in one gulp, and then put it on a shelf. He leant into his wife, as if to hug her, but instead slid his hands into her jacket pockets, pulled them inside-out, patted her down and then did the same to the child. Olive wondered what he was checking them for. Maybe he already knew his wife was up to something, couldn't be trusted.

He eventually seemed satisfied and nodded, and then Sadia and the little girl left, out of the garage and across the road, into the forest. They passed within a few feet of Olive, and she was sure that the child's eyes landed on her for a second, but she didn't say anything, and soon they disappeared into the trees.

Olive took the luck of his wife leaving the house as a divine sign. She knew she was doing the right thing. She knew that this was her chance – she only needed a few minutes – and she put her palm against a tree trunk to steady herself because she was giddy knowing that she was about to be close to him again, she'd smell his aftershave, maybe touch his chest.

He didn't notice her as she crossed the gap between them, didn't hear her footsteps because he'd turned the radio on and he had his head under the bonnet of the car, and was tinkering with something inside. She was within a foot of him before he finally noticed her, and he turned around.

When Olive saw him up close, she bathed in him. He was still so handsome, older now though, filled out and masculine in all of the places he was young and skinny before. His hair was shorter than it was when she knew him, and his skin a little paler, as if he spent less time in the sun. There were crinkles at the corner of his eyes, lines etched into his skin where there hadn't been any before, and he had a beard, short but thick, darker than his hair. He'd barely even had to shave when she knew him. He'd aged like whisky, she thought. She wanted to drink him.

When he spoke, his voice sent a tingle through her, reminding her of what it was like before, how she'd felt every time he said her name all those years ago, and she blushed.

'Olive?' he asked, a hand on his chest. She'd given him a fright.

'Hello,' Olive said, smiling and reaching out for his hand, which he let her take, looking confused.

'What are you—'

'What am I doing here?' she asked, squeezing his hand. She looked into his eyes, quicksilver, and dropped her voice to a whisper. 'Is anyone else here?'

'Er, no . . . my wife and daughter just went for a walk, just me,' he said. His eyes were slightly unfocused and he ran a hand through his hair. 'Do you want, er, do you want a cuppa?'

'Oh, I'd love one, but I can't stay, I'm afraid. I just came to – well, I just came to warn you.'

Jamie's eyebrows furrowed. 'Warn me?'

'Oh, Jamie,' Olive said, with a sad smile. She kissed his hand. 'You have no idea, do you?'

'What are you talking about, Olive?' he said, and leant against the car with one hand, pulling the other from Olive's grip to rub his eyes.

'Jamie,' she said, her voice low, 'they're plotting against you.'

'Fucking hell, man, what are you talking about?' Jamie snapped. 'Spit it out.'

Olive faltered for a second. Jamie had never spoken to her with so much scorn in his voice before. 'Listen to me, they're – they're all against you, all of these women – they're—'

'What women?' Jamie interrupted, looking unsteady now. He glanced around and picked up an axe, which was leaning against a pile of wood by his feet, and put his weight on it as if it was a walking stick.

'Oh, all of them. Your wife, for one. The young, pregnant girl. The tattooed, hoodlum one. All of these women you know. They all claim you've done terrible things to them.'

'Sadia?'

'Yes. They're trying to—'

'And you? You're plotting against me?'

'No!' she said, stepping forward and taking his face in her hands. She couldn't believe that he'd ever loved her, he was just so beautiful. 'I would never. I pray for you every day, still. Every day.'

'Right, right, so they're plotting what again?' He rubbed his face.

'Are you okay?'

'Yeah. You need to go.'

'I have no intention of being seen by your wife. They'll be after me next if they know I've been here.'

'Get on with it. I don't feel well.'

'You don't look well,' Olive said, resisting the urge to reach out and press the back of her hand against his forehead to see if he was hot, like she might have done to Kim. She wondered if he was drunk, and hoped that if he was, he would remember what she was telling him. 'Well, like I said, they gather, and they talk about you. Nasty accusations. One of them says you raped her. Your wife has been going around telling people you beat her. So they're planning on some sort of revenge, a punishment, but they can't agree on how. The tattooed girl, she keeps saying that the only way to stop you is to kill you. The rest, I think, want to go to the police.'

Jamie sneered, and stumbled, losing his grip on the axe, which clattered to the ground. Olive picked it up to hand it back to him but he waved her away.

'You can sneer all you like, but I'm worried that if they all go to the police, organised, with their tall tales, the police might listen.'

'I'm not worried,' Jamie said, slurring.

'I think you should be.'

He laughed, and Olive noticed that he had a tooth missing at the back.

'Jamie, you need to take this seriously.'

'No, you need to shut up,' he said, a mean look in his eyes. He lurched forwards and poked her in the chest. 'Remember what happened to the last little piggy who cried wee-wee-wee all the way to the police station.'

Olive rubbed her chest and found nothing to say before he carried on.

'Remember little Kimmy. Naughty little Kimmy who wouldn't let me fuck her,' he said, and Olive took a step back, confused, felt her fingers tighten around the wooden handle of the axe.

'Jamie, you're drunk, you don't know what you're saying,' Olive said, close to tears. 'Shall I help you to bed?'

'Little Kimmy tried to tell on me to the police too, remember. Stalking her. Wouldn't leave her alone. Wah, wah, wah. I didn't like that. So then oops-a-daisy, over the cliff Kimmy tumbled.' He grinned, and turned his palms to the ceiling. 'Oops.'

Olive wasn't aware of her decision to swing the axe, but she lifted it with a strength she didn't know she had and buried it inches deep into his throat, and his smile faltered and blood gushed down his front, more blood than she would have thought possible. He grabbed at the axe as he slid onto the ground, more blood bursting from his mouth as he tried to speak, tried to scream for help, and his eyes dimmed, and she put a foot onto his face to help her pull the axe back out of him. She felt his nose crunch beneath her heel and the axe came free, and she swung again and again and again and again until his head was separated from his body and he could not talk anymore. She stood over the pieces of him for a while, breathing hard, watching as the blood pooled across the floor, and then she pushed a button on the wall to drop the garage door and went to find where Sadia kept the bleach.

42

Nova
12th January 2000

The gravel in front of Heather Hall crunches under Nova's tyres for the second time that night. Rain is coming down in sheets, and Kaysha's car is parked outside the front door, which is still open. Nova runs the twelve feet between the car and the house and is soaked by the time she gets inside. She closes the door, and it bangs, but is barely audible over the rain.

The house feels even heavier than it did earlier, and she imagines Sarah flickering in and out of the rooms. Nova doesn't believe in ghosts, but the thought of Sarah existing one second, on the bridge, so bursting full of anger and sarcasm and love, and the next second as she hit the water, every memory and idea and half-forgotten song just blinking out of existence, seems completely unfeasible. She must be somewhere, but Nova hopes that it isn't here.

She finds Kaysha hunched over a desk upstairs reading a piece of paper, a typewriter in front of her. The room is neat, there is a single bed with navy sheets, a dresser with a stack of cobwebby textbooks, a couple of band posters and achievement badges pinned to one wall, but it feels as if it hasn't been occupied for a long time. Kaysha doesn't notice Nova at first. The lamplight makes her skin glow like burnished bronze, her lips move as she reads. Nova can't look at Kaysha's mouth without wanting to kiss it, even now. She tries to burn every part of Kaysha into her memory; the softness of her features, the way her nostrils flare when she's mad and the point of her incisors when she grins, the challenge in her eyes that only melts away when she is about to fall asleep. Nova wants to remember the way she feels when Kaysha is naked beneath her, how every scar and imperfection is impossibly beautiful, how she sometimes feels like crying because she can't imagine anything ever feeling more right. She doesn't want to break the silence, because she knows that this is the end of the blinding moment, the part of the eclipse that you can't look at because it's too bright. Kaysha is the sun.

When Kaysha finishes reading the paper, she looks up and jumps when she sees Nova in the doorway.

'Fucking hell,' she says, breath catching in her throat.

'I'm so sorry,' Nova says, and crosses the room, pulling Kaysha against her. Kaysha pushes her away, shaking her head.

'I can't,' she says, voice constricted. She takes a deep breath and wipes her eyes. 'I can't think about it yet.'

'What can I do?' Nova asks, kneeling beside Kaysha.

'Nothing,' Kaysha says. She folds the piece of paper that she is holding, and Nova realises that it is the fake confession. She doesn't want to admit to Kaysha that she bugged her, doesn't want to break whatever trust they have, though it doesn't matter now. She feels guilty for having suspected Kaysha in the first place.

'I know who it was,' Nova says, finally. The lamp flickers, and they both glance at it. Kaysha's face is unreadable, and Nova finds that she is holding her breath, about to say something that she won't be able to take back. 'Olive killed him.'

A laugh bursts from Kaysha's mouth, but the mirth quickly drops away and her face cycles through confusion and disbelief and comprehension, and Nova can see that she is weighing up possibilities, putting the pieces together the right way, finally.

'Have you arrested her?' Kaysha asks, looking at Nova in a way that seems accusatory.

'No.'

'Are you going to?'

Nova looks at the carpet. There are pencil shavings beneath the desk, and she wonders how long they've been there. She doesn't know what to do about Olive. It should be straightforward. Two weeks ago, she would have arrested her on suspicion of murder without a second thought, but she's learned so much since then – about Jamie Spellman, about the women who surrounded him, and about herself. She feels displaced by it all, as if her space in the world has shifted, and she is no longer where she should be. She wonders if Olive is her last straw – an impossible decision between what is legal and what is right.

‘Are you going to?’ Kaysha repeats, reaching a hand out and then pulling it back. ‘You know what he did to her, don’t you?’

‘Well, I heard her – she said he killed her daughter.’

Kaysha nods. ‘I’m surprised she admitted it. She’s always said he was good, that he’d never do anything to harm anyone.’

‘Olive seems . . . unstable. Why do you believe he did it if Olive has always maintained his innocence? Until now, anyway.’

‘Because I’m under no illusion that he wasn’t an evil bastard,’ Kaysha says, her expression dark.

‘Murdering a teenage girl though,’ Nova says, thinking through everything she’d learned about Jamie. He’d harmed a lot of women, but murder was another thing entirely. She sees Sarah falling through the air and wonders if he’d driven Olive’s daughter to do the same, whether that counts as murder, or whether it should. ‘Do you think she might have jumped?’

Kaysha folds her arms across her chest and looks at the ceiling. ‘No, I don’t. Look, I’ve always kept an eye on him. I knew he was up to something with them – knew it wouldn’t have been Olive he was interested in, and the girl – Kim – she was determined to do something about him. I found out afterwards that she kept going to the police saying he was following her, she wanted someone to listen to her. She’d reported him again earlier the same day she died, that’s how I know she wasn’t at the end of her rope yet.’

'What do you mean, you've *always kept an eye on him*?'

Kaysha shrugs. 'I've just always kept an eye on him.'

'But why? How did it start, how do you even know him?' Nova asks. She gets to her feet, rubbing her fizzy calves, and sits on the bed. She knows better than to push Kaysha to answer things she doesn't want to, but she has nothing to lose now.

'It doesn't matter, Nova. Just trust me for once.'

'I trust you,' Nova says, and Kaysha scoffs. 'What did he do to you?'

'I just knew he was bad news.'

'What did he do to you, Kaysha?' Nova asks again, reaching over to squeeze Kaysha's shoulder. Kaysha brushes the hand away, and Nova lets her. She doesn't like to be touched when she's upset. Kaysha doesn't say anything for a few seconds, meeting Nova's eyes, weighing something up. Nova waits.

'He raped me, okay?' Kaysha says eventually, her voice breaking as her face twists and she starts to cry. 'And before you fucking say it, I went to the police, straight away, the same night, and they didn't believe me. So I just . . . I just followed him afterwards, just kept an eye on him, but I was too late every time, I only saw the things he was doing when it was too late to stop him. I knew he was obsessed with Kim and I didn't figure out what to do about it in time and then she'd fallen off a cliff and I knew he'd pushed her. I just knew.'

Nova wraps her arms around Kaysha, and Kaysha stiffens but eventually gives in to the embrace and sobs into Nova's chest. She strokes Kaysha's hair. The rain has slowed, and through the window she catches a glimpse of the crescent moon between shifting clouds.

'You've been helping these women, haven't you?' Nova asks softly.

'He wasn't supposed to die,' Kaysha says, her breath tickling Nova's neck.

'What was supposed to happen?'

Kaysha pulls back a little and shakes her head, wipes her face. 'It depended on what everyone wanted. I thought it was best to go to the police first. Maybe we wouldn't all be ignored, if we spoke to the right person.'

'I could have helped you,' Nova says, thinking about how they weren't speaking at the time, how she'd betrayed Kaysha's trust all those months ago.

'Well, yeah,' Kaysha says. 'But before I brought you in, I needed to be sure. I needed to convince them all that if we banded together, we could do something about him. Stop him from harming anyone else. Some of them needed to hear each other's stories, realise how bad he was – that it wasn't just in their head. I knew you would be able to help. You're not like the rest of them.'

Nova feels relieved to hear Kaysha say that, to know that someone – maybe the most important someone – sees beyond the badge. 'I don't think I can keep doing it.'

'No,' Kaysha says, and seems completely unsurprised. 'No, I think you've outgrown the job.'

•

An hour later, they both leave the house. Nova has the fake suicide note in an evidence bag in her pocket. A sense of change washes through her. She'd wrap up this case, do the paperwork, and then move on. Time for a fresh start.

Kaysha doesn't say where she is going, and Nova doesn't ask, but she hopes that she goes to Olive. Someone needs to. The night is still around them, and the darkness feels viscous, like they have to wade through it into their separate lives.

'Kay,' Nova says, as Kaysha opens her car door. Kaysha looks up. *I love you*, Nova wants to say. *Run away with me*. The moment stretches out and neither of them speaks, though there is so much left to say. 'Look after yourself.'

43

Olive
31st December 1999

Olive cleaned up without thinking too much. If she started to think, she'd start to panic, so she let her body do the work, focusing on the practicality of each task as she did it rather than the consequence, hoping only that Jamie's family didn't return before she'd finished. First she went to the kitchen and brought all the cleaning supplies that she could carry and dumped them on a part of the floor that was not bloody. Then she got rid of the body. Her plan was to take it into the woods and bury it, or leave it under a bush, and she went through a door at the back of the garage to the garden, to make sure that there was a way through into the trees. There was, and she started to drag the body outside by the feet.

Jamie was heavy, and the adrenaline that had carried her through the last few minutes began to wear off as she got through the door. She avoided the patio and the stepping stones that dotted along the centre of the lawn, aware of the blood that was still seeping from the corpse's neck, hoping that the grass would swallow it. When she was halfway down the garden, she knew that she didn't have the strength to get him all the way to the woods. There was a pond a few feet away, which at a glance looked deep and murky enough to hide him.

It was beginning to snow, and she dragged him into the water, and hoped that his daughter wasn't the one to find him when he would eventually be found.

She cleaned the blood in the garage. There was a lot of blood, it took a long time to mop it all up with towels and kitchen roll and then to scrub it all with bleach, wipe down the splashes on the walls and the car. She cleaned the sloppy pieces of Jamie from the axe, rubbed the polished handle to get rid of her fingerprints and leant it against a pile of logs stacked against the wall. She put everything she'd used into a bin bag, along with her clothes. She padded through the house naked, went upstairs and turned the shower on. When she was clean, she took the plainest clothes that she could find from Sadia's wardrobe – a grey dress and a black coat – and put them on. On her way back down to the garage, she noticed a large sweet tin by the Christmas tree. It was deep and oval, embossed with all sorts of flowers, and the exact right size. She tipped the sweets into the bin bag with her clothes, and put Jamie's head inside instead. He looked awful now, pale, covered in his own gore. She put the lid on.

Olive reopened the garage door and put the bin bag of bloody things into the outside bin as she walked past, hiding it under a couple of existing bags of rubbish. Hopefully the bin men would come before it was found. It had grown dark, and snow fell in thick flurries, and twice she almost slipped and dropped the tin on the way back to the bus stop. She got onto a bus back into the city, the tin on her lap, worried the whole time that blood would start to seep out of it, but it didn't. She kept checking her hands under the yellow strip lights, but they were clean.

When she'd snuck through the back door into the hotel, like they always did, and into the usual room, she took the back off her mobile phone, unclipped the battery, and changed her SIM card for the new one she had in her bag. No one had the number. She sent a text to every phone number on Kaysha's list, including herself, summoning them urgently. She swapped her own SIM back into her phone and snapped the new one in half, wrapped it in some toilet roll and flushed it down the dirty, en-suite toilet.

She set out the seats in a half-circle and then dragged a table into the centre. There was a box of bibles, all with a burgundy leather cover and gold-edged pages, and she piled a few onto the table, opened the one on top to one of her favourite passages – Leviticus 24:19, *an eye for an eye*. She balanced his head on top of the open pages. She pulled a pillowcase over it, like they did to people who got the electric chair – hiding their guilty faces.

Olive washed out the sweet tin in the en-suite sink, dried it with a dressing gown hanging on the back of the door, careful not to touch it again with her bare hands, and then went to hide in the room next door until she heard the others arrive. She couldn't be the first in the room.

When, after an hour, Olive was back in the room, surrounded by the others, and Sarah pulled the cover from his head, Olive felt like she was seeing it with her own eyes for the first time, and screamed louder than any of them, horrified.

Acknowledgements

First and foremost, thank you to my absolute belter of an agent Kate Evans, who has been my biggest cheerleader since I walked into her office with three chapters, seven women, one severed head, and the promise that I'd somehow make them into a novel. I couldn't dream of anyone who would have been better to take this journey with.

Thank you to my lovely editors Jade Chandler and Sarah Grill, who approached my novel with such enthusiasm and support, and have polished it into something so much better than I could have imagined.

Thank you to Clairus Bearus, Eira Major, Sandy Watson, Lynn Murray, Graham Reid, Maddy Sheridon, Alex Pape, Kamila Shamsie and Horatio Clare for reading and giving feedback on various sections and versions of this book – it means the world.

Thank you to Hayley Murray and Ameera Rahman for your sage advice and shared experiences.

Thank you to Holly Rose, who has listened to every version of every chapter in this book with the patience of a saint, who weathered every writing-induced meltdown, and who believed in me on days when I didn't believe in myself.

Thank you to Hayley, Pablo, and Mouse for being my favourite distractions.

Thank you to Jeanette Winterson, without whose instruction, belief, and encouragement I probably would not have written this book at all.

Thank you, finally, to the plethora of brilliant, strong and determined girls, gays, and theys that I am lucky enough to have in my life. I couldn't wish for a better support system.

Resources

Some of the themes in this book can evoke difficult feelings. If you need help, please consider contacting one of the organisations listed below.

The Samaritans
116 123, www.samaritans.org

Mind
0300 123 3393, www.mind.org.uk

SupportLine
01708 765200, www.supportline.org.uk

Rape and Sexual Abuse Support Centre
0330 363 0063, rapecentre.org.uk

National Self Harm Network
www.nshn.co.uk

National Domestic Abuse Helpline
0808 2000 247, www.nationaldahelpline.org.uk

Switchboard LGBT+ Helpline
0300 330 0630, www.switchboard.lgbt

Cruse Bereavement Support
0808 808 1677, www.cruse.org.uk